STORM RISING

ALSO BY CHRIS HAUTY

Insurrection Day
Savage Road
Deep State

STORM RISING

A THRILLER

CHRIS HAUTY

EMILY BESTLER BOOKS
—
ATRIA

New York   London   Toronto   Sydney   New Delhi

EMILY
BESTLER
BOOKS

ATRIA

An Imprint of Simon & Schuster, Inc.
1230 Avenue of the Americas
New York, NY 10020

First Emily Bestler Books/Atria Books hardcover edition May 2022

EMILY BESTLER BOOKS/ATRIA BOOKS and colophon are trademarks of Simon & Schuster, Inc.

For information about special discounts for bulk purchases, please contact Simon & Schuster Special Sales at 1-866-506-1949 or business@simonandschuster.com.

The Simon & Schuster Speakers Bureau can bring authors to your live event. For more information or to book an event, contact the Simon & Schuster Speakers Bureau at 1-866-248-3049 or visit our website at www.simonspeakers.com.

Interior design by Erika R. Genova

Manufactured in the United States of America

1 3 5 7 9 10 8 6 4 2

Library of Congress Cataloging-in-Publication Data
Names: Hauty, Chris, author.
Title: Storm rising : a thriller / Chris Hauty.
Description: First Emily Bestler Books/Atria Books hardcover edition. | New York : Emily Bestler Books/Atria, 2022. | Series: A Hayley Chill thriller ; 3
Identifiers: LCCN 2021032646 (print) | LCCN 2021032647 (ebook) | ISBN 9781982175856 (hardcover) | ISBN 9781982175863 (paperback) | ISBN 9781982175870 (ebook)
Subjects: GSAFD: Suspense fiction.
Classification: LCC PS3608.A8766 S86 2022 (print) | LCC PS3608.A8766 (ebook) | DDC 813/.6--dc23
LC record available at https://lccn.loc.gov/2021032646
LC ebook record available at https://lccn.loc.gov/2021032647

ISBN 978-1-9821-7585-6
ISBN 978-1-9821-7587-0 (ebook)

For Lauren

It proves more forcibly the necessity of obliging every citizen to be a soldier. This was the case with the Greeks and Romans and must be that of every free state.

—THOMAS JEFFERSON, LETTER TO JAMES MONROE,
JUNE 19, 1813

PROLOGUE

Waking from a sleep without dreams, the immigrant lies on his back with arms and legs outstretched. Above him, the sky is black and moonless. It's night? Since when? The rotten-egg smell of hydrogen sulfide is a clue to his general location. El Norte. But that journey derailed long before now, hadn't it? Thirst forces its way into his consciousness, tongue thick inside his mouth. He becomes aware of an object in his right hand and, seeing the cheap revolver, cannot fathom how it came to be there. Though Luis Pineda comes from a world of many guns, he has never owned one.

He hears movement to his left and looks in that direction. Ernesto Cordón sits on the ground some ten feet away, hunched over and arms slack. Simultaneously both men become aware of the immense oil storage tank looming behind them. Of a security fence around the site's perimeter, topped with razor ribbon. The lights of a nearby town that glow in the distance.

"*What's happening? Where are we?*" asks Cordón in his native language.

He massages his head with both hands, but the throbbing pain inside his skull won't subside. Cordón has done drugs, back home, in Guatemala City's Zona Viva, and knows all too well the harsh aftereffects of home-brewed chemical inebriation. This torment is worse. He comprehends the likelihood that he and his fellow undocumented immigrant have been placed here as stooges, part of some wicked scheme. Why else waste good drugs on two *mojados*?

Luis Pineda releases his grip on the pistol and sits up, his body blocking his companion's view of the weapon. He hasn't survived this long by being incautious. The deaths of two brothers and his father—lost to warring cartel factions in Mexico—drove him north. How much can he trust the Guatemalan, whom he has known for less than a week? Before beginning the journey north, his mother implored him to put his faith in no man, only God.

Seeing the backpack, he points for the other man's benefit. *"Look."*

Twisting around, Cordón sees the bag propped against the base of the storage tank. Too dizzy to stand, he crawls across gravel to the tank.

"What is it?" asks Pineda, getting to his feet and shuffling toward his fellow immigrant.

Cordón unzips the top of the backpack, peers inside, then recoils as if from something unholy.

The top of the backpack remains open. Pineda peers inside, seeing two sticks of gelignite wired with firing system and circuit, in this case, a thirty-dollar Alcatel flip phone.

"A bomb?"

"Don't touch it!"

Back home, Ernesto Cordón had been friendly with the bomb maker employed by gangsters controlling his neighborhood. With that experience, he is an authority in comparison to Pineda.

"It could be remote-controlled," the Guatemalan says with blatant fear.

Luis Pineda scans the tank farm as if for lurking conspirators. He sees something worse.

"Son of a bitch! Another!"

The second backpack is of a different make, but as battered and dirty as the first.

Cordón sees that bag, too, and another placed at a third tank down the row. Alarmed, he pushes to his feet. *"We gotta go, man. Quickly!"*

They both look toward the fence, at the same time seeing a ladder on the ground inside the perimeter. A way out, the ladder is an unexpected miracle.

The men move toward the wire and steel fence. A coyote howls in the dark, far distance, closer to the highway perhaps. The dry wind from the west doesn't relent.

Ernesto Cordón stops, frozen in place by a sensation he has experienced before. A feeling of inexplicable dread, as with the dense seconds on a deserted city street before a gunman steps out from shadows. His grandmother, a worshipper of Maximón, proudly attributed his precognition to the family's Mayan roots. Their blood traces back six centuries to Gonzalo Guerrero, a shipwrecked Spanish conquistador and slave of Chactemal chief Nachán Can, who ultimately became the war leader for his captors' clan and fathered the first mestizo children on the continent.

In English, Cordón says, "Dude, stop."

Pineda pauses, looking over his shoulder and impatient to leave.

"Our captors drugged us. Left us here. They're watching, waiting for us to try to escape. Then they'll blow the place sky-high!"

These words fail to register with Pineda. Little of his life makes sense anymore. He is tired of taking orders from his fellow immigrant, who is two years his junior. Only escape matters. Nothing else. He must get away from the bombs. All of this oil. The conflagration to come.

He moves again in the direction of the fence. A reaction from Cordón, four inches taller and thirty pounds heavier, is immediate.

"No!"

The two men struggle. Pineda breaks free of Cordón's grasp and retrieves the gun from the ground where he left it. Delirious with the blue steel revolver's weight in his hand, the Sinaloan turns, pulling the hammer back with his thumb.

"I'm going. Stay if you like."

Gambling that Pineda is too timid to fire the revolver—a .38 Special with a four-inch barrel that began life in the US before being smuggled into Mexico—Cordón lunges to take possession of the weapon.

The loud bang startles them both, Luis having pulled the trigger by accident. Neither of the men can guess where the round traveled or its destination. Both check themselves for injury, a moment of unintentional comedy. That no one was hurt only emboldens Luis Pineda.

He is now a man who has fired a pistol.

Pointing the gun at Cordón's head, as he had watched in countless films and television shows, Pineda says, "Voy, pendejo." *I'm going, asshole.*

———————

Personnel from the FBI and ATF, accompanied by county fire investigators and local law enforcement, cannot enter the site for more than thirty-six hours after a catastrophic blast that all but obliterated the tank farm. Only two of sixteen tanks remain intact. With local resources inadequate to the task, a specially trained firefighting team from Louisiana helicoptered in, using foam and water to extinguish the blaze.

As the disgorged oil burned, sending black clouds towering overhead, the town of Wink, three miles from the site, was evacuated. The concussive blast shattered dozens of plateglass windows along the town's commercial strip, but other than the two unidentified victims inside the facility's perimeter, authorities reported no injuries. A weather front that moved into the region overnight has done the job of pushing the black, toxic air south of the border.

A crew from the coroner's office in Midland collected the bodies an hour earlier. Yellow surveyor flags that bend and snap back in the swirling, hot wind mark the locations where first responders found the victims. Investigators on the scene work methodically in pursuit of answers to a mystery that is only now emerging. As they walk the location in knee-high rubber boots and dark sunglasses, their easy banter masks a terror each of them privately entertains. All can visualize, with graphic detail, the deaths of the explosion's two nameless victims.

"We know for sure they were both males?" asks the ATF agent.

The county fire investigator nods. "The one at the fence was burnt pretty good. Not much left of that ol' boy for us to pick over."

The federal man turns away from the blackened cyclone fence topped with razor ribbon that partially melted in the fire's prolonged heat blast. He indicates a spot in the ground nearer to one of the destroyed oil tanks. The area is a swamp of partially dissolved foam, oil, and fouled water, putting the investigators' protective gear to a real test.

"But the one over that way, he must've been lyin' flat out on the ground. His front side was mostly intact."

"Mostly."

An official from the Railroad Commission of Texas squats down next to a second county fire investigator. Together they study the slight depression in the ground where Ernesto Cordón sought safety. The bits and pieces there. A fragment of clothing. Scorched boot heel. Clumps of scalp. Tuft of black hair.

The RRC official says, "Bagged a .38 over by the fence. This guy, nothing."

"Company says these two are trespassers. No employees on-site for six hours prior to the explosion. The hell they doing here?"

"No key to get in or out, just that fucked-up ladder," says the ATF man, coming over to join the discussion.

Standing a few feet away, a sheriff's deputy from neighboring Reeves County spits into a puddle of smoke-streaked oil. He drove up that morning after a pal with the Wink Police Department had called and asked him to come over for a look-see. Folks in Winkler County in West Texas are tight-knit. Prone to help one another out. Especially when the helping is from a man as trustworthy and knowledgeable as Jay Gibbs.

"These boys come over from the other side," he says, tipping his head in the general direction of south.

These are the deputy's first words to the others, though he has been on-site for more than ninety minutes.

"Wanna tell the rest of us what makes you so sure?" the RRC official asks from his heels.

The only one not wearing sunglasses, Gibbs points his chin at the ground where Ernesto Cordón died. "This one might as well wrapped himself in a Guatemalan flag, what with the gold in his mouth. Mayans have been decking out their teeth with jade and such since before there was America."

On his first assignment in West Texas, the man from DC-based Bureau of Alcohol, Tobacco, Firearms and Explosives has a low regard for local law enforcement capabilities.

He says, "All kinds of people have gold teeth."

"Yeah, well . . ."

Gibbs shrugs, not inclined to bump chests with the federal man.

The ATF agent glances to his partner, then focuses on Gibbs again.

"So, Deputy, you're thinking sabotage, then?" he asks with faux incredulity.

This low comedy draws a few snickers from the other federal investigators.

Jay Gibbs was born and raised in Pecos, about forty miles to the northeast. A pretty good tight end in high school, he made varsity as a sophomore in a year the football team went ten-and-four and undefeated in their district. He's been with the sheriff's office for three years and in the Marine Corps, MOS 5811, before that.

The deputy squares his hat and looks south again, across a scrubland of sand wash and wire grass to the distant Davis Mountains.

"Could be," he says. Playing it straight.

For as long as Gibbs can remember, hard men on both sides of the border have killed one another. For all kinds of reasons.

There's always been plenty enough death to go around.

"Question is, who's sabotaging who? Know what I mean?"

1

TATER HOLE SAVINGS & LOAN

Hayley Chill's most glaring weakness, Brazilian jiu-jitsu, has been her primary focus for the twelve weeks she's been in camp. Days start with a ten-mile run at sunrise, followed by a healthy breakfast, rest, and then four hours of skills training. Nights begin at seven after a light dinner. For warm-up, she hits pads for three rounds. Circuit training follows, with double-arm rope slams, dumbbell thrusters, two-hundred-pound sled pulls, and a sixty-yard farmer's walk with eighty-pound barbells. Twice through, before starting a second circuit.

In the last months of her tenure as an aide in the West Wing, Hayley gained fifteen pounds. Many days in that harrowing time passed without any physical exercise whatsoever. Since leaving the White House—twenty-seven years old and unemployed—Hayley Chill is determined to regain the physical fitness of her years in the US Army. Holed up in Princeton, West Virginia, and training six days a week at Elite Martial Arts Academy seems as good a way as any to accomplish that goal.

Today isn't a typical workout day, however. In anticipation of her first amateur MMA bout later that week, Hayley's coach has limited her to stretching and a single sparring session at 50 percent. The problem is her sparring partner. Almost six feet tall, with a murderous arm reach, Jewel Rollins ratchets up the intensity with every round. Flustered and stung by a snapping jab that feels like something more than 50 percent, Hayley retaliates. An amateur boxing champ in the military, she never suffered a loss in the ring. Her strategy when attacked—in the ring and outside of it—is to counterattack. Never relent.

Fuck 50 percent.

With her back foot slightly splayed for increased leverage, Hayley throws a jab, cross, and then hook at her sparring partner's head. She then feints with her left hand, drops low, and shoots a stiff right, hitting the other woman dead center in her sternum. The perfectly timed jab lands with a thud, catching Rollins as she exhales. The punch might have rocked a fighter with less experience; Hayley has put opponents on the canvas with lesser stuff. But Rollins is an NAAFS amateur women's champion. Her mixed martial arts skill set is deep. Hayley doesn't see the wheel kick coming until it's too late. If not for thickly padded headgear, the blow would have knocked her out.

Fredek Kozlov steps between the fighters to stop the session, helping Hayley to her feet. "You plan to lose, yes?"

His cartoonish Russian accent is made less comical by dint of an always-on physical intensity and Olympic gold medal for judo. A back injury short-circuited his transition to professional MMA fighter. Elite Martial Arts is the top training camp for three states around and Kozlov's ticket to prosperity in the United States.

Winded by her exertions, Hayley tucks her chin as if in preparation to throw a jab at her coach. Instead, she shakes her head and fixes her powder blue eyes on Rollins.

Her coach says, "I tell you. Fifty percent. What is wrong with you? Stupid!"

"What about her?" Hayley asks, gesturing toward her sparring partner.

"What about her? Maybe I tell her to go seventy percent. Or one hundred percent. Your directions are to go fifty percent, yes?"

Hayley stares at the mat, recognizing now that she has screwed up. Again.

"You fight your fight!" Kozlov points a sausage-size index finger at Rollins. "You don't fight her fight. Fight your fight!"

Basic stuff. The earliest lesson. Hayley can scarcely believe her embarrassing lapse.

I was played. What is wrong with me?

Kozlov says, "Angry, you are blind. Emotions, you are stupid!"

"Yes, sir."

She can think of nothing more to say, wanting only Kozlov to step aside and open a path to her sparring partner. To redeem herself. If that's possible.

But the Russian remains between the fighters. To Hayley, he says, "That's enough. Go home. We fix this tomorrow."

Rollins sneers from behind the Russian. Kozlov plants both feet on the mat and anchors his weight, anticipating Hayley's loss of temper.

"Save it for Friday, *tyolka*. You are going to need it."

HER MOTEL IS two miles east on Oakvale Road. Hayley jogs there at a comfortable pace. Past a sub shop. The local Dairy Queen. A Mitsubishi dealership. Losing fifteen pounds is only one part of the motivation for finding refuge in West Virginia. Transitioning from amateur boxing to mixed martial arts isn't the whole point, either. Hayley left a tumultuous Washington, DC, after a revelation so shattering that escape seemed the only sanity-preserving response. What she found inside a modest, brick home across the Potomac

River, in Arlington, destroyed all reverence for the one person she loved most in the world. Without a job or apparent purpose—trapped in a city that never felt like home—her emotional anguish was like a third eye. Impossible to disguise. Every waking moment after that fateful Sunday morning in Virginia was filtered through a lens of despair and loathing. Only time and distance would alleviate the pain.

The focus and discipline required by her MMA training help speed the process of mental disassociation. In the meantime, she waits for a call or message from the one man in her life who matters. Not Sam McGovern, the fireman she started seeing before she fled Washington. Not anyone from work, either. Her West Wing colleagues have dispersed, forced into exile after the historical abomination that was the Monroe administration. Future employment in government for any of her White House coworkers would be a miracle. Hayley is different. As a trained operative in a clandestine effort to preserve the nation's constitutional democracy—a kind of "deeper state"—her job as chief of staff for the president's senior advisor was only a cover. The phone call she anticipates is from her direct superior in that secret organization, Andrew Wilde.

The man who recruited her.

He represents a loose affiliation of powerful Washington emeriti—ex-presidents, former Supreme Court justices, retired NSA and CIA directors, senators, and military brass—linked by lifelong government service and unambiguous love of country. There is no official name for this group. Nor is there a definitive leader or hierarchy. All members have left their official offices, thereby guaranteeing that their motivations are pure and shorn of self-serving incentives. Few of the participants have ever met each other, their true identities hidden behind pseudonyms. An ultra-secure, cloud-based intranet run from a server farm in north-central Canada facilitates communication among members. Though the group has no name, Wilde and other

members have come to call themselves Publius, a nod to the Federal-
ist Party formed by Alexander Hamilton, James Madison Jr., and John
Jay in support of the still-unratified US Constitution. The essence
of their cause, and entire reason for being, is the protection of that
hallowed document and its tenets, no matter the origin of the threat
to its preservation.

Recruited from the US Army, Hayley joined a corps of similarly capable individuals to serve as covert agents of Publius. Her
first operation—protecting the president and turning him against
his paymasters in the Kremlin—was initially an unqualified success.
But that mission ended abruptly with Russia's exfiltration of Rich-
ard Monroe. A concurrent crisis was devastating cyberattacks that
nearly brought Washington to its knees. Had it not been for Hayley's
initiative, not to mention her extraordinary gift of eidetic memory,
the country might have stumbled into a third world war. Rescuing a
besieged US senator from the Capitol when the building was stormed
by white nationalists is a cruel punctuation mark on Hayley's recent
months as an operative for the deeper state. The stress has laid her
emotions bare, a mental state further ravaged by family revelations
almost too grotesque to imagine.

Retreat to her home state of West Virginia—in equal parts
beautiful and tragic—has been a soothing balm. God bless the Mountain State. Almost heaven, indeed.

The motor-court-style Turnpike Motel is low-slung and strenu-
ously well-kept. Older-model cars occupy one in five parking spaces.
Newer, franchise hotels can be had in town at double the price, but
Hayley prefers these modest, humdrum lodgings.

Hyperventilating slightly as she slows her pace and then stops
running entirely, the deeper state operative is surprised by her
elevated heart rate.

Hayley bends over and places her hands on her knees for support.
A wave of inexplicable fatigue washes over her. She feels sick to her
stomach.

What the hell is wrong with me?

Standing up straight, Hayley Chill waits for her heart rate to slow. The shortness of breath dissipates. She opens her room door with a key card. Stepping inside the darkened room, Hayley clocks a figure sitting in a chair by the window and drops into a defensive crouch. Only after recognizing the intruder as her fellow deeper state operative does she relax.

"Jesus. You startled me."

"I'm a spook. That's the idea, isn't it?"

April Wu's apparent ill health—pale and visibly weak—wins her little compassion from Hayley, who is displeased by the surprise visit.

"Are you comfortable? Put your feet up on the bed, why don't you?"

"Sarcasm doesn't suit you, Chill. Clashes with your unabashed earnestness."

Hayley strips off her trail pack and drops it on the bed. "What are you doing here?"

"I'm worried about you. I've seen you do this before—though usually, you're breaking stuff."

"This?"

"*This*," says April, gesturing at their surroundings.

Hayley pulls an insubstantial chair out from the sad motel desk. Sits. Her silence concedes the point.

April smiles, pleased with the win. "How was your workout?"

"Light." She considers leaving it at that but adds, "I have my first bout Friday."

"Sam coming down?"

Hayley shakes her head. "Working."

"Uh-huh."

"Will you stop? He's been here three or four times."

"Three 'or' four. Must've been extremely memorable."

Hayley resists an urge to throw a water bottle at her friend. "You look like hell, by the way."

Before her accident, April Wu had been at the mercy of fashion. Pairing ripped jeans with a James Perse T-shirt and Chanel bouclé jacket was as effortless as breathing air. The expense was never an impediment. But today, in this sad, dumpy motel room, April wears tragically banal canvas cargo pants and a black Army pullover hoodie. The dark clothing only heightens her sallowness and the circles under her eyes.

"I *feel* like hell. Wish that car landed somewhere besides on my head."

"Me too."

"Has the pope called you?" April asks, referring to their superior with the deeper state.

Andrew Wilde recruited them both, Hayley out of Fort Hood and April from Cyber Command at Fort Meade.

"Nothing."

"Maybe he can't find you."

Hayley suspects Publius has the resources to find anyone on the planet, but there's no way of knowing for sure. "I'm training, April, not hiding."

"Hard to tell the difference."

This has been their way forever. The best of friends *and* die-hard competitors.

April asks, "Wanna talk about what happened?"

"You mean that business with the president faking suicide, his exfiltration to Moscow, and unmasking as a Russian mole?"

"That was fun. But I mean the other thing."

"What other 'thing'?"

"What you found at Charlie Hicks's place," says April, referring to the house of horrors in Arlington. The world shifted on that Sunday morning. What didn't change no longer matters. Recovering in the hospital following her accident, April remembers Hayley's visit later the same day. The West Virginia native was emotionally shattered.

April Wu discovered something new about her friend that day: Hayley Chill wasn't invincible after all.

"I found Charlie Hicks. Hanging by his neck. From the bedroom door."

"Really? Is that all?"

"What do you want from me?"

"The truth."

How much April already knows or doesn't know isn't clear to Hayley. This is a given now. As an operative for the deeper state, she can trust no one. Not even good friends inside the organization. Not completely.

"Maybe I just don't want to talk about it."

Hayley stands and begins to empty the trail pack of her workout gear.

"I'm not going away, you know," says April.

"I suspected as much."

She walks a damp gym towel toward the bathroom.

"Are you going to win Friday?"

"Can't remember the last time I lost," Hayley says as she disappears into the bathroom.

———

SHE WASN'T READY, the Russian thinks as he watches Hayley Chill tap out a fraction of a second before she loses consciousness. Three months wasn't nearly enough time to transform a boxer into a mixed martial arts fighter.

I put her in there too goddamn soon.

The four hundred or so spectators at the Wytheville Meeting Center certainly got their money's worth, that's for sure. Hayley and her opponent—a skilled twenty-two-year-old Filipina with lightning bolts for hands and an impressive ground game—gave the jubilant fans three rounds of nonstop, cage-rattling warfare.

Absurdly overmatched, Hayley Chill showed a truckload of heart in the defeat. Her Russian coach can't recall another student with a greater capacity for absorbing pain. But courage can't make up for a catastrophic deficiency in expertise and spotty conditioning. Assuming she is down in points after the first two rounds and feeling an unexpected fatigue, Hayley gambled at the outset of the third round. She rolled the dice when all that matters are skills, conditioning, and talent.

Crouching below her opponent's torso level, Hayley propelled herself forward and wrapped her arms around the Filipina's thighs for a double leg takedown. Failing to work her rear leg to the outside, the deeper state operative exposed herself to an all but inevitable guillotine choke.

———————

WHAT HAPPENED?

Lying on her back, Hayley cannot process the events of the past sixty seconds. Breathing is difficult. Did the choke hold bruise her esophagus? An inexplicable exhaustion—she felt fatigued even in the earliest minutes of the bout—envelops her.

Hayley tries to speak but finds it difficult to form the words.

Kozlov crouches over her.

"Shut up. Don't try to talk," he says.

Copy that, Coach. No problemo.

Hayley has enough experience in combat trauma training to understand the Russian is assessing her ability to maintain focus on him. "She's okay," Kozlov says to someone out of view.

Her eyes are on her coach and never leave him.

The Russian observes his fighter's difficulty swallowing.

"Throat hurt? That's normal, *tyolka*. You're going to be okay."

Did I just lose? I don't lose.

Flat on her back, she is confused by an unavoidable truth.

I got beat?

"Let's move. Next fight ready to go."

Hayley can't see who says this but knows it must be the referee.

Kozlov and others get her to her feet. She experiences a fleeting victory in the ability to put one foot in front of another.

"What happened?" Hayley asks, articulating these words another small triumph.

The Russian can't hear her above the crowd's racket as they make their way up the mobbed aisle. But he can guess the nature of her question.

"Too soon. I put you in too soon, *tyolka.*"

The deeper state operative shakes her head. Angry.

I put myself in there. It was me.

Just as well she doesn't talk. Even breathing hurts.

All Hayley wants right now is to get away from the avalanche of jeers falling on her. Before walking through the doors that lead to the temporary locker room, she sees April standing next to the doorway.

Making another appearance.

Spectator to Hayley's first-ever defeat.

April Wu—sickly, pale, and looking every bit the victim of a car accident that she is—wears the most inscrutable expression. Is it pity in her eyes that Hayley sees? Or something worse than pity?

"EVERYBODY LOSES. EVERYBODY! Believing you cannot lose is the worst thing for a fighter." The Russian's thick accent undercuts the effectiveness of his consoling words.

"Yes, sir. I know." Hayley's voice is still raspy and raw. Talking makes the pain worse, but she must have this conversation. "I made one mistake. It cost me the match."

Kozlov shakes his head. Driving them home in his ten-year-old Ford Explorer, the Russian dreads what lies ahead. These forty-five miles will seem like three hundred. Having made similar drives, he is all too familiar with the elongation of time after one of his fighters loses in the octagon.

"Too soon. You were not ready."

Hayley can scarcely believe what he's saying. She has always worked hard enough to avoid this gut-wrenching disappointment with herself. Always. Until tonight.

And why couldn't she shake this goddamn fatigue during the fight?

Hayley says, "I don't understand. It happened so quickly."

Just this once, the Russian would prefer not to coach. Driving back to Princeton in silence would be the better thing. Some music perhaps. Under his breath, Kozlov says in his native language, *"Why not shut up, girl? Take pride in trying."*

"Trying isn't good enough."

He is stunned to hear his native language come out of Hayley's mouth.

"You speak Russian?"

She nods, letting him flounder in his embarrassment.

Kozlov realizes how little he knows Hayley Chill. In what other ways has he underestimated her?

Anxious to make amends, he says, "With more time and training, you can be good. Very good! But you need more time, *tyolka.*"

"How much time?"

"Six more months maybe. A year would be best." He sees enormous potential in Hayley and wouldn't have agreed to train her if he didn't. But the octagon has a way of revealing delusions for what they are. As they did tonight.

Hayley wishes she had a year. Developing expertise in mixed martial arts appeals to her sense of discipline. The world of MMA is inspiring. The people and their dedication to craft.

But a trapdoor has been sprung. April's surprise visit triggered it.

The Russian feels Hayley's impatience emanating off her like radioactivity. He was once like her. It's how he broke his back and derailed a promising professional career.

"Tishe yedesh', dal'she budesh'." In his heavily accented English, he says, "Ride slower, advance further."

The old proverb fails to resonate. Her loss tonight stings, and Hayley will feel its bite for many nights to come. She wishes she could talk with April. *Now* is the time for an honest conversation. Only her fellow deeper state operative could understand. But by the time Hayley emerged from the locker room after her match, April Wu was gone. Vanished again.

I'm a spook.

Kozlov drives them north. With a negligible moon, darkness envelops the hills and trees beyond the road's shoulders. Hayley fixes her gaze on the road ahead. Avoiding her reflection in her side window.

———————

SHE ENTERS THE cheerless motel room, her home for the past ninety-four days. Low ceiling. Puke-colored drapes pulled shut. An ice machine rumbles to a start on the other side of the wall. The mechanical racket is both sign and signal. Hayley realizes she is done here.

She recalls her friend's words . . .

I've seen you do this before—though usually, you're breaking stuff.

Hayley hoped she would find April Wu sitting in the chair by the window. The disappointment of not seeing her there is a sharp ache. She considers calling Sam—most likely asleep at this hour—but resists the impulse.

In the morning, Hayley promises herself. She will call him then.

Packing will take minutes. The roads should be clear the whole way home. If Hayley leaves in the next thirty minutes, she'll be back in Washington by sunrise. Then the real work can begin.

Ride slow? Not a chance.

THE BRICK, ONE-STORY home on Fifth Street in Arlington, Virginia, has suffered from a lack of occupancy since she was last here. A broken front bedroom window. Lawn overgrown and spiked with henbit weed. A newly planted For Sale sign swings with every gust of wind. More than dreams have died in this place. Hayley parks behind a roll-off dumpster out front. She turns off the engine and looks toward the silent house. Hoping to see what?

Four months ago, she came here to ask Charlie Hicks about her father's death in the Second Battle of Fallujah. The man had ducked her at his Pentagon office. Here, at his house, Tommy Chill's war buddy refused her entry. They conversed through the front door instead. Hicks, emotionally distressed and likely suffering from PTSD, provided no new information. Hayley left the property, resolved never to bother the man again.

But new intelligence suggesting Charlie Hicks had been directly responsible for her father's death altered that resolve.

Sitting behind the wheel of her Volkswagen, she recalls a second visit to the house last spring. National calamity had been averted, her mission for the deeper state successfully concluded. The matter of Charlie Hicks's role in her father's death, however, remained unresolved. Sam drove her across the river, but Hayley insisted he stay in the car. For this final confrontation with Tommy's war buddy, she was determined to go it alone. There was no answer when she knocked on the door, already ajar. Hayley sensed what had transpired before seeing the body.

But what she could not have predicted was finding her father hanging by the neck from a bedroom door, not Charlie Hicks.

Hayley can remember every detail of the horrific moment. Standing in the hallway, staring at the body, her mind reeled, struggling to process what her eyes were seeing. Tommy Chill didn't die in Iraq. He returned home from the war. But how? Under the assumed identity of another man? That explained why "Hicks" steadfastly avoided meeting her face-to-face. For whatever reason, her father had chosen to separate himself irrevocably from his old life—from his wife and children—and live an alternative life in Arlington, Virginia. And what of the real Charlie Hicks, Tommy's war buddy? Was it his body parts that they buried in the family plot back home in West Virginia? That possibility lent the conspiracy a deviously logical symmetry, of course.

But there was something worse, a conjecture almost too horrid to contemplate.

Did my father kill Charlie Hicks in order to steal his identity?

What circumstances would drive him to do such a thing? In the moment, Hayley was unwilling to consign the memory of her father to these shocking, shameful circumstances. Better to let Tommy Chill exist in an earlier, near-golden incarnation that she remembers from her youth. Hayley did not call the police to report his suicide, but instead fled the house and its impenetrable mysteries. Those unanswered questions chased her back to the car and away from that awful place. Ignoring them eventually drove the deeper state operative to her spider hole existence in Princeton, West Virginia.

For all of those days, weeks, and months, Hayley has avoided confronting the ambiguities of her father's suicide. She didn't know the house in Arlington was put up for sale by an untraceable trust. If Tommy inherited family members with Charlie Hicks's stolen identity, Hayley guesses they must be distant and never in her father's life in any meaningful way. How else would it have been possible to perpetuate his fraudulent scheme?

That was then. Hayley has run long enough. She's returned once again to the house of horrors, unafraid of the answers she might find there.

Exiting her car, Hayley approaches the eight-foot-tall roll-off dumpster nudged up against the curb. Gripping the top edge, she hoists herself up to look inside. The jumble of discarded furniture and other household items fill the bin to near capacity. Seeing her father's belongings reduced to this slag heap is like a knife thrust into her heart. Throwing one leg over the side of the dumpster, Hayley clambers down inside. Standing precariously on a wooden kitchen chair, she takes inventory of the rubble. A busted lamp. Stacks of smashed dinnerware. Shattered picture frames. Busted bookshelves. Hayley ignores all of it. She is in search of information. Clues. Whoever cleaned the house in preparation for its sale would have no use for her father's papers, unpaid bills, and other documentation. If they are in this dumpster, she will find them.

Working her way down the loaded container's length is dirty, hot work on a morning when the temperature is already in the high eighties. Hayley can't thoroughly inspect the bin's every nook and cranny without displacing large, often unwieldy household objects. A mattress and box spring prove especially problematic, weighed down by a two-seat sofa and collapsed bookshelf. After twenty minutes of labor, a winded and exhausted Hayley pulls free a pile of dusty curtains and reveals a large plastic trash bag underneath. Tearing a small opening in the bag confirms that she has found the final resting place of her father's papers.

Hayley tosses the bag out of the dumpster and clambers over the side. Dropping to the street's pavement, she retrieves the stuffed garbage bag and deposits it in the back seat of her car.

Having gained entry through the home's back door by breaking the lowest windowpane, Hayley smells immediately the commingled odor of disinfectant and fresh paint. All the cupboard doors are open, revealing empty shelves. Glue traps at each corner of the room lie in wait for their next rodent victim. Leaving the kitchen, the deeper state operative enters the similarly desolate living room.

There's nothing here for me.

For no better reason than morbid sentimentality, Hayley enters the hallway that leads to the two bedrooms. She stops short of the primary and experiences again what she cannot repress: her father hanging by the neck from the bedroom door, his head tilted at an unnatural angle. A chair lying on its side beneath his body. The pungent smell of his post-mortem evacuations.

Transported to the past, Hayley resists an urge to look away.

Remember this.

Another memory drops, one much older but sparked by this newer image. A recall of family lore, the idiosyncratic customs fostered by a clan. And what Hayley remembers is the place where Tommy Chill would secure cash—the family nest egg—at a time in their lives when banks were an unattainable luxury.

For as long as she can remember, that secure vault in their West Virginia home was below the kitchen floorboards.

What her father affectionately nicknamed the "Tater Hole Savings & Loan."

She retreats up the hallway, back through the living room, and into the kitchen. Dropping to her hands and knees, Hayley examines the wood flooring. At first glance, the narrow planks appear permanently seated in place. Tracing her fingers across the grooves between the planks, she applies pressure to one board after another and at different points in their lengths. One piece, of shorter dimension by virtue of its position by a far wall, flexes and shifts. With a knife she retrieves from her pocket, Hayley pries the short plank up with modest effort. A hole has been cut in the subfloor, revealing a space between the floor joists and its sole offering: a manila envelope.

Hayley removes the eight-by-ten envelope from its makeshift vault. Written in pencil across the front are two words: *The Storm.* The deeper state operative opens the envelope and removes four typewritten pages inside. A brief examination of the papers reveals their contents are composed in a "book cipher." Rows and rows of incomprehensible one-, two-, or three-digit numbers fill every page.

What do the seemingly random numbers mean? Without the cor-responding key—a unique text or document—the pages are impen-etrable. Instead of finding answers at the house in Arlington, Hayley has only generated more mystery and questions.

She replaces the floorboard and leaves the house through the kitchen door, taking the envelope with her.

———————

THE CONTENTS OF the trash bag—utility bills, financial statements, and junk mail—are now stacked and categorized on the dining table in her Logan Circle apartment. Hayley has given the most scrutiny to telephone bills and credit card statements, highlighting some entries and entering the information on her laptop. A broad outline of her father's daily life has emerged. What Tommy did on his days off. Where he shopped for groceries. How often he traveled and to what destinations. His most frequent contacts. The picture that material-izes of her father's final six months is relentlessly monotonous, the lonely existence of a solitary man. Nowhere in these scraps of paper is there clarification of why he had killed himself. Why he had taken the life and identity of Charlie Hicks.

The truth seems unknowable, like the dark side of the moon.

Tommy Chill rarely deviated from his routine. Friday dinners at Jarochita on Glebe Road. A movie every other week at the Parks Mall. An unlikely passion for Pickle-Ice Freeze Pops from Walmart. Details accumulate, forming a small mountain of data that reveals little of the man's real substance. But a few nuggets Hayley has found in the scraps of paper hold some promise. Her father made three trips to El Paso, Texas, in the past year, staying at a motel near Fort Bliss and spending some time at that military installation, as evidenced by receipts from the post exchange. Other receipts suggest three trips to a local strip joint. Hayley can find no clues that suggest Tommy visited similar establishments here in Arlington, or anywhere else for that matter. She speculates these stops at the Aphrodite Gentlemen's Club north of El Paso were meetups.

In the months since Hayley discovered her father hanging by the neck in the sad, modest house in Arlington, the most obvious questions have gone unanswered. Tommy Chill could not have assumed the identity of another Marine without help. Why do so in the first place? What is the Storm? Some kind of malevolent plot? Was her father a participant? Others must be part of the conspiracy, probably working from within the US military. The nature of the scheme and its agenda remain a complete mystery.

Might she find answers in El Paso, Texas?

––––––––––––

"You couldn't call to let me know you were back in town?"

When the intercom buzzed, announcing a visitor downstairs, Hayley knew in an instant who had come calling on a weeknight after ten p.m. Wouldn't be the first time Sam McGovern drove by her place, saw the lights on, and stopped for a surprise visit. Opening the door to him brought a rush of emotions. Their embrace was awkward. Almost tentative.

Sam knows what's coming and has known it for a long time. That awareness doesn't make it easier before she actually speaks the words. Hayley steers him away from the dining table, inundated with papers and mail from the house in Arlington, and into the living area.

"I was going to call. Tonight."

"What is all that?" he asks, gesturing toward the table.

"My dad's stuff."

Sam sits on the sofa. "You went back there?" he asks, incredulous.

Hayley remains on guard. The next several minutes are a minefield. "Yeah." She pulls over a chair from the dining area, close enough to smell the fire on him.

Sam can read her expression. He tents his T-shirt for a sniff. "Sorry. Busy night. Three jobs."

Hayley has always loved that. "Jobs" is what Sam and his cohorts from DCFD Engine Company 5 call the fires they extinguish. Car fire. Trash fire. Dwelling fire. All are jobs. And Sam? Assigned to a ladder company, he is a "truckie." From the beginning, she has envied him for his chosen profession. A firefighter's task is so unambiguous. The measure of accomplishment so clearly defined. The inherent good of what he does cannot be second-guessed, unlike the murk of her role as a deeper state operative.

Last spring, when Hayley emerged from the house in Arlington, Sam McGovern was waiting in the car. She didn't have to say what she found inside for him to know it was terrible. Hayley resisted speaking of it then. Not that day or the next. But eventually, she opened up to Sam, divulging the barest details of her father's stunning reappearance in her life and his subsequent suicide because all she had were the barest details. Hayley told him nothing about the wider conspiracy she was only now beginning to suspect might be afoot. Doing so would have necessitated informing him about her association with Publius.

And the absolute necessity of keeping her double life a secret from Sam is the most compelling reason why Hayley must stop seeing him.

"Given how upset you were that day, I'm kind of surprised you went back."

"I tried to let it go, but I can't. Not without finding out the truth."

"Sure, you can."

She shakes her head, emphatic. "That's not the way this is going. With me just rolling with it."

"And your MMA training? What was that?"

Hayley doesn't answer, not inclined to tell him she had fought her first amateur bout and lost. Sam takes her silence at face value.

"Okay. Got it. Anything else on that list?"

"What list would that be?"

"The list of all the things you can't . . . or won't . . . tell me. The secrets list."

"Oh, hell, Sam, I don't know."

"Yes, you do."

This guy, she thinks, *a real, American hero*.

"I'm sorry."

"There's nothing to be sorry about."

"I just—"

"I'm marking down an explanation as completely unnecessary," he says, more or less interrupting Hayley.

She anticipated he would be this composed. That Sam would let her off the hook. His magnanimous nature. And, of course, this fact makes having to break it off with him that much worse.

"Thank you."

Sam gestures toward the dining table and stacks of receipts, utility bills, and credit card statements.

"Find anything interesting?"

"Maybe."

"What happens after you discover the truth?"

"Nothing. Then it's over."

"No."

"No, what?"

"It's never over. The truth leaves its stink on you like three jobs did on me today."

"Have it your way, then."

"That's just the way it is." He seems cross now, passing through the phases of profound disappointment and regret at breakneck speed. "You never really gave this a fair shot, Hayley."

"Agreed. I didn't. Give a fair shot, I mean."

"Look, if it's time you need, that's cool. I get how insanely upsetting all of it must have been. Must be."

She stares at the floor between them.

He deserves my time. Sam deserves my respect.

He's one of the good ones. A real hero.

Hayley looks up again, meeting Sam's gaze. "Which is why I think I fell into this thing with you. After all of that craziness, I had to hold on to something."

Her words are hardly mollifying.

"Okay."

"Where I'm going . . ." She falters, unsure how to describe a world she can only intuit at its very broadest outlines. "I think this will be a very dark road."

"Then I should come with you."

Hayley shakes her head.

He says, "If it's so bad . . ." Stopping himself because he senses he has found the boundary between what is allowed and what is forbidden to him. Sam has always known Hayley Chill was more than a mere White House staffer. He realizes this is the reason she will go it alone. Why she has *always* been alone, even in the scattershot moments they were together.

She looks at him now, able to meet his gaze without guilt or shame. She knows he knows.

"Okay," Sam says.

Somehow saying just that much is easiest.

———

LATER, LYING IN bed, the city outside the window dark and impossibly silent, Sam asks, "So . . .. El Paso?"

"I'm not sure yet." A pause, then, "Maybe."

"And if you don't go, then what?"

"I don't know."

This is good enough, he decides.

Good enough.

Hayley says, "I need to sort it out. Tomorrow."

A promise she makes to herself.

"Whatever made your dad do what he did, it can't be good. Going down there, it's not safe."

"I can take care of myself."

He has heard this from her before. A thing between them.

"It's my nature to help." With a smile, he adds, "I'm literally a lifesaver."

"I know."

She kisses him. Again.

2

THE WAR HAWK

Sam is gone when she wakes up at five thirty the next morning. He told her he had to meet a guy about something. She understands what "meeting a guy about something" means and didn't press him on it. Hayley can't say she was especially eager for an awkward goodbye, either. With much to be done today, Hayley needs her focus uncluttered. As always, she needs her space.

Ending her training with Fredek Kozlov doesn't mean stopping her workout routine. Since her army days, Hayley has remained ferociously devoted to physical exercise. Her mental fitness depends on that relentless discipline. Chaotic events in the last months of her tenure in the West Wing interrupted those routine efforts. Despite placing herself under the Russian's tutelage, Hayley has yet to regain her previous levels of fitness. Her levels of strength and stamina remain frustratingly subpar.

The bedrock of her exercise regimen is running. When she was young, not yet a teenager, running was how she got around. To friends' houses. To school. On errands to the store for her mother. No one in her class—male or female—could run faster. As she grew older and competed in school track team events, her discipline sharpened. With coaching, technique augmented her natural talent for the sport. Other passions eventually displaced Hayley's devotion to running, extracurricular activities that were not strictly legal. But she never wholly stopped indulging in a long, solitary slog. Running was freedom. Running was sanity. Even in the worst days of her work in the Monroe White House, Hayley found fleeting respite in intermittent early-morning runs through the deserted streets of Washington.

She dresses quickly in her usual workout clothes. A cherished PT uniform from her time in the military long since become threadbare, Hayley was forced to look for an alternative. High-performance, quick-drying fabrics, stretchy lining, and pockets for keys and IDs are all improvements she accepts as a worthwhile trade-off. Dressed and out the door less than seven minutes after waking up, Hayley takes the stairs down to the first floor and bangs out the apartment building's entry door. Free again.

In the predawn silence, the rhythmic thud of her shoes hitting the pavement keeps time to her light exertion. Warm-up first. Loosen joints and muscles. Despite the early hour, the air is already thick and muggy. A good sweat is trivial work in a Washington summer.

Wait for it, Hayley reminds herself.

She heads east, on P Street, cutting through a deserted Logan Circle, to Twelfth, where she turns right and south. With two more hours before the morning rush, she can run down the middle of the street unencumbered. The domed rotunda that defines the National Museum of Natural History comes into view, thrusting above the modern architectural mess surrounding it.

Her destination is the car-free, uninterrupted paths of the National Mall. Here she can begin to push it, elevating her pace and heart rate. A full loop is 4.3 miles. Hayley plans to run it twice, her usual output. One loop is completed in about thirty-five minutes— maintaining a strong pace, just under eight minutes per mile— and takes her past all of the iconic sites, silent and shrouded in the dawn's half-light. World War II Memorial. Reflecting Pool. Washington Monument. Lincoln Memorial. Tidal Basin. White House. Empty of tourists, the scene is apocalyptic. Only a passing Metropolitan Police Department patrol car disrupts an otherwise fixed tableau.

She increases her pace for the second loop. Sweat flowing. Consciousness loosens its moorings. Thoughts swirl. Hayley makes no effort to corral her deliberations. She thinks of her father, his ugly suicide. Sam, in her arms the night before. El Paso and the near-certain pathos that await her there. Hayley imagines a storm forming on the horizon. In that vision, she sees herself running directly at the tempest. What is this compulsion? Returning to Princeton, West Virginia, and her training with Kozlov would be so much easier.

Finishing the second loop in front of the natural history museum, Hayley pauses, bent over with a hand on each knee. Her pulse seems high, far more so than usual. She's hyperventilating again, too.

What is wrong with me? Am I sick?

Hayley straightens again and resumes at a gentler tempo, heading north, up Twelfth Street. The easy jog to Logan Circle takes less than ten minutes. Hayley feels no satisfying sense of resolution, no closer to a decision than when she had set out ninety minutes earlier. Should she go to West Texas or not?

Cutting across the park, Hayley sees April Wu sitting on one of the benches. She slows to a stop.

"You again?"

April looks no healthier than she did two days ago and wears the same black hoodie and cargo pants. If anything, the morning sunlight makes her complexion seem even more pallid. She manages an impish grin anyway.

"I can't quit you, Hayley Chill."

"Very funny. That's a movie reference, right?"

"Are you okay?" asks April.

Hayley was unaware she is grimacing. "I'm fine. Calf muscles a little sore."

She sits down on the bench and massages her leg.

"C'mon, Chill. You can do better than that. *Which* calf muscles?"

"Peroneus longus. Tibialis anterior, maybe a little." Hayley traces her finger lower down the back of her leg to the heel. "Not this one."

"Extensor digitorum longus, asshole."

Hayley asks, "Why does everything have to be a competition between us?"

"Because it's fun as fuck."

"There's that."

"Pretty dope guillotine choke the other night. Too bad you were the one wearing it."

"Some friend you are."

"We're friends?" asks April.

Hayley has worked out the tightness in her calf. Sits up straight. "A wise man once said, trust no one."

"He's dead. Somebody killed him." Then, without missing a beat, "Seen Sam?"

"Yes." The silence elongates. It's up to Hayley to fill the void. "A relationship is not something I'm particularly well equipped to pull off."

"I know the feeling."

"Look. April . . ."

Hayley is distracted. Wants out of there. But her sickly friend seems in no rush to leave.

"What did you find dumpster diving at your dad's place?"

"Are you following me?" asks Hayley, irritated.

"I don't need to follow you to know what you're going to do."

"That's how it works, huh?"

"That's how it works."

Hayley feels the sweat drying from her forearms. The oaks of

Logan Circle sway in a morning breeze. She takes a deep inhale, wishing she knew what to do without talking to April Wu about it.

"My dad made multiple trips down to El Paso, Texas, contacts I haven't been able to run down yet."

"Andrew Wilde?" asks April.

"Not yet."

"Don't go rogue on us, slugger."

"*Rogue*. Gimme a break."

"Go, but don't go it alone. Get Publius behind you. Have their blessing in your hip pocket. Who knows what you're going to find down there?"

Hayley says nothing, watching the worker bees of Washington, DC, hurry past in all directions. Again, she envies them for their ordinary jobs. Their ordinary lives.

"What? Where is the problem here?" asks April.

"This is about me. What happened to my father. Someone else can save the country."

"Don't be wack."

"I'm serious."

"I know. And you're also wack."

IT'S A ONE-HOUR drive from Washington, west on the interstate and then south after passing the battlefield at Manassas. Hayley keeps the radio off and windows down, filling the car with the smells of late summer in rural Virginia. Andrew Wilde provided her with detailed directions to the location. Nothing new in that. Missing the turnoff for the farm would have been a near certainty without those careful, Wildesque instructions. Her destination discourages visitors, accidental or intended. Hayley wonders if she has gone offtrack somewhere along the line—the rutted gravel road seemingly unused in recent times—when she clocks three big, black SUVs parked on a grass-covered ridge. Hearing the fusillade of gunshots confirms that she has arrived.

Hayley parks, her Volkswagen Golf dwarfed by the hulking SUVs. The range shack is on the other side of the hill, accessed by a dirt path. The facility—bare bones in the extreme—is divided between a range for long guns on the right and an "urban" gallery to the left. As she descends the path, Hayley observes five shooters, male and female, practicing drills at the urban range's firing line. After retrieving eye and ear protection from a cardboard box on the porch of the range shack, she takes a rock stairway down and pauses at the bottom step.

The urban shooting gallery offers several different types of steel targets, silhouettes, and disks, some of which are placed behind old automobiles or partially obscured by plywood walls at distances varying between twenty and fifty feet. Working through a drill, a shooter changes positions behind several barricades that force an alteration of firing stances. The idea is the creation of a more accurate simulation of real-world combat conditions. Drawing the weapon and reloading increases the challenge of maintaining speed and accuracy.

Hayley watches shooters take turns on the firing line. Tactical holsters and magazine pouches adorn their duty belts. Pressing a button on a wrist-mounted shot timer activates a three-second delayed buzzer that signals the drill's start. The shooter fires on predetermined targets in sequence, hitting as many as possible before the end of par time, which is signaled by a second buzzer. In their current drill, the shooters—all middle-aged or older—are limited to a ten-second par time. None of them appear to work their way through the entire course of targets, barely expending an eight-round magazine and reloading before the second buzzer goes off.

One of the shooters is Andrew Wilde, wearing pressed jeans, Timberlands, and a polo shirt rather than his customary blue suit. Hayley nearly didn't recognize her superior. Having just completed his turn at the firing line—shooting a Glock 17 and hitting eleven targets in par time—he glances over his shoulder at her. Hayley offers him a polite "golf" clap. His expression isn't warm, but she wouldn't expect it to be. Possessing a brusque managerial style, Wilde has never been anything but businesslike with the deeper state operative. Hayley is confident that he respects her skills.

She simply isn't certain that he *likes* her.

The last shooter has a turn on the firing line, an elderly gentleman who appears quite spry despite his seventy-seven years. Armed with a Colt 1911–style pistol, he activates the shot timer strapped to his wrist and, with the first buzzer, draws cleanly and starts firing, hitting three targets in sequence, shifting to the other side of an obstacle and firing three more times, all direct hits. He shifts again, hits two more targets farther down range, releases the mag, and reloads. The second buzzer goes off before he can get off any more shots, ending with eight targets hit in par time. Some pretty good shooting.

The other shooters respectfully applaud. With a friendly grin, the white-haired geezer holsters his weapon. As a former US president, his name is on a major airport in his home state and almost entirely out of the current news. He takes note of their newly arrived spectator and gives her a wink. Hayley nods deferentially and remains at the bottom of the overlapping stone stairway, giving distance to the shooters and excited chatter that follows their shooting drills. A bearded, ball-capped instructor in his midthirties provides tips to his elderly clients.

Wilder gestures to Hayley. She joins him as they stroll the short distance to the long-gun shooting range for some privacy.

"We were just talking about you."

Hayley glances behind her, back toward the pistol range. The former president has interrupted the range instructor and regales his captive audience with a story they have no choice but to appreciate. "All with Publius, sir?"

Wilder nods. "You recognize—?"

"The president, of course. And Stanley Teller, former vice chairman of the Board of Governors, Federal Reserve. Major General Laurence Chambers, recently stepped down from command of Army Intelligence and Security. I'm surprised to see Senator Conkle on the range. Didn't she get a grade of F from the NRA?"

"There's the public persona, and then there's the person. Meredith has opted to let her hair down a little in her retirement." He looks Hayley up and down, his eyes hidden by dark, aviator sunglasses. "You look fit."

"MMA training, sir. In West Virginia."

He waves his hand as if swatting away a persistent mosquito. "Christ, I know all of that."

"Of course, sir."

"Get enough *time away*, Chill? Cooking up a new project for you."

"Project, sir?"

"Overseas. Our embassy in London. Your passport is in order?"

"Yes, sir." Her voice is a bit vacant.

Wilde doesn't fail to detect her subdued reaction to news of her next assignment. "What's wrong? You have something against bangers and mash?"

"I've been working on something here, sir. On my own."

A hearty round of laugher from the adjacent range distracts a visibly impatient Andrew Wilde for a brief moment. True to form, he fails to appreciate Hayley's mild pushback.

"What sort of *something*?"

"I'm not entirely sure." Hayley is aware of how evasive she sounds. "I've barely scratched the surface."

"Sounds definitive," Wilde says with acid.

Hayley finds it difficult to meet her superior's gaze and decides silence is the best option here.

Her boss digs in. "You're on the prowl, Ms. Chill. Of what?"

She hesitates. Because she is in the possession of so few hard facts?

"The truth."

Wilde's brow couldn't furrow more than it does. "What the hell is this all about?"

Choosing her words carefully, Hayley says, "Rafi Zamani, sir. The NSA contractor behind this year's cyberattacks . . ."

"I'm not senile. I remember Zamani."

"When he infiltrated Pentagon servers, sir, he weaponized the data and targeted me. To impede my pursuit of him."

Rafi Zamani. Speaking the name again brings a rush of memories. Those dark days of last spring feel as if another lifetime. But only three months have passed since the computer hacker brought Washington, DC—and much of the eastern United States—to its knees with a series of escalating cyberattacks. Hayley and April Wu, as operatives of the deeper state, identified and stopped the mentally unbalanced young man. Their efforts saved hundreds of lives, and kinetic war with Russia was averted. But the costs of their success were high. A car would not have crashed and run over April Wu were it not for Zamani's takedown of the East Coast's electrical grid. And Hayley would have remained blissfully unaware of the truth regarding her father. She could have sailed through her entire life with the belief that Tommy Chill died in Iraq.

Instead of discovering his body hanging from a bedroom door in Arlington, Virginia.

"You know, we got a look at the contents of Zamani's computer," Wilde says cryptically.

Hayley hadn't considered the possibility.

"Then, you know that Charlie Hicks was responsible for my father's death in Iraq." Testing him. Seeing how much her superior *really* knows.

Andrew Wilde couldn't care less about Hayley's shattered family history. He has a job to do.

"So. It's Hicks you're looking into. Weeks dead, by his own hand."

Hayley is oddly relieved.

He doesn't have even half of the story.

She says, "You can hardly blame me, sir. Wanting to know the truth."

Wilde is unmoved.

"We need you on a London-bound plane tonight, Chill."

Without waiting for her response, he starts back toward the other range.

Hayley is a soldier, first and foremost. She took an oath—administered to her by a former Supreme Court justice in a helicopter's jump seat—after her last day at the deeper state's training camp in Oregon. If Publius orders her to go to London, Hayley will go.

"Yes, sir."

Wilde nods as she falls in behind him, satisfied with her response. He didn't expect anything less than her total dedication and obedience. Hayley turns to climb the steps back up to the range shack.

The former president gestures toward Hayley. "This her, Andy? Is this our intrepid Hayley Chill?"

She turns and faces the great man. Arms straight at her side, she offers an almost imperceptible nod. "Mr. President."

"For gosh sake, shake an old man's hand!"

The president thrusts his hand toward Hayley, who obliges him. Andrew Wilde watches like the corner grocer over his wares.

"Did Andy fill you in? What do you think about this business in London?"

Wilde answers for her. "I'd just mentioned it, Mr. President. I have a full briefing packet for her in the car."

"Excellent!" The former president fixes his gaze on Hayley, but with his trademark grin. Folksy and mostly genuine. "The work you're doin', young lady, keepin' in the shadows, takin' no credit when credit is most certainly due, well, see, that's just part of the job. You and I, we're lifelong public servants, get me?"

"Yes, sir."

Gesturing with both hands, the former president continues, "You more than most, Hayley. Andy filled me in. Gave me the whole low-down. What you've done for your country, young lady, that personal sacrifice cannot be misoverestimated!"

Hayley maintains a placid expression and says nothing in response.

"Shall we have another go at it, sir?" asks Wilde, tilting his thumb toward the range.

"Sure, sure. Let's make some noise." He looks to Hayley again. "You do some good over there in London, okay, Hayley? Keep us posted!"

The former president turns away, heading back toward the firing line. But then stops. That down-home grin again. Got him reelected despite a war and a bad economy.

"Say, didn't I hear you know your way round a gun?" he asks.

Andrew Wilde steps between Hayley and the former president. "That's enough. Let's not keep the president from his shooting."

But the older man, with a glint in his eye, shoos away Wilde with a wave of his hand.

Hayley says, "Expert badge in the army, Mr. President. And some further tactical training at the camp in Oregon."

He grins devilishly, sensing the opportunity for a bit of fun. "Wanna have a go, pretty lady? Show us what you got."

The former senator seems perturbed by the old man's choice of words and makes a disgruntled sound that only encourages her antagonist.

"Oh, c'mon, Mere! I can't keep up with what's allowed and what's not. See, my plan is stayin' with what I'm used to. They can't exactly vote me outta office, now can they?" He turns back to the deeper state operative. "That okay with you, Hayley?"

"Yes, sir. Of course."

His grin grows even toothier.

"Then why not give the ol' War Hawk a try!"

The former president draws his handgun. Checks to see the

chamber is clear and safety is on, then offers the pistol to Hayley Chill.

She accepts the weapon and holds it admiringly in her hand.

"That is one beautiful gun, sir."

"Damn straight it is. The manufacturer, Nighthawk Custom, was kind enough to send it over on my seventy-fifth birthday. Entirely handmade by a single gunsmith. Forty-five-caliber. Light rail, as you can see . . ."

Hayley completes the inventory. "DLC finish. RailScales carbon fiber grips. 'GI-style' thumb safety. Gold bead front sight. Black ledge in back."

She rechecks the chamber, racks the slide, testing the fit of slide to frame, and then holds the gun out at arm's length. "Nice."

Based on the Colt Government designed by John Browning in 1911—hence the original model name—the handcrafted pistol is both a work of art and a fearsome weapon.

The former president is a delighted owner, gazing on the gun as if it were his firstborn.

"Go on. Take 'er for a spin. Let's see what a real shooter can do with her."

"Thank you, sir. I'd like that very much."

Andrew Wilde frowns but says nothing.

The former president unbuckles his duty belt. "Here ya go. Cinch that up a notch or two."

Hayley holsters the gun and straps on the belt, checking the location of gun and mags without looking.

"What d'ya think? Gunna work for ya, Hayley?" asks the old man.

"Yes, sir. I think I'm all set."

The former president has the shot timer on his wrist ready. He stays close behind Hayley as she approaches the firing line.

"Ten second par time. Shooter ready?" he asks.

The other shooters and their instructor watch with keen interest.

Hayley's arms hang easily at her side. She is composed. Breathing steadily. She is still.

The words of her trainer at the camp in Oregon come back to her, a mental checklist that is more about focusing her attentions than anything else. About freeing herself from the clutter in her mind and doing only this one thing.

Sights. Slack out. Pressure wall. Press. Reset.

"I'm ready."

"Go!"

The old man activates the shot timer. In three seconds the first buzzer sounds.

Hayley draws the War Hawk cleanly and brings the pistol up, favoring her dominant eye.

She fires three times, in quick succession, shifts, fires three more times, shifts, and fires two more times, releases the mag and reloads, bringing the War Hawk up and firing three more times, shifting, three more shots, moving, and a final two shots as the second buzzer sounds. Par time.

All target assignments hit.

"Hot damn!" The old man slaps his thigh. He turns to the others, grinning like a schoolkid. "Ya see that? Sixteen dingers in under ten seconds!"

Humble to a fault, Hayley says nothing, exchanging the empty mag for a full one.

Major General Chambers, previously with Army Intelligence and Security, isn't impressed. "Course record for that target sequence is nine seconds, sir."

"Oh, yeah? Hundred says she can do it, Larry."

"You got yourself a bet, Mr. President."

The old man turns to Hayley. "Ready when you are, young lady. Nine seconds par time."

Hayley is at the line. "Shooter ready."

"Go!"

Hayley draws. With additional familiarity of her equipment and the target sequence, her movements are even quicker. More efficient.

Moving through the series of targets, not a single moment goes to waste.

She finishes just as the second buzzer sounds.

"Yes, ma'am! Sixteen dingers! All of 'em, centerline!" He turns around, crouching a bit and then jetting upright, his right fist thrust into the air. "That's a hundred bucks, Larry!"

The army general is unwilling to concede defeat.

"Double or nothing? Let's see if she's got eight seconds in her."

The former president looks to Hayley. Her expression is all the confirmation the old man needs.

———————

SHE STANDS BESIDE her parked Volkswagen, watching Andrew Wilde see off the other shooters. Regardless of party affiliation and from diverse professional backgrounds, all are dedicated members of the deeper state. Though they no longer hold exalted positions of power, they remain true to the oaths they took in their earliest government service days. Above and beyond politics, the men and women of Publius are the sworn, steadfast guardians of the United States Constitution.

As he climbs into the passenger seat of his funeral-black SUV, the former president gives Hayley a friendly wave. She returns the gesture, smiling.

After the other vehicles lumber off, Wilde walks over to where Hayley waits.

He offers her a canvas range bag, a Nighthawk Custom logo embroidered on the side. "A gift from your newest admirer." His displeasure is obvious.

The deeper state operative can scarcely believe it. "Are you serious? A custom 1911 is worth thousands of dollars."

The gift isn't the reason Andrew Wilde is upset with her. "Six months sitting behind a desk is what you deserve."

"Because it's the world's first completely virtual security organization, sir, Publius doesn't have a *desk* for me to sit behind."

He ignores her jibe. "Jumping rank like that. I'd kick your ass if I thought I had half a chance against you."

"The president invited me to shoot, Mr. Wilde," says Hayley. "So, I shot."

"Afterward?"

"We got to talking about his home state," says Hayley disingenuously.

"And about Charlie Hicks. Fort Bliss. And some nebulous *Storm*, whatever the hell that is," says Wilde, making his point in no uncertain terms.

Of course, Hayley could tell him now about what she found in the brick home in Arlington, drop on Wilde the same bombshell that obliterated the memory of her father. Would revealing that secret to her superior gain his cooperation?

She decides to keep these secrets to herself. Why exactly, she's not sure. Shame? Or is she worried that her father's imperfections will cast her in a negative light?

Hayley hopes she's a better daughter than that.

"What happened to my dad, it could be part of something big, sir."

"Or it could just be another fucked-up thing that happened one day in the middle of a shitty war in Iraq."

"There's only one way to find out, sir."

"And your new pal, the former president, would like you to do just that."

"London?"

"We'll put someone else on it, wiseass." He turns for his vehicle. Walking away and not looking back. "Don't be a stranger."

———

ON THE INTERSTATE again, the road unspools with predictable monotony. Hayley considers calling Sam. With a flight booked for early tomorrow morning, she has no time to see him before leaving town. He will want to know when she'll be returning. More questions will follow, none of which come with a satisfactory response. She decides against calling him.

Despite a pang of nagging guilt, Hayley feels the relief of being unfettered.

Involving Publius in investigating the sordid mystery of her father's double life and suicide has forced her hand. What had April said? *Go, but don't go it alone.* Hayley recognizes now she needed the deeper state's official sanction. With Wilde's blessing, the two threads—personal and national—are inextricably intertwined. One cannot be unraveled without the other. In her bones, she senses the darkness that lies ahead. Her intentions are pure . . .

The pursuit of truth. And on the heads of the wicked, vengeance.

————————

HE IS DRESSED and pulling on his Nocona boots three minutes after getting the call. The sky outside his bedroom window—the same view he's enjoyed every predawn of his life except while in the Marines—is cobalt blue. A few minutes before five a.m., the moon has long since plunked below the Chihuahuan Desert horizon. Standing, sheriff's deputy Jay Gibbs retrieves his cowboy hat from the dresser, where he left it the night before—brim side up so his luck doesn't run out. He places the hat on his head and squares it. Most of the other deputies opt for the department ball cap, but his father gave him the Resistol two years before he passed. Not much keeps Gibbs from wearing the straw Cattleman twenty-four hours a day but sleep.

The screen door bangs closed behind him, like a rifle shot. He has been alone here since 2016, the summer his old man died. Two years ago, a girlfriend stayed around for a few months, but he has been on his own since then, and just as well. The job keeps him busy enough. His other passion is reading, as evidenced by the few thousand books stacked throughout the house. Mysteries. Thrillers. True crime. History and biographies. Forget about science fiction and fantasy. Gibbs never developed a taste for genres that, in his opinion, value typing over actual writing.

The department prowler, a white Chevy Tahoe with twin "high-viz" gold metallic REEVES COUNTY SHERIFF vehicle wraps covering all four doors, is parked out front. Summoned for assistance in yet another crisis, Deputy Gibbs never ceases to relish this feeling of utility—an existence imbued with civic duty—as he shoots driveway gravel from under the Tahoe's rear tires. Answering the call.

Taking 285 south to 232, he spots an orange glow in the sky. That would be in the general direction of the Maverick Cryo Facility. Gibbs overtakes other emergency vehicles and first responders rushing to the scene, swinging the SUV onto the road's shoulder and keeping his foot on the gas. He knows a couple of the guys who work in the plant, a midstream facility for natural gas processing. But Maverick hasn't worked a graveyard shift since the boom years of 2018 and 2019. The pandemic drove oil and gas prices to historic lows, valuations that haven't recovered to this day.

Hell, three-quarters of the basin is out of work.

Gibbs is confident no personnel are inside the Maverick facility, twenty-six miles northwest of Pecos.

Fire engines and sheriff department SUVs block the road as he comes within a thousand feet of the facility. Gibbs rolls to a stop off the shoulder, the prowler nearly swallowed up by a stand of blood-weed. Opening the driver's door creates an open space in the tangle of vegetation, and the deputy exits the vehicle. The conflagration's roar shocks, a noise both terrifying and mesmerizing. His nostrils fill with the tendrils of the burning, acrid plume that swirls over the entire site. An EMT truck from Pecos pulls up behind him. Gibbs shouts at the tech who spills out. "Shouldn't be no one in there, Dickie!"

The medical technician doesn't slow his pace as he runs toward the blazing facility. "Well, I hear otherwise, Deputy!"

Gibbs falls in behind the other man, jogging toward the site. He witnessed firsthand the effects of explosion and fire on a human body: Afghanistan, where a mortar's direct hit on an ammo dump ignited a massive explosion; a semi on the interstate engulfed in flames; the ranch house in Hermosa that caught fire, trapping a family of five. Those memories repeatedly return to Jay Gibbs, like blackbirds on a telephone wire. In his sleep. When patrolling dark Texas highways in the prowler. The mind's movie projector never stops casting its horror show in lurid Technicolor.

The bodies aren't recovered from the facility for another seven hours, in the cruel glare of a midday sun. Gibbs is on the scene, of course, along with many of the same investigators from the Wink fire. As with that incident, identification of the two victims won't be an easy task. At the fire's worst, temperatures inside the plant reached 750 degrees. Both corpses presented a "pugilistic attitude," with flexed elbows and knees. Calvaria were free of soft tissue, with pronounced fissures of the *tabula externa*. Body cavities burst open, revealing fire-shrunken internal organs. Flames destroyed the extremities, too, leaving only torsos that broke apart when forensics team members attempted to transfer them to body bags. Total incineration, the county coroner pronounced, was averted by Pecos Volunteer Fire Department's diligent efforts to knock down the blaze.

The same Bureau of Alcohol, Tobacco, Firearms and Explosives agent confers with the same agent from the Texas Railroad Commission, palavering separately from county authorities. Investigators from the fire marshal's office expect to arrive on-site within the hour. Texas Rangers promise to weigh in, too. The second incident of sabotage in the Permian Basin is a big deal, with global ramifications. Authorities have collected a backpack relatively undamaged by the fire as evidence. The bag and its contents—a malfunctioning improvised explosive device and sixteen-inch bowie knife—are already on their way to the ATF's field office in Dallas.

Jay Gibbs pokes his head into the still-smoldering ruins of the cryo plant as one of the volunteer firefighters is coming out.

"Where they find 'em, Alberto?"

He points to the corner of the building nearest the door. "Almost made it outta here."

Stepping inside, Gibbs visually measures the distance from the doorway to the location. The fireman, Alberto Jimenez, wants to help. Everyone watches cop and detective shows on television, right? They all think they know enough to have an idea or two about police work. At least, that's been Gibbs's experience.

Alberto says, "Maybe they got disoriented."

"Maybe."

"Didn't I see you up at the Wink fire, too?"

"Yup. You saw me."

"You hear about the bomb? The FBI already sent it off to Dallas."

He has to smile at that one. *Already sent it off to Dallas.* That's what they call a trope. In his spare time, Gibbs is trying his hand at the author business. He's read a couple of how-to books on the subject. Even took an online class he didn't quite finish. Plenty of law enforcement folks take up creative writing. Some of them have been pretty damn successful. Rich, even. No reason to think the profession is beyond him. Aim high, his daddy always told him. Don't sell yourself short. One of these days, Gibbs is going to write a short story. And once he's published a few of those tales of crime on the highways and byways of West Texas, then he'll write a novel, too.

Modern-day westerns, like that fella, CJ Box.

How many times has he said those exact words to a buddy over beers at Freddy's Ice House? Having worked for the Reeves County sheriff for the past three years, with three more in the Marine Corps Military Police before that, Gibbs believes he has amassed all the material he needs. And then some.

"What's so funny?" asks Alberto.

"Nothing's funny about two men dead, Al."

"Think them Mex drug cartels are paying us back for interdicting their shipments north?" asks the volunteer fireman, an insurance salesman by profession. "That's what I hear."

Gibbs studies the plant's interior where the two bodies had been recovered, focusing on the door leading outside. Casual inspection reveals the door is fire rated, self-closing, and equipped with a panic bar. If the Mexican drug cartels are indeed sending their foot soldiers north to wreak havoc on the Permian Basin, then it occurs to the Reeves County sheriff's deputy that they ought to be able to afford a flashlight or two. A cell phone, even.

"Shoot, Alberto, how about leavin' a little of this police work for me? What do you say?" asks Gibbs.

3

CAN YOU HELP YOUR COUNTRY OUT, BIG FELLA?

She watches the landscape go from green to brown to bone white as the plane flies over Texas. Hayley has been out west before, stationed at Fort Hood while in the army. But the desert panorama is a shock after so many years on the East Coast. She presses her head against the cold airplane window, entranced by the vast emptiness. From thirty-five thousand feet, it's possible to imagine hers is an overflight of some alien planet. Devoid of people. Peaceful. Unmarred by human intrigue. But then comes the plane's descent. The edges of habitation come into view. Roads and highways are sutures in the desert landscape. Residential neighborhoods. Shopping centers. Roads and parking lots. The works of man flatten ancient sandstone ridges and erase flood-eroded ravines.

El Paso.

Her body offers an involuntary shudder. Lifting her gaze, Hayley looks past the city. Past the Franklin Mountains that bisect it, East from West. To the south, into Mexico, and an immensity she cannot comprehend. The Chihuahuan Desert is 140 thousand square miles in size. The US and Mexican border cities on either side of the Rio Grande are merely a stain on its immense canvas.

The woman at the car rental agency gives her directions to the Beverly Crest Motor Inn, the same motel where her dad stayed in each of his three visits. Hayley pulls into the lot, a few blocks west of Dyer, less than fifteen minutes later. The single-story motel has a motor-inn-style layout with an office that shares the building with a muffler shop. But the location is good, the Patriot Freeway less than a mile away. Hayley can be at the main gate of Fort Bliss inside of ten minutes. A fitness center beckons a short jog up 9th Cavalry Circle, and for longer runs, McKelligon Canyon Road, leading into the highest reaches of the Franklin Mountains, is practically outside her door.

The manager—"Jerry," according to a name tag—handles the check-in process. He's mostly bald, with long rockabilly sideburns and dandruff on his black, Western-style shirt. Hayley isn't sure if the shirt is part of a uniform or not. The big window unit that expels chilled air rattles with a bored, never-going-to-be-repaired resignation, underscoring a vibe that is unrelentingly sub-budget. Hayley doesn't mind. She isn't here for vacation.

"We have free HBO, just so you know," says Jerry as he taps on his computer keyboard, entering Hayley's information in slow motion. Hayley recognizes this hemming and hawing as an obnoxious form of flirtation. Making nice with him when she walked through the door was an unfortunate necessity. First on her agenda was showing the motel manager a photo of her father. With only that much of an exchange between them, Jerry makes unfortunate assumptions.

And, for all of that, the skeevy dude had no fresh information for her regarding Tommy Chill. All before his time employed at the motel.

While the motel manager fiddles with his computer, Hayley leaves the counter and approaches a bulletin board on an opposite wall. Flyers advertise pancake breakfasts, garage sales, and offers of day labor, hauling, and painting services. Hayley saw enough empty storefronts and homes for sale on her drive from the airport to comprehend the economic impact of the oil market's collapse on the region. Times are tough in the Permian Basin. El Paso derives enviable financial stability from the military's presence. Fort Bliss and the eight billion dollars the army installation dumps into its host city's economy every year serve as a necessary buffer against the oil industry's vicissitudes. Nevertheless, high unemployment and economic disarray encroach even here, in El Paso. The desperation conveyed by the bulletin board's homemade flyers is ample evidence of that fact.

One flyer, in particular, catches Hayley's eye, a missing person notice. The photograph is of a fifteen-year-old girl wearing a navy UTEP hoodie. With black hair and dark eyes, the girl possesses an innocent beauty that is achingly tenuous and fragile.

"Kimberly" is missing for three months now. Her father offers five thousand dollars for information leading to her recovery. Handwritten and inelegantly photocopied, the flyer is a cry for help, steeped with pain and anguish. The deeper state operative can't drag her eyes off it. This girl. She could have been one of Hayley's sisters. She could have been Hayley.

"Work or pleasure?" asks the motel manager.

"Business," Hayley says, returning to the counter.

He pushes a sign-in card across the glass-topped counter.

Hayley signs and accepts a card key from the motel manager. Only he doesn't release his grip on it.

"Need to blow off a little steam, you know who to call."

His grin is mostly a leer.

Jerry Fishbaugh has been running things here at the Beverly Crest Motor Inn for the last five weeks, pretty much with free rein. The owner is Chinese and has never visited the United States, let alone El Paso. As long as Fishbaugh surpasses a relatively low threshold, monthly-numbers-wise, the forty-two-room motel is his kingdom, where his subjects defy him at risk of deportation. Born and raised in Tulsa, the motel manager was stationed at Fort Bliss following his enlistment and never left. His apartment is up in Northeast El Paso.

Pretty sweet place. His assistant manager—a college dropout named Boone—does all the real work. Some days, Fishbaugh doesn't bother showing his face around here. But Boone drove over to Dallas for the week, so there you go. The upside? If Fishbaugh was at home in Northeast El Paso today instead of behind the office counter, he wouldn't be here to check in this fine piece of ass.

Hayley tugs the card key free of his pincer grip and turns away from the counter without comment. The motel manager watches her to the door.

— She parks her rental car in front of room thirty-two, mercifully at the opposite end of the property from the motel office. A housekeeper's cleaning cart is positioned just outside the room door, which is ajar. Hayley grabs her travel duffel from the back seat and pokes her head inside the room. With painted cinder block walls, combo desk/dresser, campus refrigerator, microwave, framed landscape prints, and queen-size bed shrouded in a paisley comforter, the accommodations are basic.

A housekeeper—roughly Hayley's age and Hispanic—has finished cleaning the room. Gathering her supplies, she hurries to make way for a paid guest.

Hayley wants to put her at ease. "It's okay. I can wait."

"I'm sorry, miss," she says, gaze lowered. "I'm finished."

As the housekeeper exits through the open door, Hayley can see her left eye is black-and-blue with a two-day-old bruise.

———

HER INSTRUCTIONS ARE to use the Chaffee gate. It's noon when Hayley parks in the lot and enters the small, utilitarian Visitor Control Center. A civilian employee wordlessly gestures toward a stack of clipboards and official forms when Hayley suggests that Criminal Investigation Command has left a pass for her. Enlisted personnel are more helpful. The acne-scared private accesses the appropriate file on his computer and prints out the necessary paperwork. Thank-

ing the nineteen-year-old for his assistance, Hayley exits the robustly
air-conditioned visitor center and steps back outside, into the hard
sunshine. Washington, DC, in August has nothing on West Texas.
The air stings with a white heat.

Hayley calls Chief Warrant Officer Roy Pogue from her car after
leaving the Chaffee gate. An agent for the US Army Criminal Investigation Command, he gives her directions to the Seventy-Sixth Military Police Detachment headquarters and meets her out front three
minutes later, seemingly oblivious to the blast-furnace temperature.
Pogue is tall and broad shouldered, a dark-skinned black man with
warm eyes and smile. With the CID for the last seven years and a military police officer before that, Pogue is dedicated, in equal measure,
to law and order. Unlike most military personnel on the post, he is not
in uniform. His civilian clothes—suit and tie always—are spotless
and exceptionally well pressed.

He holds the door open for Hayley and directs her to his office on
the first floor, a cubicle with a window view of the parking lot. From
her seat across the CID agent's desk, Hayley can see the framed photos of Pogue's wife and two grown daughters. Nice-looking family. He
has good reason to smile, Hayley decides. A fortunate man.

"Private Timothy Hooker, absent without leave."

Pogue's declaration comes without preamble or pleasantries. The
deeper state sent Hayley to El Paso with a cover as the aide to US Senator Gordon Powell, who serves on the Committee on Armed Services.
With pending retirement from the Senate after decades of service,
Powell has already been approached by former colleagues associated
with Publius. From the great state of Kentucky and an ardent believer
in the US Constitution, the retiring senator was more than happy to
assist in the operation. If anyone bothers to call his office on Capitol Hill, Hayley Chill's credentials will be faithfully confirmed. The
deeper state operative has done her work, of course. In the first hour
of her flight west, Hayley committed to memory all the information in
a thick dossier on the senator's life and long political career.

Private Hooker's military status is unwelcome news. He became Hayley's primary person of interest with an analysis of her father's phone records. Tommy Chill made several calls in the last six months of his life to an Arizona cell phone number. Andrew Wilde had been able to put a name to the number in short order but made no mention of Hooker being AWOL.

"Since when, Mr. Pogue?"

"Three weeks ago. His company commander held off making the report until yesterday, hoping Hooker would wander back. I only found out when I called over there this morning, in anticipation of your visit."

"Article eighty-five, sir?" Hayley asks, referring to a charge of desertion.

"Too soon to say. Some of these kids get homesick. Some of 'em just get tired of being told what to do all the time. Most just need a kick in the pants. From what the company commander reports, Hooker wasn't homesick." He shrugs. "Soldier with a Problem."

"Yes, Mr. Pogue. I understand."

"You're former military."

"Third Cavalry, Chief."

"And the pride of ARSOUTH," Pogue says with a mouthful of teeth showing. He'd done his research, too.

Hayley is modest to a fault. "Yes, sir."

"Buddy of mine is CID at Fort Hood. He saw one of your fights. Said you were a real badass." He draws out the last word. Another toothy grin.

"Good times, Mr. Pogue. Glad I gave your friend a good show."

He gestures at the thin file folder on his otherwise pristine desktop. "Can I ask what this is all about?"

"I'm afraid I can't say much more than that my investigation is a committee matter, Chief. Do you think I can have a look at Private Hooker's quarters?"

The CID agent indicates a cardboard box on the floor next to the door. "From his barracks. Every personal item he didn't take with him."

"Thank you, sir," says Hayley, appreciating Pogue's intuition and efficiency.

"Okay then," he says brightly, standing to retrieve the box from the floor. He places it on the desk for Hayley's inspection. "I'll let you get to it."

Pogue pauses in the doorway. "Let us know if you locate Hooker, won't you, Ms. Chill?"

"Yes, sir. Of course."

He nods. "Happy hunting."

Once Pogue is gone, Hayley pulls the box toward her and begins to remove its contents. Hooker didn't leave much behind. Personal hygiene products. An Alamo paperweight. A few band-released thrash metal CDs. Phone charger. No pictures. No papers. Nothing that would suggest a connection to Tommy Chill or his job at the Pentagon. At the bottom of the box is one book, a battered paperback copy of *Harry Potter and the Half-Blood Prince*. Hayley is on the verge of repacking the box when she stops. Retrieving the book, she riffles through them to where she finds a folded sheet of paper wedged between the pages.

Unfolding the paper reveals that it's filled margin to margin with rows of random one-, two-, and three-digit numbers, the same type of ciphered text she found on the pages from under the floorboards in her father's kitchen.

———

AN EARLY DINNER at a Mexican joint a few blocks north on Dyer seems substantially more preferable than heating something with the microwave in her room. She has time to kill before checking out the strip joint her father visited each time he was in town. With no evidence of his being a habitué of that sort of establishment back home, Hayley is confident these trips to the Aphrodite Gentlemen's Club were somebody else's idea. Timothy Hooker, perhaps? The strip joint is worth checking out.

El Toro Negro is all but deserted at five thirty. Finishing her tamale, Hayley checks her KryptAll phone, a device used exclusively to communicate with her superior in Publius, Andrew Wilde. There are no messages from him. With the full brunt of the deeper state's resources, she hoped at least the vague outlines of a conspiracy within the military would emerge. What exactly is the Storm? How deep was Tommy Chill's involvement with the cabal? And what's their agenda?

"Want some more iced tea, honey?"

The middle-aged waitress has approached the table with a fresh pitcher. Hayley nods.

"Thank you." Hayley pushes her plate toward the server.

"Finished? Those beans are homemade."

"I'm good, ma'am. Thank you."

Juanita Cruz was born in El Paso. Her mother crossed when she was pregnant. Working at the restaurant for the past twenty-six years, Juanita has put two daughters through nursing school. El Toro Negro is a family place. Over the years, she has waited on hundreds of female soldiers from the sprawling army post. White, black, brown, or Asian, those young women are all much like Hayley. Serious. Respectful. Always leave a tip, however modest. The male soldiers can be a bit rowdier at times. But even the young men in the military are better customers to have in the restaurant than civilians. Better people.

"You like your tamale?"

"It was delicious," Hayley says, smiling.

Juanita returns the smile. "You should eat more, *mijita*. You're too skinny."

Hayley nods. She has heard this before from other mother-surrogates.

"Live music on the weekends," Juanita says over her shoulder, turning for the only other occupied table on the floor.

Checking her watch, the deeper state operative reaches inside her canvas-and-leather tote for her wallet. After many years of slinging a backpack, the bag was a gift to herself when she was promoted from White House intern to paid staffer. Hayley's nickname for the shoulder bag is "Mother." Like most women, she keeps what feels like half of her entire existence in the tote at any given time. Essential documents, laptop computer, the modest amount of makeup she typically uses, books she's reading or thinking about reading, a fighting knife (depending on the occasion), and, on this day, a pregnancy test, purchased at a Walgreens on her way to the airport back home in DC.

Touching the box while retrieving her wallet reminds Hayley of a telltale anxiety she has pushed to the furthest recesses of her consciousness. An explanation for her recent fatigue and occasional nausea. She cannot imagine that she is pregnant, the chances of it being just so incredibly slim. Hayley wishes she hadn't purchased the test kit in the first place, reassessing it now as a waste of money and evidence of needless worry. A news broadcast on the television behind the restaurant's compact bar diverts her attention. With the audio muted, captions and video tell the story of the second case of sabotage to hit the Permian Basin, on this occasion a natural-gas-processing facility outside of Pecos, Texas, two hundred miles to the east. Hayley had read early news reports about the fire and explosion at the Maverick Cryo Facility when she landed earlier.

Several hours have passed since the explosion. The breaking news now, however, is that the governor has called out the Texas National Guard to protect the state's valuable oil and gas infrastructure from alleged narco-terrorists.

Juanita has paused in her work to watch the news also. When the broadcast cuts to a commercial for a local Ford dealership, the waitress exchanges a worried look with Hayley.

Not good.

THE STRIP JOINT is seven miles north on Dyer, in a cluttered, downscale neighborhood of mobile home parks, fast-food franchises, and auto-salvage shops. Aphrodite Gentleman's Club, a one-story stucco box with a faded awning and oil-stained parking lot, is literally at civilization's edge. Outside its back door is only desert. Hundreds of square miles of chaparral, rattlesnakes, and unrelenting wind.

Hayley parks across the street at precisely seven p.m. Tommy's credit card records indicate he was at the strip joint between six and eight p.m., off-peak hours when there's no cover charge and dancers can hang with their "regulars." The deeper state operative accesses Hooker's army portrait on her phone: white male, with thinning brown hair and a feral look in eyes that are a touch too far apart, he seems to drown in his combat uniform. Hayley committed the man's face to memory when Pogue first emailed the photo but feels a need to sear the image into her brain again.

It begins, she muses.

Hayley hasn't spent much time in strip joints, but the Aphrodite matches her experience from those few previous occasions. Lights down low. Bar to the left, stage to the right, VIP booths in the rear. Polished cement floor. A pervasive odor of cheap perfume and industrial-strength cleaning fluid. Attendance is sparse. The woman onstage works the pole with athletic efficiency but wholly out of sync with the eardrum-busting beats of rap music pumping from the sound system.

A dozen customers hold court at the "rack," tables that ring the two-foot-high stage. Tipping every dance is de rigueur and wins a few moments of special attention from the performing dancer. Clusters of young men occupy all but one of the front-row tables. Their regulation haircuts, age, and physical fitness betray their military status. The club's sound system obliterates any idea of conversation. With weary smiles, women wearing G-strings work the floor. The club is its own world; outside is another.

Hayley hangs back, taking a seat at the bar. The bartender is a forty-five-year-old ex-con with the face of a middle-aged Val Kilmer and the heart of a young Mel Gibson. The dancers call him Mr. High-lights, for, well, his weakness for balayage. Only the club's owner knows his real name: Leonard Pfeifer. He's not here by dint of his mixing skills—the Aphrodite is strictly BYOB—but for his six-foot, eight-inch frame and G5 rating in Krav Maga.

Pfeifer's boyfriend appreciates the lack of competition at an all-female revue. The Aphrodite gets its share of lesbians walking through the door. More than a few. But Mr. Highlights decides the conservative-looking, flaxen-haired, powder-blue-eyed Hayley—his only customer at the bar—isn't here for the dancers. Without even looking at her, Pfeifer can sense Hayley scanning the room. She doesn't seem like the pissed-off-wife type, either.

Cop, the bartender thinks. *Maybe CID*.

He pours Hayley a tall glass of soda water with a squeeze of lime. She nods her thanks and places a twenty-dollar bill beside the glass in payment for the bar stool's short-term rental.

Pfeifer lets the twenty ride. Hayley doesn't seem the type to claw back a tip.

After four dancers have cycled through their sets and another tall glass of soda water, Hayley begins to doubt her strategy. How many nights can she camp out on this bar stool at the Aphrodite and suffer the pitying looks of the bartender? If Hooker is AWOL or Article 85, would he risk revisiting these familiar haunts? Hayley considers showing the bartender a photo. But if Hooker is a regular, he and the bartender might be pals. She'd prefer not to tip her hand.

But Hooker is a first and vital link in the chain. Without action-able information from him, there may be no further investigation. Andrew Wilde's patience isn't unlimited, and Hayley presently doesn't have any other leads.

She motions to the bartender, who ambles down to her end of the bar. Slipknot's "Nero Forte" thunders from the sound system. Hayley places her work phone on the bar, displaying Hooker's army portrait.

Pfeifer barely looks before lifting his gaze to meet Hayley's.

His expression is, *Yeah?*

She gestures for him to come closer. Mr. Highlights leans his long frame over the bar, putting his ear within shouting distance of her lips.

"I'm not a cop!"

The bartender pulls away. Shrugs. *So?*

She gestures. He leans in again. Hayley cups her hand around his ear.

"Can you help your country out, big fella?"

The bartender wasn't expecting that one. He knows Hooker, of course. The guy is a total freak. But a threat to the United States? The blonde, though, seems to be a straight arrow. No arguing that. Mr. Highlights finds himself unusually sympathetic toward his customer seated at the bar. It's nothing sexual. No reason for his boyfriend to be concerned. But this young lady possesses a seriousness that impresses the bouncer/bartender.

Leonard Pfeifer decides she is deserving of his trust.

The bartender leans over the bar again, cupping his massive hand around her ear, and says with his low voice, "He's here. You've been staring at him all night."

Hayley pulls away in surprise and looks over the room again. Not seeing Hooker.

Pfeifer points his chin at a couple seated at the rack. Heavy-set, balding guy wearing a T-shirt and his skinny, female date.

Hayley fixes her gaze on the woman and, after a few seconds of scrutiny, realizes she's looking at Tim Hooker.

By means of vigilant shaving, hiding gaff with tucking ring, high-rise padded control panties, dazzling metallic dress, black synthetic wig, drag queen strappy sandals, and a cosplay false bust, the army deserter does a reasonable job of passing himself off as a woman, however trashy. Despite generously applied facial makeup, Hayley identifies Hooker by his eyes, mouth, and jawline. Captivated by the dancer onstage, the army deserter and his companion fail to notice Hayley's preoccupation with them.

She has no idea whether Hooker's cross-dressing is a proclivity or disguise and couldn't care less either way. He doesn't appear to be leaving anytime soon. One of the dancers working the floor has sat in his lap and whispers in his ear. As a precaution, Hayley moves to the far end of the bar. From this new vantage point, at low risk of being observed by her target, she keeps watch for another hour as Hooker and his companion take turns accepting solicitations for multiple lap dances. Finally, after the army private makes five additional trips to the VIP booths in the back, the two men seem done for the night.

Hayley slides off the bar stool, looking toward the bartender and nodding her goodbye. Pfeifer strides down to the end of the bar and offers her a massive fist to bump. The deeper state operative grins and bangs with the not-so-gentle giant, leaving the twenty next to her third glass of water. The bartender cannot appreciate the impact of his small assistance to Hayley. Though they will never meet again, he will think of her often, especially after the momentous events to follow. Only then will the bartender suspect the role he may have played, an involvement he will never mention to another soul. Mr. Highlights will keep his job at the strip joint on civilization's edge for another three years, until the night he takes only his two, Hulk-size fists to a gunfight in the Aphrodite parking lot and dies on that oil-stained cement. Every dancer in the joint will attend Leonard Pfeifer's funeral, unaware of the question Hayley put to him that altered the course of history.

Can you help your country out, big fella?

FROM INSIDE HER rental car parked across the street, Hayley watches Hooker and his friend leave the gentlemen's club. The army deserter totters unsteadily on the strappy thin-heeled sandals and removes them halfway across the parking lot from his pickup truck. His buddy detours to the fifteen-year-old Cadillac STS parked in the adjacent space. Their goodbyes are perfunctory. The forlorn engine start of the two vehicles breaks the relative silence.

The STS heads north on Dyer, swallowed up by the dark Chihuahuan Desert. The battered pickup heads south, with Hayley on its tail a block behind. Hooker takes Woodrow Bean Transmountain Drive west into the Franklin Mountains that bisect the city and then transitions onto westbound Interstate 10, into New Mexico. At this late hour, the road is mostly deserted. Past Berino, Mesquite, through Las Cruces, transitioning again, to Interstate 25 and following the Rio Grande north, past Radium Springs, a closed US Border Patrol checkpoint, and Rincon, the passing landscape wider and ever more desolate, with an eternity of night sky overhead. South of Truth or Consequences, where the river is plugged by a cement barrier to create the Caballo Reservoir, Hooker's pickup leaves the interstate and sweeps past a state park campground before turning right at an unmarked county road.

Following a few hundred yards behind, Hayley continues straight, driving past the two-lane county road. Glancing to her right, she watches the pickup truck's red taillights stare back at her like devil eyes, retreating into the void of darkness until they disappear entirely. She reverses at the turnoff for the dam and backtracks to the interstate.

Confronting the army deserter in the pitch black of San Andres hill country—dug in whatever shithole redoubt he has found there— would not be smart work.

As she accelerates to a cruising speed on the interstate, heading south toward El Paso, Hayley devises her plan. After his night of carousing at the Aphrodite Gentlemen's Club, she surmises that Hooker won't be leaving his lair above the Caballo Reservoir very early in the morning. The deeper state operative expects to find him home if she returns by noon, a schedule that allows her to make a necessary stop beforehand.

4

PINK

Hayley walks through the doors at the Cabela's on Desert Boule-vard at ten a.m. She packed the War Hawk in her checked bag, of course, but ran short of time to purchase ammunition for the custom 1911 handgun.

"Federal HST forty-five-caliber, 230 grain?" she asks one of the sales agents working the floor in the roomy gun department of the vast store.

The salesman grins, appreciating a woman who knows her guns.

"Coming right up. How many boxes are we talkin'?"

"Six."

"You got it!"

The salesman gets hopping.

Another customer followed Hayley into the gun department and witnesses the speedy transaction. Stocky. Dressed in jeans and work shirt that aren't ever going to come clean of the grime accumulated from long shifts on too many Permian Basin rigs to count.

"Smart," he says to Hayley's back.

She has no other option but to engage him. "Sir?"

The scruffy chainhand gestures at the guns on display. "Putting some firepower in those pretty, little hands. That's *smart*."

Hayley nods, giving him a tight smile. One that he fails to read correctly.

"I've got my own guns, for sure. AR. My Rossi carbine. P320. But with the shit going down back home? I need to put some fire-power in my ol' lady's hands. Something she can carry to the grocery store, know what I mean? Cuz they're coming, all right. Right over the border, wall or no wall. Blowing up tank farms left and right. It's a fucking war zone . . . 'cuse my French."

"They?"

"Drug cartels, darlin'. Sinaloa. CDG. Los Zetas. Jalisco New Generation. You name it, cartel honchos are sending over their foot soldiers in retaliation for our cooperation with Mexican Armed Forces and La Chota. If this isn't a war, then I don't know what is. Why do you think the governor is sending in the Texas Army National Guard? And this is just the beginning. Better get more than six boxes, darling. I drove in all the way from Odessa. Can't buy a round of ammo for a hundred miles back home. Shelves are empty. Shit's hittin' the fan somethin' serious in the basin."

SHE WEARS HER Senate outfit: sensible flats, white sleeveless blouse, and matching gray linen pants and jacket. The effect is business casual, not cop. Hayley gave some thought to roping in Roy Pogue, the CID agent, for backup, but can't risk losing her one shot of inter-viewing Hooker without official interference.

The deeper state operative has no idea what lies in store for her up in the dry moonscape above the Caballo Reservoir and must be hyperalert. There is always the risk that Hooker will rec-ognize her from last night at the strip joint. Hayley is confident he won't, the army private being too distracted by the action onstage to have noticed her. She is too pragmatic, however, to ignore the possibility that she is wrong. That's when the War Hawk comes into play.

The county road leads into higher elevations above the dammed Rio Grande, into sparsely populated and arid hill country. The few houses Hayley passes appear abandoned, falling-down structures that have been ravaged by wind and rainstorm, wood siding sun blistered, and roofs caved in. Near what seems to be the paved road's terminus, a turnoff leads to a single dirt lane posted by a mailbox and shotgunned No Trespassing sign. She eases her rental car to a stop after turning onto the drive—no house or mobile home in sight—and shifts it into park.

Hayley performs a final check of her weapon and places the War Hawk on the front seat next to her. Exiting the car, she goes to the front left tire and crouches down to let most of the air out. From the trunk, she retrieves the jack and tosses it into the creosote bushes on the side of the road.

Underway again with a flat tire, Hayley follows the driveway up and over a ridge. Below is an occupied homestead, the first for miles. Hooker's truck is parked in front of a mobile home, in addition to a Nissan pickup and a Suzuki four-door sedan. Salvage-yard body parts are a common theme. So are missing wheel coverings, cracked windows and windshields.

The mobile home, perched on a foundation of cinder blocks, is the compound's primary structure. A thirty-two-by-sixty-foot sheet metal barn to its north is larger, but the roll-down door is missing a few panels and remains open to the elements. The barn's interior is dark, but gaps in the siding reveal what appears to be a hoarder's wet dream.

Hayley stops about twenty-five yards from the mobile home, with the barn to her right. Keeping the car's engine running, she opens her door and climbs out. From her vantage point standing next to her car, she can see a dilapidated eight-by-twenty-foot mobile construction shed positioned to the south of the trailer home. The trailer's tires have disintegrated, held together only by synthetic inner liners. Metal bars protect the shed's slider windows, and the steel door is padlocked. An odor of human waste wafts in Hayley's direction from the bright orange five-gallon "Homer" plastic bucket positioned under one corner of the construction trailer.

Only a handful of seconds have elapsed since she exited the car when the mobile home's screen door is pushed open. Tim Hooker emerges from its shadowy confines.

"Can I help you?" he asks in a way that suggests he's not particularly interested in helping at all.

The army deserter has swapped metallic dress and strappy heels for dusty blue jeans, cowboy shirt, and dirty white T-shirt. His snapback cap advertises a bar in Wink called the Dog-House. No saying if Timothy Hooker knows the name refers to the room on a drill floor, an oil rig's command central.

Hayley points semi-helplessly at the front flat tire on her car. "Got a flat. Some damn fool before me must've stole the jack."

Hooker says nothing. Just nods, bobblehead-like.

The deeper state operative squints one eye and cocks her head in a way she's seen in the movies. "Think I can borrow yours?"

"What're you doin' way up here? That is, if you don't mind me askin'."

Hayley sees the curtain in one of the trailer windows move slightly. Suzuki perhaps. Or Nissan truck. Maybe both are in there.

Hayley feels the cold weight of the War Hawk, riding in the "inside the waistband" holster she purchased once she'd shaken loose the overly friendly Odessa chainhand. An IWB carry seemed the best approach, given the situation: relatively quick draw, thin profile, and highly concealable. More important, she can still access her weapon if there's a struggle and she ends up on her back.

"Looking at some property to buy, back down the road a mile."

"Conway place? White-and-blue trailer?" asks Hooker.

She draws a blank.

Hayley knows there's no white-and-blue trailer on the unmarked county road. Because she paid attention when heading up.

She says, "Fitzgerald's. Rusted-out stock tank on the knoll up above the stove-in ranch house." The mailbox had been missing a couple of press-on letters, but she was able to *Wheel of Fortune* a guess. "Ten acres. Good piece of land."

A second man joins Hooker in the doorway of the trailer. No shirt, rat beard, and scraggly chest hair. His jeans are more grease-smeared than blue. Bandages wrap his left hand.

He says, "Help the lady out, Tim."

Nissan Truck, Hayley designates him.

Where's Suzuki?

Hooker mutters something in the other man's ear, eyes on Hayley, then leaves the mobile home's open doorway. He comes down the two homemade steps, walking toward the rental car.

Did he recognize me? From last night?

The army deserter stops at the front of the rental car and, hands on his hips, stares at the tire.

Nissan Truck steps through the open doorway and stops on the small landing, made from scrap plywood and cinder blocks. "Lookin' at it ain't gonna fix it, dummy."

Hooker shoots a pissed-off look back in the other man's direction, then stomps to the back of the car and pops the trunk. Hayley is confident he won't likely discover boxes of ammo she hid under the passenger seat.

The army deserter excavates the doughnut spare from its secured placement under the trunk mat and throws it in the dirt near the car's front. Hayley watches him stride off toward the metal barn, where he intends to fish a jack from somewhere within its bowels.

"Come inside. Get out of the sun." Nissan Truck's smile reveals lackadaisical dentistry.

"I'm good," Hayley says with reasonable casualness.

"Come on, now. No sense standin' out there sweatin' in the hot sun."

Hayley prefers her chances outside, but confirming Suzuki's whereabouts is the more significant priority. If there are more than three of them, the odds begin to shift against her.

The deeper state operative walks to the steps leading up into the trailer home. The shirtless desert rat moves aside, with surprising courtliness, to facilitate her entry. Hayley climbs the two steps and enters the mobile hovel.

The large Nazi flag hanging on one wall would be difficult to miss were it not for an even more distracting bearded fat man, naked except for black thong bikini underwear, seated below it in a recliner chair. The combination of the two—Nazi flag and nude, fat man—is a shock that Hayley manages to mask with nothing more than a raised eyebrow.

They just keep getting naked-er and naked-er.

Suzuki, she decides. With luck, there are no other people elsewhere inside the trailer.

The fat man doesn't look like he'd be much in a fight . . . unless he has a gun hidden somewhere between his voluminous body mass and the recliner's seat cushion.

"We don't get many visitors up here at Rancho Cocoa Puffs." Suzuki's phlegmatic voice comes from somewhere deep within all of that flesh. Hayley is now certain there is a gun beneath his right thigh, observing a hint of blue steel peeking out from beneath the fat man's hairy leg. Drawing it will take some doing, she calculates, and puts most of her concern in the more agile Nissan Truck, who has shifted his position to outflank her. The doorway is effectively blocked.

Suzuki watches her closely. She orients her gaze on the Nazi banner. Staring at the nude bearded fat man would be the alternative.

"You ain't Jewish, are ya?" asks the seated man.

Hayley meets his taunting gaze.

"Is it that obvious?"

The right-handed Nissan Truck grabs an aluminum baseball bat propped against the wall and raises it over his head, lunging toward Hayley. She draws and raises the War Hawk, nearly poking the charging man in his right eye with the barrel end. But as Nissan Truck shrinks from the gun pointed at his head, Hayley hears the low squeal of ancient recliner chair groaning under the obese weight of Suzuki. Knows, too, that the fat man is going for another gun and not the one under his elephantine thigh.

The backup gun.

Turning and acquiring her target before she fires, Hayley takes the trigger to the wall and then some. . . .

The 230-grain jacketed hollow point round does the sort of damage to a human head its engineers envisioned.

Which is to say, total damage.

And she hopes, frankly, that she hadn't made a mistake in *thinking* she saw him bringing up the hand cannon. Because, though she has killed, she has never killed casually. Never without cause. No time to verify any of that now because Nissan Truck, with the gun off him, comes back at her, swinging his bat.

Wishing it were his right hand that was bandaged and out of commission, Hayley ducks below the arcing bat. Strike one.

"Stop!" She has a gun, after all, and Nissan Truck only a baseball bat. Hayley had displayed her willingness to use it. The headless Suzuki—his bloody beard splattered across the Nazi flag—is proof positive of that.

Nevertheless, Nissan Truck presses forward with his attack. Driven by what? Revenge? He brings his bat down, missing Hayley and demolishing a rickety TV tray table instead.

Strike two.

"Damn it! Drop the fucking bat."

Hayley has had her shot all this time, but has held fire.

The skinny shirtless man raises the bat again, breathing heavily from his exertions, and howls like a Viking berserker.

Hayley shoots the man, center mass, throwing him backward against the opposite wall, the exit wound in his back leaving a bloody skid mark all the way down.

Called strike three. *You're out.*

———————

THERE'S NO SIGN of Hooker outside. Having taken the precaution of hiding both of Suzuki's firearms—he had indeed retrieved a sawed-off shotgun from the floor when Hayley blew his head off—Hayley walks down the steps and across the gravel drive to her rental car. She checks the back seat and under the vehicle. Nothing. If Hooker is hightailing it on foot, she would see him on the road leading up the opposite ridge. Her eyes fall on the cavernous metal barn with the fucked-up roll-down door off its tracks.

He's in there and it's up to me to get him out.

The War Hawk held down at her side, Hayley strides toward the barn. Her desire is to take the army deserter alive. And not get killed. In that order.

As she approaches the barn's nonfunctioning door, her worst fears about what's inside are confirmed. The barnlike structure's entire interior is crammed with a hodgepodge of junk stacked in piles that reach halfway to the ceiling.

Hayley stops in the open doorway, raising the War Hawk and gripping it with both hands.

"Tim Hooker!"

Only the sound of wind rattling the metal barn's loose joints is the response.

"C'mon out, Private. Taking you back to the post. I'm not here to hurt you."

The mobile home's screen door behind her bangs open and shut in the gusty, desert breeze. That and the squawking of the barn's wind-buffeted sheet metal panels are the only sounds Hayley hears in response.

She's got to go in there.

The deeper state operative enters the barn. If there's a light switch somewhere, she's not going to find it easily. Or quickly.

Hayley wishes she had a weapon light for the War Hawk's recon rail and silently reprimands herself for not buying one in town. Or at least a goddamn flashlight!

Narrow passages lead deeper into a darkness that grows more intense with every step away from the open doorway. Plastic water barrels, dusty computer components, stacks and stacks of half-collapsed cardboard boxes, crates of empty beer bottles, piles of cast-off clothing, piles of construction supplies, tools, random car parts, household and office furniture, more cardboard boxes, a small mountain of mannequins, and then it becomes too dark to see what forms the walls of her passageway. Hayley can only sense—and smell—the presence of more and more chaotic debris.

She keeps her gun ready, listening for the slightest sound that might betray Hooker's location.

Hayley stops, sensing danger. The hairs on her forearms stand up in prophetic alarm.

Slowly inhale and then exhale.

The barn's metal walls and roof continue to rattle and groan.

Hooker's faint footfalls betray his location to her immediate right. His form *almost* visible. Something raised over his head *barely* distinct.

Hayley pivots, at the same time aiming for what she estimates will be his shoulder, and fires. The flash briefly illuminates Hooker advancing on her with a machete, poised to strike. He goes down.

The deeper state operative holsters her sidearm and drags

a wailing Hooker to just inside the doorway, needing light if there's any hope of saving him. "Any" is the operative word. Hayley now sees the .45-caliber hollow point slug has demolished the army deserter's shoulder, all but separating his arm at the glenoid socket. The glistening head of his right humerus juts from the mess of tissue that dangles from what's left of clavicle and deltoid muscle.

———————

BOTH OF HIS parents were drug addicts who died from accidental overdoses within two months of each other. Raised by Bible-thumping grandparents in Sacramento, California, fourteen-year-old Tim Hooker clashed with their strident disciplinary beliefs. The rebellious teenager soon took to the streets. Cycling in and out of juvenile hall, young Hooker fell in with a skinhead gang that offered him family and unqualified acceptance. Espousing the most rudimentary racist beliefs, the all-white gang engaged in bloody, ongoing turf wars with the Pope Street Crips and Barrio Pachuco Nortenos.

The day after his nineteenth birthday, he participated in the ritualistic murder of a former member who tried to leave the gang. Police apprehended most of the offenders, but Hooker, the triggerman, managed to escape by hiding from police in a dumpster. Without money, his street "family" in jail, and grandparents long since washed their hands of him, Tim Hooker enlisted in the US Army and was on a bus heading to basic training the following morning.

———————

HAYLEY ESTIMATES THAT Hooker has less than two minutes to live.

She retrieves a cotton shirt from a pile of old clothing and folds it into the semblance of a dressing, compressing it against his subclavian artery. The army deserter screams.

"You're gonna be okay."

His eyes find hers. Panicking.

"Calm down, man."

Hooker grits against the pain, subsiding as he goes into hypovolemic shock. Blood pressure plummets. Adrenal glands go into hyperdrive.

He's dying. Fast.

Hayley brings her face to only inches from his.

She says, "You knew my father."

No response.

"Charlie Hicks."

Nothing.

Then, as a question. "Tommy Chill?"

Still nothing.

Hayley knows she is losing him. Losing her chance.

She says, emphatically, "Charles Hicks. Works at the Pentagon. You met him three times at the Aphrodite in the last year."

His eyelids flutter as life ebbs. Too much blood lost.

Hooker's jaw barely moves.

". . . white . . . nation . . ."

Hayley clocks what he has said, the searing hate that motivates these words. And eases off her pressure on his injury.

The faintest of smiles appears on Hooker's face. Eyes are almost closed now.

"Storm rising."

———

Sitting back on her heels, she looks up from the dead man. Her eyes fall on the construction shed to the left of the mobile home. She needs to know what's inside. The smell drifting from that direction is strong evidence of human habitation. Or imprisonment?

Hayley stands and reenters the barn, reemerging seconds later with a crowbar.

The construction shed is accessed by three metal-grate steps. Its door is secured with a heavy-duty hasp and shrouded padlock. Hayley bangs on the door. Twice. Hard.

"Anybody in there?"

No answer.

"I'm coming in." A beat. "I've got a gun."

Yeah, if anybody's in there, they've probably gotten that idea, she thinks with a wry half grin.

Hayley jams the end of the crowbar in the thin gap between the door and frame. Her leverage isn't enough to pull the door out, but the padlock hasp loses some of its purchase. She focuses her energies there, prying the hasp from the steel door. With a few minutes of effort, it swings open. The deeper state operative backs away, returning to the top step, and draws her weapon, pointing it into the construction shed.

She sees:

The detritus of human confinement, including scattered clothing, eating implements, empty and half-full gallon water jugs.

Graffiti and messages scrawled on the interior walls.

A man lying on his back, wearing only pants and motionless near the doorway.

Another man—Hispanic, no more than twenty years old—crouched in the farthest corner of the shed, staring back at Hayley. Wide-eyed. Terrified.

The smell that wafts from the shed's interior is far worse than the stink outside. Death and decomposition.

Hayley holds her position, keeping the gun trained on the crouching man while she processes exactly what she is seeing.

"I'm not going to hurt you."

The young man's expression doesn't seem to register her words.

He can't speak English.

She gestures for him to come out.

The man tentatively stands up from his crouch. Hayley walks backward down the steps, lowering her weapon but keeping it at her side.

She points. "Over there, please. Stand there."

Blinking as he steps into the sunlight, the man seems to understand. He shuffles on unsteady legs to a piece of shade cast by the adjacent mobile home.

Hayley climbs the steps again, peers inside the gloomy shed, then looks down to the man lying on his back. He's dead. A couple of days, at least, she guesses.

Hayley backs out and goes down the steps again. The prisoner stares at the .45-caliber pistol in her hand. His fear is palpable. She holds out her hands in response, so he can see the gun, and then holsters it again.

"I'm not going to hurt you. I want to help. I'm here to help." She leans heavily into the last word, drawing it out so that the young man understands.

"*Are they gone? The men? Are they all gone?*" he asks, in his rapid-fire Spanish.

Hayley may speak fluent Russian, but her Spanish comprehension is nonexistent beyond the obvious phrases and words.

"*The men imprisoned so many of us. . . . Are they dead? Where are the others? I'm afraid they're dead. The North Americans captured us coming over the border. They imprisoned us here. These men are very bad. Are they dead? Did you kill them all? Where are the other immigrants? They must dead. All dead.*"

The deeper state operative picks out enough words to understand he is talking about Hooker and the other men she killed. Her gift for extraordinary memorization isn't limited to visual triggers. With echoic memory—associated with auditory stimuli—she retains every word the prisoner says. Each inflection. Hayley locks it down.

GETTING UNDERWAY ON the gravel road is simple business after finding an operational tire inflator in the barn. She keeps all the car windows open driving back over the ridge and down the gravel road toward the interstate three miles west, an absolute necessity with the odor coming off the disheveled young man sitting next to her.

His name is Diego. That much Hayley was able to figure out on her own. She suspects he is in a state of shock and probably suffering from the effects of severe dehydration. The man requires immediate medical attention.

Hayley checks her phone for a signal. Once she contacts CID agent Roy Pogue, the deeper state operative intends to return immediately to Timothy Hooker's hideout on the other side of the hill. Searching the compound for more clues before other authorities arrive is absolutely essential.

Diego, once started, can't stop talking. To Hayley's ear, seemingly without punctuation.

In his excited Spanish, he says, "*Three men, all bad. They would feed us only rice and beans once a day and at times not even that much. In the beginning, there were ten of us. We came from everywhere south. From Mexico, like me. But also from El Salvador . . . Guatemala . . . Honduras. I was the last one taken captive. I cannot remember how many days ago it was. I crossed over in May. What month is it now? Are you with the police? Border Patrol? The men would come just after sundown and they would select two of us. Taken away and driven somewhere. We would never see them again. One morning, only a few days ago, one of our captors—tall and skinny white man—his hand was badly injured. I could see, through a crack in the wall. He was in a lot of pain. His hand, his arm, very badly burned. A little doctor came later that day to help him, wearing the uniform of your army, camouflaged, two black bars here . . .*"

He points to the center of his chest. *"The little doctor who helped the injured man came into our cell, and he tried to help us. I do not speak English, but I know the bad men told the little doctor not to bother with us. We were going to die anyway."*

Hayley checks her phone again. Seeing that she has a signal, she gestures to Diego to stop talking. She has committed everything he has said to memory, without comprehension.

"Wait, okay. Just let me make this call." Feeling ridiculous. She knows he has no idea what she's saying.

Hayley pulls over to the side of the two-lane road. The interstate is visible in the distance. Without one leaf of vegetation for miles, steep ravines and fissures fracture the descending hillside. The road seems precarious and temporary. A gusting wind, of course.

The deeper state operative pops her door open and turns to Diego. "I'll be right back. Two minutes." She holds up two fingers. "Two. Two minutes."

Sitting in his cubicle, the CID agent answers on the third ring. "Pogue."

"Mr. Pogue, this is Hayley Chill."

"Are you in a wind tunnel, Ms. Chill?"

Hayley stands at the front of the car, staring out over the lunar landscape. "In a way. New Mexico, sir. I located Hooker."

"No kidding? I'll send some officers right over."

"Chief, I think you better come out, too."

Pogue senses what he couldn't possibly imagine. Cop instincts kicking in.

"What the hell happened?"

"He's dead, sir."

Hayley frowns as the line goes quiet.

How long is this going to take? How much time do I lose having to deal with local authorities?

Finally, Pogue says, "Give me your exact location, Ms. Chill." His tone of voice is flat.

He's pissed.

"Exit 59 off Interstate 25. You want the access road that takes you to the east side of the reservoir. At the terminus of an unmarked county road you'll find at Pulido Canyon."

"Got it. Sit tight. We'll be there in ninety minutes."

Pogue disconnects.

Anticipating the paperwork, interviews, and red tape that the shoot-out will generate, Hayley suffers a brief agony.

I don't have time for this shit!

The deeper state operative turns to get back in the car and sees that Diego is gone.

She checks the vehicle's interior, looks up the road, and then scans the open country on either side.

In a few seconds, she clocks him. The undocumented immigrant runs at the bottom of a deep wash, heading south. He has about a two-hundred-yard head start on her.

Hayley starts to give chase but then stops only a few feet from the road's edge. She looks down at her shoes and then up at the rugged terrain.

There's no way.

She says, "Shit!"

Hayley watches the young man scurrying off, quickly lost in the vast landscape, and turns back toward the car.

———————

TELL ME SOMETHING *I don't already know.*

Hayley listens patiently as Chief Warrant Officer Roy Pogue, wearing one of a dozen tailored dark suits he owns, explains what he and other investigative authorities have uncovered in their preliminary search of the mobile home, barn, and constructions shed. The compound swarms with uniformed New Mexico State Police and agents from US Army Criminal Investigation Command. Though it's after six p.m., the sun is still high enough that mismatched chairs have been retrieved from the barn and set up outside in any available shade. Hayley has been sitting in one of these wooden, straight-back chairs for the past two hours, watching Pogue and his colleagues work the site. Before they arrived, she thoroughly searched the mobile home herself, taking care to wear gloves while accessing boxes of papers and more than one computer device.

The CID agent takes a seat, enjoying the respite of shade.

He says, "Some kind of satanic death cult is the best I can ascertain right now. The Nazi memorabilia is fairly obvious evidence for affinity with white supremacist beliefs."

Hayley is way ahead of him but plays dumb.

"The other two men?"

"The big boy whose head you splattered all over his pretty flag was Charles Henry Wilcox, medical discharged more than five years ago. Never served overseas. His skinny friend was Anthony Joseph Fermin. Did a couple tours in the sandbox. BCD, with three years in Leavenworth," says Pogue, referring to a bad conduct discharge.

"For?"

"Aggravated assault on an officer."

She just looks at him, waiting for it.

"Yes, Ms. Chill. A black officer."

Hayley notes Pogue's admission of this fact with a brief silence. Changes tact.

"What about the undocumented immigrant? His dead friend in the construction shed. There's evidence of several others having been confined in that box."

"Criminal Investigation Command wouldn't wish to speculate." His grin is mirthless. Dire, even. "But if you were to ask Roy Pogue, he might say this is some kind of sex-cult thing."

The deeper state operative nods, almost imperceptibly. "Okay."

Wouldn't be my first guess.

Pogue adds, "Lot of places up in these hills to bury the bodies."

Hayley takes a breath and looks around. The New Mexico State Police are being particularly methodical in their investigation and evidence collecting.

Making no effort to disguise her impatience, she asks, "Who's running the show here, Chief?"

"You have someplace to be?"

"As a matter of fact, I do." Her decision not to elaborate appears deliberate. Pointed, even.

County coroner personnel choose this moment to haul one of the sheet-covered bodies from the trailer. Their van is parked next to the beat-to-shit Nissan pickup truck.

Pogue looks over his shoulder and eyes the procedure, then returns his attention to Hayley.

He says, "Pretty fancy shootin' for a Senate aide, I'd say."

"I know my way around a firearm, Mr. Pogue. Earning a blue cord will do that," she says, referring to the fourragère in light blue awarded to infantry-qualified soldiers in the US Army. Hayley Chill was among the first women to complete all Infantry Training Brigade requirements successfully.

"And you say you bought the forty-five today?"

"No, Chief. Just the ammo. I'm licensed to conceal carry in Virginia and the District of Columbia. The paperwork is in the car. Shall I get it for you?" Andrew Wilde made it possible for her to obtain the necessary licenses in a few hours, just one of the many perks associated with being an active member of the deeper state.

The CID agent waves off the offer. "I think you'll be able to leave directly, Ms. Chill. But maybe you can share a little bit more about the nature of the committee's investigation. Tracking Hooker to his hideout was risky, to say the least. I'm curious what compelled you to do such a thing, without backup."

She isn't prepared to reveal any specifics of her mission to Pogue, not until she knows more. The truth is, Hayley doesn't know the subject of her investigation. Only a sense of the thing has emerged since her confrontation with Hooker and his cohorts. The broadest of out-lines. One hint was a self-published copy of the Declaration of Inde-pendence by the Republic of Texas, signed in 1836, that she found on top of a stack of pornographic magazines in the bedroom. The Nazi artifacts. The men's toxic racism.

What did Tommy Chill have to do with someone like Hooker? She's certain the two men met on three occasions at the strip joint. If Hayley is to have any understanding of her father's fate—of the document she found hidden under the floor in his kitchen—she must plunge deeper into the abyss.

"The senator and his committee are investigating white suprem-acy in the military, Mr. Pogue. I can't go into any more detail than that." This sounds plausible enough to Hayley's ear as she says it.

The CID agent is somber as he processes the deeper state oper-ative's vague response.

"Okay. Well, anything I can do to help," he says, matching her level of candor.

Hayley offers a tight smile, but something behind Pogue's back has caught her attention. "Who's that, do you think?" she asks.

———————

HE HAD BRAKED at first sight of the mess of vehicles and authori-ties assembled at the compound. Putting the truck in reverse, Peter Oswald backed up fifteen yards, over the other side of the ridgeline. Wearing loose-fitting black khaki trousers and a black button-down cotton shirt, he exits the truck and walks back to the rise. Even the cotton twill safari fedora he wears on his head is black. With bland facial features and expressionless eyes, Oswald seems from neither this region nor any other, for that matter. By design, he is nebulous. His clothes are a costume, purchased at a JCPenney in Midland. He bought the twelve-year-old Ford F-150 pickup truck for two thousand dollars in Kermit. This morning's breakfast came from Dewey's, in

Odessa, a nearly six-hour drive east. The Swarovski EL 15x56 HD binoculars strapped snugly in the harness he wears across his chest matter most. Texas being a state of vast reaches, Oswald has found practical use for the high-end field glasses. Through them, he has observed every incident of sabotage that has taken place in the state over the past two weeks.

Oswald is especially glad to have the binoculars upon discovering the New Mexico compound overrun with local and military police.

Within moments of his leaving the air-conditioned truck cab, sweat pricks the skin above his eyebrows. His lower back is killing him after several hours behind the wheel, not unusual for a man near his sixtieth birthday. He remembers when his body was strong and his stamina seemed boundless. This physical degradation has weighed heavily on his emotional well-being in the past years. The breakup of his marriage and estrangement from his three grown children have taken a toll, too. Middle age is one long suck. This is why Oswald has seized this current operation with the zeal of a man with nothing to lose, breathing fire into a life that has become increasingly without meaning.

The Storm has given him reason to hope.

But even that sense of renewed optimism can't restore the deteriorating L1 and L2 spinal segments of his lumbar vertebrae.

Once atop the ridge, Oswald has an excellent vantage point over the compound in the wash below. Ignoring the numbness in his left foot, a symptom of his sciatica that rarely eases, he removes the binoculars from their harness and puts glass on the investigators, committing their faces to memory. Differentiating the military personnel from the local authorities is a trivial task. Oswald spent enough time in the US Army to recognize a CID agent when he sees one. Is it the squared shoulders? Trimly cropped haircuts? Makes no difference anyway. That the compound was compromised is bad business. Judging by the bodies being carted away by the county medical examiner and lack of arrested suspects, all of his people down below are now dead.

Just as well. Their roles in the operation are all but over and done. Low-level players in the plot. Whoever killed them did the cause a considerable favor. Their deaths save Oswald the trouble of killing them himself.

HAYLEY POINTS TO the hill that rises above the compound and the road out. She can just barely make out a man standing on the rise about a mile off. The occasional sun flare off what must be binoculars is the beacon.

CID agent Roy Pogue squints, trying to bring the individual into focus. "The hell if I know."

"Who's got a pair of binoculars?" Hayley asks the investigators within earshot.

She stands and follows a state police officer to his cruiser. The officer retrieves a pair of binoculars and hands them to Hayley.

But putting glass on the ridgeline, she sees that the individual observing them has fled.

And reacts with exasperation.

"Fuck!"

PETE OSWALD IS back on the interstate in fifteen minutes, heading south. Back into Texas. As he drives, he calculates how much significant information the authorities might find at the site. Hooker and the others had a limited function in the overall operation. Their awareness of the organization beyond their individual cell was limited, as was their specific mission. Consequently, any exposure is contained. The paraphernalia discovered in the mobile home is not atypical for the region and the dead men's socioeconomic background. Oswald made sure Hooker and the others kept incriminating evidence to a minimum in the compound.

The men had drawn a hard line in the sand when it came to the Nazi flag.

A wild card is whether or not any of the undocumented immigrants were still on-site at the time of the police raid. Hooker assured Oswald only yesterday that all of the captives were deceased. He certainly hopes so. The security breach is a textbook lesson in the value of compartmentalization. Oswald will make sure everyone at the ranch is aware of the situation. Any investigation by local authorities and the CID will require monitoring. The young blond woman's presence was a surprise.

Who the hell is she?

Oswald decides the rental car must be hers. With only a few phone calls, he will have the woman's name and driver's license number, as well as her home address. And with not much more effort than that, Pete Oswald will know everything else there is to possibly know about the woman who seemed to exhibit authority over male investigators twice her age.

HOLDING THE PREGNANCY test in her urine stream, she realizes she hasn't called Sam since arriving in Texas. When was the last time they talked, anyway? Events of the previous thirty-six hours make her last night in Washington seem like another lifetime ago. The relationship with Sam was complicated almost before it could even be called one. As an operative for the deeper state, Hayley's duties preclude a normal life. The fireman has been a unique and happy discovery: a romantic partner who gave her all the leeway she needed. Hayley is strongly attracted to him. Theirs is a connection of significant fondness and affinity. Perhaps, under other circumstances, Hayley could fall in love with Sam McGovern. Her involvement with Publius prevents that level of commitment. Dedication to the nation's constitution is her destiny.

With enlistment in the army and embarking on her amateur boxing career, Hayley stopped ovulating. Gradually, at first, and then completely. Hormonal messages sent to her pituitary gland and ovaries were interrupted by a combination of nonstop military training and a strenuous exercise regime. The long-term failure to ovulate gave her a false sense of security. Practicing safe sex was a given. But with Sam, after a short time, the deeper state operative tended to be less vigilant. It has been almost two years since she had her period.

Hayley realizes now that all-consuming duties at the White House during the previous spring had enabled her hypothalamus to do its thing getting her cycle going again.

The earliest suspicion she might be pregnant arose only in the past week or so. Hayley never felt so tired as during her last bout. Workouts seemed much more difficult, too. As a high-level athlete, she has always been keenly attuned to the subtle changes in her body. An increased pulse rate. Hyperventilation. Clothes just a little snug. Sporadic sluggishness. All were signs of something amiss. The thought occurred to her she might have started ovulating again, in not-so-perfect timing with her intimate relationship with Sam.

Hence the pregnancy test from Walgreens.

Sitting on the toilet in the bathroom of her motel room, Hayley places the test stick on "a dry, flat surface" as instructed, in this case, the bathroom sink basin.

If one line appears in the result window, she is not pregnant. If two pink lines appear, then, well, she's screwed.

In less than forty-five seconds, Hayley will have the results.

She doesn't check her phone while she waits. She doesn't gaze out the open bathroom door and let her mind drift. Hayley stares at the test stick. Or, to be exact, at the result window. And commands it to obey.

One line. Not pregnant.

One line. Save the country.

One—

Two pink lines appear in the test window.

5

EL PEQUEÑO DOCTOR

Leaving the motel room at nine on Wednesday morning for the short drive to Fort Bliss, she sees the housekeeper pushing a cleaning trolley up the walkway. The notion of seeking the other woman's help occurred to Hayley on the drive back to El Paso from the compound in New Mexico. The deeper state operative's gift of echoic memory had allowed Hayley to memorize the entirety of Diego's ramblings.

She only needs someone to translate it all for her. And quickly. Discreetly.

"Excuse me?"

The housekeeper stops, the skin around her left eye slightly less black-and-blue. Lina Campos has a dozen rooms to clean in the next two hours. Warned against any type of interactions with guests in the past, she would prefer to carry on with her work. But *la chele* has an honest face. Unlike most of the "USAmerican" motel guests who scowl when catching her eye, this one smiled warmly at Lina while checking in two days ago. Therefore, the room cleaner will not fake a language failure. She leaves her trolley and turns toward Hayley Chill.

"Yes, miss? How can I help you?" she asks in her lightly accented English.

––––––––––––

CID AGENT ROY Pogue sees the Senate aide approaching from across Ricker Road and mutters a curse. He has decided that Hayley Chill is more trouble than she's worth. The last thing anybody needs is a senator in Washington, DC, standing before a scrum of reporters in the Capitol Rotunda, soapboxing about white supremacy at Fort Bliss. As he steps gingerly over the extended arm of the dead corporal, a victim of overdose, Pogue reminds himself to be cool. The young Senate aide won't be departing anytime soon, not after the multiple fatalities in New Mexico. Roy Pogue can only hope Hayley won't kill anybody else.

She joins the military police officers and CID investigators crowded inside the visitor's dugout at Finney Field, home to the Fort Bliss Desert Knights baseball team. The dead man lies facedown in the dirt, arms outstretched, a needle and other drug paraphernalia scattered on the ground around him. Pogue expects a van to arrive any minute from Beaumont, the army medical center. Hayley called his cell phone twice in the past hour, which the CID agent resolutely ignored. He reminds himself to strangle whoever it was back at the office that told the Senate aide where to find him.

Hayley glances down at the body. With the dead man's head turned to the side, she regards a startlingly young and angelic black face. The deeper state operative is no stranger to the ravages of narcotics addiction. She has lost family members and close friends to the scourge of drugs. Enlisting in the army while still a senior in high school was her tactic to escape that fate. The untimely death of the young man at her feet—and likely dozens more every year at military bases across the country and around the globe—is hard evidence the strategy isn't foolproof.

"Chief, can I have a word?"

Pogue turns and works his way through the huddle of military investigators, following Hayley out of the dugout. She leads him toward the pitcher's mound, out of earshot of the others.

The housekeeper at her motel had been an enormous help. Even with her gift of echoic memory, Hayley's recall of Diego's frantic words during their brief car ride together is incomplete. But the deeper state operative had retained enough of the migrant's testimony to recite so that Lina—their introduction a first time any motel guest asked the housekeeper for her name—could provide a paraphrased translation.

Hayley learned that Timothy Hooker and the other two men at the New Mexico compound had held as many as ten immigrants at the site. That the captives were taken away in pairs, never to be seen again. Diego spoke of watching the gringos' preparations from the construction shed, that bombs of some sort were an element of their mysterious operation. Crucially, he recalled one of their captors appearing a few days earlier with a badly burned hand and forearm, possibly the result of an errant explosion.

"The injury was treated by a fourth man, sir, who visited the site specifically for that purpose. This fourth man was in uniform, with two black bars here." Hayley points to the center of her chest, where military insignia would be located. "A captain, Mr. Pogue."

CID agent Pogue frowns. *This is exactly the kinda shit . . .*

"You think personnel from Beaumont have something to do with these jokers in New Mexico?" he asks, referring to the William Beaumont Army Medical Center.

"That would seem to be the case, sir. Yes. The undocumented immigrant said he was small."

"Small?"

"Yes, sir. He called him *el pequeño doctor*."

Pogue exhales, noncommittal.

He asks, "You think I can get back to my overdose?"

"Put me in front of ten doctors on staff at Beaumont with the shortest heights. I'll limit my interviews to less than five minutes."

"Cardiologists? Podiatrists?" he asks with exasperation.

"Please, Chief."

"I'm too busy to be chasing short doctors all over the medical center, okay?"

"Get me the list. I'll do the legwork."

Pogue understands he can't throw her off course. Not easily, at least.

He nods, winning a smile from her.

"Tomorrow." He jerks his thumb in the direction of the dead body in the dugout. "I'm kinda busy today."

———————

ONE VICTIM WAS a fifteen-year-old high school sophomore who loved to play soccer. Another was a fifty-nine-year-old husband in the self-checkout line. A couple in their twenties left behind an infant son. A sixty-three-year-old military veteran died shielding his family from the gunman. A grandmother was shot in the head, having just hung up from a phone call with her son. Several of the dead were Mexican nationals. From Ciudad Juárez, Yepómera, and Chihuahua. A ninety-year-old woman died. In all, the gunman shot dead twenty-three people. He wounded twenty-three more.

After leaving the post, Hayley stopped by the Walmart near the Cielo Vista Mall, south of the airport. She needs a few things, having packed for only a short stay. New Mexico Police made it clear they expected her to remain in the area until their investigation was complete. Not that she needs to be convinced. Her plan is simple: follow the cabal's chain of command, as high as it goes, until the truth reveals itself.

A memorial at one end of the Walmart parking lot reminds Hayley of the location's tragic significance. On August 3, 2019, a twenty-one-year-old man drove 650 miles from his home in Dallas, walked into the mega-store just before 10:40 a.m., and began firing from the shoulder with an AK-47, targeting people of Latino ethnicity. He had posted a manifesto with white nationalist and anti-immigrant themes on an online message board shortly before the attack. First responders arrived on the scene within six minutes of the initial 911 call. Fleeing the scene, the gunman surrendered to law enforcement officers a few blocks away.

Hayley falters at the store's entrance. Shoppers stream in and out the doors, seemingly oblivious to tragedy. Old and young. White, brown, and black. Families and individuals. The deeper state operative watches two young siblings squealing with laughter, avoiding their mother's attempts to corral them. How can these extremes—love and hate—coexist in the world? Thoughts Hayley had driven from her consciousness over the last twelve hours come flooding back. Of her unplanned pregnancy. Of what to do.

STANDING BESIDE HIS prowler parked at the top of the off-ramp for Collie Road, just east of town, Reeves County sheriff's deputy Jay Gibbs heard the four CH-47 Chinook helicopters long before he could locate them in a cloudless sky. He watches the heavy-lift workhorses wheel south, heading toward EagleClaw's processing complex outside of town. The governor's order to move National Guard units into the Permian Basin is less than twenty-four hours old, and life in West Texas hasn't been the same since. Gibbs's assignment today is to facilitate the flow of civilian traffic on Interstate 20 as troop transportation and supply vehicles from Camp Mabry, in Austin, flood the region. Earlier in the day, he helped divert passenger cars off the interstate entirely. With the operation to emplace the National Guard troops and their equipment almost complete, however, civilian traffic can return to the area's roadways.

Having done a tour in Iraq, Gibbs isn't easily impressed by a show of military might. But even he couldn't resist standing in awe of the convoy of Stryker combat vehicles that rolled through town earlier in the day. Given the Thirty-Sixth Infantry Division's Seventy-Second Brigade's conversion to a Stryker combat team—one of only three in the entire Army National Guard—the fearsome eight-wheeled armored vehicles have joined what commanders dubbed Operation Valiant Resolve. Equipped with M2 machine gun and Mk44 Bushmaster II cannons, the personnel carriers take positions at dozens of sites throughout the region as a deterrent against further sabotage of the state's oil and gas infrastructure. In an instant, the department-issued Smith & Wesson 9 millimeter on Gibbs's utility belt feels no better than a peashooter.

The radio call comes in less than three minutes after the flyover by the National Guard helicopters. Shots fired. A possible intruder down. At EagleClaw.

That didn't take long.

From the Love's Travel Stop, Gibbs takes 118 south, hitting more than one hundred miles an hour on the straight two-lane pavement. He is the closest unit to the incident and expects to be first on the scene, within a few minutes of dispatch's alert. He strongly disapproves of the National Guard's involvement in bringing an end to the bombings. Like many of his colleagues—all of them natives of West Texas—Gibbs considers the army brigade from Austin, four hundred miles east, to be invaders. It matters not one whit that they are units of the Texas Army National Guard. Only a small fraction of the soldiers are from *here*.

Like one of his colleagues at the sheriff's department said, "If you need a Stryker combat vehicle to solve your problems, well, buddy, you're too fucked to be helped."

Jay Gibbs no longer believes the ongoing sabotage in the basin is the Mexican drug cartels' handiwork. He possesses no proof to say otherwise, only his common sense. How could these drug lords be so inept as to hire saboteurs who keep on getting themselves killed? In every instance? As an aspiring writer and fan of the crime genre, the sheriff's deputy finds the coincidence of these "accidental" deaths to be an affront to his creative instincts.

Hells bells, couldn't they be just a little bit more artful?

But enough people in the country are preloaded with the assumption that criminal elements from south of the Rio Grande are itching to invade these United States of America that it's short work to make these fabrications seem legitimate. For years now, the National Guard has assisted local law enforcement and Homeland Security at an increasingly militarized border. With the governor's order, that battlefield has expanded into Texas itself.

Overkill, he muses, pedal pressed to the floor and siren wailing. *And why?*

Gibbs can't begin to guess who's responsible for the bombings or their agenda.

He clocks the Stryker stopped up ahead, a quarter mile north of the EagleClaw facility, disgorged of its personnel. Army National Guard soldiers from two Humvees join those from the combat vehicle in the road. When he brings the prowler to a stop, Gibbs can see the body lying facedown in the dirt at the side of the road. Getting out of his vehicle and jogging toward the soldiers, he clocks the M16A2 rifles carried by all of them.

Hand-me-downs for weekend warriors.

"Unit nine on scene. EMT support and backup!"

Radio call made, Gibbs approaches the soldiers. No one pays any attention to the downed man, who wears running shorts and a T-shirt, but instead scan the area in every direction, on alert. The Chinooks lift off from the nearby parking lot of the EagleClaw facility. Apache helicopters circle overhead, making conversation difficult.

Gibbs crouches beside the injured man. Blood pools on the ground from beneath the body.

"What happened?" he asks the soldiers standing closest. No answer is immediately forthcoming.

Turning the man over reveals a shirtfront drenched in blood. Brown skin caked with red dirt.

The deputy's throat nearly seizes at the sight. "What . . . happened? How was this man shot?"

One of the soldiers moves to stand over Gibbs and the shooting victim. Sunglasses. Red haired. Sunburned face and sweating. His voice is barely audible with the *whomp whomp whomp* of the helicopters circling overhead.

"He was running away." Pointing toward the gas compressor station, the guardsman says, "Running from the plant."

"Goddamn fool!" Gibbs puts his fingers to the victim's carotid artery for a pulse. Nothing.

He places his hand over the dead man's inert heart, glaring at the soldiers arrayed around the body. "This is Alberto Jimenez! He's a Reeves County volunteer firefighter and triathlete!"

SAM CALLS AFTER seven that evening, when Hayley is in her cinder block bunker of a motel room reviewing files on the doctors she will be interviewing tomorrow.

"I was worried. Hadn't heard from you."

She had considered not picking up the phone. Should she tell Sam about the incident in New Mexico? Or the pregnancy? About that, Hayley hasn't even taken the time to sort out her feelings. But she feels some guilt for leaving Washington without saying goodbye. For the way she left things between them. After the fourth, insistent ring, Hayley felt compelled at least to say hello. But discuss with him these other weightier topics? What's going on in her life?

Not a chance.

"Sorry, Sam. Busy."

"Sounds like it's going nuts down there. This dead jogger? Shot by National Guardsmen? Crazy. Are you all right?"

The work Hayley must finish tonight isn't going anywhere. The papers, files, and laptop computer spread out before her on the bed of her banal motel room demand her attention. She now regrets answering Sam's call. As gracefully as possible, Hayley will endeavor to make their conversation brief.

"That was over two hundred miles east of El Paso. I'm fine."

"Really? You sound . . . weird."

"I appreciate your concern, Sam." She instantly rues the formality of her statement. So cold.

"But you have to go."

Compassion for him gets the better of her. "How's it going for you? How's work?"

"It's okay. Same. How long do you think you're going to be out there?"

"Sam . . ."

"I know. We broke up. But that doesn't mean I stop worrying about you." He pauses, then plunges forward with a confession he didn't anticipate making. "I spoke to your trainer. That Russian dude in West Virginia."

This is not good. Hayley can't have anyone from her "normal" life checking up on her. Running down her story.

"You shouldn't have done that."

"When I stopped by your apartment the other night, you didn't look well. You seemed tired."

"I'm fine," she says again.

"Your coach. Kozlov. He told me about your bout. He feels terrible for putting you in there. He says it was too soon. Have you thought about going to a doctor, at least?"

She wishes a fight injury was her only physical issue.

The boundaries she drew between her work for Publius and

a normal life are being erased. A pregnancy upends her performance as an operative for the deeper state in a dozen obvious
ways. Hayley can't even imagine how motherhood would impact
those responsibilities. Having to choose between her work and
having a child seems antiquated and unnecessary in the first quarter of the twenty-first century. But as an agent for Publius, her
dilemma is all too real. This awkward business with Sam under-
scores the point.

Hayley must be one or the other. Not both.

Do it. Now. Just do it.

"I don't think we should talk anymore, Sam. A no-contact policy
is probably best."

He is silent for a moment. "Okay." And then, "Yes. I think so,
too."

After Sam disconnects the call, he remains standing on the
sidewalk outside the bar on Twentieth Street, just off Washington's
Dupont Circle. They met at the Darlington House, more than a year
ago. Morbid sentimentality compelled him to stop by tonight. Raise a
glass in a toast to their failed relationship. The fireman hates himself
for being such a chump. For calling her. Love makes asses of us all,
doesn't it? He respects her strength, one greater than his own, for
doing what is right.

Probably best.

Sam has been through this particular ringer before. His emotional maturity is more advanced than many of his peers', whether
male or female. This, too, he will survive.

The relationship was doomed from the start, he decides.

Sam returns to the house he shares with two other firefighters.
His roommates are rewatching *Tiger King* for what seems like the
tenth time on the big-screen TV in the living room, and Sam finds
himself immersed in the bizarre world of "murder, mayhem, and mad-
ness" depicted in the documentary series. Bingeing one episode after
another, fortified by repeated shots from the bottle of Maker's Mark

on the coffee table, the firefighter momentarily forgets about Hayley and the disappointment of their busted relationship. He sleeps well that night but wakes the next morning with a headache and renewed remorse. But the day continues.

And the day after.

One following another, again and again. Other ecstasies and dramas ensue. Sam is a good-natured and handsome man, kind to animals and people alike. He will not be single for long. Living in an apartment in Brookland with his new girlfriend—Carole, a schoolteacher and fierce competitor on the softball field—he climbs the fire department's hierarchy. By the time he and Carole are married and seeing their youngest of three kids off to college, Sam McGovern is the assistant fire chief in charge of operations, second in command to only the DC FEMS chief. His oldest boy plays ball for the Dodger organization. Carole, armed with a PhD in education, teaches at nearby Trinity Washington University. Life, by any measure, is astoundingly good.

He never sees or hears from Hayley again. Without fail, geographical places will induce memory of her. Darlington House, where they met and now an Indian restaurant. Her old apartment building. Favorite restaurants gone thirty years on, but their addresses still loaded with significance. Driving or walking past these sites conjure the dull ache of emotions, completely raw again. Painful. Despite the many years of separation, those moments when he recalls her and their brief time together can still turn his stomach inside out. No one in his life is aware of these intermittently disinterred feelings for Hayley Chill that he carries with him every single day. Sam is confident their doomed love poses no threat to his marriage. With his complete and utter happiness in life.

It simply is.

And always will be, until AFC Sam McGovern collapses and dies in his kitchen, on a Saturday morning, in the fifty-ninth year of his quietly remarkable life.

HAYLEY SITS IN the small, windowless office, waiting for her tenth and last interview of the day. Like most hospitals, the army medical center at Fort Bliss is a hectic facility, teeming with hospital staff, patients, and visitors. Snagging a few minutes of her busy interview subjects' time has been an enormous challenge, an experience something like having ten different doctor appointments in a day. The wait times intolerable. For a person who thrives on *doing things*, the morning has been Hayley's idea of hell.

After twenty-five minutes of agonizing idleness, the door swings open and a balding, middle-aged man enters the room, wearing a doctor's white coat and camouflage trousers from his combat uniform. He leaves the door open, anticipating a short interruption in the day's crammed schedule. Captain Chris Hall, an internist at William Beaumont Army Medical Center, is five foot nine and white with a slim build, matching the undocumented immigrant's general physical description.

It's Thursday, her fourth day in El Paso.

Hayley believes she will recognize *el pequeño doctor* when she sees him. Her gut instincts are that good. And the man standing before her doesn't fit the bill. While small and slight of stature, the doctor's gruff impatience belies a description of "little." His personality is too large. She girds herself for the difficult interview that will surely follow.

"What's this about?" Hall asks.

"Thank you for your time, sir." Hayley takes a small breath before launching into her inquisition. "Captain, I'm looking into an incident that occurred a few days ago in New Mexico."

He stares at her, blank faced. Checks his watch. Waiting for her elaboration.

"Have you been in New Mexico in the last seven days, Captain Hall? Did you treat a patient there by the name of Joseph Fermin?"

"No." Describing his response as curt would be generous. "Will that be all?"

She knows Hall isn't her man. But his manner is so dismissive, so outrageously rude, she feels compelled to push harder at him. This is her last shot, the tenth interview subject. Pogue is unlikely to permit access to more doctors.

What's my next move? God, do I even have one?

"Captain Hall, do you have any affiliation with white supremacist or white nationalist organizations?"

"Pardon . . . ?"

Her mind races, an interior monologue that is increasingly difficult to mask with a bland expression.

What am I doing? No one will talk to me now. They'll run me off the post.

"Well?" the doctor asks, indignant. He heard her the first time.

"I asked if you belong to any groups that embrace an intolerance for people of color, sir. Do you believe in a 'white' agenda?"

He leaves without further comment. The sound of his footsteps retreating down the hallway is an indictment of Hayley's absurd and futile effort.

What the hell is wrong with me?

Hayley sits motionless for almost a full minute. The thread of her investigation is embarrassingly tenuous. The self-destructive nature of this final interview proves her ineptitude. After today's performance, Roy Pogue will surely deny her access to the post.

Hayley tries and fails to imagine what she will write in her report to Andrew Wilde.

She exits the doctor's office and heads down the hallway toward an elevator bank. The entrance to the Department of Behavioral Health clinic is at the end of the corridor. Passing the wide entryway, Hayley glances inside the clinic's waiting room and sees that patients occupy every chair. More soldiers stand along the walls. The uniformed men and women waiting for appointments, while ambulatory, all share a haggard expression. She's seen it before, back home in West Virginia. The active-duty service members gathered in the clinic's reception area seek placement in the army's substance use disorder in-patient care. Their medical plight is painful for anyone to witness, but especially for Hayley Chill, who has lost family and friends to the disease of addiction.

Pausing at the department's entrance before continuing to the elevators, she watches as a doctor emerges from an office suite beyond the waiting room and confers with one of the nurses behind the admissions desk.

Captain Christian Libby is *small*, standing at five-seven and weighing less than 140 pounds. Hayley can't fathom why the doctor wasn't on the list provided to her by the Criminal Investigations Command.

But she knows that she wants to talk to him.

Hayley marches into the waiting room and approaches the admissions desk.

"Excuse me?"

Libby, wearing a doctor's white coat over a camouflage uniform, looks up from his conversation with the nurse.

"Can I help you?" His name is stenciled below the lapel of his white coat.

"Captain Libby? Do you have a minute, sir?"

"What is this about? As you can see, I'm very busy."

"Is there someplace we can talk?" she asks, persisting.

"You can take a seat and wait your turn, thank you." He focuses again on the nurse's computer screen.

Hayley asks, "Did you treat a burn injury recently? In New Mexico, Captain? Patient name, Joseph Fermin."

Libby goes rigid. Even the nurse with whom he has been conferring takes note of his sudden discomfort.

"Sir?"

He stands bolt upright and turns away from the admissions desk, fleeing for the offices in the back without another word.

Hayley gives chase. "Captain Libby?"

The nurse jumps out of her seat to stop Hayley. "Ma'am, you can't go back there!"

The deeper state operative easily sidesteps the woman and continues down the corridor after the fleeing doctor.

"Sir, we need to talk!"

Libby breaks out into a shuffling jog, with Hayley in pursuit. She follows the frantic doctor, passing a series of examination rooms, to his office in the suite's farthest corner. He tries to slam the door closed behind him, but Hayley jams her foot in the way, pushing against the door. Libby is no match against her. *El pequeño doctor* gives up and retreats to his office chair behind a cluttered desk. Hayley remains standing, blocking the doorway.

"What is the 'Storm'?"

"Who are you?" Libby asks. "Who sent you?"

"The men at the compound in New Mexico, Captain. Private Hooker. Wilcox and Fermin. Are they connected to the explosions in the Permian Basin?"

"I don't know what you're talking about."

"You were at that compound, sir. One of the undocumented immigrants Hooker was holding captive survived. We have him in protective custody. When he picks you out of a lineup, maybe then your memory will improve."

He cannot confirm or disprove Hayley's fabrication in the moment. And it is completely devastating.

In his mind's eye, Christian Libby sees the entirety of his life collapse into a thundering ruin.

———————

HIS GRANDFATHER WAS an infamous proponent of eugenics in the 1930s and '40s, gaining widespread popularity with his racist advocacy until the Second World War's unequivocal result reversed his stunning rise. Christian Libby's parents—both doctors who similarly embraced genetic determinism—kept these controversial beliefs to themselves, but enthusiastically indoctrinated their only child. When Libby was a teenager, a mugger killed his mother and father in downtown St. Louis. Raised in affluence his entire childhood, Libby's standard of living declined substantially following his parents' deaths. The attack only intensified his racist views.

In emulation of his parents and his grandfather before them, Libby desired a career in medicine. A ward of the state, the eighteen-year-old's only possible way to afford medical school was with the army's Health Professions Scholarship Program. Too busy for romantic relationships and without surviving immediate family members, the army doctor was hardwired for recruitment by a variety of fringe, white supremacist organizations. If anything, Libby developed these associations out of a basic human necessity for social engagement. All he wants is to be comfortable, financially well-off, and completely removed from those things of the world that frighten him. Money and a safe harbor. To be left alone.

CHRISTIAN LIBBY HADN'T figured on an eyewitness who could identify him. He hadn't anticipated any of this mess. Talked into participating by stronger personalities, the neurologist shudders when imagining the professional and personal humiliation that lies ahead.

"I didn't understand . . ." His voice falters. Unable to continue.

Hayley has so many questions. But one is foremost in her mind.

"Did you know Tommy Chill, sir? He worked at the Pentagon, under the name of Charles Hicks. Did you have any contact with a Charlie Hicks or Tommy Chill?"

Libby stares at her with a vague expression. "No. Neither name is familiar to me."

Disappointed, the deeper state operative retrieves her cell phone from her tote. "What were Hooker and the other men doing with the imprisoned migrant workers?"

No response. Hayley starts punching numbers into her phone.

She sits in the chair opposite his desk. "How did Joseph Fermin burn his hand?"

"Who are you calling?" he asks.

"CID."

The army doctor reacts as if hit with a cattle prod. Dismayed.

Hayley connects a call. "Mr. Pogue . . ."

Christian Libby springs from his seat and charges toward the open doorway.

"Captain, sir! Stop!"

But the doctor flees out the door. Without bothering to disconnect her phone call with the CID agent, Hayley stands and again gives chase.

Libby pushes past a patient in the corridor, knocking him on his ass, and hits a stairwell doorway at full speed.

Hayley enters the stairwell and hears footsteps heading up. She follows, taking two steps at a time.

Her quarry reaches the top landing of the building's interior stairwell and bangs out an emergency exit door that leads out onto the medical center's roof. The army captain continues at full speed toward the low wall of the building's edge.

Hayley struggles to maintain a fast pace with the last set of stairs, suffering from an immediate fatigue and shortness of breath. Reaching the top landing, she exits through the fire door . . .

And sees the doctor sitting astride the low wall at the roof's edge.

Approaching slowly, the deeper state operative holds both hands out wide.

"Captain Libby . . . don't . . ."

He is beyond consoling. *El pequeño doctor* is at the end of a life he could never quite master.

Libby says, "Stay back."

Hayley doesn't stop moving forward.

She doesn't want to see the man die.

But more crucially, she wants the information inside his head.

Military police sirens echo in the distance. Libby throws his left leg over the wall so that both hang over the edge. Twelve stories below, the cement plaza promises eternal release.

"Whatever it is that you've gotten yourself into, sir, it's not too late to stop. You can make it right again."

Libby shakes his head no.

Only a few yards separate Hayley from the man on the ledge . . .

She says, "I'm here, sir. I can help you. I promise, I will help you."

That's not enough. He leans toward the abyss.

Hayley throws herself forward, gripping the doctor's left wrist as he pushes off the wall.

With her hold on his arm, she stops his descent. Libby is of slight frame, but 135 pounds of deadweight isn't insignificant. Hayley levers her body against the wall and adds her other hand to her grip on the army doctor's arm.

Dangling from the great height and imagining the horrid moment of impact, the neurologist has second thoughts of killing himself.

They look to each other—an absurd situation, really—on either side of the low wall. Hayley sees the fear in his eyes. Struggling to keep her hold on him, she attempts to haul the man back over the wall. But can't. She's not strong enough.

"You have to help, Captain! Help yourself!" His eyes register his confusion. "With your free hand, sir!"

Libby's head bobbles in acknowledgment. He raises his right hand, grips the ledge, and throws his right leg up and over the wall. Hayley slowly—painfully—hauls the army doctor over the wall and onto the roof with his assistance.

Sprawled on the gravel-covered rooftop, they are exhausted. And relieved.

After a few moments, Libby manages to speak again.

"I'm . . . I'm so ashamed."

Both sit up, backs leaning against the low wall.

Hayley says, "It's okay, sir. It's going to be okay."

"The explosions in the Permian . . ." He pauses, finding it difficult to go on. But he does. "Hooker and the others were responsible."

She takes a moment to process what Libby has revealed.

"The sabotaged tank farms in the news?"

The doctor nods. "The migrants were left behind to deflect blame onto the cartels."

"My God. Why?" asks Hayley. Before Libby can respond, she answers her own question. "Pretext to bring in the National Guard."

Libby says nothing, and in that way all but confirms her hunch.

A conspiracy, then.

As if reading her mind, the doctor mutters a single word.

"Culberson."

"Sir?"

"Nathaniel Culberson. He . . . is . . ." His voice catches. Tries again, with a mountain of regret. "I only knew Culberson."

Hayley has gotten control of her heart rate. Streaks of blood begin to well from the scratches on her arm.

She can't believe her shoulder wasn't dislocated.

"Culberson."

He nods, feeling the sudden rush of a vast relief. Like the first hit of heroin. A confession made.

Libby says, "In six days."

Hayley forgets all about her arm. The abrasions.

"What about six days, sir? What's happening in *six* days? Is it another bombing?"

The diminutive army doctor meets her gaze. His eyes express deep remorse. A weary sadness. His mouth opens to speak . . .

Behind them, the stairwell emergency exit door opens. Hayley looks over her shoulder and sees the two uniformed MPs, in the same moment registering a desperate act she wishes she had done more to prevent. The crunch of roof gravel. A sense of adjacent movement. And shouting from one of the military policemen that now charge toward them.

She knows what has happened without having to confirm it with her eyes . . .

Christian Libby has scrambled to his feet and leaped over the low wall.

6

BALMORHEA

She crossed the border at San Antonio del Bravo with her mother the day after she turned sixteen and, therefore, is not eligible for consideration of legal residency under the Deferred Action for Childhood Arrivals immigration policy. That was fifteen years ago. Lina Campos, undocumented and now a mother herself, has worked at the Beverly Crest Motor Inn for three years, a shift that begins at seven a.m. and ends at four in the afternoon. Afterward, she picks up Diana, her three-year-old daughter, from day care, treasuring these late-afternoon and evening hours with her. The granny who lives in the apartment below comes upstairs at seven. Lina, changed and barely rested, then heads off to her other job as a waitress at Teddy's Flame Room. Located in a Best Western (Plus!) south of the airport, Teddy's isn't a half-bad job. The bouncers keep the drunks off her back, and the tips, due in no small part to her warm smile, are fantastic. If only her take-home pay from the dance club were enough, Lina would happily quit her job cleaning rooms at the motor inn.

The trouble began six weeks ago, the day Jerry Fishbaugh started as day-shift manager. Before that date, the job had been a grind but blissfully uneventful. Lina would spend the first two hours cleaning common areas. As guests check out, she and the other housekeeper would start turning over rooms for incoming customers. Sometimes the messes left by guests were disgusting, so much so that Lina augmented her heavy-duty rubber gloves with plastic goggles she purchased with her own money. That was the worst of it, however. Many guests might leave a few bucks behind as a tip, in appreciation of Lina's diligence. No customers had a reason to complain about the cleanliness of their rooms. The work was hard and unrelentingly dull, but Lina Campos considered herself fortunate to have steady employment given her immigration status.

The arrival of the new daytime manager changed all of that. Fishbaugh introduced himself to the staff—two housekeepers and a full-time maintenance man—at the start of his first day on-site. Lina thought nothing more or less about the man. He struck her as just another brash gringo who had never experienced the ever-present fear of arrest and deportation. After five minutes of talk, Fishbaugh sent the staff on their way and retreated into the small office behind the registration desk. Lina didn't see him again until a few hours later when he surprised her by abruptly entering the guest room she was cleaning and closing the door behind him. Without uttering a word, he threw himself on her and attempted to push her on the bed.

Even as a teenager, Lina Campos was someone who could defend herself. On the journey north with her mother from the southern state of Oaxaca, another emigrant in their group attacked Lina—a brute almost twice her size—and she successfully defended herself with a tree branch. Her assailant was taken to the hospital and never seen again. Fifteen years removed from that scrap, Lina possesses the same fierce willpower. Jerry Fishbaugh took nothing from her on that morning or during the attempted assaults that followed. These incidents, while infrequent, occur with a randomness that defies pre-diction or logic. The terror is real.

Lina would quit, of course, if she could afford to do so. But jobs for an undocumented worker are almost impossible to find. She just manages to pay the bills, every month a challenge to keep a roof over her daughter's head. The standoff with the daytime manager continues. Fishbaugh's threats to alert Immigration and Customs Enforcement of Lina's status is his carefully calibrated control over her. The fight between them two days before Hayley Chill checked in had been one of the worst yet, with the house-keeper suffering a bruised eye. Lina doesn't know how much lon-ger she can resist Fishbaugh's demands. He has told her that if she would only give him what he wants—once—then he will cease tormenting her.

The wretch even offered to raise her hourly wage by a dollar. If she would only give herself to him.

HAYLEY AWOKE BEFORE dawn on Friday and quickly dressed in her running clothes, in need of the emotional release that only physical exertion could provide. Given the time of year and her intended route, she must get started before sunrise. The North Mount Frank-lin Trail is 7.2 miles out and back, with an elevation gain of 2,408 feet. Parked at the trailhead, a fifteen-minute drive from the Beverly Crest Motor Inn, hers is the only car in the Tom Mays Unit lot. For hydration, she hand-carries two twenty-ounce water bottles. With a couple of deep leg stretches, Hayley starts running. The sky is dark overhead, and the moon has long since set. A starry canopy illumi-nates the way ahead.

Witnessing Captain Libby's suicide is a trauma that will stay with her as long as she will live. One moment he was sitting beside her—their backs braced against the low, roof wall of the medical center—

and in the next instant, he was gone. The rocky terrain of the trail's first mile is her hope of an antidote to her obsessive self-recriminations. Attention must remain laser focused on securely planting one step after another, bounding from rock to rock in a dynamic ballet of balance and momentum.

The dawn's gradual glimmering light reveals more and more of the rugged Chihuahuan Desert landscape. Barrel cactus and yucca dot the steep hillside. Deep within these canyons are pictographs and mortar pits, the residue of human habitation more than ten thousand years ago. Somewhere a mountain lion feeds on the carcass of a mule deer. Bound for Los Angeles by way of Miami, an American Airlines 737 streams west at thirty-five thousand feet, silent and relentless. Unobserved by the single-minded trail runner.

She reaches the summit in an hour and pauses to enjoy a view that stretches in every direction. The city huddles against the mountain range just below, quickly giving way to the unspoiled desert. Hands on her hips and witnessing the sun's rise over the Guadalupe Mountains more than one hundred miles to the east, Hayley's thoughts return to the matters of the day. CID agent Roy Pogue wants her in his office at ten a.m. He had interviewed her yesterday, of course, at the hospital. To say he was displeased with the consequences of her interaction with Captain Libby is an understatement. Hayley's proximity to violence seems a recurring theme.

But her questioning of the army neurologist had not been unproductive.

I only knew Culberson.

The lead was a solid one. Having returned to her motel late last night, Hayley spent hours on the computer vetting the most likely candidates for Libby's alleged contact. Assuming it's not an insurance salesman in Houston with the same name, her most promising determination is that the doctor had been referring to a

Major Nathaniel Culberson, with the Texas Army National Guard, Thirty-Sixth Infantry Division. News reports suggest that elements from the division are among those National Guard units deployed to the Permian Basin over the past twenty-four hours. Culberson may be in West Texas, which will make questioning him that much easier.

But first, she has to mollify Roy Pogue. As the sun makes a full appearance over the distant mountain range to the east, Hayley starts back down the trail. Descending requires even more focused concentration than her ascent. The last thing she needs now is a broken leg or collarbone. Reaching the desert floor a few minutes after seven, the deeper state operative sees her rental car is still the only vehicle in the parking lot. Including the few minutes she spent ruminating on the summit, Hayley completed the seven-mile run in less than two hours. The temperature is a manageable seventy-eight degrees and rising. Both water bottles are empty. Time to go.

Pulling into the motel driveway and parking in front of her room, Hayley glances in her rearview mirror and catches sight of an altercation inside a room on the opposite side of the lot. She sits a moment and watches, the time required to confirm that the housekeeper is being knocked around by a man wearing a light blue polo shirt.

Hayley bails out of her rental car and strides across the broken black asphalt.

"Hey!"

Jerry Fishbaugh is too focused on his prey, Lina Campos, to notice Hayley's arrival on the other side of the parking lot. Hearing the shout, he is surprised he'd neglected to shut the door behind him.

Stupid!

Looking over his shoulder and seeing Hayley approach, he releases his grip on the Campos woman and backtracks, ducking out the door and up the walkway with his gaze fixed down at his feet.

Once he is safely inside his cramped office behind the registration desk, the Beverly Crest Motor Inn's daytime manager, humiliated and enraged, picks up the landline phone and dials the toll-free number for making anonymous tips to U.S. Immigration and Customs Enforcement. He keeps the number written on a desk blotter, tempted to make the call a dozen times in the past year. The sharp sting on his cheek where that bitch scratched him is impetus enough to make the phone call that will result in her deportation. Fishbaugh knows Lina Campos is undocumented because the previous manager—a mild-mannered, kindhearted elderly man from Taiwan inherited from the motel's previous owner and since moved to Scottsdale, Arizona, for a well-deserved retirement—told him as much. He must teach the evil bitch a lesson she won't soon forget.

But Fishbaugh hangs up after the first ring. Getting the Campos woman hauled off by ICE without even a chance to hug her daughter goodbye is an undeniably enticing prospect. But doing so would deprive him of what he has long wanted of the housekeeper. He'll make that call *after* he takes that satisfaction. Only then will he have her ass deported. The same day would be best. A one-two punch.

Does he have any reason to fear the female guest in room thirty-two seeing a small part of his fight with Campos? Fishbaugh doesn't think so. People don't care. And they care even less than that about some *mojada*.

Stepping out of his manager's office and into the registration area, he sees a fifteen-year-old Dodge minivan with California plates pull into the drive. An elderly couple is visible through the windshield. Fishbaugh checks his polo shirt for any rips or other signs of his struggle with his obstinate housekeeper. Satisfied he is presentable, he readies himself to greet the old people tumbling out from their vehicle. For $39 a night, one cannot expect much from the Beverly Crest Motor Inn, but a friendly smile is certainly a guaranteed perk.

―――――――――

SHOWERED AND DRESSED, Hayley is back in her rental car and on the road less than forty minutes after returning from her dash up Franklin Mountain. Lina Campos refused her attempts to intervene further on her behalf, beseeching Hayley not to call the police. No need to tell the deeper state operative why.

The clinic is in Sunland Park, New Mexico, one mile from El Paso, a nondescript one-story structure of recent construction. A single car claims one of eight available parking spaces of the Women's Reproductive Clinic of New Mexico, most likely not belonging to any of the six protesters posted out front on the opposite side of the public sidewalk. Parking the rental car, Hayley briefly regards the protesters in her rearview mirror and steels herself. She's out the door and walking quickly toward the clinic entrance, head held high. The judgment of others will not cow Hayley. Her choices—always reasoned, always methodically decided, and guided by personal notions of right and wrong—are hers to make.

For reasons Hayley believes to be obvious, she doesn't want anyone associated with Publius to know about this particular life event. Andrew Wilde and the others will hold it against her, view the unplanned pregnancy as a failure not only of character, but efficiency.

As always, trust no one.

After a urine test and ultrasound, Hayley waits in the lobby. No one else is present in the snug, carpeted waiting room. The receptionist is behind a thick, clear acrylic "bandit barrier" typically found in banks. A bulletin board hangs on the wall to her left. Informational posters with the common theme of women's health occupy most of the real estate on the corkboard, but some homemade flyers are also present. Hayley recognizes the missing person flyer for "Kimberly." Pretty teenage girl. Black hair and dark eyes. Navy UTEP hoodie. Missing three months. The handwritten and poorly photocopied flyer is an echo of a father's anguish. Hayley feels herself again spellbound by the familiar leaflet.

The door opens, and the nurse practitioner pokes her head into the room. "Hayley?"

Hayley stands and follows the NP, wearing jeans and a concert T-shirt for Austin-based band Balmorhea, through the door and down the short corridor to an examination room. Rose Blackwell is a grandmother, pilot, landscape photographer, and haphazard French chef, with a concealed carry permit who prefers wearing her Glock 19 on her hip. She carries the pistol everywhere, except in bed or while swimming at the local YMCA.

Blackwell takes shit from no one, which in no way prevents her from rewarding Hayley with a warm smile as they sit in their respective plastic molded chairs.

Still grinning, she says, "Well, you sure are pregnant. But you already know that."

"Yes, ma'am."

"No need to ma'am me, darlin'." The nurse practitioner indicates the rose tattoo on the weathered skin of her right forearm. "Rose."

Hayley says nothing. Blackwell shrugs. It was worth a try.

"Okay, then, your options. I refer you to a few pretty good ob-gyns. That's number one. Number two, we schedule you for surgical termination. With anesthesia, we only do those procedures on Fridays. Since you're less than nine weeks in, a third option is—"

"Misoprostol."

"Good! You've done your homework."

"Yes, ma'am."

"Less than one percent risk for complications that could put you in the ER. With your general health and age, I'd say much less than one percent. Four 200 mcg tablets under your tongue. Hold 'em in your mouth for thirty minutes. Swallow what doesn't dissolve with some water. Repeat with four more tablets. That's pretty much that. You'll likely have bleeding that's heavier than a period. Perfectly normal."

Hayley nods her head.

"Was that a yes? Go with the misoprostol?"

"Yes, ma'am."

Blackwell turns to write the prescription. Hayley's gaze finds a framed photo on the wall to her right. A desert landscape of wind-rippled dunes, massive and undulating.

Without looking up from her Rx pad, the nurse practitioner says, "Los Médanos."

"Ma'am?"

"Samalayuca Dune Fields, southwest of Juárez. Ever been?"

"No, ma'am."

Rose finishes writing out the prescription, tearing the page off the pad and offering it to Hayley.

"You're not from around here. Military?"

"I was, ma'am. Live and work in Washington, DC, now."

Hayley senses the other woman wants her to talk. She has no time for any of that. Neither does the busy nurse practitioner, for that matter. But something about the young woman from the nation's capital demands attention. Discovery. Unexpectedly, the mundane appointment has achieved something unique in Rose Blackwell's daily routine. The older woman needs something from Hayley. What exactly, she cannot parse except for a vague sense of not wanting the moment to end.

The deeper state operative cannot miss Blackwell's perplexed countenance.

"Ma'am?"

Focusing her full attention on Hayley, the nurse practitioner folds her hands in her lap and leans forward as if in supplication. Making herself vulnerable isn't a default mode. She's forcing herself to go through with it here. To confess.

"My mother, God rest her soul, she was one-quarter Comanche. Family legend has it she was directly related to the great Penateka Comanche chief and medicine man, Mukwooᴙ. Is it true? Maybe. I know that sometimes I feel as if I have Nᴗmᴗnᴗᴗ blood in me. A rage just thinking about the Council House Massacre, know what I mean? But, anyway, my momma could 'see.' Get me? She was born with a power of prophecy. Just like her ancestors. I feel it sometimes, too. A sense for things to come. Ol' Mukwooᴙ. Spirit Talker. I'll tell you what, honey. I'm feelin' a dark foreboding right now. Sitting here across from you. An approaching storm."

"Is this part of the medical examination, ma'am? Like an ultrasound?"

The nurse practitioner doesn't exactly regret going to this place—revealing herself like that—as much as being surprised that she did.

"I just felt I should say something, darlin'."

Later, back in the car and heading toward Fort Bliss, having filled the prescription in Sunland Park, she ruminates on what the nurse practitioner said. Hayley has no false illusion. Rose Blackwell's premonition had nothing to do with an unwanted pregnancy. She will put her emotions in a box, to be dealt with in due time. Has she considered for a moment having a child? Being a single mother is a fate she has evaded since the day she got on a bus bound for Fort Benning and basic training. How could she expect to be an operative for Publius while parenting a young child?

Boyfriend. Husband. Children. Family. Friends. Community. Church. All go in the same box. Ahead of all these things, Country.

What the nurse practitioner alluded to—*an approaching storm*—is something entirely different. Hayley Chill feels it, too. No need for the lineage of indigenous ancestors. Of the Nᴗmᴗnᴗᴗ. She has felt the same foreboding since the day she first entered the house on Fifth Street, in Arlington, Virginia, and found her father's body hanging from a bedroom door. The malevolent forces that drove Tommy Chill to commit suicide are at work here, in this parched and windswept terrain of West Texas.

———————

"THE OD FROM the ball field, Mr. Pogue. Was he a patient of Captain Libby's?"

Hayley remains expressionless while Pogue frames his response. She contacted Andrew Wilde last night. Spoke at length about everything that had transpired so far in her investigation. Through the resources at Publius's disposal—contacts inside the Pentagon and, no doubt, hackers otherwise in the employ of the US intelligence agencies—Wilde had returned a treasure trove of data and factual histories on all of the individuals with whom Hayley had linked to the violence and sabotage.

Actions behind an agenda that remains a complete mystery to her.

"So, what if he was?" This from Warrant Officer Angelica Lopez, another CID agent in Pogue's office, sitting in the other chair opposite his desk.

Hayley asks her, "Have you accessed the medical records, ma'am? Why do you think Captain Libby was prescribing buprenorphine to the enlisted personnel as a treatment for heroin addiction? Non-opioid medications are available. Lofexidine, for instance. Or clonidine."

"How do *you* know about the buprenorphine, Ms. Chill?" asks the female CID agent, and not in a friendly manner. "We only received those records a half hour ago."

Hayley is cool and modulated, putting no more emphasis into her answer than is needed.

"I was in that dugout, ma'am. I saw a vial on the ground next to the deceased."

Pogue can't not be impressed by the Senate aide's powers of observation. He doesn't think Hayley was in the dugout with the OD victim longer than ten or fifteen seconds. The more he becomes familiar with the young woman from Washington, the more Roy Pogue admires her skills. Nevertheless, the CID agent resents Hayley's intrusion on his turf.

"What exactly are you inferring? Captain Libby was intentionally stringing out his patients? Why on earth would he be doing that?"

"That's what the senator sent me to Texas to find out, Mr. Pogue. An African American corporal overdosing in the dugout of a baseball field who was in the care of a white army doctor deserves attention, don't you think?"

She has no idea if the soldier's overdose has anything to do with the still-unidentified conspiracy. Libby's role is unclear. But he was remorseful enough about *something* to jump off a twelve-story building. As of now, Hayley is in the dark. And she isn't getting any closer to the truth sitting in this office with CID agents Pogue and Lopez.

"You said Captain Libby mentioned a Major Culberson before he jumped," says Angelica Lopez.

"Major Nathaniel Culberson, ma'am, with the Texas Army National Guard. He's been deployed to the Permian Basin, along with elements from the Thirty-Sixth Infantry Division."

"And how is *he* supposed to be involved in all of this?" Pogue asks, incredulous.

"I don't know, Chief. Libby didn't live long enough to tell me." She stands up from her seat. "But it'll be the first question that I ask Major Culberson."

"You're going to Reeves County?" Pogue doesn't seem exactly thrilled by the prospect.

Hayley's silence is answer enough. She doesn't need their permission.

The CID agents exchange a look.

Lopez looks to her colleague and says, "She's not *my* problem."

Pogue expels an exasperated sigh and turns his focus on Hayley again.

"We're still in the middle of investigating the incident in New Mexico. And now this insanity over at Beaumont." The CID agent is aware of how weak his protest is coming off. He adds, "There are jurisdiction issues here, Ms. Chill. By the precise letter of the law, the Army National Guard doesn't have to cooperate with Criminal Investigation Command."

Hayley is unruffled. "How does the Texas Army National Guard feel about the jurisdictional authority of the United States Senate, sir?"

———————

SHE STOPS BY the motel for a change of clothes and the War Hawk. On the interstate by six p.m., heading east, Hayley stops in Sierra Blanca to eat. Less a town than an off-ramp, the offerings are slim. She chooses Delfina's Restaurant. Walking through the door, she finds a small restaurant space that lacks the warmth and charm of El Toro Negro, her go-to Tex-Mex joint back in El Paso. Seven tables are clustered around a center island for red and green sauces. The largest tub serves as a glistening reservoir for sriracha mayonnaise. One corner of the dining room once housed a gift shop and now serves as a haphazard storage area. Hayley is okay with the downscale vibe. The War Hawk rides snugly in her IWB holster. A bad batch of gorditas is about the only thing that could bother her.

Hayley opts for an omelet with black beans. Despite her trail run to the summit of Franklin Mountain and back in the predawn hours that morning, she only finishes half of the food on her plate. Reaching in her tote for her wallet, she sees the bottle of misoprostol nestled with other personal items. Hayley would have taken her first dose this evening were it not for the last-minute drive to Reeves County. Andrew Wilde verified Culberson's current location in Balmorhea and forwarded it via text while Hayley was with the nurse practitioner. Despite her urgency to put the pregnancy behind her, questioning the National Guard major is a greater priority. She can only hope that tomorrow will be a quieter day.

Pushing her anxieties regarding the pregnancy to the back of her mind, Hayley gestures to Delfina, the server/cook/cashier/owner, that she would like her check. At that same moment, the door opens and a uniformed Reeves County sheriff's deputy strides into the dining room.

Deputy Jay Gibbs is traveling east, too, returning home after a day in El Paso where he provided testimony at the US district court there. A routine traffic stop on the interstate south of Toyah led to the discovery of 200,000 dosage units of hydrocodone and 145,000 of carisoprodol, smuggled into the country from Mexico and destined for "pill mills" in El Paso. The deputy is a regular at Delfina's—one of the few nonfranchise restaurants open for dinner between Van Horn and El Paso—and the proprietress greets him with something more than the grunt that the deeper state operative received.

Delfina places salsa and chips on a table next to Hayley's, apparently Gibbs's customary spot. He touches the brim of his Resistol when exchanging a glance with the young woman who in no way appears to be a local.

"Ma'am." He looks to the middle-aged proprietor. "How are you doin', Delfina?"

But she has disappeared into the kitchen to prepare Gibbs's food and fails to answer. The sheriff's deputy is a regular enough customer that ordering isn't necessary.

He sits, removing his straw cowboy hat and placing it on the other chair. Smoothing down his hair signals the favorable impression Hayley must have made on him with that one glance.

They face each other from their adjoining tables to the left of the serving island of many sauces. Gibbs's arrival has interrupted Delfina getting the check prepared.

"Something wrong?" he asks.

Hayley is surprised her annoyance was so obvious. "It's nothing."

"You want to get back on the road. But Delfina forgot all about you." He looks over his shoulder toward the kitchen, then lets his gaze settle on the slender young woman with blue eyes again.

Gibbs confirms then and there that looking at her is not an unpleasant experience.

"I could say something, but it wouldn't do much good," he confesses. "Ol' Delfina has been running this place single-handed for years. Used to doin' things *her* way."

"Yeah, I got that sense."

"Pretty good food, though. Did you try the gorditas?"

"No. Played it safe and got the omelet."

Gibbs chuckles easily and lowers his eyes to the floor. Hayley can't help but experience an Easterner's romantic preoccupation with the American cowboy archetype. In a flash of memory, she recalls the old Westerns she would watch with her father on television. *Shane. Rio Bravo. Butch Cassidy and the Sundance Kid.* Her dad had a deep affection for those classics and an aversion for more revisionist fare. Hayley can almost smell the popcorn her mother would make on the stove in preparation of these family movie nights. The arrival of two or three red envelopes from Netflix containing the DVDs of Tommy Chill's latest finds was cause for quiet celebration. No doubt, Hayley is self-reflective enough to understand that the idealization of her father—until the discovery of his suicide and abandonment of the family—was inextricably intertwined with the western movie heroes he worshipped. If she has a type, it's of the strong and silent persuasion that was made emblematic by those wonderful, classic movies.

That said, the modern-day cowboy sitting across from her at the other table is anything but silent. He's downright chatty.

"Next time you come through, gotta try the gorditas."

She grins, the good sport.

"That's what I'll do."

Gibbs noted the slight bulge of her gun at her waistline when he entered.

She ain't no tourist, he mused.

And endeavored to find out more.

He asks, "You're not from around here, I wager."

"Nope."

"I guess I'm wondering if you have a concealed carry permit in your home state."

Hayley thought her IWB conceal more effective than what is now apparent. But she recovers quickly enough.

"I do. Would you like to see it, Deputy?"

"What state would that be, ma'am?"

"Virginia. Full reciprocity with Texas."

"Virginia, then," says Gibbs.

"Sure was a long way around to figure out where I come from."

"Maybe. Maybe it was." He likes her eyes and hasn't quite decided yet if he's talking here professionally or personally. Which is the problem. With being a sheriff's deputy. He knows there are a few bad apples—not necessarily in his office, but maybe—who might use the uniform to coerce and manipulate women. That's not his way, of course. Gibbs met his last girlfriend at the gun range. Wasn't even in uniform at the time and didn't tell the woman he was law enforcement until after a couple of nights out together.

Another flash of those powder blue eyes convinces him. She's no outlaw. Or some wild-ass cosmopolitan from California blowing through West Texas on her way to Marfa and the degenerates who congregate there. No, sir, he can't put his finger on what she does or what about her sticks on him like a mesquite thorn. But without a doubt, Gibbs would like to know more. He already hates that she will soon be walking out the door of this godforsaken little Tex-Mex joint. That he'll never see her again. Assessing all of these thoughts and emotions in the few seconds since he last spoke, Reeves County sheriff's deputy Jay Gibbs deduces his interest in the woman with the concealed handgun is an entirely personal one.

She indicates the paperback in his right hand he forgot was even there. "Whatcha reading?" Hayley asks.

"Oh," he exclaims, marveling at the well-thumbed novel like it's a baby porcupine that curled up in his palm without his knowing it. "Elmore Leonard. *Hombre*."

"Don't know that one."

If someone bothered to ask her, she would confess to not knowing any of them.

Gibbs says, "It's good. Set in the ol' West. Stagecoach is robbed by outlaws and the passengers are left in a hard way. Up to this Apache fella, John Russell, to save everyone."

"Okay. But what's it really about?"

The deputy pauses a moment to think.

"Well, I guess you could say it's about civilization. The fake kind we see all 'round us and the one that's real."

Hayley grins. "Nice."

"Which is your favorite? *LaBrava*? *Rum Punch*? *Out of Sight*, maybe. You strike me as a Karen Sisco type."

She doesn't know what a Karen Sisco type is and, in that way, is oblivious to Gibbs's intent to flatter. Instead, she takes it as her cue to leave.

Hayley stands, dropping a twenty she extracted from her wallet on the table.

"Tell Delfina the omelet was delicious."

Without lowering his eyes to the table, instead keeping his gaze fixed on her face, Gibbs says, "That's a pretty hefty tip by Sierra Blanca standards."

She rewards his good nature with a smile.

"Guess I just set the new standard, then."

The Reeves County sheriff's deputy feels the breeze of her passing by his table.

And so, as he feared, in a short moment, she will be out of his life. Purely gone.

"Adios," Gibbs says without turning around to watch her out the door. After all, a man has his pride, if nothing else.

7

THE LAKE OF FIRE

The fiery glow is visible for miles. Hayley considers the possibility that saboteurs have taken out another tank farm despite the deployment of National Guard troops. She witnessed evidence of the military intervention soon after leaving the Tex-Mex café in Sierra Blanca. A column of Humvees, rolling west. The thump of helicopters overhead, unseen in the night sky. Dozens of military 6 x 6 trucks transporting supplies. Soldiers with M16 rifles standing guard on overpasses, in rest stop parking lots, or watching from the back of five-ton troop haulers.

The conflagration's glow increases in size as she drives east on the interstate. Reeves County sheriff's deputies direct traffic on the interstate, allowing civilian vehicles to continue in both directions but at reduced speeds. Seeing the uniformed deputies standing beside their department SUVs, Hayley thinks of the cowboy-handsome, gorditas-loving, Elmore Leonard fan she left back in Sierra Blanca. She had felt that surge within her and silently upbraids herself.

What the hell's wrong with you?

Pregnant by another man and on an operation to expose an imminent threat of potentially national proportions . . . and she entertains all-new amorous thoughts? She dismisses the inclination quickly enough, gone moments after it abruptly appeared. But even if the notion was only a blip, the deeper state operative can't quite believe the ill-discipline of her inclinations.

Black smoke intermittently obscures the road ahead. So surreal. Otherworldly. Hayley is not drawn here by the fire, but in pursuit of her quarry. Andrew Wilde's sources suggested that Nathaniel Culberson is in the area. But what exactly is ablaze? She sees a cluster of National Guard soldiers standing at the top of an off-ramp, cast in a sickly yellow glow by the overhead streetlight. The turnoff for Balmorhea.

In the most recent run-up of oil prices—peaking in 2019—the region, somewhat south of the more bountiful Permian Basin, proved a productive terrain for fracking. A significant percentage of those newly developed wells were abandoned after the market's collapse in 2020. With the Trans-Pecos Pipeline traversing the region on its path to Mexico, though, targets for would-be saboteurs are abundant. Hayley steers her rental car off the interstate and stops at the end of the off-ramp.

Hayley rolls down her window as a corporal approaches the car. His sandy hair frames a round, sunburned face that is far from friendly.

"You can't be here. Gotta get back on the highway." The corporal indicates the on-ramp entrance across the road.

Hayley has her identification—prepared by the deeper state within hours of her mission assignment—ready.

"My name is Hayley Chill. I'm an aide for US Senator Gordon Powell, on the Armed Services Committee."

The National Guard corporal doesn't bother looking at the identification she proffers. His expression is stone.

Hayley tries again.

"I'm here on official business, Corporal. I'm looking for a Major Nathaniel Culberson, Seventy-Second Brigade."

The guardsman sneers and turns his head to spit. Hayley notices that the other soldiers have surrounded her vehicle, their weapons held at ready. One of the guardsmen uses a powerful flashlight to illuminate the car's interior. Hayley shields her eyes from its bright white beam. Black smoke wafting across the roadway fills the car with its dank, chemical odor.

"Park over there." The corporal points to the shoulder of the road that passes over the interstate.

"Corporal?" Hayley hasn't a clue what the guardsman intends to do with her.

He gestures again, impatient and hostile. "Over there! Get this vehicle off the ramp!"

Hayley does as she's told. The military is in control, not civilian authorities. Customary laws no longer apply. She opts to leave the War Hawk locked up in the trunk.

She rejoins the soldiers grouped under the streetlight. None of the guardsmen look toward her, conversing among themselves as if the deeper state operative isn't even there. Hayley gets the impression, though, that a vehicle is coming for her. She welcomes their casual disregard. After ten minutes of waiting, a Humvee approaches from town and stops beside the soldiers standing on the top of the off-ramp.

The corporal silently—menacingly—points at the military vehicle. As Hayley clambers into the Humvee, she hears lewd snickering from the men behind her.

Inside the troop carrier, armed guardsmen stare at her with blatant hostility.

"You with the fuckin' *New York Times*?" the private behind the wheel asks as he makes a U-turn and heads back toward town, two miles to the south.

"No." Hayley feels no need to explain herself to the guardsman. She assumes that moment will come soon enough with someone of higher rank.

Barely satisfied, he says, "Too many fuckin' journalists round here, if you ask me."

The soldier riding shotgun ignores Hayley entirely. He says to the driver, "They caught a dozen more of those fuckers coming over the border. Two hours ago, at Hackberry Arroyo. My buddy said they had fifty pounds of plastic explosives on 'em."

"Motherfuckers."

Through the windshield, just beyond the town ahead, the fire's glow fills the sky. Acrid smoke hovers at ground level, heavy with particulates. Balmorhea is decidedly rural. Many residents on the town's dozen or so streets keep pens for horses and goats. Less than 250 acres in size, the town is home to 612 souls. Passing the darkened post office and the Eleven Inn—taken over by the National Guard troops—the Humvee turns left on Galveston, right on First Street, and then stops in front of the mostly dark high school.

Hayley isn't sure what the soldiers expect of her.

"Go on. Get inside, sunshine." The driver gestures toward the school's front entrance.

Two soldiers holding M16s stand guard at the door. Inside a classroom next to the building entrance, Hayley finds a chaotic scene. Local officials, including authorities from the Texas Railroad Commission and Reeves County Fire, argue for access to the fire site and are met with stony indifference by the military officers. Within seconds, Hayley comprehends the reality of her situation. The soldiers didn't bring her here to meet with Major Culberson. The Texas Army National Guard lieutenants tangling with the incensed civilian authorities are flak catchers.

She's been sidelined.

For the moment, the three officers arguing with the civilian authorities ignore Hayley. She backtracks out of the classroom and retreats up the dark corridor, avoiding the soldiers standing sentry at the school's entrance. The deeper state operative finds a door leading to the school's athletic field, but it's chained shut. Entering an empty classroom next to the exit, Hayley goes to one of the windows, discovering it opens just wide enough for her to slip through and outside.

Sulfurous fumes drift from south of the high school campus, bringing tears to her eyes. Thick clouds of churning smoke reflect the fire's glow to the ground and cast the scene in a ghoulish light. Heading in that direction, Hayley jogs past a collection of storage sheds and across the bedraggled football field, then hops over a low fence on the other side. She traverses the four blocks of residential streets of mobile homes, chicken coops, and empty lots at a steady run.

Crossing Railroad Avenue Hayley finds herself in open ground. Like the surrounding thousands of square miles, it is a desert landscape of switchgrass, lotebush, and mesquite. Everywhere there is the chemical smell of petrol extraction.

She calculates the fire to be less than two miles away, south of her location. A road to the east leads in that direction but is busy with military trucks and Humvees. Hayley resumes running again, across the open ground, dodging the cholla branches that threaten to snag her. Swirling winds carry most of the smoke away from her, into Mexico. What could be the source of the conflagration? Only as she draws nearer and can see above the tall brush does Hayley comprehend what has occurred.

Balmorhea Lake, fed by San Solomon Springs and more than five hundred acres in size, is on fire. Similarly to the infamous fire on Cleveland's Cuyahoga River, churning flames cover nearly the entire surface of the shallow body of water. Hayley can see no sign of interventions to combat the fire. Military vehicles drive past the site without slowing. A collection of trailer homes and vacation cabins on the lake's north shore appear abandoned. But from this new vantage point on a small knoll above the expanse, Hayley can see a large gathering of military vehicles and tents amassed a couple of miles to the southeast.

She starts jogging in that direction.

Rounding the northern end of the lake of fire, Hayley comes upon a white pickup truck stopped near the water's edge. The driver's door is open. A middle-aged man wearing the uniform of Texas Parks and Wildlife Department stands to one side of the vehicle, staring abjectly at the unfolding ecological catastrophe. The fire's lurid glow bathes him in a garish light. The deep lines in his face and ruddy complexion betray a life lived outdoors. As Hayley draws nearer to the park ranger, she can see he is quietly sobbing. Only after he notices her approach does the man compose himself.

"Sir?" Hayley pauses, despite her urgency. "Are you okay?"

The ranger, his white hair matted from his hat left on the passenger seat, gestures helplessly at the blazing lake. Words fail.

Hayley asks, "Why is it burning, sir? What happened here?"

"Comanche Corporation happened. They started developing the Alpine High field in 2018. Found fifteen billion barrels under this ground. Five formations. Bone Springs. Wolfcamp. Barnett and Woodford. The Pennsylvanian. More than three hundred thousand contiguous net acres in wet gas and oil windows. In less than two years, they drilled nineteen wells. Some sites pulling out seventeen thousand cubic feet of natural gas . . . a *day*! One over that hill to the east there. Next to the outlet canal. After the collapse—the pandemic and such—they went bust. Just cleared out. Drill sites abandoned. Orphan wells, they call 'em. Leaked into the canal is what they did, see. Into the Toyah Creek. Into the groundwater. San Solomon Springs. Folks round here, we tried to stop the development. To save the springs." He shakes his head. "Didn't do no good. They still drilled."

Hayley stares out over the lake of flame.

"How did it catch fire, sir?"

The park ranger shrugs, casting his gaze to his feet. Humiliated. "Nobody knows. Sabotage, maybe."

Hayley registers that he says this without conviction.

She asks, "But can't someone do something to put it out?"

"National Guard won't let the county bring in the fire teams. 'Security risk,' they said. Tried to scare me off. Fat chance. Nobody knows these backroads and trails like me. Had to come out to see for myself. Been looking after things here for close to thirteen years. I taught my kids how to fish on this goddamn lake. Just look at it now."

Hayley recalls the Bible lessons delivered by her grandmother. Something about a false prophet. The mark of the beast. And a lake of fire burning with brimstone. Where and when will this hellish night end? What has been done to the world?

"Everything is dead." This from the park ranger. He has already forgotten about the young woman's intrusion on his private memorial service. Makes no effort to mask his pain. The man is crushed.

"All dead," he says.

———————

BIG GAME HUNTERS sought sustenance from San Solomon Springs more than eleven thousand years ago. Animals have watered there for countless centuries more. First known as Mescalero Springs, after the Mescalero Apache, who used it as a water source, Mexican farmers rechristened the place "San Solomon Springs." The canals they gouged from the dark gray silty clay loam exist to this day, irrigation for crops they sold to the inhabitants of Fort Davis. An abundance of water and the railroad's arrival lured a thriving cattle ranching industry. The Bureau of Reclamation power shoveled the springs in 1927 and dug an additional canal to extend the water's reach to thousands of acres of alfalfa and cotton. The Civilian Conservation Corps arrived in 1934, roughly two hundred men who constructed a 1.3-acre pool around the springs, and a concession building, bathhouses, and the surrounding Balmorhea State Park.

In the 1930s, troops and horses of the First Cavalry from Fort Bliss were the earliest visitors to camp at the new park. Tonight, more than ninety years later, elements from Thirty-Sixth Infantry Division's Seventy-Second Brigade of the Texas Army National Guard have made the site their base of operations. Their tents, supplies depot, and motor pool occupy nearly the park's entire forty-six acres.

Hayley enters the camp from the east, barely winded from her jog. Encountering few soldiers at this far corner of the park, she checks her watch. It's only a few minutes past ten. Where is everybody? That question is soon answered. Drawn by the noise of a crowd—volume rising and lowering in waves—she walks south through the temporary encampment, past parked tactical vehicles and Stryker combat vehicles, until she comes to an open area.

The boxing "ring" is a sixteen-by-twenty-foot area defined by fuel drums at each corner. Spectators form a stricter boundary, more than one hundred uniformed soldiers pressing in for a better vantage point of the ongoing combat in the ring—black faces to one side, with white and brown faces a clear majority opposite them. Two male soldiers fight in the arena, one black and one white. They wear no headgear or gloves. Stripped to their waists and barefoot, the boxers are engaged in a brutal, bare-fisted slugfest. Looming over the spectacle is the SkyWatch, a mobile surveillance tower, its occupants hidden from view by the large, tinted windows on four sides.

Hayley is stunned by the fight's level of violence, and the blood-lust of the onlookers. The bout is lopsided, the white fighter using an advantage in arm's length to repeatedly land jabs to his opponent's bloodied face. The deeper state operative has witnessed plenty of brawls in her childhood and in the army. She has seen the damage a sufficiently motivated sadist can inflict with a closed fist. Nothing in her personal experience, however, prepares her for the ferocity of an organized bare-knuckles fight.

There is no art or sweet science. No rounds or neutral corner. Only one rule exists: the bout continues until one fighter fails to get back up.

Having waged a minutes-long, losing battle, the black fighter staggers and drops to his knees. There is no referee in the ring. The other soldier swings from his feet, landing an uppercut on his opponent that lifts him off the ground and puts him on his back with arms splayed. One side is deliriously satisfied with the fight's outcome, while on the other side of the ring, silence and sullen faces result. Supporters mob the victor. Black soldiers tend to their fallen comrade. He is soon back on his feet, badly bloodied but ambulatory.

Hayley turns to address a white female corporal standing next to her in the crowd of riotous spectators.

"What is all of this?" she asks.

"Brigade tradition. At least for as long as I've been around. Last Friday of every month. That's how it got its name. 'Last Friday Fights.' Back in Austin, this is the biggest underground draw in town."

"While deployed?"

The corporal smirks. "This bullshit mission? Gimme a break. We're jacking off out here, with nothin' to do." She shrugs. "The major wanted Last Friday, whether deployed or not."

"Major Nathaniel Culberson?"

The female corporal sizes Hayley up. "Who are you, anyway? You're ARNG, right?" she asks, using the acronym for Army National Guard.

"He's here? The major?"

Realizing she's said too much to someone who might be an outsider, the corporal slides a telltale glance over her right shoulder. Up at the SkyWatch tower. Following her gaze, Hayley sees the bout's winner climbing a set of external stairs up to the mobile guard tower. To be congratulated by the event's VIP attendees? A phalanx of guardsmen prevents intruders from following their champion to that lofty perch.

When Hayley lowers her gaze, she discovers the corporal has skulked off. Another fight is about to commence, one combatant already having already entered the "arena." The deeper state operative regards the soldier waiting for her opponent to join her on the patch of oil- and blood-soaked dirt. She is a giant of a woman, Hispanic, with close-cropped black hair and wearing ACU pants and a filthy T-shirt. The long shape of her head and narrowly spaced eyes suggests a praying mantis. Enough so, at least, to have earned the nickname her supporters repeatedly call out.

Mantis Religiosa! Mantis Religiosa!

With sinewy biceps and ham hocks for fists, she is the white and Hispanic soldiers' favorite.

Hayley scans the side of the ring, where the black soldiers have closed ranks around their next fighter. She is also tall—almost six feet—and solidly proportioned. Athleticism isn't a problem. The black soldier, wearing ACU pants and a military "sand" T-shirt, would intimidate most opponents with the sheer menace of her powerful physique. At issue is her head. Like everyone else in the crowd of spectators, she watched the destruction of the last fighter. In addition to the jeers of the white and brown spectators, that punishment had an unnerving effect.

Mantis Religiosa has that kind of "Mike Tyson effect." Her reputation as a brawling, relentless assassin precedes her.

The prospect of a bloody fracas between women has driven the crowd into a frenzy, one that only intensifies when the white and Latino spectators register the black fighter's reluctance to enter the ring. Those spectators release an avalanche of ridicule and obscenities on the woman, encouraged by Mantis Religiosa, whose derision takes flight in a rapid-fire mix of Spanish and English. The black fighter recoils as her supporters on that side of the ring nevertheless push her forward, into the ring.

Hayley glances up at the SkyWatch box, anticipating some reaction or intervention. None is forthcoming. The tinted windows hide the VIP spectators from view, silent and accusatory.

The deeper state operative sees no movement behind the tower's windows. The door remains closed.

She pushes through the crowd and enters the ring.

"I'll do it."

At first, no one in the crowd pays Hayley any mind, their clamor too distracted. She crosses the makeshift arena and stands in front of the black fighter, blocking her way forward.

"I'll fight her," she says to the other woman.

Once the spectators comprehend Hayley's intention, their scorn rises to an even higher pitch. The deeper state operative is nearly a foot shorter than the Hispanic fighter and thirty pounds lighter. Wearing light cotton pants, long-sleeve shirt, and sensible flats, Hayley hardly presents herself as a "ready fighter."

The black boxer resents what she perceives as pity. Her eyes blaze. "Don't need you fightin' for me."

Hayley is unwavering. "You can't fight scared. She'll maul you. Scared never wins."

They can hardly hear each other over the howling mob. But Hayley's words sink in with the black fighter, pushing their way past her pride and humiliation. And landing.

She *is* scared.

The black fighter turns abruptly and disappears into the crowd behind her.

One of the black soldiers stares angrily at Hayley, rebelling against the white woman's intrusion. "Not really the idea, if you know what I mean." The tone of her voice isn't friendly.

"What is the idea?" Hayley asks.

No response comes quickly enough to stop her from slipping off her shoes. Someone in the back of the crowd throws a dirty T-shirt forward. Hayley catches it on the fly and looks hard into the eyes of the soldier who had spoken. Understanding what is needed, the female guardsman steps forward, close to Hayley, who quickly unbuttons her shirt.

The crowd roars in approval over what they view as libidinous performance. Only her back is revealed to the mob as she removes her shirt, tosses it to the ground, and pulls on the T-shirt. Turning then, dressed for the combat, Hayley faces her opponent. She does not consider herself a savior. The deeper state operative has one goal: win, and climb the stairs to the SkyWatch box. To earn an audience with Nathaniel Culberson.

She has fought with only her fists more times than she can count. As a kid growing up in Lincoln County, West Virginia. While an amateur boxer in the US Army. In backyards, street alleys, and recreational halls. Hayley has the necessary skills to punish an opponent into submission. Yet, despite this multitude of scraps, no previous bout seems more significant than the one she now faces.

There is no bell or facsimile of one. The moment both fighters in the ring toe their respective lines scratched in the dirt signifies the bout's start. Hayley's adversary is ready. Mantis Religiosa watches Hayley with cold, Tyson-like menace, devoid of emotion. Waiting for the moment. Primed to strike.

Hayley is warmed up from her two runs, from town to the lake and then to the ARNG site at Balmorhea State Park. But one crucial element is missing. Before every fight as an amateur, she would clench a jagged, walnut-size rock in her hand so fiercely as to bring blood. After that private ritual was completed, Hayley knew she was ready. There was nothing to fear. Blood was drawn. She could fight.

With the crowd screaming for the start of the bout, Hayley turns her back on her opponent. Many of the spectators believe she has lost her nerve, the same as the first fighter. But the deeper state operative doesn't leave the ring. Instead, she beckons the same female soldier who had challenged her decision to fight.

"Hit me!" Hayley says to her, shouting over the crowd noise.

"Come again?"

"Hit me." She points at her face. "Hit me hard."

The female soldier, raised in a neighborhood south of downtown Houston ranked as one of the most dangerous in the entire nation, doesn't need to be asked twice.

"Fuck yeah."

The soldier pulls back her right elbow and bops Hayley in the nose.

Blood immediately pours from Hayley's left nostril. She puts her fingers to the blood. And nods, satisfied.

There is nothing to fear. Blood flows.

Now I can fight.

Hayley turns and charges forward. Before the Hispanic fighter has time to cover, she connects with a rock-solid left hook. Mantis Religiosa, stunned by the blow, is temporarily incapacitated. Time ceases to exist, and the crowd's clamoring fills her ears. Brain functions are on the fritz. Mantis Religiosa puts the deeper state operative in a clinch to save herself.

Hayley pushes her opponent off and charges forward again. The Hispanic fighter backpedals into the surrounding crowd. Spectators propel Mantis Religiosa—unused to being on the defensive—forward again. Hayley traps her just inside the ring's perimeter and throws a rocketing left uppercut that is followed immediately by a thundering right to the body.

The right jab is a finisher.

For the first time in her fighting career—whether in a sanctioned amateur bout or a similar illegal fight like tonight's—Mantis Religiosa takes a knee. Hayley steps back away from her adversary, unwilling to press her attack despite an obvious "no rules" situation.

Ridicule and obscene mockery fall on the champion in a deluge of verbal abuse. Her supporters are in a riot over their fighter's apparent surrender. Mantis Religiosa's pride wins the internal conflict with her sense of self-preservation. After five seconds on her knee, the Hispanic fighter stands again. And goes on the attack. Hayley is ready for the swinging right hand and ducks under it, answering with a sharp left-right combination to her opponent's cheek.

Mantis Religiosa crumples to the ground, knocked out. She failed to connect with a single punch. In contrast to the remainder of the crowd's sullen and stunned silence, the black spectators celebrate Hayley's shocking victory. The deeper state operative checks her hands for broken bones. The fight lasted less than ninety seconds. Her jog from the lake was a greater exertion.

Standing at the center of the crude boxing ring, Hayley glances up at the expressionless, tinted windows of the SkyWatch. The door of the tower box opens, and a soldier scuttles out, coming down the stairs and gesturing to the crowd to make way for their new champion, the vanquisher of Mantis Religiosa. For Hayley Chill.

———————

WATCHING HER FIGHT, he was almost sure the young woman in the ersatz boxing ring below was the same person he saw with investigators at the New Mexico compound. With his powerful binoculars, he had committed her features to memory. The only woman in the scrum of investigators was difficult to forget.

For Oswald, watching her demolition of the Hispanic boxer was unsurprising. Once he recognized her and witnessed the ease with which she commanded the boxing ring, Oswald knew who would be victorious. His father had been a true aficionado of the sport. Both he and his dad were enormous fans of Cassius Clay—not ever referred to by them as Muhammad Ali—though that champion's politics made it almost impossible to acknowledge his support in public. The fights with Frazier, though, swept aside any disapproval eight-year-old Pete Oswald inherited from his dad of Clay's activist beliefs. And the bout against Foreman in Zaire? My God. *That* was boxing!

The way this blond fighter moved in the ring suggested just a hint of that poise and speed.

But now isn't the time or the place to rekindle childhood passions. Oswald hasn't watched a full bout of professional boxing in more than a decade. He had come to Balmorhea to assess Culberson's performance and capabilities. A civilian's shooting death at the hands of Texas Army National Guard personnel brought unwanted media attention at a particularly sensitive phase of the operation. That incident and the shoot-out at the New Mexico compound have raised concerns. Zero hour nears. The Storm's goals are on the cusp of becoming something much more than a pipe dream. Every operational element of the conspiracy must avoid further mishaps.

Which is why Oswald argued strenuously with the major to

cancel this ridiculous event, to no avail. A born narcissist and preening military man, Culberson had flatly refused to listen to reason.

And now this.

When the young woman is ushered into the tower box to meet the major, Pete Oswald knows her plan with absolute certainty. . . .

So, she has come this far in her investigation. This high in our chain of command.

Then a second, even more shocking realization . . .

She was involved in Libby's untimely demise!

Oswald stands at the rear of the box, behind three seats that afford the best view. As she enters, the young woman's eyes fall on the major and his aides. He pretends to check his phone for messages, turning his face away in the unlikely event she is able to connect him with the incident in New Mexico. Pete Oswald can't help but be impressed by her cunning and persistence, defeating the Hispanic fighter to win an audience with Culberson.

Without a doubt, her investigation represents the gravest threat to their effort.

She must be destroyed.

———————

MAJOR NATHANIEL CULBERSON sits in a swivel chair at the big window that affords a generous vantage point over the surrounding area below. Like the two junior National Guard officers seated on either side of him, he wears his combat uniform and is identifiable by rank insignia at the center of his jacket and name tape above the right pocket.

Having established Culberson's presence, Hayley shifts her focus to the man in civilian clothing—black khaki pants and button-down shirt, and with a bit of a paunch—engrossed with a phone call at the back of the tower box. She senses that he is avoiding her gaze. Why is he acting so weird? Where have they met before?

"Outstanding performance, young lady!" says the major. "That was quite a show you put on!"

Culberson had stood upon Hayley's arrival and now offers his hand to shake. The deeper state operative swings her attention off the man in black civilian clothing and accepts the major's hand.

"Thank you, sir."

"You've obviously had experience in the ring. The benefit of professional instruction. What's your name? Where have you fought?"

"Hayley Chill, Major. Before leaving the army, I was stationed at Fort Hood."

Culberson's face lights up with recognition. "Chill? You fought Marcela Rivas a few years back." He addresses his two aides excitedly, gesturing toward Hayley. "Beat a two-time Golden Gloves champ with the First Armored. Come-from-behind KO!"

"Yes, sir. Rivas is a good fighter."

"But not good enough. Not that night."

Hayley nods. Her nose hurts like hell where she took the ritualistic punch just prior to the bout. The dried blood inside her nostrils makes it difficult to breathe except through her mouth. She can't remember the last time she slept for more than a few hours.

Without looking his way, Hayley feels the eyes of the civilian standing behind Culberson on her now. Sizing her up.

Why? Who is he?

The major asks, "What I want to know, however, is what the hell you're doing here in my camp?"

The mood in the cramped confines of the guard tower shifts abruptly. The easy grin has disappeared from the major's face. She clocked the Sig Sauer P320 handgun on the narrow shelf in front of Culberson upon entering the tower a few moments earlier. The guardsmen who stand sentry at the bottom of the stairs haven't gone anywhere. Should she require escape, her options are limited.

"I'm in Texas on behalf of Senator Gordon Powell and the Senate

Armed Services Committee. The senator, and many of his colleagues, have become concerned, Major, about reports of white supremacy within the US military. At all levels, sir."

Culberson doesn't so much as flinch, absorbing Hayley's direct challenge without overt reaction. His face is immobile, with eyes that seem without a bottom. Twin pinholes that empty into a corrupted, pitiless soul.

"You didn't have to whip ass on one of the brigade's best fighters to get a meeting with me, Ms. Chill. That's why God . . . and the Pentagon . . . created public affairs representatives."

"Precisely, sir."

"Then what the actual *fuck* did you hope to gain by confronting me directly?"

Hayley glances toward the man in black, who no longer feigns interest in his smartphone.

His seeming recognition of her and his blatant, predatory stare— lacking any other plausible explanation—incontrovertibly designate him as another player in the game.

The first place her mind goes is the ridgeline above the New Mexico compound and the road out. Someone watching them, standing on the rise above. The occasional sun flare off what must have been binoculars.

And dressed all in black, just like here.

He is a person of interest. A factor to be considered. But not now. At this charged moment, Nathaniel Culberson is her target. His role in the unnamed conspiracy. What he might know about her father and how he was involved.

Hayley turns her gaze to the major again. "Sir, what do you know about the participation by members of the US military in the recent incidents of sabotage in the Permian Basin?"

His voice rises an octave with mock incredulity. "The sabotage we've been deployed to prevent?"

"What about the Storm, Major?"

The major guffaws and exchanges a dubious look with one of his aides.

Before Culberson can frame his response, they all hear the altercation from down below.

———————

IN HOUSTON, ON August 23, 1917, black soldiers guarding the construction of Camp Logan fought city police and local residents in a series of pitched gun battles that lasted hours. The arrest of a black soldier for allegedly interfering in the detention of a black woman ignited the riot. Sixteen white city residents died, including five police officers. Four black soldiers were killed. Martial law eventually restored order to the city after a full day of chaos. Sixty-four black soldiers were tried in the subsequent court martial, the largest in US military history. Thirteen were found guilty of murder and hanged without the chance to appeal.

On Guam, Christmas Day 1944, white and black soldiers fired on one another with their service weapons in a quarrel that began the day before over a Chamoru woman. Tensions had been rising between the two groups on the island—taken from the Japanese Army six months earlier, at the cost of almost two thousand American lives—after a series of racially charged incidents.

A violent disturbance occurred at Camp Lejeune on July 20, 1969—the night Neil Armstrong first set foot on the moon—when a black Marine tried to cut into a white Marine dancing with a black female Marine at the NCO Club. The twenty-year-old white corporal, Edward Bankston, who survived multiple combat-related injuries in Vietnam, was beaten to death.

In October 1972, black and white sailors armed with broom handles, wrenches, and pieces of pipe fought one another aboard the US carrier *Kitty Hawk*. Fifty sailors were evacuated to onshore hospitals. The chaos began when a black sailor requested two sandwiches from an unreceptive white cook. A shouting match ensued after the black sailor reached across the food-service line and took two sandwiches anyway. With 4,500 sailors aboard and only 302 of them black, the ship was a racial tinderbox, due in no small part to the civil rights movement going on at the time back home.

THE FIGHTING AT the National Guard encampment between black and white soldiers erupts over an unpaid bet. Passions had already been stirred, of course, by the racially demarcated bare-knuckle bouts that led up to the altercation. Pushing and shoving leads to a thrown punch. Initially, the scuffle is limited to the two original combatants. With the white soldier losing to his black adversary, other white and brown soldiers jump to his defense. A free-for-all ensues. Fortunately, the risk of gunplay in the escalating fracas is limited. After the accidental shooting of the local resident earlier in the week, officers confiscated most if not all ammunition. Improvised weapons, however, are quickly taken up as the situation spirals out of control.

Hayley emerges from the surveillance tower and descends the external stairway, following Major Culberson and the two junior officers. The violent brawl swirls around them. Military police are nowhere to be seen.

Culberson, the senior officer on-site, raises his arms and tries to be heard over the mob. "Stop! Stop fighting, goddammit!"

No one pays him any mind. The fracas intensifies. Officers try to control the soldiers, to little or no effect. Many combatants have armed themselves with lengths of pipe, wooden stakes, and glass bottles. These improvised weapons inflict terrible, bloody injuries.

Hayley sees Culberson give up and retreat from the chaos. Needing to question him, she starts after the major but is stopped by a group of frenzied soldiers who recognize her as the winner of the last fight. They block her path, converging on her. Hayley strikes out at her attackers, deflecting their blows, but there are too many of them. Knocked to the ground, she draws her knees to her head, protecting her face and abdomen from their kicks and punches.

One soldier stands over her with a length of pipe, poised to slam it on her skull.

Hayley sees the blow coming out of the corner of her eye and braces for it. There's nowhere to go. Nothing to be done. Too many of them.

But the jolt never comes.

When she uncovers her head, Hayley sees that several Reeves County sheriff's personnel have waded into the crowd and are in the process of restoring order. The same deputy she spoke with briefly at the Tex-Mex joint in Sierra Blanco disarmed the soldier who was moments from attacking her with a pipe.

I guess you could say it's about civilization. The fake kind we see all 'round us and the one that's real.

Deputy Jay Gibbs puts cuffs on Hayley's would-be attacker. The deeper state operative gets to her feet without anyone's help.

From her new perspective on the scene, she sees the Reeves County sheriff prowlers stopped just outside the scrum of soldiers, LED light bars flashing. With cooler heads on both sides prevailing, altercations between the National Guard troops have mostly ended. Several soldiers remain down on the ground, bleeding from various injuries . . . but alive.

Gibbs toggles his radio as another deputy takes control of the handcuffed soldier.

"We're gonna need EMT response."

Once that's done, he turns his attention to the blond woman with the powder blue eyes.

HE DIDN'T REALIZE it was her at first. Seeing the soldier raising the pipe to strike someone—just another body down on the ground—

Gibbs moved quickly to stop the attack. But once he had immobilized the frenzied soldier, the deputy recognized his victim. *Her.* How
often does anything like that ever happen? They had exchanged a few
words at Delfina's only an hour or so earlier. And then she left. Out of
his life forever, or so he imagined at the time.

Gibbs thought about the woman on the rest of the drive home
after his meal. Like a love-addled schoolkid, he daydreamed of various scenarios in which he might run into her again. Helping her out
with a flat tire. Seeing her at the local Family Dollar store, or when he
stopped in for a cold beer at Pop A Top after his shift. In his mind's
eye, the sheriff's deputy saw how that scene would play out, pretty
much in its entirety. The mild surprise and bashful grins. An offer to
join her at the bar. He would buy the next round, and she would tease
him about being a cop. He would tell her about his writerly aspirations in a thinly veiled attempt to gain her interest.

The radio call requesting immediate assistance with a disturbance at the National Guard's temporary camp at Balmorhea State
Park cut short these idle fantasies. He was on Interstate 10, less than
five minutes from the scene, having avoided construction on the
more direct route. Had he taken his usual route, up Interstate 20,
Gibbs would've missed out.

He would never have seen her. Not ever again.

———————

HAYLEY DOESN'T KNOW where her tote bag is. Or her shoes and shirt.
Wearing her scuffed linen pants and dirty T-shirt, barefoot and aching
from the blows she took to her side, hips, and back, she wonders where
Culberson has fled. She didn't go through everything she has in the past
six hours—the long drive from El Paso, detained by the National Guard
troops on the highway, slipping away from the high school, her run to
the burning lake, and, finally, winning a bare-knuckles bout to gain an
audience with the major—only to lose him so easily.

Looking in all directions for Culberson, Hayley finally registers that her rescuer is speaking. To her.

"Ma'am? Are you okay?" he asks for the third time.

The deeper state operative finally locks her eyes on Gibbs.

"Yes. Thank you." Not acknowledging she recognizes him from the Tex-Mex place. No time for that now.

"You sure? Look a bit beat-up there."

Hayley's mind is elsewhere. She realizes the solicitous deputy might be useful to her cause.

"Major Culberson. He's the senior officer in camp."

The sheriff's deputy needs to be sure he understands what Hayley is saying.

"He . . . ?"

"Culberson organized the bare-knuckle boxing matches, Deputy. He's responsible for all of this."

"What bare-knuckle boxing matches?"

JAY GIBBS HAS experienced much in his thirty-two years. Growing up in hardscrabble West Texas. Tours in Afghanistan and Iraq. Patrolling highways on the front lines of the drug war. But when Hayley gives him a sharp look the likes of which he has never experienced, his knees could buckle.

He toggles his radio. "Anybody see a major tryin' to get on outta here, stop him for questioning."

"Thank you," she says.

Gibbs nods and taps the brim of his straw Resistol. "Ma'am."

The black female soldier who bopped her in the nose, at Hayley's behest, approaches, carrying the deeper state operative's personal belongings: shoes, shirt, and tote bag.

Grateful, Hayley accepts her things. "Are you okay?" she asks the soldier.

The woman is unsmiling. "Lady, we're a long way from 'okay.'"

Hayley says nothing. She can't disagree.

SHE CLOCKS THE UH-60 Blackhawk helicopter approaching from the west, swooping overhead, and landing in the open area between the National Guard camp and the diversion canal.

Meaning Hayley only has a few minutes to question Culberson without Pogue's interference.

Jay Gibbs has proved himself to be of invaluable assistance. The National Guard major was stopped by Reeves County sheriff's deputies at the interstate on-ramp, heading east. Back to Austin, presumably. He hadn't accepted his detainment in good humor. Only a stern phone call from the governor himself—Deputy Gibbs, again—was enough to shut down Culberson's protestations and guarantee his cooperation with local law enforcement.

Overhead halogens illuminating their walk to the sheriff's department SUV stopped near the park's entrance off State Highway 17. Hayley glances to her left, to Gibbs, as they approach the vehicle where Culberson is being held. Despite the circumstances—the litany of promises she had made to herself not to have such thoughts—she can't help but admire the cut of his profile in the half-light.

Hayley recognizes the attention he's given her can't be entirely official.

And has to remind herself. Again. For the umpteenth time.

Not now, idiot. Not now.

As they near the SUV, Gibbs says, "The man isn't overjoyed with the situation, such as it is." Two other sheriff's deputies stand guard outside.

Hayley nods.

Such as it is.

He asks, "You want me—?"

"I'll be fine, Deputy. Thank you."

Gibbs's grin is as wrinkled as his department-issued, khaki shirt. He had taken care to put on a freshly laundered, adequately ironed shirt in the morning for his court appearance. But that was a lifetime ago. Enough has transpired in the last sixteen hours to make a wreck of his best efforts at a buttoned-down presentability.

"Yeah. I'm pretty sure you will be."

One of the deputies regards Hayley skeptically as they walk up to the parked vehicle.

"Who's she?" he asks Gibbs.

"Not your business, slick." He opens the front passenger-side door for Hayley. "That's who."

Hayley says, "Thank you again, Deputy Gibbs."

She climbs into the SUV, the sheriff's deputy closing the door behind her.

Nathaniel Culberson sits in the back seat, sufficiently caged behind wire mesh cargo and side window barriers. Hayley, in front, turns to face him, her left elbow resting on the seat back.

"Hello, Major."

His ego is bruised. And he's scared. Frantic for a way out.

"Satisfied? We were only having a little fun. Working off some stress."

"The five soldiers in your command that were sent to the hospital are the least of your problems, sir."

Culberson shrugs, a poor attempt at feigning a cavalier attitude.

"Did you know a Charles Hicks, Major? Former Marine who worked at the Pentagon. Or Tommy Chill?"

He seems offended by her presence. By her persistent harangue.

"You have no rights here. No jurisdiction. Nor do these deputies!"

"Captain Christian Libby gave you up, sir. Before jumping from the roof of the William Beaumont Army Medical Center to his death."

Mere mention of the captain's name takes Culberson's legs out from underneath him.

"Libby . . . ?"

"Yes, sir."

He processes these revelations. Understands now the meaning of the phrase "walls closing in."

Hayley asks, "Who's involved, Major? What's the plan? The goals of your group?"

"Group?"

"Yes, sir." She takes a stab in the dark. "The Storm."

He grins, his eyes watery and vague. Hayley wonders if he is under the influence of drugs.

"It's not too late, Major. There're other ways out than the one taken by Captain Libby."

Culberson seems to mentally shift gears, giving his interrogator a quizzical look.

He says, "Tommy Chill."

Hayley can't not react.

"Sir . . . ?"

"You asked me a minute ago about Tommy Chill."

She feels as if her heart might thump its way out of her chest. Glancing out the windshield, the deeper state operative sees CID agents Roy Pogue and Angelica Lopez approaching from the road leading into the temporary garrison. A clutch of somber-looking National Guard officers accompany them.

Hayley turns her focus on Culberson again. She estimates she has less than a minute.

"What do you know about Tommy Chill, Major?"

"Your father?"

Hayley remembers using her real name with Culberson when she entered the guard tower.

Fucking stupid.

"Yes. He was my father."

Culberson smirks.

"Well, Tommy . . . he was more than a footnote."

"Sir?"

She can hear their voices outside the car. Gibbs trying to buy her more time.

"The guy in charge? Our George Washington? He and Tommy were like this," he says, wrapping his two index fingers.

One of the rear doors is pulled open. Pogue peers inside the SUV, seeing both Culberson and Hayley.

"Ms. Chill."

Pogue knew Hayley was on-site. As her contact at Fort Bliss, he was summoned to the location because of her involvement in the incident. But the CID agent hoped not to find her questioning the National Guard officer before Criminal Investigation Command.

In fact, nothing would please him more than to see her on a plane to Washington, DC.

"Chief," says Hayley, in that Chill way.

POGUE AND LOPEZ walk Culberson through camp, to the open ground on the opposite side of the state park. The major suffers every step of that forced march, in full display before the troops in his command. Hayley, a few paces behind him, can almost see the humiliation and dread shed off the senior officer like a fever's sweat. Midnight has come and gone. With a cooling trend in the offing, temperatures hover in the low seventies. The late-night's weather could be described as pleasant, except for the fire's smoke drifting from the east.

Her work isn't over, not by a long shot. Hayley Chill can barely recall how the day began.

As they approach the waiting chopper that will take Culberson to Fort Bliss, she sees the man in black from the guard tower, standing in the back of a silent crowd of soldiers. But in the blink of an eye, he disappears from view. Had she seen him? Who is he? That the man is connected in some way to the conspiracy—the Storm—is certain.

Hayley considers her initial hunch that he is the same individual she spied standing on the ridge at the New Mexico compound. Now that she has seen him up close, the deeper state operative has committed his features to memory.

The CID agents prepare to load Culberson into the Blackhawk. He hesitates, wanting a word with Hayley.

"Get in the chopper, sir," Pogue orders, keeping a firm grip on the major's arm.

The National Guard major turns to Hayley, leaning toward her in a last-ditch attempt for private conversation.

"Three words . . ."

"Sir?"

"Clemency, witness protection." His gaze has an unhinged intensity. "Believe me, whoever you really work for *wants* to hear what I've got to say."

Pogue shoves Culberson toward the open doorway in the side of the helicopter.

"Now, Major! Hop in."

The detainee climbs aboard, followed by Lopez. Twin General Electric T700 turboshaft engines turn over and roar to a start. The chopper's four-blade main rotor begins to turn.

Pogue pauses before joining the others inside the Blackhawk.

"Sure you wouldn't prefer riding back with us? I can have one of the MPs here sort out your vehicle."

Hayley shakes her head. "I'll be okay, sir. See you back at Fort Bliss. Ten hundred hours?"

The CID agent is anxious to be off. "You got it."

Within seconds of Pogue climbing aboard and pulling the chopper's hatch closed, the Blackhawk lifts off and flies west.

———

SHE CHECKS HER watch. Five minutes past two a.m. Having spent the last two hours interviewing both ARNG enlisted personnel and officers at the temporary garrison in Balmorhea, Hayley is satisfied that awareness of the Storm and its agenda is limited. As best as she's been able to ascertain, only Culberson is involved. The two junior officers Hayley found in the guard tower with the major will be questioned further by CID, but only regarding their role in the bare-knuckle brawls organized by their superior officer. For the time being, Hayley is withholding any details of the Storm from the army's Criminal Investigation Command.

No one Hayley interviews seems to know the identity of the man in black or where he might have gone.

Gibbs stands at the open driver's-side window of the rental car parked on the interstate's overpass, where Hayley had left it hours earlier. Behind the wheel, the deeper state operative wishes she could just stop and rest. Wake up after a decent amount of sleep and meet the deputy someplace for breakfast. Drink a cup of coffee. Talk about books. The weather. About anything but the darkness that infuses her every waking thought. A growing sense of dread.

But that is only fantasy. Hayley has the long drive back to El Paso. She needs to make calls regarding Culberson's demands for clemency and wonders who in Andrew Wilde's Rolodex will be able to swing it.

Other business requires Hayley's attention, too, before she can steal an hour or two of sleep.

"Personally, I think it's not too smart driving back at this hour of the night. Some of the things I've seen on this road after midnight you wouldn't believe."

Gibbs only just met Hayley Chill, but already has her measure. He knows he's wasting perfectly good oxygen with these words.

She smiles wearily, grateful as a person can be for his friendly offer of help.

"Deputy Gibbs—"

"Jay."

". . . I appreciate your assistance tonight."

Assistance.

He nods and taps the brim of his hat. "Next time, try them gorditas."

"I will," says Hayley. "Maybe you can join me."

Jay Gibbs strives to keep his grin under wraps and mostly fails.

———————

OSWALD DRIVES NORTH on Ranch Road, takes the interstate west to the next exit, and doubles back, pulling over to the shoulder so he has a decent vantage point on the overpass. He passed several cars parked there and found the blue-eyed woman's rental vehicle among them, having committed the make, color, and model to memory when he observed it at the New Mexico compound. He switches off the engine and kills the lights. His binoculars are on the seat next to him. All he has to do now is wait.

He argued strenuously with Culberson to cancel the bare-knuckles event. All of this unnecessary attention. Oswald dreads making his report to the Storm's ideological leader. James Earl Woodside is an unforgiving man with a hyperbolic temper. The best strategy is to deliver the unvarnished truth. Embellishing or spinning a false representation of events only made matters worse.

Oswald knows this from experience. Another man—a member of the inner circle like him, with oversight on several elements of the movement simultaneously—attempted to cover up his failure by shifting responsibility to others. Woodside exposed the falsehood easily enough and summoned the man for a late-night meeting. Faced with a more dire fate, the shamed conspirator performed *seppuku*, with the broad elements of that Japanese ritual of honor suicide observed, down to cloth-wrapped *tantō*, spectators, and the traditional left-to-right cutting open of the abdomen.

That night—less than two weeks ago—Oswald was more than convinced James Woodside meant business. The offender's honor suicide had the desired impact. Message received, loud and clear. Their cause was "do or die." No half measures would be tolerated. Surrender was not an option. Under Woodside's leadership, and by dint of his sheer willpower, the movement would go forward and achieve its stated goals . . . or they will all die trying.

Oswald first met the movement's leader in Iraq. The war was how many of the organization's core members had met, had their eyes opened to the truth. Of what had become of America. The corruption of its Founding Fathers' ideals. And, most important, shown them a path to starting over. Most of these original conspirators have since left the military, though a valuable contingent remains with combat forces. No one in the movement is higher in its rigid hierarchy than Woodside. The movement *is* Woodside. He has led them to within sight of the promised land. He is their *new* founding father.

Pete Oswald, one of Woodside's first acolytes, has been a fervent and devoted servant of their ideological leader. He has served as a kind of factotum for the congressman, willing and able to fulfill any need. Complete any mission, no matter what. His high rank in the organization and unshakable faith in its cause have given Oswald a reason to live. The Storm, in almost every way possible, has become his life.

He will make a full and accurate report of what happened here in Balmorhea and accept his fate.

After waiting nearly an hour, Oswald sees a sheriff's department SUV stop on the overpass and the young blond woman get out. She speaks to the deputy behind the wheel briefly and then walks to her car parked on the side of the road just short of the overpass. He watches with his binoculars as she pulls away from the shoulder and takes the on-ramp for the westbound interstate. Once she has entered the highway and attained cruising speed, Oswald hits the ignition and merges onto the mostly deserted interstate. He takes the off-ramp for Balmorhea, crosses the same overpass, and turns for the westbound on-ramp.

He doesn't know where the Senate aide is going, but he sure as hell wants to find out.

8

THE WHITE RAJAHS OF SARAWAK

She drives back into town at dawn, her sixth day in West Texas. The fatigue that weighs on her is like one she has never experienced before. No doubt, Hayley surmises, the unplanned pregnancy has something to do with this unfamiliar lethargy. What compels her to push through this exhausted, sleep-deprived state is a sense she is getting closer to the truth. To answers. Of making the history right.

As always, the accoutrements of a "normal" life seem of secondary importance. Hayley accepts this sacrifice. She must if she is to continue her work for the deeper state. Her relationship with Sam was a casualty of that dedication. To the country and its Constitution. The same must be true for an unwanted pregnancy. Pushing her conflicted emotions into the recesses of her active consciousness, Hayley narrows her focus as if through a Leupold rifle scope. On target. She is an operative, not a mother.

Hayley reckons that later today will be the best time to take the pills. After she is confident that Culberson's cooperation has been secured.

On a Saturday at daybreak, El Paso is a slumbering, low-lying rattletrap of tire joints, strip malls, transmission shops, and fast-food franchises, hours from opening for the day's trade. The sky is a vast, cyan-blue scrim, nearly indistinguishable from the dark Franklin Mountains to the west. A relentless sun will soon breach the placid, predawn gloom, and August will again broil all in its grip. Until then, the city broods.

Hayley clocked the dude slinging dope from under the shuttered restaurant's red-and-white-striped awning on Dyer Street while out for a predawn run earlier during her stay. Sorrento Italian Restaurant is permanently closed, another casualty of the pandemic and collapsed oil prices. The scrawny white kid wearing baggy cargo shorts, Nikes, and a Houston Astros jersey uses its doorway as a place of business. His NY Mets snapback hat suggests a casual degree of team loyalty.

Confirming the drug dealer is at his usual spot, Hayley drives past the location and turns right at Fred Wilson Avenue. Right again at Lackland, to an alley that takes her into the parking lot behind the restaurant. If she had the money, Hayley would avoid the hassle of robbing the guy. But she doesn't have the extra cash. The War Hawk in her trunk will have to do.

In a way, the deeper state operative reasons, she's doing the city of El Paso a favor. A little less dope on the street.

Hayley doesn't bother with the holster. Holding the .45-caliber handgun down at her right thigh, she walks quickly up the side of the squat, adobe-style building, to where the squirrelly drug dealer waits for his next drive-up customer. He prefers selling to the working schmucks of the world who require a boost before putting in at the nine-to-five. These customers tend to be of a higher-caliber human being than the dope fiends who venture out later in the day or at night. A lot less dangerous, too.

"Hey," she says, raising the gun to chest level.

The look on the guy's face confirms he didn't register her approach until Hayley is essentially on him. Total compliance is his only option.

He has never been robbed before. Not on the morning shift. Not by anyone but the cops.

Words seize in his throat and come out as a garbled shout.

Hayley grips his shirtfront and hauls him back into the recessed entryway. She wonders if the guy is cold, standing outside in his goofy cargo shorts. A weather front has moved into the region, dropping early-morning temperatures into the fifties. On the horizon to the west, a wall of clouds looms ever closer.

She says, "I want all of it."

"Fuck you!"

His exclamation has a plaintive tenor. Hayley recognizes a young man who has been beaten down repeatedly in his short, brutal life. A human punching bag. Where she grew up, you were prey or a predator. If she hadn't escaped the world of her upbringing, the deeper state operative wonders what role she would have played.

"All of it," she repeats.

"I don't even have the stuff on me, dumbass."

"It's not far away, though. And if you don't take me to it in the next three seconds, I'll blow your shit-for-brains out the backside of your head."

The drug dealer blinks, calculating the odds she's bluffing.

"One . . ."

"Okay, okay!"

"Let's go." Hayley gestures with the gun.

Cargo shorts sliding off his nonexistent hips, the drug dealer leads the way from the restaurant's entrance and around the corner of the building. Halfway down its length, on the ground, is a Taco Bell box. It's not the only piece of discarded garbage to catch Hayley's eye. Assessing the amount of trash in the parking lot, she concludes that El Paso suffers from either a scarcity of public trash receptacles or a doesn't-give-a-shit populace.

The drug dealer stops a few feet from the grease-spotted carton and points at it with the toe of his stained Nike. "There."

"Pick it up and hand it over."

He obeys. Hayley accepts the box and, keeping the guy covered with her gun, cracks the lid open. She seems satisfied with what she sees inside.

"Go on. Get the hell out of here."

The drug dealer pops the briefest of sneers, relieved she isn't robbing him of the 243 bucks in his pockets.

He hesitates before hauling ass out of there. "You don't strike me as the average jibbhead."

Hayley needs him gone before she can return to her car parked behind the building.

She says, "Two . . ."

Taking the hint, the drug dealer pivots and starts running, crossing the street and heading south on Dyer.

———————

THE MOTEL MANAGER's Suzuki Forenza occupies its usual spot behind the office. Jerry Fishbaugh has covered the skeleton shift for the last several days, his regular guy delayed while visiting family in Fort Worth. Something about a sick grandmother. Hayley received this information from the motel manager two days ago when stopping by the office to pay for an additional week's stay. His chattiness was too obviously a ploy to keep her at the counter for longer than necessary, Fishbaugh's gaze baldly rapacious. Hayley tolerated the motel manager's leer only as long as she needed to gather intel. She devised an action plan then and there.

Pulling into the property at the first driveway, Hayley parks behind the office and exits her rental car. She opens the driver's-side door of the Suzuki, using a slim jim she fashioned from the bracket of a hanging file folder. Popping the trunk lid with a release button on the driver's door, the deeper state operative stows the Taco Bell box inside and locks up the car again. The El Paso Police Department receives her anonymous tip before she pulls into the parking space in front of her motel room.

Lina Campos, thirty minutes into her shift, pushes a cleaning trolley up the walkway. Hayley gives her a friendly wave as she exits the rental car.

Entering her motel room, Hayley instinctively drops to a half-crouch upon seeing April Wu in the reclining chair between the bed and front window.

"Goddammit!"

"What?" asks April innocently.

Hayley knows better.

"You've got to stop doing that. Seriously."

April, wearing the same cargo pants and black Army Knights hoodie as before, shrugs. Even in the bad light, her sickly pallor is pronounced.

"Gotta admire the tradecraft, right?" she asks.

"No one should take any pride in defeating the security measures in place at the Beverly Crest Motor Inn, April."

"I do." Her cocky grin is proof.

"*You* would."

Hayley turns to pull open the blinds, flooding the room with the first, unimpeded rays of the morning sun. The dinginess of the motel room is hardly alleviated.

"What are you doing here?" she asks without warmth.

April gestures toward Jerry Fishbaugh's heap across the parking lot. "A better question is to ask why you're breaking into cars."

Hayley releases an exasperated sigh she wishes she could have back.

Her friend's mocking grin is savage. "Save yourself the heartache, slugger. Assume I know and see everything."

A police cruiser stops behind the Suzuki, visible through the motel room's window. Two El Paso patrol officers exit the vehicle and give the motel manager's car a good walk-around.

Hayley, distracted by April's intrusion, can't fully observe the conclusion of her mission to rid Lina Campos of her abuser.

"Let's get back to what *you're* doing here."

"I'm not the only one who's concerned about you." After a pause, April adds, "Looking like shit, by the way."

"*I* look like shit?"

April says, "I've got the gold-plated excuse, Chill. Never forget that."

Outside in the parking lot, the two cops leave the Suzuki and walk toward the office door, disappearing from view.

The deeper state operative experiences another surge of weariness. She craves sleep. April is the only thing between Hayley and a few hours of much-needed rest. Getting rid of her becomes an acute priority.

"I'm pregnant." Simple and direct. Like a .45-caliber round right between the eyes.

"I know."

Hayley's sleep-deprived state aggravates a preexisting annoyance with her friend, but not by much.

"*Fuck!*"

"Relax. The receipt for misoprostol you left crumpled up in the trash can." April gestures at the receptacle next to the bed. "Tell the world, why don't you?"

Hayley can only blame herself for this unintentional reveal. She retrieves the prescription bottle from her tote and stashes it unceremoniously in a toiletry travel bag in the bathroom. As if *that* would make the whole business disappear from her life.

"What's the plan?" asks April.

A flustered Hayley reenters the room.

"With the pregnancy? What do you think? People like us, we can't keep tropical fish."

"You had a dog."

"For two minutes. Sam took Yazat."

"Sam." The expression on April's face asks the obvious question.

"No. I haven't told him. And I don't plan to."

"Okay." April's head bobs with a judgmental cadence.

"Look. I haven't slept in more than twenty-four hours. Today isn't going to be any less challenging. You should probably go."

"I just got here. What else am I going to do in fucking El Paso . . . ?"

"But bother me."

"But bother you."

With morose resignation, Hayley accepts that she has zero control over what her friend does or doesn't do.

Waving her hands in front of her like she's walked into a swarm of houseflies, she says, "Really not in the mood, ya know."

"Copy that." April pauses ever so briefly, then says, "New topic. This business here. Who's blowing up the Permian Basin?"

"I'm working on it."

"What can I do to help?" She gestures to herself, relaxing comfortably in Hayley's motel room. "You've seen my work."

"You know as well as I do that you can't do *anything* to help me."

"Andrew Wilde?"

"Reluctantly cooperative."

"Having a few ex-presidents backstopping you doesn't hurt."

Through the window, Hayley sees the two El Paso patrol officers following Jerry Fishbaugh back to his car. The motel manager seems agitated.

"What's that all about?" asks April, gesturing at the unfolding scene without actually looking in the cops' direction.

Hayley, however, watches the investigation with great intensity. "Helping a friend."

"You don't have friends."

April joins Hayley at the window. They watch the motel manager, at the cops' direction, unlock the Suzuki. One of the patrol officers pops the trunk and searches it. Within seconds, she emerges from behind the raised trunk lid with the Taco Bell carton. Her partner cuffs an apoplectic Fishbaugh, ignoring his histrionics.

"Well, well, well . . . another win for the good guys," says April.

Hayley remains silent, watching the spectacle without expression. She feels more tired than ever.

April has been staring at her for these last few seconds.

She asks, "Should they be worried about you?"

"Who?" asks Hayley.

"*Everybody.*"

With April's unwelcome intrusion, Hayley relinquishes any hope for sleep. She steps out of the motel room, heading to her rental car parked directly in front of the door.

"Hey!"

Lina Campos stands in the open doorway of the room next to Hayley's. The expression on her face is neither friendly nor hostile.

"Hi" is the best Hayley can manage. Did the room cleaner see her plant the drugs in her boss's car?

"He's gone. The police took him away."

"Yes. I saw." Hayley pauses. Then, "He won't bother you anymore."

Lina has said all that she is going to say. Fixing her gaze on the deeper state operative for another few moments, she betrays no sign of appreciation or gratitude for Hayley's intervention.

The silence hangs between them, an awkward indictment of the white woman's privilege. A stray dog enters the motel's parking lot from the street, taking a shortcut to the alley that runs behind the north wing. From one of the rooms farther east, a loud argument erupts between a recently married couple.

Hayley nods by way of goodbye and turns for her car.

The housekeeper disappears inside the recently vacated room.

Fishbaugh or no Fishbaugh, she has only fifteen minutes to prepare it for the next guest.

———————

SITTING BEHIND THE wheel of the fifth-hand pickup truck, stopped across Dyer from the motel, Oswald watches the young woman get in her rental car. He has no clue what she said to the motel housekeeper. Something about cleaning her room? He witnessed the robbery of the drug dealer and subsequent framing of the motel desk clerk. None of it makes much sense to Oswald. What exactly is Hayley Chill's fucking game? His contacts have already provided him with her name and recent work history. Her position in Senator Powell's office might go some way to explaining her activities . . . *but not quite*. Raised in relative poverty in West Virginia, a veteran of the US Army, and a former, low-level aide in the disgraced Monroe administration . . . Hayley Chill's story is a collection of odd, mismatched parts. An enigma, she seems to have a knack for being in the wrong place at the wrong time.

Oswald has a hunch she is something other than a scrubby Senate aide. What exactly, he has no idea. As his target pulls out of the parking lot and heads south on Dyer, he buries his face in his right shoulder and starts his car's engine only after she has turned right out of the lot entrance and cleared the immediate area. He hopes like hell she doesn't note his necessary U-turn in her rearview mirror.

———————

IN FACT, HAYLEY clocked the old pickup as she climbed behind the wheel of her rental car. Even from that distance, she recognized the driver as the man in black from the National Guard camp in Balmorhea. As she pulls out onto Dyer Street, Hayley doesn't even bother checking her rearview mirror. She knows he will follow her once she is underway. Hayley is surprised by the sloppiness of her adversary's tradecraft. Did he think the old Ford made him less conspicuous? That he isn't trained—at least with a basic understanding of espionage—is a given. But that incompetence doesn't necessarily lessen the threat he poses.

Surveillance requires finesse and skill, but any asshole can pull the trigger of a gun.

Hayley mulls the possibility of dropping her pursuer, doubling back, and putting a tail on *him*. But the greater priority is nailing down Culberson's cooperation. Drive time to Fort Bliss is twelve minutes. She doesn't again consider the ramifications of the man tailing her, even though he follows her the entire way to the gate at Chaffee Road. Too much else on her mind. Always too much.

———

POGUE CALLED EARLIER with confirmation that Criminal Investigation Command was holding the National Guard major at the Ninety-Third Military Police headquarters. Having passed through the Chaffee gate with the credentials provided to her by the CID agent, Hayley proceeds to the location on Cassidy Road. The army post hums with activity, awash in pale, August sunlight. A respite from the summer's heat can't last long, and people seem to relish the relatively cool temperatures, pausing to chat on the sidewalk or sitting on benches outside. Hayley clocks the increased activity on base and makes a mental note to ask her CID contact about it.

Parking in front of the MP headquarters, she sees Pogue exiting his car. They meet on the walkway leading to the building entrance.

"Chief."

"Ms. Chill, you look like shit, if you don't mind me saying."

"I don't mind. It seems to be a popular opinion."

"Working on a weekend will do that to you. Why not get some rest? Culberson isn't going anywhere soon. Jurisdictional issues still need to be resolved."

"I spoke with Washington earlier this morning, Mr. Pogue. The senator has taken a personal interest in the matter."

"Fantastic," the chief warrant officer says dryly.

Hayley gestures toward the building. "Let's get inside, sir. Talk to the man."

The deeper state operative hadn't talked with the senator from Kentucky, of course. She made her first and only call of the morning to Andrew Wilde. Her direct superior with Publius made the subsequent requests of sympathetic contacts at the Pentagon and within the Judge Advocate General's Corps. Hayley was inclined to marvel at the reach and persuasive powers of the deeper state. Culberson's proposed clemency could not have come without a price. Judging by Wilde's demeanor, Culberson's cooperation better be worth the horse-trading it required. In their encrypted email exchange following the call to her request, she assured her superior the stakes were exceedingly high.

They're met just inside the doors by Command Sergeant Major Joseph Johnson. With Chief Warrant Officer Pogue in civilian clothes, as is customary for CID military investigators, Johnson does not offer a salute.

"Chief."

Johnson's back is pool-cue straight, his combat uniform pressed and starched. One glance at him and his surroundings confirms that he runs a tight outfit as the principal aide to the battalion commander. The building's entry lobby is orderly and gleamingly clean. Enlisted men at their desks work diligently regardless of the disruption.

"Sergeant Johnson, this is Hayley Chill, from Senator Powell's office in Washington. She's here to speak with the detainee."

"He's in one of our holding rooms. Follow me, please."

HIS FATHER, TRAVIS County judge Roy Culberson, was a lifelong Democrat with an innate compassion for the underdog that he

shared with Nat's mother, Betty. Within the liberal-leaning and cul-
turally sophisticated Culberson clan, Nathaniel was something of an
outlier. Embracing a more rough-hewn, conventionally Texan (i.e.,
hell-raising) attitude, the oldest of four Culberson children relied on
his father's prominent status within Austin's law enforcement circles
to skate over legal troubles. Drunk driving arrests. Bar brawls. An
arrest for joyriding. The judge pulled the necessary strings to extricate
Nathaniel from jam after jam that he prayed would be the last. Rock
bottom took the form of expulsion from the University of Texas for
theft of another student's property. The judge refused to make the
problem go away.

Disowned, the lifelong hellion found God and went in search
of a new patron. A woman he met at church was the daughter of
the largest car dealer in the state, precisely the kind of father-in-law
that Nathaniel Culberson needed. With marriage and the arrival of
a couple kids, the rehabilitated carouser rose through the dealership's ranks. At the encouragement of his father-in-law, a shameless
racist, he joined the Texas Army National Guard, first as an enlisted
citizen solider and then as a commissioned officer at the age of
thirty-five.

Culberson was not well-liked or much admired by those in
his command. Deployed to Iraq and assigned to the quartermaster
branch, he strove to line his own pockets. That baldly larcenous activity resulted in a breakdown in the supply chain and a dire scarcity of
ammunition at some forward operations bases deep in-country. Three
soldiers died as a direct result of these shortages. A skillful bureau-
cratic manipulator, Major Culberson implicated junior officers in the
brigade, who unwittingly took the fall for him to cover up his crimes.

The bare-knuckle bouts he has staged for the past eighteen
months are yet another illicit moneymaking scheme, gambling opportunities that afforded Culberson a healthy cut of the action. That
these gladiatorial contests exploit preexisting, racial animosities are
exactly the point. Preexisting ethnic tensions are the juice. Never an

ideologue, believing in nothing besides the accumulation of money, Culberson paid only lip service to his father-in-law's white nationalist beliefs. If there are financial opportunities in advancing white supremacy, then the liberal judge's son is all for it. Submerging himself in his wife's extended family, Nathaniel Culberson rarely spoke to his parents or siblings following the wedding ceremony. He has gone his own way. Found a separate path.

And that journey has taken him here, to a holding cell at the MP headquarters at Fort Bliss.

THE SERGEANT LEADS Hayley and Pogue down a corridor of gleaming linoleum. Holding cells line the hallway to the left. Hayley observes the detainees' faces framed by the narrow windows in the steel doors as she passes and ponders on what infractions landed the prisoners in this unenviable place. Their gazes are accusatory, as if the deeper state operative were responsible for their misfortune. Loss of rank, dishonorable discharge, or, worse, long-term incarceration at US Disciplinary Barracks at Fort Leavenworth are just a few of the consequences these detainees can expect as they move through the army's legal system like so many sausages in a meat-processing plant.

"Poor bastards," says Pogue as they walk past those distraught gazes.

"Only gettin' what they deserve, Chief." Command Sergeant Major Johnson stops at the last door, key in hand. He glances through the window to determine Culberson's position on the other side of the door.

"Oh, fuck!"

The military policeman fumbles with his keys to unlock the door, dropping them in his haste. Pogue and Hayley peer through the door window to see inside the holding cell as he bends down to pick them up. They see Culberson lying on the narrow cot, wrists slit. Blood floods across the green-tile floor like a toilet's overflow.

"Open the door, Sergeant!" the CID agent bellows.

Johnson inserts the key in the lock. Hayley follows the two men into the holding cell. The only object inside the eight-by-ten room is a cot. Any bathroom needs are handled by taking prisoners out in handcuffs to restrooms at the other end of the corridor. Hayley stands aside while the others ascertain Culberson's condition. A spectator. Nothing she can do to help the man.

The military policeman barks into his radio, requesting EMT response, while Pogue checks Culberson for a pulse.

Hayley watches as the CID agent lifts Culberson's arms in a vain attempt to slow the blood loss. She doesn't have to take the major's heart rate to know he's dead. And not by his own hand, despite the safety razor on the floor almost submerged by the blood.

Culberson represented her best shot thus far at explaining the mystery surrounding her father's inexplicable fate. He had *known* Tommy Chill, or at least, of him. Those truths died with the major.

Kneeling at the prisoner's side, Pogue looks back over his shoulder at Hayley. His expression telegraphs what she already assumed: the major is a goner. Blood smeared on the walls next to the cot suggests an unquiet death. She imagines Culberson's terror, held down by conspirators while an assassin carved each wrist open.

In their efforts to resuscitate the major, Pogue and the military policeman fail to see what Hayley only now notices herself: a few words scratched into the paint where baseboard meets the wall, across the room from the cot.

———

"WHY WASN'T THE prisoner issued attire during processing? I don't understand."

"Chief, the major was brought into the facility at an hour when we have a quarter of our regular personnel on staff. Culberson would've received standard-issue detainee uniform this morning."

"It's almost eleven hundred hours!" bellows the criminal investigations agent.

Hayley watches from the doorway of the CSM's office as Pogue grinds a baleful Johnson. Lieutenant Colonel Oscar Wainwright, commander of the Ninety-Third Military Police Battalion, leans with his back against the wall. He knows his turn is next. Culberson's death while in the battalion's custody is an insoluble black mark. Wainwright is experiencing the dread that comes with the realization that years of hard work building a military career have imploded.

"Is she necessary to the discussion?" he says to Pogue, referring to Hayley.

"*Yes, sir.*"

The intensity of Roy Pogue's fury is notable, given that Wainwright outranks him. But Criminal Investigation Command enjoys unique privileges within the army's vast bureaucracy. The Ninety-Third Military Police Battalion might be in the same business, but there is no question which command carries more weight. The power dynamic in the room would be apparent to a child. Chief Warrant Officer Pogue is in charge here.

"You really think a major in the Texas Army National Guard took the trouble to hide a blade in his clothing, in case of arrest?" an incredulous Pogue asks the battalion commander.

"If that's what my people believe, then yes. How else did it get there?"

The CID agent employs his silence with devastating effect.

Wainwright thrusts his index finger at Pogue like a bayonet. "Cut the BS, Pogue. I've got control of this command!"

Hayley Chill observes the exchange with a detached air. Culberson is dead. But in the final act of a man who realized his end was near, the major left a valuable clue, one that only she noticed. While Pogue and Johnson were futilely rendering aid to Culberson, Hayley crouched down to read the words the detainee had crudely scratched into the baseboard, the tiny incisions obviously freshly made . . .

Cecil X Drummond III

She wants to follow up on the lead and is keen to extricate herself from the blame game at the MP headquarters. Hayley anticipates increased resistance from her CID contact. Pogue's attitude toward her has become one of intensifying aggravation. The deeper state operative can hardly fault him. Since arriving in West Texas, she has left a trail of dead bodies in her wake. That incidental mayhem would go a long way toward explaining his increasingly cantankerous behavior around her.

Or he simply dislikes her. Either way, Hayley needs to get going.

Clearing her throat to draw the attention of the three men in the cramped office, Hayley says, "Videotape doesn't lie. Not typically, at least."

Command Sergeant Major Johnson frowns for dramatic effect. "Unfortunately, our surveillance cams on this floor went down late yesterday. Still waiting for tech."

Johnson's commander mutters an obscenity. Pogue shakes his head in disgust, seemingly unsurprised. He exchanges a pissed-off look with Hayley, despite his growing animosity toward her. Looking for sympathy? She has no time for it.

Hayley gestures with a tilt of her head, letting the CID agent know she is intent on leaving.

Pogue looks to Wainwright. "Gimme a second, Colonel?"

He follows Hayley into the corridor.

"I'm sorry, Chief. The senator is after me for a report of everything that's occurred in the last twenty-four hours."

"Fine. We'll get back to you later?"

"Of course, sir."

The CID agent shakes his head, glancing back toward the doorway to Johnson's office. "This shit ain't straight."

"No, sir."

"And so what're you going to say to your boss, Ms. Chill?"

"The truth, Mr. Pogue."

He grimaces. Somehow, the warrant officer knew she was going to say that.

THE SCHEDULED FLIGHT time between Dallas and El Paso is one hour and thirty-four minutes. Hayley hopes to close her eyes for some of that time. Though the pandemic is long over, air travel has yet to return to normalcy. Consequently, the plane is barely half-full and the two seats next to her unoccupied. The prospects for sleep are good were it not for her growing excitement.

Hayley feels she is close, if not to a resolution, then to a better idea of what exactly is happening here in Texas. And her father's role in the plot. The higher up the chain of command she climbs, the more determined to hunt down the truth she becomes.

This is big.

Hayley is almost afraid to close her eyes. Will she dream again of her father hanging by the neck in the doorway of his disheveled bedroom? These recurrent nightmares have been a torment since that awful Sunday morning. But without sleep, her operational abilities degrade by the hour. As the airliner tilts up into its ascent over the cluttered expanse that is the city of El Paso, Hayley forces her eyes closed.

Let the visions come. Bring it.

WHEN HAYLEY CHILL drives off base, Peter Oswald is fifty miles east on the interstate. Duties elsewhere demanded his attention. The organization has more than enough sympathizers to handle any job, activated with a single phone call. Before he hit the road—in response to James Woodside's last-minute request for a meeting of the conspiracy's captains—Oswald dialed a certain phone number. Within ten minutes, Storm operatives were posted outside every gate leading out of Fort Bliss, watching for their target's rental car and ready to follow. Oswald suspects Hayley Chill "made" him while leaving the Beverly Crest Motor Inn or on the drive to the base. Fresh eyes on her is a good thing.

As he drives, the thump of truck tires passing over drainage seams in the roadway keeping a steady beat, Oswald reflects on the loss of Nathaniel Culberson. The major's role in the organization was a vital one. Given the fact that the conspiracy is on the verge of reaching its critical phase, a replacement immediately assumed Culberson's responsibilities. Oswald can only hope that the new man—and he must acknowledge that most, if not all of the Storm's senior leadership are male—possesses fewer of the personal flaws that led to the major's downfall. The stakes are too high for any more near exposures. Culberson has been handled. But Hayley Chill remains an unknown and potentially catastrophic threat.

Oswald must decide quickly how best to proceed. Reflecting on his first sight of the young woman at the New Mexico compound, he comprehends how far she has come in her ad hoc investigation. The Senate aide from Washington—if that is, indeed, her real job—is drawing far too close to the organization's highest ranks. A few minutes earlier, his cell phone rang with news that Hayley Chill has boarded a flight for Dallas. Pete Oswald instantly understood why she was going to that destination.

He knows what must be done.

———

IRONICALLY, AN ARMY base has more restrictive regulations regarding personal weapons than the civilian world. Consequently, Hayley left the War Hawk hidden in her room at the Beverly Crest Motor Inn when she visited Fort Bliss that morning. Not having the time to swing by the motel before catching her flight meant leaving the gun behind. Given the events of the past few days—but most acutely Culberson's probable murder—the deeper state operative feels vulnerable and exposed without a weapon as her plane lands in Dallas. Mindful of possible surveillance, Hayley takes the rental car shuttle bus to the DFW Rental Car Center, where she merges with a throng of departing passengers climbing aboard a shuttle *back* to the airport Terminal A. Once there, she catches a Dallas Area Rapid Transit train into the city.

Renting a vehicle downtown takes only a few minutes. Within an hour of landing, Hayley is behind the wheel of a Hyundai Accent and navigating to the Cedar Grove Country Club north of the city. After walking out of the military police headquarters at Fort Bliss, she called Andrew Wilde from her parked car with Cecil Drummond's name. Five minutes later, her deeper state superior called back with the thumbnail biography. Previous to his current position as a "wealth manager," Drummond was a North Carolina–based financial con artist who ran a boiler room operation that directed minority borrowers toward unnecessary and punitive subprime loans. The 2008 real estate crash, and subsequent FBI investigations, brought an end to that rapacious, illegal operation. Following that debacle, Drummond moved to Texas and, in the ensuing thirteen years, amassed a sizable number of affluent clients whose assets he manages for substantial fees.

Cedar Grove is one of the city's most exclusive country clubs, founded exactly fifty years ago and constructed on two hundred acres of cotton fields and pasture. In the 1800s, the Shawnee Trail traversed these same lands, the principal route by which Texan longhorn cattle were delivered to railheads north of the Red River. Today, golfers wearing pastel-colored short pants walk these same grounds. Hayley is stopped at the gate and tells the guard she is an employee of Cecil Drummond's, carrying materials he needs for a presentation that has already commenced. She implies a sense of urgency, and the guard, swayed in no small part by her powder blue eyes, instructs Hayley to leave her car near the front entrance of the main building.

Having parked the rental Hyundai in an exclusive hub of gleaming Bentleys, Mercedes, and Jaguars, Hayley heads inside the casually opulent club and is mostly ignored. Dressed as she is and younger than most members, she looks like staff. Her demeanor, however, suggests something other than servile obedience. A hardness has come to her gaze. Sullen determination in the firmness of her jaw. Despite Hayley's best efforts on the short flight, she hasn't slept in thirty hours. With a sense that events are coming to a head, the deeper state operative has lost all patience.

A sign in the lobby—"Financial Opportunities in Year Zero"— indicates that the seminar is located in the Honey Springs meeting room. Hayley heads in that direction. Walking down a long, carpeted hallway, past the club's main dining room, she clocks two security men—wearing dark blazers and pants—keeping guard of the doors leading into the conference room. She stops, pondering her next move, and sees unmarked service doors on the same side of the hallway as the meeting venue.

Fatigue grinding her down and battling a persistent mental fog, Hayley enters the club's service corridor and discovers it connects the kitchen with the main dining room, as well as every meeting room in the wing. Finding the rear service entrance into the Honey Springs room, she pulls the door open and slips inside.

White tablecloths drape the twenty-two round dining tables spaced throughout the expansive room. Club staff has already cleared lunch service. The 180 guests in attendance—all white and over the age of fifty—enjoy coffee and iced tea as they listen with rapt attention to the luncheon's speaker standing at the front of the semi-darkened room, Cecil X. Drummond III. With an athletic physique secured by his regular triathlon training and generously highlighted by a handsomely tailored suit, the wealth manager makes his pitch to the well-heeled crowd. A sprawling thirty-foot LED wall and a high-volume, low-profile array speakers behind him lend a corporate gloss to the presentation.

Hanging back to one side of the meeting room and ignored by all in attendance, Hayley Chill studies a map of North America currently depicted on the video wall. The borders, as drawn, are like none that she has seen before. The states of Texas, New Mexico, and much of Arizona, Oklahoma, and Kansas comprise one, national identity separate from the remainder of the substantially diminished United States.

Divided into five new states—each retaining their original names—the name of this new nation is Free States of America.

The deeper state operative retrieves her cell phone and discreetly begins recording.

"Together, strong. Together, united. Together, philosophically pure. The Free States of America will be a nation of commonality. A nation created so that all of its citizens are joined together in one purpose. One party. One belief, under one God."

As Drummond speaks, the LED wall displays new images, replacing the map. The scenes depicted are uniformly prosperous, revealing a world of happy privilege. The actors and models from the blatantly staged shots are unvaryingly white. Smiles abound.

"We are not alone. The philosophies we embrace are shared by the citizens of other countries around the word. Our leaders have already been in discussion and formed robust alliances with the Russian government, as well as powerful political parties in Germany, Australia, France, Italy, Turkey, and Greece. A coalition of like-minded international powers will arise in the course of only a few years, separate but equal. We will be joined together in our shared beliefs, a new kind of union of nations and nationalist parties. We are strong, ladies and gentlemen, and getting stronger. Our self-determination will be ironclad, that is my guarantee to you today. The Free States of America will be a shining example on this continent, the envy of the entire world once again."

Drummond has learned to pause for the applause he receives with this line from his speech. He has delivered these words in dozens of banquet halls, living rooms, and financial workshops these past few months. He knows when he has an audience on the hook, as he does today.

"Prosperity doesn't come cheap, friends. It takes money to make money, am I right? And it takes a whole lot of money to make a whole new country! The FSA requires the cooperation and direct participation of several thousand individuals just like you good people. New FSA citizens who will cement the nation's success through their *investment* in it. Ladies and gentlemen, the future is bright. Our cause has adherents throughout the US military branches, ready and willing to do what's necessary to advance our patriotic vision. But these brave men and women cannot do their jobs without your generous support. And don't for a minute think that your contributions are a charitable gift. No, my friends. This is an opportunity to get in on the ground floor . . . of a *new country*. An investment at Year Zero. Imagine those families of the eighteenth century who foresaw the business opportunities available in an emergent United States and acted. Your investment today in the FSA, ladies and gentlemen, is your toehold in a future of unlimited potential."

The crowd hoots and applauds as the video wall displays a diagram that suggests a nationalized oil and natural gas industry. Figures presented are in the billions of dollars.

Drummond must shout over the audience's handclapping and joyful roar. "Like the White Rajahs of Sarawak, you and your descendants will be the benevolent rulers of this wondrous, new realm!"

Ovation washes over the beaming wealth manager.

"Join us!" he shouts over the clamor.

The lights come up. The attendees, buzzing with excitement, stand or otherwise prepare to leave.

Drummond remains at the front of the room. "Feel free to come on up, friends. I'm here to answer any of your questions. Grab the information packet on the way out. But please, and I can't emphasize this point too strongly, keep those materials and our discussion private." He pauses again, with polished comedic timing. "Rival producers would love to steal our movie idea!"

Appreciative laughter greets the wealth manager's tongue-in-cheek stab at deniability. A cluster of older men and women line up for a word with the luncheon's speaker. The spot to the side of the room where Hayley had been watching the proceedings is now empty.

CECIL DRUMMOND FINISHES packing up his materials and gear. The meeting room is otherwise empty. The voice from behind startles him.

"You're selling treason."

Hayley has emerged from the rear service door and approaches to within only a few feet of where the wealth manager loads the last items into his briefcase. Whether it's the snake oil smile or Bruno Magli loafers, his physical proximity alone is enough to stoke her growing fury. But what the man sells with his slick presentation is the most vexing. Hayley Chill has forfeited everything she has in the world to preserve and protect the United States of America and its Constitution. Untold thousands of brave men and women have fought and died in wars defending that sacred document.

Drummond traffics in the crass betrayal of those grave sacrifices. And takes a percentage on every share he sells. She has never despised anyone more in her life.

"Excuse me?"

"Who is in charge? I want the names. All of them."

The words themselves are sharp edged.

"Look, young lady—"

She snaps. Though Drummond's more than six inches taller than the deeper state operative, is physically fit, and outweighs her by a good seventy pounds, Hayley moves on him with shocking speed. The wealth manager reacts by throwing a weak right hand. Hayley deflects the punch with both hands, sweeping his arm down. She buries a jab in his abdomen and then pushes the wealth manager over her extended right leg, putting him on the ground.

Standing over Drummond and gripping his thumb with her left hand, Hayley retrieves an S. T. Dupont fountain pen from his inside jacket pocket, flips the cap off her thumb and presses the 14-karat, solid gold nib into his ear.

"Stop! Why are you doing this? I'm a wealth manager!"

Hayley releases her grip on Drummond's thumb and retrieves her phone from her tote on the floor where she dropped it, pressing play on the video she recorded of Drummond's sales pitch . . .

"But please, and I can't emphasize this point too strongly, keep those materials and our discussion private."

Hayley stops playback and leans into him.

"Your secret *isn't* good with me." She asks, "Who hired you?"

"Fuck you!"

Drummond struggles to escape. Hayley responds by pushing the pen deeper into his ear. The wealth manager ceases trying to escape.

"Okay, okay, okay . . ."

"Who hired you? Who's in charge? Tell me the plan."

"I don't know anything."

She presses the nib deeper into Drummond's ear, piercing his eardrum and pushing into the tympanic cavity. He yowls in pain.

"Stop!"

But she's over waiting. Done bargaining.

No clemency. No mercy. Not anymore.

"I'll stop when you talk. Tell me what I want to know."

Drummond resists the urge to talk. More dominant than the pain Hayley inflicts on him are his fears. The wealth manager is aware of the consequences if he betrays the cause. Like Pete Oswald, he has witnessed the cruelty of their leader.

The wealth manager begins to sob, helpless. His predicament is inescapable.

"Someone calls and tells me where to go. I don't know who it is."

His fear and panic cause him to lose control of his bowels. He blubbers like a helpless baby. Utterly in her control.

"I'm just a salesman, for Christ's sake!"

Hayley twists the expensive fountain pen inside his ear, the nib ravaging the malleus, incus, and stapes. All destroyed. Blood flows freely now as the man shrieks in pain.

"Killebrew . . . !"

"What?"

"Killebrew. Two star at Fort Bliss. Killebrew is in charge. He runs the whole operation."

Hayley nods, withdrawing the pen from Drummond's ear. She looks up for the first time since initiating her interrogation and only then sees the busboy standing in the doorway leading into the service corridor.

The look of repulsed horror on the busboy's face clues Hayley to the depths of her descent.

What have I done?

The busboy turns and flees the scene through the service door. Hayley can hear his shouts of alarm from where she crouches over Drummond. She knows club security will be swarming the room and corridor outside soon enough, with local law enforcement arriving not long after.

The deeper state operative stands and grabs a slightly soiled, white cloth napkin from the nearest table and tosses it at the wealth manager.

"Press it against your ear. You're fine."

Not all that fine, she muses. But people who are hopelessly fucked still seem to like hearing such bromides.

Drummond sits up, palming the napkin to his ruined ear.

"You fucking bitch."

"Don't push your luck. I've got enough time before the cavalry arrives to make it a matching pair."

The wealth manager suddenly realizes he has more to worry about than the loss of hearing in one ear. This most unfortunate incident will bring an excessive amount of attention to a movement that is unlikely to be confused for the concept of a Hollywood movie. This being Texas, he's carrying just the tool he needs to extricate himself from a bad situation.

Drummond hikes up his left pant leg, revealing a Smith & Wesson M&P Shield subcompact 9-millimeter pistol in an ankle holster. He draws the gun and points it at Hayley.

"By God, I oughta shoot your ass."

Hayley is confident he won't. The wealth manager probably has a small arsenal at home, in his car and office, but she apprises him as a range shooter. Plenty of men will plug a woman at close range; Drummond isn't one of them, in her estimation.

As he struggles to get to his feet, keeping pressure on his injured ear with his left and gripping the gun in his right, Hayley makes her move. Unspectacularly armed with her cell phone in one hand and expensive fountain pen in the other, she drops a shoulder to knock him flat.

Drummond fires.

So much for her snap judgment of his character.

Luckily, the wealth manager's marksmanship, even at this close range, is errant. The shot is an inch wide of his target. Hayley turns and runs for the service entrance at the back of the room as Drummond fires repeatedly, narrowly missing with each shot.

Hayley bangs through the service door and takes cover in the hallway as a final round follows her out, burrowing into the opposite wall, followed by silence. Has Drummond left the scene? She sees security personnel coming her way at a dead run from the other end of the corridor, near the main dining room. The wealth manager remains a prize, his knowledge of the plot obviously high-level. Ignoring the security guards' shouted orders to stay where she is, Hayley tosses the fountain pen and charges toward the service door again. Barging back into the meeting, she confirms her suspicion: the meeting room is empty.

Turning to retrieve her tote, Hayley sees that it's gone.

Cecil Drummond speed walks up the corridor, heading toward the club entrance. He feels the startled gazes of the members he passes. No doubt he must look a sight, disheveled as he is and pressing the blood-soaked napkin to the side of his head. The gun in his right hand only adds to what must be an outrageous display of plans-gone-horribly-wrong.

So what? One thought dominates: get the fuck out of here while he still can.

He has the woman's bag looped around his shoulder. Drummond took the tote as a precaution in case she had a weapon inside, as well as for possible clues to her identity. Those above him in the organization will want an explanation for the afternoon's mayhem. Drummond hopes giving them the bag will go some ways to assuaging their displeasure with him.

Looking over his shoulder, he sees the blond woman emerge from the meeting room back down the carpeted hallway. He pauses to raise the S&W subcompact and point it in her direction, but she keeps coming on at a run.

Of course she would know he has emptied the magazine.

Fucking bitch!

The wealth manager barrels through the club entrance's open doorway, laying eyes on the valet.

The valet?

Waiting for his car to be retrieved is out of the question. The thought makes him laugh as he skids to a stop outside the entrance and short of the valet stand. Then, with the sort of fast-footed ingenuity that has been the hallmark of his prolonged, prosperous survival in the cutthroat world of asset management, Drummond remembers the woman's tote under his arm.

With precious seconds ticking past, he searches the bag's interior and comes across the plastic car rental tag and Hyundai key fob. Looking up, the wealth manager sees the incongruent Accent sandwiched between an Aston Martin and gleaming Range Rover.

The Hyundai has got to be hers!

Drummond dumps his gun in the tote and, key fob in hand, runs up the circular drive to the VIP parking area.

Hayley exits the club seconds later and, clocking him, continues her pursuit. As she runs, the deeper state operative sees him approaching her rental car, unlocking its doors with the fob, and climbing in behind the wheel. She is less than fifty yards away, then, as Drummond fires up the car's ignition and the vehicle explodes in an expanding ball of flame outpacing the spray of ripped-apart automobile and human flesh by microseconds.

9

BATTLE CRY

Sleep comes, at long last, in the cell of a dormitory unit of the Dallas County jail, North Tower, where Hayley mercifully finds solitude and relative safety behind a time-lock door. Knocked flat by the car bomb's blast and possibly concussed, she was arrested by detectives from the Richardson Police Department. The busboy who had witnessed her brutal interrogation of Cecil Drummond provided police with a detailed description of the "crazy woman" in the Honey Springs meeting room.

Charged with aggravated assault, Hayley Chill suspects the Storm has already made arrangements for her execution. Sunday is her seventh day in West Texas, but will be one of little rest.

The tank has fourteen cells, with a dayroom and lavatory/shower. Hayley arrived at eight p.m. the previous evening and kept to herself in the otherwise unoccupied cell. Only after lights-out and the sound of automatic door locks engaged did she finally close her eyes. Those same locks open at seven a.m. the following morning.

Whoever tried to kill her with the car bomb won't stop after one failed attempt. Hayley assumes trouble will come in the dayroom or lavatory just off that unit's central area. She had reached out to Andrew Wilde—before the police confiscated her phone—and left a message. When and if Publius can free her before she's killed is an anxiety Hayley tries to suppress. Until then, survival is her own responsibility.

The other inmates have been up and out of their cells for more than two hours before Hayley's need for the bathroom necessitates leaving her sanctuary. All eyes fall on the deeper state operative as she enters the dayroom, wearing jail-issued blue coveralls and flip-flops. Hayley assumes all of the other women in the tank are, like her, charged with violent offences. They certainly have that appearance, brazenly watching the new inmate with predatory gazes intended to intimidate. The filth and disrepair of the facility is impossible to miss. A male correctional officer occupies a protected cubicle—the "pod"—at one end of the dayroom.

Ignoring the other hard looks, Hayley focuses instead on the doorway that leads into the bathroom. She finds no other inmate inside. There are no stalls, of course. Sitting on the toilet farthest from the doorway, Hayley is grateful to have gotten some sleep the previous night. Arriving at the jail, she felt at the end of her rope. Depleted and emotionally frayed. With rest, however, she feels more like herself. Psychologically and physically renewed.

Ready for the worst of what Lew Sterrett North Tower can throw at her.

Hayley stands up from the toilet as the two inmates enter the bathroom and walk directly at her. Both women hold their right hands down and slightly behind them, leading with their left hands out. The deeper state operative assumes their other hands hold shanks. She has no way to evade the attack she knows is coming.

There's no time to confirm their intentions or the existence of weapons. Raising both hands, Hayley centers on the larger of the two inmates.

As the woman draws within range, she reaches with her left, leveraging hand to grab hold of Hayley and pull her toward the shank—a sharpened toothbrush—that only now appears in her lowered right hand.

Hayley traps the woman's knife hand, guiding it away while driving her knee into her attacker's abdomen. She then spins the woman in the direction of the other inmate, who has simultaneously launched her attack by raising her shank overhead. The first woman absorbs two blows of the makeshift knife before her cohort realizes her mistake.

Both thrusts hit the first inmate on the back of her neck, piercing the least-resistant part of the skull at the squamous part of the temporal bone. These violent stabbing wounds completely sever the brain stem and basilar artery.

The first inmate drops to her knees and falls over, leaking blood and mortally injured.

Hayley faces off with the remaining attacker, who adopts a more measured strategy now that her adversary has proved herself an adept fighter. The deeper state operative experiences a moment of optimism, having achieved some parity.

But it's brief.

She sees three more inmates enter the bathroom. None appear eager to stop the fight. To the contrary. The other women are without question reinforcements of the first two.

At least I can go down fighting.

Hayley centers her weight over her feet as the prisoners converge on her position.

Take out the biggest first, she strategizes. *Maybe I can scare off the more diffident ones.*

No one makes a move to help the injured woman on the filthy, piss-stained bathroom floor bleeding out from her neck wound and thrashing around in the throes of her demise.

Her story is over.

Hayley savors one, last second of tranquility before the onslaught of violence. One last breath. There will be more bloodshed. Soon, there will be death.

"What the hell's going on in here?"

The voice—male, authoritative, pissed off—comes from behind the female inmates. It belongs to the pod officer, come to retrieve the newest inmate in the unit.

Come to fetch Hayley Chill.

———————

ANDREW WILDE TAKES her to eat at Slow Bone, more of an insiders' hang than one of the more touristy barbecue joints in town. Most of the customers—both white and black—are wearing their best church clothes. Hayley's deeper state superior manages to eat a half rack of pork ribs without so much as the slightest smear of sauce on his face or hands. Dressed, as usual, in what must be one of a dozen blue suits, Wilde's bland emotions and placid expression betray no sign of concern over the traumatic events in his operative's past eighteen hours.

Hayley pauses over her plate of skinless chicken thighs to watch her boss polish a rib bone clean.

"Can I ask you a question, sir?"

He twists off another succulent rib from what remains of the rack. "Shoot."

"Are you ever *not* tan?"

His color is indeed a wholly unnatural shade of orange. Hayley has speculated whether the soles of her superior's feet are similarly bronzed.

The question fails to register with Wilde, who gestures at Hayley with the pork rib held confidently between his index finger and thumb. "We're bringing you out."

"What?" She thinks he is joshing. It dawns on her that he's entirely serious. *"Why?"*

"Because they're running out of body bags down here, that's why."

"Mr. Wilde—"

"Not open to discussion, Chill. You've left quite a swath of destruction in your wake. How many more messes do you expect us to clean up after you?"

"I'm making progress, sir. These people are advocating separation from the United States. Their goal is the creation of a nation built on a foundation of white supremacy." She gestures at her cellphone on the table. "You saw the recording of Drummond's presentation."

"Come on. Texans have been talking secessionism since there was a Texas. Bunch of wing nuts. We have files on this already. It's nothing new."

By "we," Hayley assumes he means Publius.

"Sir, what if the sabotage events in the Permian Basin were just a ruse to get the National Guard deployed there? That's hardly theoretical grandstanding. What was started with the storming of the Capitol gets finished here. In West Texas."

Wilde scoffs. "A few elements from the National Guard are going to effect the military occupation of eighty-six thousand square miles of territory? A region inhabited by a bunch of ornery, pissed-off Texans?"

"Then what are they doing there?" asks Hayley.

"Besides staging bare-knuckle fistfights? I'm not sure. And I don't care. Your antics have made it difficult for Senator Powell to preserve any semblance of legitimacy. He's asked that you no longer be associated with his office in any capacity." He drops the rib bone in the basket and wipes his fingers on a napkin. "In other words, Chill, you've been fired from the job you never had."

Hayley goes quiet. She knows from experience that there's no point arguing with Andrew Wilde.

He says, "We're still working on the authorities in New Mexico. Now this business in Dallas. Despite my best efforts, you can't leave the state just yet."

She remains silent, sensing an opening.

"Go back to El Paso. Sit tight."

Hayley lifts her gaze to meet his. A lingering glance they exchange transmits a message of some significance. Andrew Wilde's typically mild expression seems to perk up. A lightness in his eyes.

He says, "Cheer up. You're going home soon. What's your final verdict on the hush puppies? West Virginia girl is the expert on down-home cooking. Up to snuff, Chill?"

The deeper state operative nods. She suspects that her boss is wired, another layer of surveillance. One more version of not being able to trust anyone in this business. He has delivered the official decision from *his* superiors within the deeper state. But she fully comprehends his unspoken desire.

Andrew Wilde wants her to keep going.

"The hush puppies were pretty damn good, sir."

―――――――

OSWALD HEARS THE news from Dallas after leaving the meeting at the ranch and is already halfway through the long drive to Austin. His lower back is killing him, and he hasn't been able to take a decent shit in three days. He wonders at times if he is too old for all of this. Too old for an active role in the second Civil War. On the other hand, however, he cannot imagine sitting this one out. Of all the wars and battles in which he has shed blood and sweat (never tears), the aspirations of this fight are too grand. A once-in-a-lifetime chance to be James Woodside's Himmler. Is he a firm proponent of the racist philosophies of the majority of conspirators? Not particularly. Oswald knows why he is here, lower-back issues or not.

To make *history*.

The death of one of the movement's best fundraisers is a blow, but certainly survivable. The bulk of the conspiracy's underwriting comes from a Texas-based multibillionaire entrepreneur and recent refugee from the Socialist State of California. Drummond's work was an ongoing effort to match the mercurial and headstrong billionaire's investments in case he suddenly decamped for even more laissez-faire environs like Switzerland . . . or Mars, for that matter. In any event, plenty of candidates are prepared to take Cecil Drummond's place. Any public exposure that arises because of the incident is of small consequence, too. With the operation well underway, events will soon outpace any future investigations mounted by local authorities. In only a matter of hours, the FSA will be in charge.

What remains a significant concern is Hayley Chill, if that is indeed her true identity.

With her survival of two assassination attempts, Oswald now understands that the young woman is something more than a lowly Senate aide. Other conspirators have queried FBI agents sympathetic to the cause. They confirmed that the young woman isn't an undercover operative from that federal agency. If not with the Bureau, then what? And how to explain her tenacity? The woman operates as if on a personal mission, relentless in her pursuit of the Storm's hierarchy. He can't help but be intrigued by her. And impressed.

It's a shame, then, that he must kill her. Getting to know something of Hayley Chill's story would have been preferable. To understand what makes her tick.

A call comes not long after the first, informing him that the Senate aide has boarded a flight at DFW. Oswald wastes no time making a series of calls that allow him to change directions on the interstate and head west again, back toward El Paso. He was on his way for an overnight trip to Austin to monitor an operation that will culminate in the arrest and detention of the governor, then immediately return to the Permian Basin midday tomorrow. That responsibility will now be delegated to others.

If someone must kill her, then he is the man to do the job. As a Marine Raider who saw action in Iraq during the earliest years of the war there, followed by a decade with the CIA's old Special Activities

Division, Oswald has the experience and skill set to get the job done. Nearing sixty years of age, he thought all that wet work was behind him; his duties with the Storm have been more supervisory, and he's been okay with that. But the blond-haired Senate aide has stirred a longing in him. A desire long dormant.

Monumental shifts are afoot. Most of America eases blithely into its Sunday evening without awareness of the machinations now in place to irrevocably alter her. As he drives west, Peter Oswald experiences the delectable surge of bloodlust. The entrance of a worthy adversary into the arena.

He must kill Hayley Chill if only to prove his mettle.

RETURNING TO THE Beverly Crest Motor Inn after ten that night, she isn't surprised to find April Wu gone. Hayley can't imagine her former colleague's frustration. What to do with all of the downtime? Being reduced to the role of spectator. For an alpha female like April, the inactivity must be torture. Hayley has enormous sympathy for her friend and misses their rivalry as Publius's preeminent covert agents. At the same time, however, the deeper state operative is relieved to find her motel room empty. She isn't in the mood for putting up with April's needling questions. The sardonic observations that pick apart Hayley's motivations and lay bare her emotional incapacities.

Her personal failures. Sam McGovern. The unplanned pregnancy.

Hayley returned to El Paso with little more than the clothes on her back, of course. Her tote bag was destroyed in the car bomb blast; she was fortunate to have held on to her phone. The rental agency representative met her at the airport with replacement keys for the car Hayley had left in the parking lot. She lost her tablet in the explosion but nothing else of significance. Along with the War Hawk, Hayley left her father's coded document behind in her motel room, behind the vent and past a turn of the heating duct. Retrieving the items, she flips through the pages of cryptic passages. Will she ever decipher their meaning?

Hayley hides the envelope again. She is at a crossroads. Whoever occupies the deeper state's command level has decided to end her investigation of the Storm. Andrew Wilde faithfully delivered that order, but with the implicit understanding that he was giving her a way to remain in the game. Without the deeper state's support.

She's on her own.

Hayley enters the bathroom. The prescription bottle is nestled inside her open toiletry travel bag where she left it. Almost dying—twice!—in the last twenty-four hours has had a strangely calming effect on her. She feels strong. Not invincible, but extraordinarily capable. What circumstances seemed impossible only a few days before now appear less monumentally intolerable. No one can question her dedication to Publius. To her country.

Retrieving the vial from the travel bag, Hayley uncaps it and dumps the eight tablets of misoprostol into the toilet, flushing it for good measure. She then climbs into bed, checks to see that the War Hawk is loaded, with a round in the chamber, and slides the gun under her pillow.

Hayley is fully asleep within sixty seconds of lying down.

———————

OSWALD IS ACROSS the street, sitting behind the wheel of his pickup truck and keeping an eye on the motel room. On the passenger seat next to him is a standard Colt M45A1 CQBP pistol. Though not the M45 MEU(SOC) model he had carried while a Marine Raider in Afghanistan, the M45A1 was its official replacement in 2012 and familiar enough for Oswald's daily carry. His old Colt had gotten him out of plenty of jams during his two tours with the Marines Special Forces, and he feels a strong loyalty to the manufacturer and its reliability. He intends to wait ninety minutes since lights-out inside

Hayley Chill's room and then enter using a master key derived by hacking the Vision software used in hotel locking systems worldwide.

He considers the possibility of interrogating his target before executing her—shooting her in the head through a pillow to muffle the sound—but doesn't count on having that opportunity. Oswald imagines she has taken the precaution of keeping a weapon within reach as she sleeps. If Hayley Chill makes any move for a gun, he'll shoot her where she lies and then run like hell.

The Senate aide has earned his respect.

The lights were turned off more than an hour ago. Oswald is ready. He watches the motel parking lot and periodically checks the same Casio G-Shock DW-6900 wristwatch he's had for fifteen years, purchased between deployments. Oswald feels sentimental toward the cheap timepiece and considers it something of a good luck charm.

Three minutes to jump-off.

Oswald puts eyes back on the motel parking lot. An older Latino man leaves the sidewalk, a pouch slung over his shoulder. He approaches the nearest parked car in the lot and slips a leaflet under the windshield wiper. Withdrawing another circular, the man— in his sixties, though the dim light makes a confident guess nearly impossible—continues to the next car and repeats the process until he has leafleted every vehicle in the lot. He turns now and approaches the street again.

The man locks eyes with Oswald sitting in his car across the street and turns in his direction. Juan Lugo, in his late sixties, has lived in West Texas his entire life, twenty years of which were spent working on the JW7 Ranch, near Balmorhea. He walks with a proud, erect gait, his straw hat crisp and clean despite the countless hours spent under a relentless sun. Clearly, Lugo wants a word with the gringo dressed in black sitting behind the wheel of his vehicle, stopped directly across the street from the motel. At this hour, they are the only people present in a world that seems all postapocalyptic.

Oswald only has a few seconds to make his decision: Should he kill the man there in the street and continue with his original plan or should he abort the mission and leave now? Simply waving him off is not an option; the man could be questioned eventually by the police and identify Oswald or his vehicle. Shooting him would leave a body in the street while he carries out the hit on Hayley Chill, an agonizing span of time to be exposed and vulnerable. Attempting to move his body runs the risk of creating additional incriminating evidence.

What to do?!

Oswald realizes with not a small amount of shame that his indecision is just another indication of his age degrading operational performance. He frets that he won't live long enough to truly enjoy the fruits of his labors, to fully enjoy his status as a revolutionary hero and potential founding father of a new nation. If only he were ten or fifteen years younger!

As the leafleting Juan Lugo closes the distance between them, Oswald hits the ignition and pulls away at high speed. Of all the fucking bad luck.

———————

THE NEXT MORNING, Hayley makes the short drive to the base. On the seat next to her is the flyer she removed from her windshield. "Kimberly." Still missing. Black hair and dark eyes. Wearing a navy UTEP hoodie. Fifteen years old. Her family has increased the reward for information leading to her recovery to ten thousand dollars. Seeing the flyer again—a constant motif since her arrival in El Paso—only stokes her growing outrage.

The higher she has climbed in her furious ascent of the Storm's hierarchy, the graver her descent into what Hayley perceives as a corruption of the country's ideals. What it is to be an American. And why the people of the United States should "form a more perfect Union." The leaflet for the missing teenage girl, like a constant drumbeat of despair that keeps time with Hayley's unyielding investigation, is a reminder that suffering and loss are everywhere around her.

The missing girl might seem insignificant compared to civil war, but Hayley Chill can't avoid sensing a connection between these two disparate incidents. By what correlation, however? She might ponder it longer, but not a quarter mile after leaving the motel, she sees the familiarly old and battered Ford F-150 following her. There are two vehicles between her and her pursuer, but the deeper state operative is able to make out the license plate. She remembers it, of course. After seeing the man in black sitting in the pickup across the street from the motel on Saturday morning, Hayley had sent the plate number to Wilde. The answer that came back wasn't useful. The Ford was registered to an eighty-two-year-old widow in Kermit who lives alone. The man driving the truck—white, in his late fifties or early sixties— had either stolen the vehicle or bought it without title transfer. Cash transaction. Off the books.

That's one way to do it.

Seeing him back there and not making much effort to conceal himself only pisses Hayley off more. And it's not even eight in the morning.

———————

HE RETURNED TO the Beverly Crest Motor Inn a little after sunrise. Seeing her car in the lot, Oswald waited halfway down the block. Made some calls. Checked in via text messages with some of Storm's other supervisory captains. He regrets missing out on taking down the governor. Fucking guy wasn't even born in Texas. Yeah, that's going to be a real party. Oswald's lieutenant, who has inherited the operation, promised to get the whole thing on video. The look on that Okie son of a bitch's face when they come for him is going to be priceless. Missing out on that piece of business gives Pete Oswald another reason to hate Hayley Chill, or whatever her real name is.

His plan is simple enough: Oswald intends to drop the hammer on the purported Senate aide before she gets to Fort Bliss. Taking her out while she's on the post isn't an option. Oswald can't even get past the gates. No, the time is now. Pull up alongside her at a stoplight and start blasting, Mexican-cartel-style. He'll have to ditch the truck, but the old biddy who sold it to him for two thousand bucks won't have much of anything actionable to say about him. Nice, white man. Fifties, maybe. Did I mention he was awful nice?

But then, just like that, Oswald loses sight of her rental car. For some reason, she had stayed on Dyer instead of hopping on southbound Gateway Boulevard. Had she spotted him following her? Passing the high school on his left, he can't locate Hayley Chill's rental car anywhere on the six-lane divided road.

He's passing through the light at Ellerthorpe Avenue when the impact from the rear of his vehicle causes his head to pitch forward and smack the top of the steering wheel.

———————

HAYLEY HAD TAKEN advantage of a slight bend in the road just before passing underneath the freeway to speed ahead and take a hard right—cutting off two lanes of oncoming traffic—to enter the high school grounds. Via the school road—speeding past sports fields and parking lots—she was able to reenter southbound lanes on Dyer and fall in behind the F-150 unnoticed. Hayley could see her pursuer behind the wheel of the beat-to-shit Ford pickup truck, his head swiveling from left to right in search of her. She waited until he merged into the right-hand lane before accelerating and bashing into the rear bumper of the pickup.

When Hayley gets to the open driver's window—both vehicles stopped in the right lane, cars whizzing past behind them—they have each other dead to rights. With their respective 1911 handguns held at point-blank range, pulling the trigger is as good as suicide.

Oswald asks, "Who the fuck are you?"

"I was going to ask you the same question."

"Who do you work for? What do you want?"

Hayley says, "You first."

His eyes take in the magnificent, clean lines of the Nighthawk .45-caliber 1911 pointed at his head, a more impressive weapon than his Colt—at least if measured by purchase price. Oswald's 1911 costs a quarter of the custom handgun in Hayley's grip.

"Fancy gun. Too big in your hands?"

"Ask your friends in New Mexico."

Oswald's mouth forms a perfect O. So, she did make him from more than a quarter mile off. How—?

She interrupts his idle speculation with, "I already know more than you think."

"But you don't have it all. *I* don't even have the whole picture."

Hayley wonders if this guy knew her father. Odds are they both walk away from this. Or they both die. She entertains no illusion of taking her adversary into custody. Not now. Not this morning. The deeper state operative has a bigger fish on the line.

No doubt, the man in black has done his due diligence and most likely knows her name. He probably thinks it's made-up, just like everything else he'd learned about her. Funny, huh?

Hayley decides to split the difference.

"Did you know Charlie Hicks?" Watching his face for a reaction. And intentionally *not* asking about Tommy Chill.

Oswald's face remains impassive. "Never heard of him. My turn?"

"You don't get a turn."

He scoffs and shakes his head. "You remind me of my kid sister. She was a pain in the ass, too."

"I like her already."

A passing Good Samaritan slows to a near stop, his passenger-side window down. The smoke from his cigarette wafts out of his brand-new Ford pickup truck with a languid insouciance.

"You folks need a hand?" the Good Samaritan asks from behind all of that blue smoke.

Oswald glares at the man with an impatient menace that prompts quick reconsideration. Soon enough, he and Hayley have the shoulder of the road to themselves again.

"She was the one with the grades. Apple of the old man's eye," he says, furiously scratching his chin. "My parents didn't even try to encourage me to go to college. Marines was good enough for me. Let her be the 'good' one. Getting into trouble was more fun. And even as a kid, Amy had to be the cop. The moralist. Used to follow me. To keep tabs on her fuck-up big brother and report back to Dad. This one time, Amy sees that I'd taken the shotgun out of the old man's closet. Follows me in her car, right? My friends and I were going to boost the local McDonald's. When my sister figured out what was going down, she went inside to warn the burger flippers. Told them not to answer any knock at the back door. That we were out there, with our ski masks and shotgun. I didn't realize it until later why no one ever came to the door, when she told me that she'd ratted us out. My sister, she had the same expression on her face that you do now. Like she *knew* she was better. That she would always be better."

The muscles in his face set like concrete. The bitterness still fresh all these years later.

Oswald says, "Too bad one of my buddies found out what she'd done. I hated what happened to Amy after that. The old man, he was just brokenhearted."

Hayley says nothing. The wind created by the cars rushing past behind her is infused with grit and sand from miles of desert in every direction. A stray dog scurries over the rock-strewn frontage area bordering the road, beneath a sky clogged with ominous clouds. How did she not hear about a storm in the forecast?

"Wherever you come from? Go back. Leave this alone." He says, his words knocking her out of her split-second reverie. "You know what happens to good girls."

This dude doesn't have a freaking clue.

She says, "I got some advice for you, too."

Oswald raises his eyebrows by way of inquiry.

Hayley shoots her left hand into the car, rips the key from the ignition, and says, "Don't be such a perfect shit."

With her left fist clutching the truck's ignition key, she punches him in the right eye.

"That's for Amy."

Hayley leaves the window and walks quickly back to her idling rental car.

SHE FINDS ROY Pogue in a treatment cubicle at the emergency center of the Beaumont Army Medical Center. The last time she was at this hospital, Hayley watched Christian Libby jump over the low wall on the building's rooftop. Feels like ages ago, though only four days have passed since that event. The CID agent sits on the examination table while a young army doctor stitches up a nasty gash on the right side of his head, just above the ear. Nursing staff have yet to clean his neck of dried blood.

He can't suppress a baleful expression.

"They got me in the parking lot of a Starbucks on Lee Trevino."

"They?" Hayley asks. She learned Pogue had been assaulted and was receiving treatment when she called his office just before passing through the Cassidy Gate.

"Three guys."

"Military?"

Pogue shrugs. "I didn't recognize any of 'em."

"White men, sir?"

The young captain wearing scrubs shoots her a glance.

"We almost done here?" the CID agent asks the doctor, pointedly ignoring Hayley.

Low, DARK CLOUDS threaten rain. Wind whips in one direction and then another, kicking up dirt and debris. Temperature spiking and then dropping again within an hour or two. Weird weather in many places, but not West Texas.

Hayley and Pogue walk in the hospital lot toward her car.

"I know who's in charge."

The CID agent seems less than thrilled to hear Hayley's announcement.

"In charge of what?" he asks testily.

"Mr. Pogue, I witnessed a sales pitch in Dallas to potential investors for a proposed nation to be carved from Texas, New Mexico, Oklahoma, and parts of Kansas and Arizona. A secessionist movement, sir, founded on a political philosophy of white supremacy. According to my sources, a small but far-reaching conspiracy exists within the US military in support of this movement."

"That . . . is . . . absurd."

"I was followed here, Chief. By a man who had every intention of killing me. My rental car in Dallas was booby-trapped. I was attacked in the Dallas County jail. They want me dead for a reason, sir. The threat is real. It's happening *now*."

They stop in front of her vehicle. Ramming her pursuer's truck has left the front bumper and hood bashed.

Pogue takes in the damage.

"You're hell on rental cars, know that, right?"

Hayley ignores his effort at levity. Or is it simply evasion?

"I need your help, sir."

Whether it's that he was mugged in a Starbucks parking lot an hour earlier or he has simply had enough of Hayley's relentless pushing and prodding, Roy Pogue seems at the end of his rope with her.

"What do you want from me? I investigate drug dealers and car thieves. Maybe a sexual assault now and then. I chase homesick privates halfway across the state to their grandmas' homes in Houston. What do you expect *me* to do about any of this other shit?"

The deeper state operative is characteristically undeterred.

"General Killebrew. I'm following up on the military aspect of this thing."

Pogue's head swings back and forth as if slapped. "No. No, no, no, no."

"My source in Dallas. The guy selling time-shares for treason." Hayley pauses, considering how best to describe her interrogation methods. Decides that omission is the best strategy. "He wouldn't talk. And then he did. Killebrew is at the top of this."

All of which compels the CID agent to draw the proverbial line.

"In no universe will I deliver up General Killebrew to you so that your crazy ass can accuse him of heading up a military-led secession-ist movement. That, my friend, is not going to happen."

He climbs into the car. Hayley does the same on the driver's side.

"Chief, I just want to talk to him."

"Like every other poor motherfucker you've had a 'talk' with? No. I'm not doing it."

"Chief . . ."

"Open your eyes, lady! Half the base is mobilizing for Operation Battle Cry. Killebrew doesn't have time for your shit."

Hayley recalls the increased activity around the base and in town over the last couple of days.

"I saw a bunch of equipment on the highway. And down by the rail yards."

"Correct. What you're seeing is prep for the largest military exercise in Europe in twenty-five years. Participating units from Bliss, Hood, Stewart, and Fort Polk are loading vehicles, heavy equipment, and material for rail transport and onward shipping. Twenty thousand soldiers and that many pieces of equipment deploying from the United States, bound for Europe. Kickoff was yesterday."

Hayley ponders this news. Then asks, "Southeast, through San Antonio, to the Port of Houston?"

"That's right. Port of Houston. Half a division is on the move."

Putting the pieces together inside her head, Hayley doesn't like what she sees.

With even more than her usual conviction, she says, "I've got to talk to the general."

"Take me to my car." Pogue folds his arms across his chest, just as adamant. Hayley had offered to return the CID agent to his car at the location of his mugging.

"Chief . . ."

"Drive, dammit! Take me back to my car!"

———————

NOT WAITING FOR permission is standard operating procedure. In William Killebrew, Hayley Chill's hunch is that she has found the apex of the conspiracy. The plot's architect and commander. Operation Battle Cry is too convenient an opportunity. The war could be over before Washington even knows it's started. Hayley forwarded her twelve-sentence report to Andrew Wilde and hopped in the car without waiting for an answer. She doesn't need help from Roy Pogue or the deeper state to find the general.

On the first day of the monumental military exercise, there's only one place he's going to be.

———————

THE STRAUSS RAIL Yard just outside Santa Teresa, New Mexico, is twenty miles northwest of El Paso, completed in 2014 as a modernization effort of the region's commercial transport infrastructure. The facility was designed with intermodal shipping—moving freight via two or more modes of transportation—as its primary improvement over older, existing facilities in the city. The transfer of forty-foot containers from truck to rail and onto ocean carriers is the most visible component of Operation Battle Cry in the United States, representing a crucial test of the nation's ability to project a military presence anywhere in the world and in the shortest amount of time.

Siting of the Union Pacific facility in the open desert outside of tiny Santa Teresa and within a short driving distance to Fort Bliss was undoubtedly a significant consideration.

Heading due west on the highway, Hayley passes dozens of tractor trailer rigs heading in the same direction. In the far right-hand lane, convoys of heavy-haul flatbed trailers loaded with M1 Abrams tanks, Bradley Fighting Vehicles, general-purpose Cougars, Strykers, M-ATVs, and RG-31 armored trucks travel in a nearly continuous line toward the rail yards on the outskirts of Santa Teresa. Storm clouds continue to pile up and collide above the town's industrial landscape. Hayley joins the convoy transitioning onto Airport Road—intersections under military police control—and heads north,toward the intermodal facility and rail yards a few miles in that direction.

Union Pacific security guards and military police protect the facility's gated entrance. Numerous other armed personnel patrol the tracks and surrounding area for miles, on foot and in expanded-capacity M1113 Humvees. Pausing in her vehicle on Airport Road outside the rail yard's main gate, Hayley assesses the security presence and realizes her chances of gaining unauthorized entry are close to nil. With nothing to lose, the deeper state operative pulls into the visitors' entry driveway, separate from the entrance used by freight-bearing tractor-trailers lining the road behind her.

The gate is down, denying entry. A uniformed Union Pacific police officer steps up to Hayley's open window while another, with a guard dog on a short leash, performs a walk-around of the car. Two military policemen hang back, maintaining their position at the gate.

The UP man says, "Sorry, ma'am, no visitors."

Hayley has her identification ready, including her Senate credentials Wilde had provided her within twenty-four hours of her arrival in Texas.

"I'm Hayley Chill, aide to Senator Powell, on the Committee on Armed Services. Here on oversight."

"Well, ma'am, I don't care if you're here on cocaine. You're not coming on facility premises without prior authorization."

Hayley isn't willing to let it go, not so easily.

"Look, if you just call—"

The security guard steps back, putting a hand on a Glock 22 in its holster on his equipment belt. A trio of military police approach the car, their M4 carbines pointed down at the ground but ready.

"There a problem here?" asks one of the MPs.

The UP officer, a veteran of the Fort Worth Police Department, ignores his military counterpart. "Turn around, ma'am, or you *will* be arrested for trespassing. The entire facility is on lockdown for the duration of the army's load-in."

Hayley says nothing but pleads her case with those powder blue eyes.

The Union Pacific officer is immune to her appeal.

"Ma'am, I advise you to turn your car around and go. We just sent a TV news team from KTSM up to Doña Ana County Detention Center thirty minutes ago."

———————

SANTA TERESA ISN'T much of a town. Not nearly as sweetly spiritual as its name implies. Thanks to Union Pacific's move from East El Paso to the new facility on Airport Road, the entire municipality is one massive warehouse after another, a grid of tan office buildings erected seemingly overnight in a once-empty expanse of sand and sagebrush. Many of these warehouses contain raw materials awaiting transport over the nearby border to factories in Mexico. The finished products are moved north again and stored in these very same warehouses before loading onto trains for shipment all over the United States.

Hayley stops at Penny's Diner, which shares a large parking lot with a Travelodge on Airport Road. A little before five p.m., the joint is almost empty. She chooses a booth farthest from the front door, next to the restrooms. A waitress—Hayley's age, with a cheerful manner and eager to please—approaches with a carafe of coffee. She wordlessly holds it aloft, and the deeper state operative nods.

"Figured. You had that 'gimme coffee' look," the waitress says as she snags a cup and saucer, placing them on the table in front of Hayley. "Fixin's?"

"Black is fine. Thank you."

"Long day?" asks the waitress.

"You could say that. Long week."

The other young woman nods sympathetically. "Eating?"

"Just coffee for now. If I change my mind, I'll let you know."

The waitress smiles and turns to attend to other duties.

Hayley watches her go, reflecting on the utter grace of people. *Some* people. With precious little conversation, the other woman intuited exactly what Hayley needed. And all with a kind smile. Perfect. She ponders the beauty of that uncomplicated, human interaction. Hayley indulges a moment of envying the other woman, with full awareness she's being delusional in doing so. That Hayley comprehends nothing of the waitress's actual life—the full spectrum that may include dissatisfactions and unhappiness—makes no difference. Not while enjoying the brief moment of their simple, elegant exchange.

Hayley had entered the café in a low mood, in full retreat after her recent setback. That weight has at least partially lifted.

Checking her phone, she finds no message from Andrew Wilde in response to her concerns regarding the massive military exercise. As outlandish as her suspicions might seem, Hayley now suspects the secessionists intend to take advantage of Operation Battle Cry and combine elements of the First Armored Division with the Texas Army National Guard's Seventy-Second Brigade as an occupying force of the Permian Basin. But the railway route to the port in Houston passes hundreds of miles south of Midland and the ARNG deployment. Is she being paranoid? What real evidence does she possess that might convince Wilde and her superiors in Publius of the imminent danger? Despite her successes in climbing the cabal's chain of command, Hayley has learned almost nothing about Tommy Chill's role. Why he stole Charlie Hicks's identity. What compelled him to abandon his family.

After only a few minutes of sitting in the booth and staring out the window that faces Airport Road, Hayley sees an HMMWV pull into the lot. Three officers exit the vehicle and stroll toward the café's entrance.

Though the two men and one woman wear the same combat uniform in camo pattern, the oldest among them—walking a pace in front—has unmistakable authority over the others. No matter how subdued the grade insignia, his two stars embroidered on a matching camouflage pattern are impossible to miss.

General Killebrew's cranium seems as if carved from an oak stump. Hayley doesn't think she has seen a more massive head in her life. Coarse gray bristle emerges from below the bottom of the general's camouflage field cap, ending with a sharp edge at the base of his neck. With long arms swinging confidently, punctuated by enormous, pendulous hands, the general's gait is simultaneously adamant and jagged.

Killebrew is a born warrior, someone who would be at home on the fields of Thermopylae. At Baba Wali Pass. On Pork Chop Hill.

Hayley watches the army officers approach the door. Denied entry to the rail yard where she had hoped to find the general, she only needed a coffee stop at Penny's Diner for William Killebrew to come to her.

The smile, Hayley muses. The waitress's friendly greeting was an act of grace.

Killebrew and his staff officers enter the café and take the first booth by the entrance. Hayley cannot make out much of their subdued conversation. They're talking shop, that much is obvious. The logistics of Operation Battle Cry require herculean management attention. Hayley surmises that Killebrew and his staff have escaped to the quiet confines of Penny's Diner for some privacy to confer.

Pouring coffee for the officers, the waitress glances in her direction.

Hayley nods, their wordless communication continuing unabated.

With her coffee cup refreshed, she locks her gaze on Killebrew at the other end of the room, deep in conversation with his two staff officers. The .45-caliber War Hawk rides comfortably on her strong side, inside the waistband holster. What she doesn't have is a plan.

But there's no way Killebrew is leaving the premises without a confrontation. Hayley Chill will wait for her moment.

That opportunity comes soon enough. After the army officers have ordered, Killebrew stands up from the booth and walks in Hayley's direction, heading to the restroom, she assumes. The deeper state operative weighs the timing of her challenging Killebrew in the next few seconds. How will his junior officers react? Are they even aware of the Storm and its agenda? She feels her pulse quicken and works to control it. Calm is needed. Calculation.

Follow him into the men's restroom. Confront him there.

Hayley resists the urge to study the general more closely, keeping her eyes locked forward. She feels the general's gaze fall on her briefly as he passes her in the booth.

But he doesn't turn left, toward the restrooms. Instead, Killebrew continues past Hayley's booth and exits the diner through a rear emergency door.

Hayley remains motionless for a beat, looking toward the two junior officers at the other end of the diner. They converse quietly, as if nothing is amiss. Do they even know the general has left the premises? Is he coming back?

She doesn't want to lose her chance to interrogate Killebrew. She can't allow that to happen. Not when she's so close.

Sliding out of the booth, Hayley glances toward the other end of the room. Confirming that the two junior officers remain seated, Hayley turns and exits through the same emergency door Killebrew exited.

Stepping outside, she feels her hair grasped and wrenched backward. Hayley loses consciousness—for seconds only—as the back of her skull slams against the metal door frame. Despite her incapacitation, the deeper state operative fully comprehends what is happening. Though she has yet to see her assailant, Hayley knows it must be Killebrew who has her hair in his grip. She can intuit his sheer *size*.

Her training kicks in. Hayley reaches for the War Hawk, and her fingers touch the empty IWB holster.

Killebrew has her gun.

With his massive fingers gripping her hair, the general wrenches Hayley's head down and around, putting an unnatural torque on her upper vertebrae, and then propels her across what must be the rear parking lot. In his lumberjack's grip, she is utterly in his control. Her mind races as Killebrew bum-rushes her to God knows where.

So far, Hayley and the general have exchanged no words. Just the assault and then being dragged across the parking lot. Recalling that the café shares its parking lot with a budget motel, Hayley wonders how her abduction can be happening without witnesses.

Where is everyone?

———————

HE WAS BORN and raised in New Hampshire. His father, Jack, was a teacher at the high school. An only child and unusually introverted, William Killebrew was closer to his mother, Carol, a deeply religious homemaker. More at ease prowling in the woods than engaging in the normal teenage activities of his peers, a thirteen-year-old William was devastated by the shocking breakup of his parents' marriage. Challenging his father in the driveway of the family home—one which the elder Killebrew would never set foot in again—the teenager did not receive the answers he desperately needed to hear. Why was he leaving the family? What possibly could justify this unpardonable betrayal of mother and son?

William resorted to surveilling his dad until the source of the breakup was uncovered: Jack Killebrew had fallen in love with a fellow teacher at the high school. This warm and vivacious black woman was the polar opposite of his soon-to-be ex-wife in every way imaginable. William's mother soon left for North Carolina, taking her only son with her. She remarried, her new husband the single father to a boy eleven years younger than William and the sibling he always wanted.

For Carol, there was no greater priority in life than indoctrinating both sons—biological and step—with her fiery racist beliefs. William Killebrew carried that extreme, xenophobic ideology with him through high school and afterward, while attending West Point. Cautious in revealing these hatreds, Killebrew served his country with honor.

But waiting. For the opportunity to bring his ideas into the open. And make them a reality.

———————

THE GENERAL STANDS six feet, four inches tall, with shoulders like a crucifix's crosspiece. His eyes blaze with belief in a cause that can only be just. Kicking open the gate to the trash bin enclosure at the edge of the rear parking lot, he flings Hayley Chill to the ground inside. As if she were Azazel, a fallen angel.

Knocked semiconscious again, Hayley attempts to focus her eyes on the giant standing over her. The War Hawk is in his right hand.

Pointed at her.

Killebrew says, "You don't even know."

His voice is hoarse. Perennially, she's sure. A soldier's voice, blown out in battle. From making order of chaos.

"You killed him, damn you. You killed my only brother."

Hayley has been a witness to several deaths in the last week. She can only remember killing three men, the AWOL soldiers at the New Mexico compound.

His brother was one of them?

"How . . . ?" she asks.

"Christ, I saw you coming from a mile away." He takes a less casual aim on her. "You've caused enough trouble."

"Your brother?" she asks, buying time.

Devise a plan. Something!

"Cecil Drummond. My stepbrother."

Hayley's expression reveals enough to tell him that he was right about one thing: she didn't know.

Despite his father's betrayal, William Killebrew found solace in the combined family provided by his mother's second marriage. With the mentoring of a younger stepbrother. As much as his limited emotional boundaries allow, Killebrew loved Cecil Drummond. He rescued him from his numerous legal troubles and gave him a new sense of purpose in the noble cause of creating a better and thoroughly white nation.

"Tortured him. Then chased him to his death."

Hayley feels a moment of sheer desperation that she struggles to dampen. And also some shame with the extreme measures she had taken.

Calmly she says, "One of your people placed the bomb in that car, not me."

"What does that matter?" he asks.

Killebrew's smile is mostly a sneer, confessing a propensity for sadism. Will this be for pleasure or revenge?

His finger curves around the trigger, applying the necessary pressure to initiate the mechanism's pretravel sequence. Only the slightest additional force is needed to engage the 1911's mainspring.

That is, when things go boom.

A man's voice interjects first. "General?"

Hayley's gaze lands first, a split second before Killebrew's . . .

CID agent Roy Pogue, in his two-piece suit, is a welcome sight. A familiar face in an otherwise hellacious ordeal.

Pogue speaks again, his voice firmer.

"Sir, what is this?"

Killebrew's expression is mostly one of embarrassed consternation. As if he's been caught masturbating.

Hayley seizes on this opportunity provided by her attacker's fluster.

"Chief, please! Help me!"

Now the general grins, enjoying her plight. The fire in his eyes undiminished. Only heightened.

"Help you?" Killebrew barks a laugh. "How do you think I knew what you looked like? Who gave me a photo of you."

Hayley stares incredulously at the CID agent, unable to process the reality of what Killebrew is saying.

The general says, "In the new order of things, they get their own country. Gulf states. Louisiana. They recognize the need for separation, just like we do."

"They?"

Pogue has no issue with meeting her gaze. There's a hardness in his eyes. Generations of indignities and humiliations earned him that much.

He says, "I told you to stop."

Killebrew gestures toward the enclosure gate that Pogue had pushed open as he entered. "Close that damn thing. Let's finish this."

The general takes aim again on Hayley with her own gun.

Almost softly, Pogue says, "No."

He has drawn his Sig P320, holding it out and grasped with both hands. The sight picture is Killebrew's enormous, Frankenstein head.

In the tight confines of the dumpster enclosure, less than six feet separate the two men.

"My God, soldier, are you fucking insane?" asks Killebrew, swinging the War Hawk around and gun blasts cracking almost simultaneously.

HE WAS A middling football player and slightly above-average student. Raised in Sunnyside, a neighborhood south of downtown Houston, Roy Pogue mostly avoided trouble and the gangs that infested the community. Enlisting in the US Army after graduation from high school, he continued to make concerted efforts to "better himself." Soon after basic and occupational training, Pogue applied to join the military police and then Criminal Investigation Division Command. In the army, his closest buddy was another guy from the neighborhood, Micah Johnson, a more charismatic individual. Batman to Pogue's Robin. Both Johnson and Pogue attained ranks of sergeant, with Micah opting for straight infantry.

Frustrated in his pursuit of advancement and at the mercy of hostile, mostly white, superiors, Johnson grew increasingly radicalized in his political beliefs. A girlfriend introduced him to the Israelite Church of God in Jesus Christ, an organization of Black Hebrew Israelites that the Southern Poverty Law Center has labeled an active hate group that espouses black supremacist beliefs.

Always the follower, Roy Pogue joined his friend at the twice-weekly services held in the living room of a local priest of the controversial church. The CID agent embraced the sect's ideas of Ten Lost Tribes and black superiority more out of loyalty than for anything resembling conviction. Several years passed. Pogue remained on the political movement's fringes.

Many of the church's followers drifted away from active participation. Pogue would have lost interest, too, were it not for his close
friendship with Micah, whose radicalization had only increased.
The police shooting deaths of two local black teens finally triggered the most virulent form of this extremism. A planned protest
of police violence in Dallas inspired the army sergeant to go "cop
hunting." In a rare act of defiance, Pogue refused to join Johnson.
After killing five police officers in a gun rampage, Micah Johnson was shot and mortally injured by members of Dallas SWAT
unit.

Following his best friend's death, Pogue recommitted himself
wholeheartedly to the principles of black nationalism and the Israelite Church of God in Jesus Christ.

HAYLEY GETS TO her knees and looks to her left. Toward the felled
giant. The blood pooling rapidly beneath his face suggests a shot to
the head. So does the missing left backside of his skull. No one has
ever been more dead than this guy.

She lifts her gaze and pivots, looking behind her. To where Roy
Pogue sits on the ground near the enclosure's gate. Shoulders slumped
and chin nearly on his chest, the CID agent plants his hands on the
stained pavement at either side. The Sig 320 lies at his feet.

Hayley retrieves the War Hawk from the ground next to Killebrew's
corpse—first things first—then crawls to where Pogue sits. She sees
no blood on the CID agent.

"Chief, are you hit?"

His head comes up, engaged now. Like a ventriloquist's dummy.
All muscles slack except in the jaw. Pogue is determined to speak.

"Killebrew?" he asks.

"Dead. Headshot."

Pogue nods. Satisfied. "Not to be ugly, but kinda hard to miss."

Hayley smiles despite the circumstances. That the warrant officer saved her life is a jewel to be admired later.

Assess the situation, then act on that assessment.

"Mr. Pogue, tell me where you're hurt."

Growing weaker, he moves his head back and forth.

Only then does Hayley see the blood seeping through his shirt to his suit jacket. She reaches to render medical assistance. To do *something*.

The CID agent pushes her hands away.

"Enough."

He's going to die and knows it.

"Why did you help me?" she asks.

Pogue struggles to sit up, grimaces, and settles back again. "Anything to put it to these racist fucks."

"Including you, right?" Hayley asks pointedly.

His smile vaporizes.

"Maybe." Then, "Funny what hate can do to a man."

She follows his gaze to where the general's body lies facedown on the filthy cement.

"End on a high note, right?" asks Pogue.

Indeed. Hayley regrets lumping the CID agent in with the likes of Killebrew.

"You stopped it. It's over."

"No. Not over. Everything . . . in motion. Only Woodside has the whole thing in his head. Only him."

"Woodside? Killebrew wasn't the top?"

Pogue shakes his head no. "Take my phone. Go. Don't stop."

Though he knows he doesn't have to tell her, of all people, he does so anyway.

He says, "Never stop."

The CID agent reaches into his suit jacket pocket and offers his smartphone to her. "Nine-nine-six-six. Everything you need is on that phone."

She takes the phone. "Why, sir? Why did you help me?"

Does he even know why?

"Maybe . . . maybe I'm just . . . so tired."

Hayley has seen enough men die to know Roy Pogue's time is close. The question she has raised at each rung of the ladder must be asked.

"Did you know Tommy Chill? He was involved in all of this. Maybe went by the name of Charlie Hicks. Worked at the Pentagon. Did you know him, Chief?"

But the light in Pogue's eyes is mostly extinguished.

Talking has taken such an effort. He no longer feels the cold of lurking death, replaced by a surging, warm glow. There is goodness still in these last few moments of life. Peace. Despite the stench emanating from the dumpster bins and grease-stained pavement under his hands, Roy Pogue can almost smile. For real. Experiencing the heady rush of grace.

Of making amends.

"Nine-nine-six-six."

10

LIBERTY DAY

She cleans her face and hair of Killebrew's gore in the bathroom of a gas station a few blocks away. The cashier freaked when Hayley walked in, blood splattered as she was, but Hayley smiled as if nothing at all was amiss and received the bathroom key with a wink. News of the double shooting appears on her phone's news feed by the time she climbs back inside the car. The victims are not yet identified. She estimates the police investigation is only now getting underway. The Pentagon will weigh in, of course. A perfect shitstorm will ensue. But will the load-in of materials and supplies for Operation Battle Cry stall with General Killebrew's death? She doubts it. The military exercise is a multinational effort involving the cooperation of several NATO allies.

Pogue was right. Killebrew's demise will stop nothing.

It's half past seven. The evening sky has darkened, heavy with a roiling mass of matte black clouds. Wind swirls, kicking up dust and debris. Rain hasn't fallen in the area for weeks. Hayley turns the ignition and drives back into El Paso, finding a budget motel not far from the Beverly Crest Motor Inn. SuperLodge Motel is also on Dyer

Street but two miles north. Checking in and parking, she doesn't bother entering the room. Hayley only needs a place to lie low for the night.

She takes residential streets east of the main drag, doubling the walking distance between the two motels with a zigzag route. But keeping out of sight. A scruffy cemetery and busy car wash are located directly across Dyer from the Beverly Crest. Between those two addresses is a cement-lined storm-drainage ditch that Hayley accesses from Guadalupe Drive. The culvert is deep enough so that when she approaches the busy avenue, she is below ground level.

With a gopher's-eye view, the deeper state operative has a good vantage point on the entire motel parking lot and surrounding street.

Identifying the hit team's vehicle is trivial business. Parked in the same location opposite the motel driveway that the man in black had favored is a dark blue, '90s model Chevrolet Suburban. Hayley sees one operator behind the wheel of the generously dented SUV and another in the shotgun seat. More men might be sitting in the back seat; she's not sure. Despite the dying light, they wear sunglasses, a fact that brings a grin to Hayley's face. The men—white, short hair, wearing civilian clothing—talk easily among themselves. Passing the time. Waiting. For her.

She isn't surprised the man in black, having been badly humiliated, has passed the job of eliminating her to others. With their action-movie eyewear and lax security measures, the hit team impresses Hayley as near amateurs. She doesn't take it personally; given the scope of the conspiracy, the deeper state operative is the lowest of priorities.

Without a doubt, the men have searched her room already. Hayley is reasonably confident the envelope containing the ciphered pages is still safe, secure in its hiding place. However, her clothes and personal items in the motel room have clued the hit team to her inevitable return. They won't be leaving their stakeout of the Beverly Crest anytime soon.

So, how to retrieve the encrypted pages?

Backing away from her vantage point, Hayley turns and walks quickly back up the drainage culvert. She has much to do in the next several hours. The pieces are falling into place. Roy Pogue's cell phone was a treasure trove of information. She had accessed the device after driving only a few blocks east on Airport Road, away from Penny's Diner.

What motivated the CID agent to give her the phone's unlock code? His fringe separatist movement shared only racial bias with the group that Killebrew had joined. Cooperation between the two groups was fraught with tension from the beginning, their mutual enmity an obvious stumbling block. Hayley will never know if it was Roy Pogue's hatred of Killebrew, a disillusionment with the separatist fantasy, or some emerging affinity for her that compelled his change of heart. Ultimately, it makes no difference. Maybe it was a merging of all three impulses.

Moments before his demise, Roy Pogue decided to die a patriot.

Nine-nine-six-six accessed the phone and revealed all of its secrets.

One photo, in particular, was more shocking than any other clue contained on the cell phone's storage chip.

Hayley had learned the identity of the secessionist plot's true leader.

But also revealed was a path forward of taking him down.

———————

THE FAST-FOOD MEALS he has consumed over the past twenty hours have left several stains on his Punisher T-shirt. Jack in the Box. 7-Eleven coffee. More Jack in the Box. And even more coffee. The hit team's driver and de facto leader is sick-and-fucking-tired of sitting in the Suburban with the other three guys. Inhaling their bad breath and all-too-frequent farts. Listening to their inane conversations and intermittent snoring. Waiting. For this stupid bitch to show up. Hayley whatever-her-fucked-up-fucking-name-is. Thrill? Pill? Kill? Who the fuck knows? Or *cares*? Let's get it on already!

Around eight a.m., while everyone else in the SUV is still asleep, Busby watches the housekeeper making her rounds. To be honest, a nice piece of ass. For a hotel maid. The hired hit man—his last job as a motorcycle mechanic at the local Harley-Davidson dealership a victim of the pandemic and subsequent crash in oil prices—entertains a brief notion of jacking off to this dizzying sight of the maid's butt while the others sleep but dismisses the thought just as quickly. Busby is anxious to make a good impression on his new employers, whoever the hell they may be. The dude who hired him—wearing all black like some kind of low-rent Johnny Cash—had approached him at Mulligan's, on Dieter. This guy in black—no name, sixty maybe, bitching about his lower back half the time—promised more work if this job was a success.

Born Henry Thomas Cahill, "Busby" is a probationary member of the Kinfolk Motorcycle Club. Most of the guys in the set barely tolerate the wannabe biker outlaw, but he's willing to wait them out. Getting a reputation around town as a cold-blooded killer for hire is a fast track, Busby imagines, of getting patched. The other three guys in the fifteen-year-old GMC are also vying for their club colors. Forever Kinfolk, Kinfolk Forever! They're armed, of course, with cheap .38s and Busby's newer Glock 17 stolen from an ex-girlfriend's ex-boyfriend's pad.

Their instructions are straightforward enough.

Kill the blonde on sight. Then skedaddle.

The guy riding shotgun sits up, blinking against the morning sunlight. Registers Busby's alert attention.

"What the fuck is happening? Something I hope."

THE BLOND GUEST with the friendly smile approached her car at a stoplight on Dyer a couple of blocks north of the Beverly Crest. Lina Campos was already a few minutes late for work—her daughter, Diana, fussing and resistant to being dropped off at day care—and so any further delay was irritating. Lowering her window, Lina made no effort to mask her impatience. The blond woman wasted no time getting to the point. Hearing her out, the room cleaner made her decision before the traffic signal changed.

Now, an hour later, as she approaches Hayley Chill's room with the cleaning cart, Lina wonders if she has made a mistake getting wrapped up in this crazy business. The Chevrolet Suburban, as anticipated, is still parked across the street. Lina can feel the driver's eyes on her as she walks toward room thirty-two. How will the gunmen respond when she stops to enter? She could have refused to help *la chele*, despite what the motel guest had done to rid Lina of Jerry Fishbaugh's vile harassment. But, in truth, the undocumented Honduran volunteered for this more hazardous operation. Hayley had requested only that the housekeeper confirm the envelope was still in its place until a better plan could be devised to retrieve it.

Lina offered to do more. She owes the blond woman that much.

The Honduran stops at Hayley's room door and knocks, announcing her presence with the expected declaration. "Housekeeping!" Waiting a few seconds, Lina opens the door with her master key. Leaving the cart outside and the door open behind her, as is customary, she enters the room.

Judging from the disarray, Lina surmises the men searched the room at some point the previous night. She glances at the front window to her right and sees damage to the frame that suggests a method of forced entry.

The men know the condition of the room.

That "cleaning" it is next to impossible.

When hotel staff encounters disarray of this extent in a room, a change of bath linens is the most a guest can expect. The men in the Suburban are aware of all of these things.

She hasn't much time.

———————

BUSBY AND THE others are on the move moments after the motel housekeeper enters the room. Triggered by Lina's presence—and in no small part because he's sick of doing nothing—the out-of-work motorcycle mechanic is determined to act decisively. He isn't going to earn his patch by drinking convenience store coffee for another twenty hours.

The wannabe hitmen jog across Dyer and toward room thirty-two's open door. If anyone inside the office is watching, there's little expectation of them interfering with this crew. They may only be prospects, but they look the part of motorcycle outlaws.

Lina steps outside with an armful of dirty bath linens as the men converge at the door.

"Get in the room!"

One of the other men knocks the dirty linens out of her arms. Lina seems far too quick to crouch down to gather up the towels again.

Before she can gather up the linens, another man pushes her on her ass. "What do you got in there?!"

Lina scrambles to her feet again as the thug bends over to search the towels, casting them aside as he inspects each one.

"What do you think you're doin'?" Busby demands.

The housekeeper crosses her arms over her chest and hunches her shoulders, girding for attack. Her silence is all the more damning.

Busby takes a threatening step toward her, pushing Lina against the wall.

"Fuckin' bitch! You're hiding something!"

He slams his fists down on her crossed arms, knocking them

apart. Two of the other men put hands on the housekeeper. She struggles to break free of them.

One of the men has run his hands across her front and around to her backside. Shakes his head. "She's got nothin'."

Busby feels his bravado siphoning off. Lamely he says, "This bitch is hiding *something*."

"*Gilipollas!*" Lina pushes past Busby and the other men, exiting through the room door and striding up the walkway.

APPROACHING THE REAR of the motel from the west, the deeper state operative remains hidden from view. Though the men in the old Suburban were amateurish poseurs, they were still a threat. Even stupid can kill.

The weed-choked lot behind the motel is strewn with trash, broken furniture, and empty paint cans. Hayley stops below the bathroom window of her room.

"Come on. Let's get the fuck outta here."

Hayley listens as they troop out of her room, their disgruntled voices receding as they retreat into the parking lot. A few moments later, Lina's head appears in the bathroom window. She passes Hayley the envelope retrieved from its hiding place deep inside the room's heating duct.

"Thank you."

The room cleaner nods in response, her head quickly dropping from view.

Hayley remains below the window for a few seconds longer and listens to make sure Lina is okay. It is a needless gesture. As throughout her life, the room cleaner is more than capable of taking care of herself.

The undocumented Honduran will work at the Beverly Crest Motor Inn for another year, long after the colossal events in which she had tangential involvement pass into the history books. Securing an assistant manager position at Teddy's Flame Room, she will quit the housekeeping job, accepting with it a living wage and health benefits. The man Lina meets there—a US citizen born in Honduras—makes good money as a builder in Boulder, Colorado, and she will subsequently quit the bar manager job, too. Her daughter, Diana, will graduate from Fairview High School and attend the University of Colorado Boulder, as a premed student. The former motel housekeeper's life will be indisputably good, one built upon the all-American foundations of opportunity, hard work, and perseverance. No part of that bright future would have been possible had she failed to help *la chele* in a moment of tremendous need. To her dying day—a winter Sunday morning, following church in the year 2100, exactly one hundred years after her birth in La Ceiba, Honduras—Lina Campos, the matriarch of a proudly prosperous American family, will remain unaware of the pivotal role she played in securing a future for herself and Diana.

As well as every man, woman, and child in the country.

———

OSWALD WAS RELUCTANT to delegate the responsibility of assassinating Hayley Chill, preferring to do it himself. But General Killebrew's shocking murder by another conspirator, a CID agent by the name of Roy Pogue, has the potential of throwing operations into disarray. What had prompted a deadly argument between the two men? Leaving Sierra Blanca and driving east on the interstate for an emergency meeting with Woodside and other high officers of the cabal, Oswald runs the possible scenarios in his head. The alliance between white and black nationalists in a movement that envisions a "two-state solution" is not a dependably easy one. Distrust preexists between the two groups. But natural foes can work together to pursue a common goal, right? Liberation! Did Killebrew and the black CID agent have a personal beef with each other? Legitimate law enforcement authorities, including some sympathetic to the cause, investigate that possibility. Time will tell.

He considers another possibility. Was Hayley Chill somehow involved? The two junior officers who accompanied Killebrew to the diner in Santa Teresa—not participants in the movement and unaware of its intentions—provided similar testimonies. Killebrew had excused himself to go to the restroom. His failure to return after several minutes prompted them to go in search of him. The young lieutenant found the two dead men in the dumpster enclosure at the rear of the parking lot. A waitress corroborated what the army officers reported: the only other customer in the café at the time was a woman loosely matching Hayley's description, unavailable for questioning and still unidentified.

Something doesn't seem right. Oswald continues to brood as the miles of flat Texas landscape fly past his window. The men he hired to take care of Hayley Chill reported that she hadn't checked out of the budget motel on Dyer Street. Their instructions are to continue their surveillance. Oswald is all-too aware of their probable ineptitude. With the operation's jump-off only hours away, time and manpower are suddenly in limited supply. The first railcars from El Paso are due to arrive in Sierra Blanca within the hour. Personnel is in place at the rail yard there. He hasn't a clue if he'll be successful in eliminating the threat posed by Hayley Chill. At the very least, Oswald imagines he has placed additional obstacles in her path.

But if she *was* somehow responsible for the death of William Killebrew, one of the cause's most important actors? Well, then perhaps he and the movement are truly fucked.

———

HER ATTIRE, ACQUIRED the previous night, suggests an evolution of tactics in her investigation. Unable to retrieve a change of clothes from her room at the Beverly Crest, Hayley went shopping at a Walmart Supercenter on Gateway Boulevard. Besides a couple of changes of underwear and socks, she purchased a cotton camisole and men's flannel shirt, Dickies carpenter pants, Merrell boots, and a Levi's denim trucker jacket. More comfortable, in more practical clothing, Hayley has shed her cover identity as a Senate aide.

She arrives in Sierra Blanca shortly after two p.m. Driving past Delfina's, Hayley recalls her meal there four days earlier. Remembers meeting the sheriff's deputy and aspiring crime novelist, Jay Gibbs.

Would be nice to stop in for a bite to eat.

Even better if, by chance, Gibbs has also stopped in. Almost in the same instant, the deeper state operative rolls her eyes in reaction to these frivolous daydreams. Who is she kidding? Hayley glances to her right, toward the old man sitting next to her in the front seat. Thank God that despite Juan Lugo's many talents and skills, reading minds is not one of them. She focuses again on the matter at hand, attention jogged by a glimpse of the M1 carbine the old man cradles in his lap.

Traveling on the Union Pacific "Sunset" route—paralleling the interstate for much of its journey between El Paso and Sierra Blanca—the massively long train is visible from the roadway. Seven diesel-electric locomotives interspersed through the train with a total length of nearly three miles. More than five hundred double-stacked container flatcars and wagons laden with the First Armored Division's supplies, vehicles, and material roll east across the Rio Grande Valley.

From Sierra Blanca, the train can switch to a line that follows a southeasterly direction or transition to the northeast, on the "Fort Worth" line and into the heart of the Permian Basin. The first dozen railcars have passed over the crossing Archie Avenue, where the two routes diverge, as Hayley pulls the rental car into the lot of the Pecos County State Bank, parks, and gets out.

Her companion—weathered brown skin and eyes like galactic black holes expressive of a sadness so profound that no light can escape them—gets out of the car as well. Having left the carbine on the vehicle's front seat, Lugo slips his pristine, ivory-colored Cavender's straw cowboy hat on his head and follows Hayley across the parking lot, to the crossing on Archie. The deeper state operative stops and watches the passing massive freight cars roll steadily past, heading east and shunning the tracks that peel off toward the south on a rail line that leads to the port in Houston.

What she feared has come to pass. With the train diverting from its planned route—one dictated by the Pentagon under Operation Battle Cry—the secessionists have hijacked an entire army division for their traitorous activities. Retrieving her smartphone, Hayley takes a short video of the train's movement due east. She will send it immediately via encrypted text to Andrew Wilde. But what can Publius expect to do now? Can anyone stop rebels who are backed by armored elements from both US Army and National Guard? Nothing Hayley has witnessed in the past week suggests that enlisted personnel are party to the rebellion. Rather, the conspiracy seems to be the concerted effort of a small cabal much higher in the military hierarchy, a plot that is enabled by civilian sympathizers.

And at the top? Something worse, she has learned. A *politician*.

Hayley has seen enough. She gestures to the Hispanic, middle-aged man who stands mutely beside her, watching the passing train.

"Let's go."

The old man, wearing a plaid shirt, Bodie wool vest, and dusty canvas pants, nods and turns for the car. But Hayley hesitates, reaching out and touching the man on his elbow.

He turns to face her again.

"You sure you want to do this? It's . . . it will be dangerous."

The old man, who has spent a lifetime outdoors and mostly without the company of others, as is his preference, says nothing. His eyes speak for him. Hayley doesn't think she has witnessed a greater resolve than the one she reads on his face.

They walk back to the car together.

JUAN LUGO WORKED at the spread for twenty years before being fired
last June. The JW7 Ranch in the Davis Mountains is thirty-seven
thousand acres of open and mountainous terrain, sitting on top of the
Capitan Reef Complex Aquifer. The main residence, built in 1890, is
a ten-thousand-square-foot stone edifice renovated with every modern convenience. The trophy bass lake, within view of the wraparound
porch, is spring fed. US Congressman James Woodside bought the
ranch out of foreclosure in the depths of the pandemic a few years
earlier and resides there when not in Washington, DC. Lugo, a loyal
and beloved employee of the previous owner, clashed with Woodside
over various issues, not the least of which was the congressman's decision to sell an excessive amount of the ranch's abundant frac water to
operators in the Permian Basin. Partial to his opinions regarding the
matter, Juan Lugo accepted termination in lieu of his silence.

Fortunately for the United States of America, he kept the keys.

Roy Pogue's phone provided Hayley with enough evidence to
indisputably identify Congressman Woodside as the Storm's spiritual leader and chief architect of a new white nation. Unencrypted
emails on the CID agent's device confirmed as much. Hayley had
time only for a cursory investigation of the congressman. Information available online revealed that Woodside was born and raised in
Howard County, the son of a struggling cattle rancher. Following high
school graduation and a few years helping his dad out on the ranch,
he received his degree from UTEP and then immediately joined the
Marines and its Officer Candidate Course. After a tour in Iraq and
one back in the States, Woodside left the military and partnered
with a Marine buddy in a lucrative oil business in Midland. His first
attempt running for public office, a highly contentious election to rep-
resent Texas's Twenty-Third Congressional District, was successful.
Divorced, Congressman Woodside's advertised hobbies are hunting,
fishing, and "loving the proud state of Texas."

On the drive from El Paso, Lugo provided Hayley with a detailed briefing of the ranch and the main residence's layout. He described the round-the-clock security team that keeps watch of the ranch's entry gate and the compound situated two miles up a private road. Given the emergent conspiracy, it's not a stretch to imagine Woodside has augmented his personal security team with troops from the National Guard. Hayley has no way of knowing for sure. She hopes Andrew Wilde will come through with promised satellite imaging, but stopping to wait for it isn't an option. Hayley is determined to get to Woodside with or without help from the deeper state.

Once the secessionists have all of their elements in place, the congressman and his cabal will be extremely difficult to dislodge. And untouchable. She'll never again get the opportunity to confront Woodside with questions about her dad.

The JW7 Ranch's ex-foreman is intimately familiar with every acre of the entire spread. No one knows the place and its secrets better than Juan Lugo. Without him, Hayley has no idea how she could put Woodside in the War Hawk's iron sights. But the plan—devised on the drive from Sierra Blanca to Balmorhea—is a good one.

"Get me inside the fence. You can stay with the vehicles. Then I'll come back to you."

Juan Lugo is seventy-two years old. He favors the M1 because he carried the carbine in the Vietnam War. Fighting and living alongside Popular Forces militia members in rural hamlets as a Marine in the Combined Action Program, Lugo traded for the weapon with a militia member who carried the WWII-era rifle. Fifty years ago, he preferred the carbine's reliable, lightweight simplicity, and today he still does. IBM manufactured the M1 he carried in Vietnam. After returning from that conflict, Lugo bought one made by Rock-Ola, a company more famously known for making jukeboxes.

Beyond answering Hayley's numerous questions about the ranch and offering his thoughts on their improvised operation, Juan Lugo has barely spoken a dozen words. Lost in his thoughts, he's a pres-

sure cooker of barely contained fury. Hayley can see she is wasting
her breath by suggesting he stay in the car; the old man will do as
he wishes. With this common resolve, Hayley Chill and the old man
share an affinity for vengeance.

As they drive in silence, the deeper state operative recalls the
tumultuous events of the past nine days. The shoot-out in Timothy
Hooker's trailer in New Mexico. Christian Libby's leap off the army
hospital rooftop. The gladiatorial games staged by the Texas Army
National Guard major, Nathaniel Culberson. Cecil Drummond's gold-
tipped pen as she jammed it into his ear. These grim memories—and
the more recent deaths of General Killebrew and Roy Pogue—seem
a high price to pay for James Woodside's name.

So be it.

Hayley has come this far. Her objective is clear: to slow or stop
the secessionist movement with a decapitation strike.

But time is short. The full brunt of the First Armored Division
will be in Midland/Odessa within hours. Once military personnel
are in place, the game is essentially over; the Permian Basin's vast
oil riches will be in rebels' hands by sunrise tomorrow. Dislodging
those elements will be a terrible, bloody, and drawn-out affair. Hayley would not be surprised if she learns the secessionists have active
sympathizers among the tactical-fighter wing at Holloman Air Force
Base, less than ninety miles north of Fort Bliss. What a few F-16
Fighting Falcons could do for the secessionists' cause is frightening
to imagine.

Will Congressman Woodside have any information to impart
about her father? The fact that both served in Iraq as Marines holds
promise of new revelations. Hayley Chill tempers those expecta-
tions, however. Stay focused on the task at hand. Be prepared for all
contingencies.

And, as her father would say, hope for a little luck.

H<small>E WAITS IN</small> the library of the stone manor. The decor is a comfort to Oswald, feeling a deep resonance with the unabashed masculinity expressed by the leather upholstery, muted light, and glassy-eyed animal heads mounted on the paneled walls. Despite the room's welcoming comfort, however, the former Marine is anxious in these long minutes of waiting for US Congressman James Woodside to enter. The Storm's unquestioned leader presided over a larger meeting an hour earlier, in a basement conference room meticulously designed to resemble the Situation Room in the White House. In that gathering, Woodside attempted to calm the nerves of the movement's top commanders, all of whom were unsettled by the deaths of General Killebrew and other Storm sympathizers so close to operational jump-off.

The congressman has always been a charismatic and persuasive speaker. He was able to soothe the anxieties of his commanders and effectively delegate those mission responsibilities left exposed by the general's death. Afterward, as the others quickly departed the ranch to attend their assigned duties, Woodside asked Oswald to wait for additional instructions in the private library upstairs.

Sitting on the leather couch, he studies framed photographs on the opposite wall that are a testament to James Woodside's meteoric rise since his return from Iraq. Framed photographs capture his intense gaze and inscrutable smile, with the Texas congressman in the company of presidents, industry titans, athletic superstars, and Hollywood celebrities. Not bad for a former Marine officer representing a hardscrabble district in Congress. But Woodside's magnetic personality and ability to connect with an audience is the rocket fuel of his ascendency. Like Alexandria Ocasio-Cortez, at least when measured by political and cultural impact, the freshman congressman from Texas's Twenty-Third District is a proficient master of social media and catnip for cable news producers everywhere.

Articulate, his message is reducible to a few easily digested ideas. "Washington, DC, isn't America." "The government has forsaken us." "Self-determination is the consequence of a determined self." These pithy messages, coupled with Woodside's dynamic presence, find resonance with a formidable percentage of the country's adult population and political intelligentsia. The debacle of the Monroe administration and chaos resulting from the global pandemic have only intensified the congressman's appeal, creating a hospitable environment for anti-government sentiment. Sustained instability in the US was too perfect an opportunity for a man of Woodside's megalomania to ignore. But mere politics—the slog of congressional debate and compromise—is an insufficient tool with which to make significant change.

Brute force is required. Insurrection the only way forward.

In the Storm movement, Woodside's singular genius was an instinct to meld the primal motivations of nationalism, white supremacy, and a long-standing "otherness" of the people in the region. In fact, the congressman harbors no racist inclination, but rather exploits that passion as a fuel to further his own ambitions. Hate as a useful intoxicant. By his estimation, people are small things. The victims of their own fears and inbred prejudices. James Woodside's drive comes from an insatiable desire for power. For immortality. A city named after him. A state. His face on paper money. What his father forever denied him: approval and respect.

The great man and founding father of the Free States of America enters the library—as with every room and situation—having the intention of making history. His aura is undeniable. So, too, an impenetrable force field of self-confidence.

"Thanks for staying, Peter. I know you have a lot to do over the next twenty-four hours."

James Woodside is not a tall man, but trim and fit. His amber eyes are golden marbles that capture anyone in their gaze and hold them with an otherworldly, gravitational pull. That allure comes not only from his physical appearance, one shared with any number of former military types who see the denial of the aging process as a matter of arrogant pride. Woodside commands via his psychological presence, a man who inhabits every moment as if it's his last. In his orbit, one comprehends the omnipresent authority of a gargantuan, outsize willpower.

That he lost the thumb on his left hand in Iraq hasn't slowed him down one bit.

Oswald leaps to his feet with the arrival of Woodside, who is at least twenty years his junior.

"Thank you, sir. Happy to be here. How can I be of service?"

The great man sits in an old Morris chair that belonged to his father, upholstered in leather, of course. Oswald takes his seat again after a deferential pause.

"As we discussed downstairs, losing General Killebrew has presented several challenges, given the timing, of course."

"Yes, sir."

"He was also like a father to me, you understand? My real dad never . . ." Woodside doesn't finish the thought.

Oswald respectfully stares down at the floor, giving the great man his moment.

The congressman takes it to compose himself.

Clear-eyed again, Woodside says, "I'm certain these next few hours will proceed as planned, thanks to the efforts of brave men and women like you."

"Thank you, sir. It's an incredible honor to play a role of any significance in the movement."

"Project Ace In The Hole, Peter. That element of the operation requires real dedication. An unshakable belief in our cause."

"Yes, sir."

"I'd like you to be in charge of it, my friend. I want you to be our ace in the hole."

Oswald strives to mask his surprise.

"I was set to transition to overseeing the Morale Operations Branch, sir. Troops on civilian train transports will be arriving in

Midland/Odessa tomorrow, 0700 hours." He pauses, then says with more emphasis, "Congressman, these folks need to be told what the hell they're doing there."

James Woodside nods gravely.

"Swaying our enlisted men to our cause is vital to ensuring the success of our overall operation, of course. But this other assignment, Peter, without it, we face inevitable defeat . . . despite all of our achievements thus far."

Oswald stands, spine straight and arms flattened to his sides. At attention.

"I'd be more than honored to have that duty. For you, sir, anything."

"Not me, my friend. For the cause. For the Free States of America."

"Yes, sir. Yes, of course."

Out of the corner of his eye, Oswald sees a young woman standing in a doorway that leads toward a part of the house he had never seen in a dozen visits. He had observed the girl at the ranch before on those occasions and wondered who she was.

When Oswald glances in that direction, the figure has disappeared.

Sensing the same presence, James Woodside stands to his feet as well. Oswald follows the great man toward the doors that lead to the home's entry hall, where three private contractors—all with Special Forces backgrounds—wait for the Storm's founder to emerge.

Woodside walks Oswald to the big double doors that lead outside.

"We are on the cusp of realizing all our dreams, Peter. We are not only witnesses to history, but the creators of our destiny."

Though Oswald has heard the great man utter these words on multiple occasions in the past few months, he feels his heart rate quicken. Arrested by those strange, golden eyes, he can only nod gravely and affirm. "Yes, sir. Yes."

Stepping out onto the massive, wraparound porch, Oswald leans into a buffeting gust of wind. The sky at dusk is a shroud of fast-moving black clouds.

Going to storm, he thinks. *Better get on the road.*

———————

FIVE HUNDRED AND forty miles to the northeast, Greg Lyle sits before a bank of computer monitors in the Storm Prediction Center on the campus of the University of Oklahoma in Norman. Thin, bald, and bespectacled, he has worked for the Weather Service for twenty-nine years. Forecasting weather is his occupation and his passion, buttressed by talents that are considerable. For all of those reasons, his managers tend to listen when Greg Lyle talks. Which isn't all that often. He's more interested in studying satellite pictures, forecasting models, surface observations, and radar data than trading the scuttlebutt with office colleagues or visiting in the chat rooms that link Weather Service offices across the country.

Lyle prefers to go it alone, feeling a personal connection with a galaxy of data that goes with predicting the weather.

For the past two hours, information being sent to Weather Service computers every two seconds by instruments affixed to a six-foot-wide, latex weather balloon released by the NWS office in El Paso has captured the forecaster's attention. Lyle has seen every kind of severe weather event one can expect to see in a lifetime of study. And what he sees on his monitors—in the satellite imagery and reports from the ground—registers in his facial expression.

Greg Lyle, NWS veteran, is deeply concerned.

The main room in the Storm Prediction Center resembles NASA's Mission Control, with forecasters and researchers seated at long tables. Communication and the sharing of ideas is encouraged by the layout. The forecaster at the next station over from Lyle's is a relative newcomer, with only ten years of experience. Margie O'Keefe suspects her colleague's reticence around her is due to his distrust of a woman in the SPC. She is wrong in this assumption; Lyle is simply shy.

Despite their less-than-convivial work relationship, O'Keefe is compelled to speak when she sees the look on the veteran forecaster's face.

"Greg? What's up?"

But Lyle doesn't answer. He's already picking up the phone to call the chief of forecast operations. A bulletin needs to be issued. Immediately. Warning of the high risk for extreme weather in Reeves County, Texas.

The Storm Prediction Center has issued similar "High Risk day" bulletins seven times in the past decade.

———————

THE RENTAL CAR won't be able to handle the unimproved roads they need to traverse in their final approach to the ranch, a fact made only more obvious by low storm clouds hurtling overhead and intermittent rain squalls. The old man called before they left El Paso and made arrangements with a former employee who could lend them the use of a John Deere Gator all-terrain utility vehicle. Stopping in front of the man's brick-and-wood ranch-style home outside Balmorhea, Hayley puts the rental car in park and turns off the ignition as Juan Lugo climbs out, carbine in hand. He walks to the Gator parked on the driveway and checks the contents of a gunnysack in the cargo bin. The utility vehicle's owner—a thin, wiry man of indeterminate age with a long beard and wild hair—steps out of the house and, without a word of greeting, tosses his former boss the keys. Hayley joins the old man in the Gator, her .45-caliber again riding comfortably in its holster.

Hunched against a now-drenching rain, Hayley buttons the freshly store-bought Levi's jacket to her neck. In her head, she works through an impromptu plan conceived during the ride east. Juan

Lugo stows the M1 carbine in the gap between the two, molded plastic seats. Within moments of arriving in the staid rental car, they're off and running in the feisty all-terrain vehicle.

A stiff wind blows, kicking up debris. Taking FM 3078 south, the two-lane farm-to-market road runs to the east of vast JW7 Ranch. Crossing the Woulfter Draw, the old man steers the Gator off the pavement two miles short of the gravel road that leads to the ranch's seldom-used east gate and continues west, across the desert and hidden from the view of roving security personnel. Though the all-terrain vehicle bounces over the rutted and rock-strewn open ground without a problem, Hayley is relieved when they transition to an actual packed-dirt road the width of a single car. The ex-foreman knows every path and roadway the ranch has to offer.

Though the rain has stopped for now, overall the weather has deteriorated. Worse is yet to come. Any water that has already fallen from the sky was absorbed by the parched earth.

Lugo registers Hayley's anxiety. Gesturing at the angry clouds swirling overhead, he says, *"Derecho."*

The word is new to her.

"Spanish for 'straight.' A straight-line windstorm. Very sudden. Widespread. Comes with tremendous winds. Torrential rain. Hail. And tornadoes." He points to what looks like a miles-long, towering black shelf in the sky to the west. *"Derecho."*

Hayley nods, no less determined than before. Relieved the old man is similarly undeterred. With the deeper state operative shielding her eyes against swirling particulates in the air, Lugo reaches into a door compartment and fishes out a pair of cheap, plastic goggles.

She is inclined to decline the gift but registers disapproval in his facial expression.

Slipping on the goggles brings immediate relief. Hayley glances toward the old man, who seems oblivious to the blast of sand and grit, imagining his eyes are made of dark, hard glass.

Ten minutes after following the single-track west, it peters out. The old man confidently steers the Gator over open ground until they come to a high game fence composed of high-tensile steel mesh. The gate is padlocked, and an abundance of overgrown weeds suggests infrequent use.

Juan Lugo climbs out and approaches the gate while Hayley slides over behind the wheel of the Gator. Once he has opened the padlock and swung the gate wide, she drives through as he closes it behind her. Hayley slides back over as the old man gets back behind the ATV's steering wheel.

"I'd asked the previous owner to install six additional access gates, in addition to the three on the paved roads leading onto the property. Didn't want to have to drive four miles in either direction if there was a good reason to get on the other side of the fence. I'm the only one who has a key. Woodside probably doesn't even know these extra gates exist."

Inside the ranch's perimeter, finally, the main residence is still three miles distant.

Lugo points to the northwest. "The main road, coming south from the interstate, is that way. They'll have that road guarded. Behind us, the road coming from the east? They'll be watching that one, too. We're due east of the house now. Between us and them is the hydrofracking well." Hayley nods. For the time being, she is only a passenger.

IF ANY STRUCTURE can withstand the damaging high winds brought on by a West Texas "high risk" storm, it's the main residence of the JW7 Ranch. Sturdy as a blockhouse, the thick, stone walls are impervious to the tempest's blast. But the roof's hold on the structure is less secure. Windows, too, seem of insufficient sturdiness. James Woodside has retired to his bedroom suite upstairs after an abbreviated meal, leaving the private security contractors to gather on the porch and bear witness to the weather's burgeoning fury.

Buffeted by the gusts, the men grip a handrail for support. Each man is armed with holstered pistols, slung long guns, or both. Their demeanor is relaxed. Miles from the closest public road and with both gates guarded, their biggest worry is the weather. The rumble of thunder gathers until it reaches a violent crescendo, a clattering noise that bounces across the surrounding hills.

One and all, the operators feel almost like young boys again.

"Jesus."

Wind swirls. Undulating clouds the color of bruised flesh threaten to funnel. Rain again begins to pelt the ground, kicking up minute explosions of mud.

"Anybody ever ride out a tornado before?"

None of the mercenaries seem particularly keen about the prospect, despite the great home's stone walls. These men have seen combat. All have killed other men in battle. They are familiar with the stink, sweat, and spurting blood of close-quarters combat. But this night of multiple storms is a different experience. A power over which they have no control has rattled them.

One beyond the reach of their weapons.

Craving the relative security of the indoors, they turn for the home's entrance. A much different rumbling noise from over the hills to the east stops them in their tracks.

"What the hell was that?"

The unit leader—known only as "Jones"—returns to the porch railing and peers in the direction where the rumble continues to echo.

"That's an explosion."

Another rolling thunder clap unravels overhead from the west. Are their senses deceiving them?

"I'm not sure," says one of the men. "Sounded just like thunder."

Another says, "The fucking wind playing tricks."

Jones looks like every other Special Forces veteran: ball cap, beard, athletic build. Intense. Survival doesn't happen by accident.

Preparation. Planning. Execution. The unit leader isn't only good. Jones excels in all aspects of security and military operations. Protecting James Woodside isn't ideological for him or any of the others.

Professional pride is at stake.

They don't even know about the cabal's agenda or planned secession from the United States. Would it make any difference to the operators if they did? Most likely not. None of the men are familiar with Woodside or his ambitions. They only know the man has a taste for young women. They may judge him for those proclivities but keep those thoughts to themselves.

After all, they're professionals.

Jones retrieves his cell phone and is relieved to see he has a signal, despite the foul weather. Whether thunder or explosion, he's unwilling to roll the dice. His lieutenant at the north gate answers after one ring.

"Leave two men there. The rest of you come to the main house." He disconnects the call and is turning to speak with the man standing next to him when the .30 carbine 110-grain full metal jacket round, traveling at slightly under 1,500 feet per second, strikes Jones in the side of his head, just above the right ear, and pulverizes much of the cranium. With kinetic energy to spare, the projectile ricochets off the vestiges of Jones's cranial plate and hits another mercenary in the neck and buries itself in his spine. The man is immediately paralyzed. Within minutes he will be dead.

A second shot and third shot from Juan Lugo's M1 carbine follow in rapid succession, each finding a target in the heads of a third and fourth security contractor. The old man has rarely let a week pass by since his days as a Marine sniper in Vietnam without a few hours on the range. He has never forgotten the words of the Rifleman's Creed and lives by them still.

My rifle is human, even as I, because it is my life.

Lugo's connection with his near-ancient carbine is real. Today it serves him—and Hayley Chill—as well can be expected, given the circumstances. Fourth, fifth, and sixth shots miss the two surviving mercenaries, who drop to the porch floor and push open the front door to reenter the residence.

In the few seconds of that journey from outside to inside the house, the surviving mercenaries comprehend some obvious facts. That they are under attack. That they were foolish to gather on the porch. Grouped together like idiots. These survivors of the initial surprise attack cling to the expectation of reinforcements their now-slain unit leader summoned from the main gate only moments earlier, unaware the explosion they all heard has released a fresh torrent across the private road from the gate. Those reinforcements will never come. They are also unaware, only for another moment longer, that a woman—with blond hair and powder blue eyes—stands over them now, War Hawk in hand. Waiting for them inside their false sanctuary.

"Don't move." Then, more emphatically, "Don't do it."

She holds her aim between them, finger off the trigger. Waiting for their reaction. What's it going to be? Smart or not?

The old man had provided her with the key and a detailed description of the house's layout. Basement door at the rear of the structure unlocked, Hayley had crept upstairs undetected and stayed out of sight until she heard the distant, wireless detonation of a single C-4 block provided to Lugo by his former ranch hand. After leaving the fence line and crossing rows of chaparral-covered hills, Hayley and the old man stopped at the hydrofracking water well site. Lugo set explosives at the wellhead and at the bases of twin mammoth galvanized steel water tanks holding a combined nine hundred thousand gallons of water. Between the sudden release from the destroyed tanks and ruptured wellhead, the water flooding the road below ensured no one would be accessing the ranch's main residence anytime soon. Once they arrived within a quarter mile of the big house, Lugo set up a sniper hide in the wooded hill above while Hayley approached from a seasonally dry creek bed to the rear. The old man remotely detonated the explosives only when he had a clear shot at the men gathered recklessly on the porch.

Having taken refuge inside the great house's entry hall, one of the two operators rolls at the sound of the female intruder's voice and brings his M16 around. Hayley shoots him in the top of his skull. The other man, lying on his Glock in a side holster, reaches for a backup gun barely visible under his right pant cuff.

"Are they paying you enough to die?" Hayley asks him, then puts another round into the chest of the first man. Making sure.

Making a point.

The second operator says nothing.

"You are *paid*, right? Do you even know what these people are trying to do?"

He is former Special Missions Unit, Delta Force. On Sundays, back home in Florida, he likes to golf with army buddies. Has an ex-wife and one current. His daughter starts at the University of Miami in the fall. A guilty pleasure is *The Masked Singer*. Moments before the diversionary explosion, the man was thinking about an omelet he had had for breakfast in Balmorhea. That it had been pretty damn good.

The mercenary decides he isn't being paid enough to die. Nope.

He slowly moves his hand as far away as possible from the gun strapped to his ankle.

Hayley says, "Good."

Juan Lugo enters through the front door, M1 carbine in hand and backpack strung over his shoulders. The storm's wind blast and a renewed torrential rain follows him inside, abated only by the old man closing the door behind him.

He exchanges a look with Hayley and then silently collects the weapons scattered on the floor.

"Roll over," he says to the sole surviving mercenary, retrieving the Glock and then the Sig P365 backup.

Working quickly—no doubt displaying skills acquired from a lifetime working on farms and ranches throughout the state—Lugo hog-ties the mercenary with rope from his backpack.

Hayley squats down beside the man.

"Is he armed?" she asks him.

The operator is merely glad to be alive. "Isn't everybody?"

Hayley nods, barely.

"Where?"

"Upstairs, last I knew. He could be in Timbuktu by now, for all I know."

She stands. Looks to the old man. His expression telegraphs sadness. An infinity of pain.

"You ready, sir?"

"Yes."

Leaving the mercenary tied up on the entry hall floor, Hayley and Juan Lugo turn and climb the staircase.

They find James Woodside in the master bedroom. The girl with black hair and dark eyes barely looks her fifteen years. They sit on the end of the king-size bed, facing the door. The revolver in his hand is ornate, almost ceremonial. His left arm is draped casually—proprietarily—around her shoulders.

Hayley looks to the old man, gauging his reaction to the sight before them.

Lugo is without words, tears filling his eyes.

The girl is crying as well.

She says, "Grandpa."

"Kimberly," says the old man.

Kimberly of the flyers. On leaflets left throughout El Paso. A motif of Hayley Chill's journey through the looking glass. Kimberly, the teenage runaway. Of navy UTEP hoodie. Possessing the kind of innocent, sweet beauty that is achingly tenuous and fragile. All there still. Almost intact. Under Woodside's arm, his pistol pointing at her gut.

Hayley recognized her almost immediately when reviewing photos she had found on Roy Pogue's phone. She has no idea how the CID agent came to have the photographs in his possession. Given the innate antagonism between a black man and someone trying to create an all-white nation, it's easy to comprehend why Pogue might gather *kompromat* on the FSA's presumptive president. The girl's haunting photograph on leaflets all over El Paso was an apparition that followed Hayley throughout her investigation. An obscene snapshot—of the teenager with Woodside—was the vital connection to Juan Lugo, who answered the phone when she called the number listed on the flyer in her car.

Without Lugo, Hayley would not be here. The truth within reach.

She says, "Let her go."

With these words, the deeper state operative takes aim on the ethmoid bone in Woodside's face.

From ten feet, she will not miss.

To everyone's surprise but his own, Woodside removes his left arm from the girl's shoulders and drops his right hand down so that the revolver is pointed at the floor.

"Of course."

The teenager stands and runs to her grandfather, folding into his embrace. As one, they turn and disappear out the door, trailed by the eruption of her sobs.

Hayley listens to their footsteps down the grand staircase just outside the master bedroom door. She has not moved the gun off target. Her finger remains on the trigger. Through the pretravel, to the wall.

"Drop the gun on the floor . . . *slowly*."

Woodside does as he's commanded, carefully bending over to place the pistol on the rug at the bed's foot.

Rain and wind crash against the six windows that line the two walls of the expansive bedroom. The storm outside rages. Another crash of thunder. A flash of lightning. Even more wind and rain.

Hayley recalls her last image of her father. Hanging by his neck from his bedroom door. Shirtless. An ignoble death.

James Woodside knows the why and what of Tommy Chill's death.

She has never been more confident of a hunch than this one.

He *knows*.

———————

HE WAS BORN and raised in West Texas, his father owning a ranch north of Big Spring where he bred quarter horses and black-and-white tobiano paint horses. Jim Woodside was a confident, happy-go-lucky child, sharing with his fun-loving mother a natural gift for singing. The family fortunes changed in an instant with the death of his younger brother, kicked in the head by a surly mare. Jim's mother took off for Florida six months later, and then it was just the two of them: a suddenly morose boy and his mostly silent father. Badgering his remaining son to help out with the livestock, Earl Woodside imagined they might still make a go of a diminished enterprise. To his eternal dismay, however, the boy never relinquished a dream of becoming a country western singer. Their battles were epic. Only with the onset of his father's stage four pancreatic cancer was James Woodside free to pursue his musical aspirations.

Unfortunately, with no more than a mediocre talent, the young man's artistic goals went unrealized. He spent many months as a vagabond and found mentorship with Carter Shaw, a white supremacist and ex-con who gave the nineteen-year-old a sense of belonging. Virulently racist, Shaw strove to indoctrinate Woodside with his beliefs. His charge, however, was more preoccupied with his unrequited desires for fame and fortune. The nineteen-year-old country crooner paid only lip service to the idolatry of hatred. It was that diffidence—and an opportune flu bug—that kept the future congressman from joining his mentor and two friends in the "lynching-by-dragging" murder of a local black man.

But the die was cast. James Woodside joined the military and excelled, ultimately applying for Officer Candidate School and attaining the rank of major in Iraq, enduringly cognizant of the energizing and dynamic power of a racist message.

———————

WOODSIDE ASKS, "WHO are you?"

The silence between them lasted only a few moments, but Hayley felt as if an eternity had passed. Juan Lugo will return. For unfinished business. She doesn't have much time.

"I'm Hayley Chill. My father was Thomas Chill. He lived for the last fifteen years of his life, give or take, as Charles Hicks, working as a civilian in the Pentagon. Before that, he was a Marine with two tours in Iraq. You're going to tell me what happened to my dad. And you're going to stop whatever it is your group has planned here, in the Permian."

If Woodside is surprised by any part of Hayley's statement, he doesn't betray it. He is utterly calm and composed, having the attitude of a man who has accomplished his ultimate goals.

"There's no stopping it. The machine is in motion, designed to operate autonomously. Killing me will not affect the outcome."

"Well, I guess we'll see about that." She bends down to retrieve his revolver from the floor. Stands erect again. "And my father? You knew him."

Woodside says, "Tommy was my friend. Saved my life, in fact. It was on our first deployment, the invasion of Iraq in 2003. We had taken Baghdad, the Army's Third Infantry and us. Five days after entering the city, there was a rumor that Saddam Hussein and his top aides were holed up in a mosque in the Al Az'Amiyah District. Three companies went in. All came under heavy fire. Rocket-propelled grenades, mortars, and assault rifles. One of our guys killed. Twenty wounded. Never found Saddam anywhere. Tommy pushed me behind a wall and fell on top of me when an RPG nearly took off the back of my skull. The blast did a number on both of us, but we were good to go after a few minutes. Your dad was a good Marine. Anybody over there would say that."

Hayley hears this with a placid expression. She hasn't chased Woodside through hell for war stories. "What happened over there? What *really* happened?"

Woodside stares at her, mute.

She asks, "How was he part of this? My father was no racist."

"No, Tommy wasn't a racist. But he came to understand what his government had done to him. How it used him. Used all of us. He and Charlie wanted to do something about it."

Charlie Hicks.

Hayley's last vestiges of hope begin to crumble away. Her father died a traitor to the country she loves. He betrayed every ideal she holds dear.

Oh God, did dad kill a fellow Marine?

"Why . . . why did he take Charles Hicks's identity? Why abandon his family?"

Woodside's face registers his surprise.

"You don't know . . ."

"I don't know what?"

He sighs, the awareness of his imminent, glorious demise settling on him like a warm blanket. The congressman from Texas will always be remembered as the founding father of a new and prosperous nation.

As George Washington's name is for the ages, so will be the name James Earl Woodside.

"Tommy backed out. Charlie, too. Once they understood. When they saw how far we wanted to take this. After we folded in the fellows with white nationalist agendas. Tommy and Charlie wanted no part of the Storm or its goals after that. Of seceding from the United States. But they knew too much by that point. They were too involved. Others in our movement wanted them dead, a trivial matter in the theater of war. We eliminated many of our adversaries in a similar fashion. KIA, as it were. But I owed your father my life. I considered him a friend."

Juan Lugo appears in the doorway behind Hayley. Alone. She feels his presence there. Waiting. Woodside sees him, too, of course.

Her prayers have been answered. Too soon, though, to process it all. Not yet. But her relief is apparent.

"My father didn't abandon his family. He *saved* us."

James Woodside says nothing. His silence is answer enough.

Lugo takes a step forward. He draws a hunting knife—the four-inch blade of Damascus steel—from a sheath on his leather belt.

The deeper state operative holds out her hand, not finished with Woodside. Something she can't understand.

"He came west. To Texas."

"Tommy sniffed out our plans. Like you, on his fishing expedition. Putting his nose where it didn't belong. I couldn't protect him any longer. After that point, no one could've helped Tommy."

She understands now. What she had always desired is now hers. The truth.

"He didn't kill himself?"

The possibility reverberates from the soles of her feet to the top of her skull. Becomes conviction.

He didn't kill himself.

Woodside's eyes leave Hayley and shifts to the old man standing next to her. Of grave expression. He with the remorseless gaze. A dire wolf.

"Hello, Juan. It's good to see you again, my friend."

"Who?" Hayley asks Woodside. "Who did you send?"

He moves his gaze off the old man and back on her. As if describing the weather. Or a particularly ordinary day on the golf course.

"For Tommy? One of my best men. Obedient. Loyal. You'll never find him." The congressman considers leaving it at that, but arrogance gets the better of him. A supreme faith in his chosen apostles. "Oswald. So extraordinarily ordinary. Has that elusive quality. Like smoke."

Hayley stands still for another moment, the scene too difficult to break in its perfect, triangulating symmetry.

Then she steps backward, turns, and walks out of the room. Leaving fury to do its work.

———

KIMBERLY IS WAITING for Hayley in the library. Though the worst of the storm has passed to the northeast, strong winds and rain continue to pound the windows. Lamps with dark, heavy shades cast the room in a masculine gloom.

The teenager seems to be okay. Eyes are red from crying, and her hair is a mess. But Kimberly Chacon is a strong, young woman who was pulled into the unyielding darkness . . . and survived.

Hayley stops in the open doorway, glancing back over her shoulder to the one surviving mercenary who lies tied up at the foot of the staircase. He remains securely immobilized. But God only knows what noises will descend from the upstairs bedroom in the next seconds.

Not the soundtrack a teenage girl needs to carry with her through the rest of her life.

Hayley gestures to Kimberly.

"We should wait outside."

But the teenager remains rooted in place, staring at an artifact hanging on the wall. Hayley enters the room and joins Kimberly in front of what she can see now is a historical document framed and under protective glass.

Within a few seconds, Hayley comprehends that she is looking at an original manuscript of the Declaration of Independence by the Republic of Texas, signed in 1836.

"This," says the girl. "You want this."

Hayley is puzzled, not understanding why Kimberly has brought the artifact to her attention. But then she recalls seeing the same document, cheaply self-published and of recent vintage in the trailer at the New Mexico compound.

And she gets it.

Retrieving her phone, the deeper state operative snaps three photographs of the framed document. Satisfied she has captured every word, Hayley puts her hand lightly on the girl's arm.

"Let's go."

11

ATOMIC DEMOLITION

Juan Lugo maneuvers the Gator across a black landscape. Time has lost meaning except for the most fundamental evidence of night. All three on board are soaked and cold, the wind-driven rain blowing nonstop during their traverse of the West Texas ranch. Hayley took the narrow back seat—if that's what it can be called—so the girl could sit next to her grandfather.

From her vantage point in the back, she watches the interplay of glances between Kimberly Chacon and the old man.

Words that go unspoken. Of bottomless pain. And relief.

Emotions rise within Hayley as well. Too soon to comprehend all that has happened. How her world shifted again. All that James Woodside said. Those revelations will take time to parse fully. What impacts now are the foundational realizations. That her father wasn't part of a white nationalist movement. He didn't desert his family, but rather stayed away to protect them. And, the biggest shock, Tommy Chill didn't hang himself.

Her father was murdered.

The same organization that killed him survives Woodside's demise.

And Hayley intends to destroy it. How isn't clear.

Lowering her gaze, she sees the old man holding Kimberly's hand in his. A small gesture that is nevertheless profoundly moving. What is the familial bond if not the strongest connection between two people? Hayley remembers with a start that a human life exists within her, intrinsically of her blood. She tries to imagine herself as a mother, and fails. That adventure awaits. The anticipation of it, however, brings a new emotion.

One that Hayley hasn't experienced in what feels like a thousand yesterdays.

She feels joy.

Hunched over and arms locked around herself for warmth—the all-terrain Gator bouncing over the roadless, barren expanse of the JW7 Ranch—Hayley recognizes her elation as if an old friend had entered the room. Rain-lashed and cold, she is happy nonetheless. The deeper state operative thinks of April Wu and envisions announcing news of her decision next time she sees her friend. Anticipating April's inevitable and sardonic teasing, Hayley hopes the moment comes soon. The thought of it brings another smile to her face.

———————

THE LANKY RANCH hand steps outside the door as the Gator pulls into the gravel driveway. Seeing Kimberly in the front seat, he nods and raises his fist in acknowledgment of the old man's success. Climbing out of the ATV, Hayley checks her watch. It's a few minutes before midnight. The worst of high winds have moved north, but squall lines continue to release scattered, violent downbursts over the entire Permian Basin.

No one is doing anything in the region tonight but seeking shelter.

Lugo guides his granddaughter toward the house. Hayley hangs back. Her rental car is parked at the curb.

"Got a trailer round back. You're welcome to it." The ranch hand, cigarette dangling from his lips, gestures toward the door. "Dryer for your clothes. Wife can fix you up with something to wear in the meanwhile. Got a pot of stew on the stove, too."

The old man has walked Kimberly inside the modest, brick home. Lights glow warmly within. The road behind her, alternatively, is wet, windswept, and dark.

Hayley nods, grateful for the kindness.

"Okay," she says. "Thank you."

———————

LATER, AFTER EATING her fill and retrieving her clothes from the dryer, Hayley lies on the platform bed inside the backyard trailer. The metallic ping of hail on the roof convinces her that she made the right call. Her natural inclination is to press forward. To never relent. But for this last part of her mission, she needs to prepare herself. Rest and recharge. The framed document on Woodside's library wall is the cipher's code, used to communicate orders to the secessionists' operational cells. She's sure of this. Deciphering the coded document, recovered from under the floorboards of her father's kitchen, will be her first task in the morning.

Before that, however, Hayley needs to sleep.

———————

AT DAWN, HER tenth day in West Texas, the sky is low and the color of lead when the deeper state operative pulls away from the curb. A truck stop off the highway on the outskirts of town is open, of course, and she takes a booth in the back of the restaurant. A desultory waitress pours indifferent coffee into a barely clean mug.

Hayley, who couldn't care less about the café's offerings, sets to work.

The Declaration of Independence by the Republic of Texas, signed in 1836, is the cipher's key. Utilizing her host's printer the night before, she generated paper copies of the digital photos she had taken in Woodside's library and numbered every word in the 1,249-word declaration. With her pencil poised over a legal pad, Hayley begins to decode the encrypted document she had removed from under her dad's kitchen floor. The first number in the dizzying rows of seemingly random numbers is 272. Hayley counts the words in the Republic of Texas's Declaration of Independence and determines that "political" is number 272. The first letter of the secret message is "P."

Assigning an alphabetic value to each number in the encrypted document is laborious, but the encrypted document's contents begin to take shape.

What her father managed to obtain on his trips out west was the secessionists' battle plan. Hayley has already uncovered many of these strategic objectives in her relentless investigation. But within the encrypted document that Tommy Chill acquired is a more detailed description of something called "Project Ace In The Hole." With a second and third full reading of the encrypted document, Hayley now understands the movement of National Guard and US Army troops and equipment into the Permian Basin is the lesser half of the secessionists' mission equation.

Project Ace In The Hole is what will make a break from the United States stick.

THE MAIN THOROUGHFARE through Monahans isn't exactly Times Square. Not at seven a.m., and Pete Oswald guesses probably not at midday or five p.m., either. Just off the interstate, halfway between

Odessa and Pecos, the town of seven thousand souls appears beaten down by the pandemic and subsequent collapse in oil prices. As Oswald drives down Sealy Avenue, the main drag through town, and passes by a string of brick, one-story commercial buildings, he counts more vacancies than on-going businesses.

With more than a passing interest in history, Oswald knows that the Spanish explorer Antonio de Espejo "discovered" the region on his way to present-day New Mexico. The historical record suggests further exploration of Los Médanos (the sand dunes) outside of town in the 1770s. The Texas and Pacific Railroad brought limited development to the region in 1881, but it was John Thomas Monahan who dug a water well that produced an abundance of good water and created the justification for a city at this location. Adios, Comanches and Lipan Apaches. Howdy, small-plot farmers and ranchers. The discovery of oil changed all of that, too. The wheel turns and turns as it continues to turn today.

Unofficially, Monahans is "The Center of the Permian Basin," and for that reason Oswald selects the town for his initial hideout. In the first minutes after leaving the JW7 Ranch the previous evening—wind and rain flooding low-lying portions of the roadway and dropping power lines by the dozens—he worries the weight of responsibility delegated to him by James Woodside might be too great a burden. *Everything* depends on the viability of Project Ace In The Hole. Like others in the movement, he had worried all along that despite the presence of the First Armored Division and the elements of the Texas Army National Guard's Thirty-Sixth Infantry Division, the full brunt of the US military would push the insurrectionists out of the Permian Basin and end their dreams of seccession from the United States.

Project Ace In The Hole levels the playing field. The eighty-pound device in the trunk of Oswald's car effectively places the Free States of America in the rarified league of nuclear powers. Washington will have no alternative but to reach a peace accord with the insurrectionists under threat of a bomb explosion that would kill almost ten thousand people in an instant and leave ten times that number with potentially fatal radioactive poisoning. As was the case with the Chernobyl disaster and its Exclusion Zone, the region for twenty miles in every direction would be rendered uninhabitable for hundreds of years. The nation's capacity to produce oil would be severely impacted, and its economy wrecked for generations. Every component of the insurrectionists' strategy to successfully break away from the Union depends on a sustained nuclear threat. By taking possession of the vast oil resources of the region, the Free States of America will inherit the world's most valuable bargaining chip.

If the United States wants another drop of Permian oil—currently representing 95 percent of its oil reserves—it will have to sign whatever peace agreement the FSA puts in front of Congress.

And he, Pete Oswald, is responsible for the safekeeping of this all-important fail-safe device. He must remain autonomous. Anonymous. Always on the move. Untouchable. Most important, his orders are to remain ready, willing, and able to detonate the device if ordered to do so. Are there others like him, in charge of other bombs? Oswald has no idea. His instructions are to disappear somewhere in the dozens of towns or midsize cities in the region, telling absolutely no one his precise location. And to keep moving.

He picked up the device late last night, meeting a group of uniformed soldiers in the parking lot of a United supermarket on Eighth Street in Odessa. Oswald was shocked by the nuclear weapon's compact size. Based on the W54 Special Atomic Demolition Munition developed by Los Alamos Scientific Laboratory in the 1950s, the sturdy ruck contains awe-inspiring destructive power. Research and deployment of SADM weapons was *officially* discontinued by the United States in the 1960s. However, anyone with a healthy dose of skepticism would assume all superpowers continued development of these tactical, man-delivered nukes.

He guesses that the weapon's latest incarnation stowed in his car trunk is much more powerful than its predecessor.

The soldiers provided detailed instructions on the operation and maintenance of the nuclear device, and a cell phone. They instructed Oswald to carry the phone on his person at all times and at all costs. If it ever rings, a voice on the other end will order him to detonate the bomb immediately. There will be no second call. His directions are clear. Will he be willing to vaporize thousands of human beings? Oswald has nothing but complete confidence in his ability to do the right thing. The threat isn't real without a total commitment.

Pulling into the parking lot of a derelict motel a few miles east of town, he wonders how the Morale Operations Branch's work is getting on. If not for this new assignment, Oswald would be in Midland at this very minute, as soldiers from Fort Bliss disembark from civilian passenger trains. Under the supervision of the MOB, their commanding officers will issue new orders that may require the soldiers to wage combat with other US military forces. The troops undoubtedly will be confused. Their bewilderment is understandable. But they are soldiers. They will obey their superiors. Gradually these dedicated military men and women will come to appreciate the merits of citizenship in a *new* country. Nonwhite personnel will be shifted east or to the west. Gradually. Safely. All of this will take time.

Parking in the debris-strewn lot of the abandoned motel—the Sunset Motel, according to the decaying and rusting roadside sign—Oswald feels a swelling within him. Of pride. Accomplishment. Of being part of something big.

One thousand suns.

That will be the message. His orders to detonate. He will do his duty. He has zero qualms about causing the deaths of so many people, including his own.

Pete Oswald will only be following orders.

Sitting in the back booth of the truck stop café and brooding on the contents of the newly unencrypted document, Hayley recognizes the *real* strategy of the secessionists: the army and National Guard troops, with their hardware and equipment, are in place to protect the nuclear device and its human handler, not the other way around. The bomb truly is an ace in the hole. A compact nuclear device in the possession of a committed human carrier creates a weapon that is far more intelligent than any computer-laden "smart bomb." Ingenious, really. The device's handler can adapt to a rapidly changing situation, problem-solve with intuition that a machine doesn't possess.

How much of this new information should she tell Andrew Wilde? Is there time for Publius to provide meaningful assistance? When will the secessionists announce their intentions to the entire world? How will Washington react? These questions might normally plague Hayley Chill. Give her pause from taking immediate action.

But the revelations concerning her father—his sacrifice for family and country—have had an odd, calming effect on Hayley.

Only she can stop the insurrection at its birth. Having worked her way through the cabal's levels of authority, she has full comprehension of the conspiracy's inner workings from top to bottom. And she is already on the ground. But the deeper state operative must act quickly, before all components of the secessionists' battle plan are in place.

Hayley has no idea how she will stop the Storm conspirators. She doesn't know where to begin her search for the bomb's handler. Nor does she have any idea what to do if she finds him. Or even if a man is indeed her target.

The only thing Hayley knows for sure in these early moments of contrasting emotions—determination and bewilderment—is an immediate recognition of the customer who enters the truck stop café at this precise moment.

A familiarity that brings her some relief.

She is not alone after all.

"SOMETHING OF A habit, then," says Gibbs, having spied her in the back booth upon entering the almost-deserted café and turning to saunter in her direction. He stops a yard or two short, hesitant to loom over her. A tall man's inclination. "Meeting in roadside spots, I mean."

"Deputy," she says, by way of hello.

For a brief moment, neither knows what to say and for entirely different reasons. Hayley is busily calculating the deputy's usefulness to her cause. Whether she can trust him. And how far. Gibbs's excuse is less strategic. He's merely tongue-tied.

"Sit down, Deputy Gibbs. Join me."

Of course she remembers his name. Not only does she possess an eidetic memory, but the deeper state operative also holds a fondness for Jay Gibbs, one that she valiantly keeps at arm's length.

The window next to the booth wobbles with wind gusts, the unstable weather pattern having stalled over the region. Sporadic raindrops splatter across the broken macadam parking lot, fissures in its surface flowing with oily water. Though the sun rose thirty minutes ago, the light is murky. Profane. The perfect weather for civil war.

"I'm just getting a coffee for the road. All hell's breakin' lose."

"Something about the JW7 Ranch?"

Gibbs gives her a queer look. "Among other things."

"Sit down, Deputy. I promise, you'll be glad you did."

He takes a seat. The same tired waitress appears, as if by magic, with coffee.

"Eating, Jay?"

The sheriff's deputy shakes his head. "Thanks, Janice. Just coffee."

Once the waitress clears off, he levels Hayley with a flat look.

"What do you know about the Woodside place?"

"The ranch is the least of your problems today, Deputy."

"I'd like to know what sorta problem you're gonna be, Ms. Chill."

"I'm an operative for an organization you've never heard of, Deputy Gibbs. You will never hear its name, in public or private, because it doesn't have one. We're good guys, though. You have my word about that."

He pulls at his chin and glances out the window to his left, debating whether or not her "word" is worth more than the tepid coffee in his mug. With short consideration, Gibbs decides the blond woman with the powder blue eyes is probably more trustworthy than just about anyone he has encountered in his thirty-two years.

Instinct tells him as much. A feeling that rings true.

"What? Like some 'deep state' sorta thing?"

"Deeper than that." She offers the barest of grins, one that's returned by the Reeves County sheriff's deputy.

"What the hell's going on? I've got a buddy up in Ector County. He says there are two trains stopped in Midland carrying all kinds of military hardware outta Fort Bliss. Troops arriving, too. Who's invadin' who is what I wanna know."

Hayley tells him as much as she thinks he can absorb in one sitting.

Gibbs listens, rarely asking a question for clarification. The deeper state operative has a knack for concise and clear expression. She speaks for several minutes, the wind and rain outside lending the appropriate mood. Other customers come and go, served with minimum hospitality by the long-suffering truck stop waitress with an asphalt heart. Hayley's tale doesn't stint on violence or drama. The picture she paints for him is factually dire.

Details of Project Ace In The Hole are the most difficult for Gibbs to hear. Of course, invasion and occupation by outsiders of a land where he was born does not sit well. But taking its inhabitants—family, friends, and neighbors—hostage with the threat of nuclear obliteration brings his simmering rage to a boil.

Jay Gibbs is Permian proud.

Reeves. Pecos. Brewster. Ward and Winkler. Crane. Upton.

Midland and Ector. These West Texas counties are as different from Travis County, the state's seat of government, as any place possibly can be.

Hell, Austin might as well be in Suffolk County. Or Sonoma.

Hayley clocks the brooding rage behind his silence after she finishes talking.

"We can still beat them, Deputy. Stop this business before it gets started. There's still time," she tells him.

But Gibbs needs no bucking up.

"They won't win. Not here. Not on land my family has lived and died on for five generations."

"Good. Yes."

The sheriff's deputy clenches his hands, emotions getting the better of him.

"I didn't go over to Iraq—watch buddies die—white, black, brown . . ." His voice tremors. Gibbs pauses, regrouping. Steadier now, he continues, "Maimed for life, so that these sonsabitches could tear my country apart. No. Not while I still draw a breath."

Hayley says, "We need everyone to be looking for this guy. Without the threat of this nuke—"

"And we sure there's just one?"

"According to the encrypted document I read, yes, just a single device."

"One document."

"It's all we've got to go by now, Deputy."

Gibbs nods.

"I can call a few buddies I have in some of these counties. Other deputies. Keep it on the down-low."

"The sheriffs might be part of all of this. Some of your buddies, too."

"Not these boys. They'll reach out to other deputies. Only the good ones."

"Okay. Tell them to look for any strangers who seem to be loitering in the area for no particular reason. Our target may be military but out of uniform. The idea is to blend in."

"Not easily done in the small towns out here. Midland and Odessa is another matter. What else do you know about their plan? Who exactly are we looking for? 'A stranger' is not a lot to go on."

Hayley shakes her head.

"We don't have a description. Accept it. But as an alternative, we can try to locate our suspect from the perspective of their agenda. That much we *do* know."

But she's lost Gibbs, who remains silent.

Hayley says, "I don't think they're targeting people specifically. As collateral damage, yes, but I think the actual hostage is infrastructure. The Permian Basin surpassed Saudi Arabia's Ghawar field as the world's highest oil supplier. Before the pandemic, it was producing almost six million barrels a day. That's nearly half of the country's total crude output. The radioactive fallout from a nuclear device—even a small tactical weapon similar to a SADM—would render a huge portion of the basin's oil infrastructure unusable for centuries."

"SADM?" asks the deputy.

"Special Atomic Demolition Munition. Backpack nukes. In the fifties and sixties, the US and USSR developed and produced hundreds of them. They were eventually phased out, but it's common knowledge that our military and Russia's continued development of these evil, little bastards. My guess is sympathizers in the US Army managed to provide the secessionists with one from their secure stockpile."

"Okay. So, what're you saying?"

"Where would a bomb this size cause the most damage?"

"The Permian is tens of thousands of square miles in size. Different oil fields, from the Val Verde Basin to the Matador Arch up north. Take a thousand backpack nukes to shut down the whole thing."

The sheriff's deputy makes a valid point. Hayley realizes the bomb is a symbolic threat. While capable of killing thousands of innocent people and destroying several dozen square miles of infrastructure, the intimidation is emblematic. Classic terrorism.

"What is the center of the Permian?"

Gibbs doesn't even have to think about it. "Monahans."

"Monahans?" Hayley has never heard of the place.

"Between Pecos and Odessa. Little town of six thousand." He laughs, without mirth. "I mean, literally calls itself 'The Center of the Permian Basin.'"

As THEY WALK toward his prowler, he asks, "You carrying?"

Hayley nods. "That a problem?"

Before climbing in behind the wheel, Gibbs removes the straw Resistol his father had gifted him two short years before dying. Lung cancer. At the Reeves County Hospital in Pecos. "Be a bigger problem if you weren't."

THE PRAIRIE ON either side of Texas State Highway 17 is a tabletop of wind-twisted pappusgrass and churning pumpjacks. Wipers work at a furious pace to maintain visibility through the rain-spattered windshield. Despite somewhat cooler temperatures, the SUV's air conditioner heaves at full blast; cracking a window for circulation would leave the vehicle's back seat drenched in minutes.

Gibbs uses his personal phone to call his contacts with sheriff's departments in the neighboring counties. As he calmly and matter-of-factly relates the shocking facts of the situation to his fellow law enforcement officers, Hayley quietly listens. With these precious minutes—Monahans is an hour's drive north and northeast—she reflects on the good fortune of meeting the sheriff's deputy five days earlier at the Tex-Mex joint in Sierra Blanca. His assistance in these crucial hours will be invaluable.

But more than his help, Hayley appreciates the temporary partnership. The company.

Her life as a deeper state operative is, by definition, a solitary one. In the vast emptiness of the Texas grasslands, under a black, thunderous sky, Hayley experiences an aching need for human connection.

In Jay Gibbs she could not have found a companion more trustworthy. More essentially competent. No one is perfect, but the sheriff's deputy has lived—in the balance—a life of grace and honesty.

Violence is sure to come. In the quiet prelude before an inevitable fight, Hayley takes comfort in the deputy's low voice, a murmuring song without melody. The future is dire.

For a moment, why not breathe? Why not feel alive?

———————

No ONE NOTICES the rental car parked in the abandoned motel's lot, partially obscured as it is from the road by overgrown weeds and the untended shrubs that front the roadway. Oswald checks the time and sees it's a few minutes past eight. Stomach growling, he thinks about breakfast. What is he supposed to do with the nuclear device if he wants something to eat? A decent hot breakfast? Does he leave the thing in his trunk while he stops in a café for thirty minutes? Or does he bring the bomb in and place it on the seat next to him?

Massaging these anxieties in his head, Oswald recalls images and tales of the military aides who carry the nuclear "football" whenever the US president leaves fixed command centers. In those instances, of course, the briefcase contains the authentication codes necessary to launch a nuclear attack, not an actual *nuke*. His role for the Storm is much weightier.

Cool, ain't it?

Despite these ego-boosting thoughts, he remains hungry. Starving, in fact. With the bad weather and last-minute summons to the ranch the previous night, Oswald failed to eat dinner. He realizes with a shock that it has been almost twenty hours since his last meal. And that was only a convenience-store burrito.

Oswald appreciates the strategy of a lone and anonymous carrier, a job tailor-made for a man of his extraordinary ordinariness. No sense drawing attention to the device with an SUV jammed with SOF types.

Ball caps and scruffy beards the dead giveaway, a neon sign that spells out "S P E C I A L O P S!!!!"

But only now, in the deepening gloom of this rainy, forlorn morning, does Ace In The Hole's practical drawbacks sink in. His isolation and vulnerability, not to mention the impracticalities. Is he supposed to bring the damn thing into a gas station bathroom with him?

That's one thing you never see in the movies, he muses. *When the good guy has to take a dump.*

Oswald wishes he could get some advice and further clarification of his orders. The problem is, however, he doesn't know who to contact. General Killebrew was his only superior whose identity had been revealed to him, and he's dead. From its founding, the Storm existed as an amalgamation of distinct, operational cells. Oswald never even knew the other captains' names and was never provided with their contact information. James Woodside is their spiritual leader and founder, but not an operations guy. All tactical information flowed through the recently deceased army general.

Oswald was told they would track him with the burner phone's geolocation. In other words, "don't call us, we'll call you." There is no exact time frame for the mission. Only after the higher-ups—presumably Killebrew's staff officers and Woodside—decide the FSA is secure from invasion by the United States will his mission be completed. Only then will Pete Oswald be able to come in from the cold.

But in the meantime, he wants breakfast!

In the past hour, Oswald has watched three military convoys pass his location, two heading east toward Midland/Odessa and the other west, toward Pecos. Light-armored Humvees jammed with soldiers. Gun trucks. Big M35 2 ½-ton cargo trucks. Even some M2 and M3 Bradleys. So the troops have been deployed. Oswald imagines their confusion. What the hell are they still doing in West Texas? They're supposed to be on their way to Europe. No doubt, it will take time to process this new, truly bizarre reality. Their commanders won't reveal the full scope of the operation immediately. Not for a day or two, at least. As a key member of the Morale Operations Branch, Oswald is privy to the propaganda techniques to be employed on military personnel. Dissenters can leave at any time. He knows most will elect to stay with their respective units. Such is the way of soldiers. They are loyal to their fellow warriors. Not to a flag. To a piece of paper.

The birth of a nation takes time. The bomb inside his rental car's trunk is a guarantee of having the time needed to finish the job.

Oswald sees confusion on the faces of the troops, a bewilderment that is exceeded by that of civilians stopping to watch the passing parade of military vehicles.

What in hell must they be thinking?

He knows enough of the overall plan to understand the cabal's military commanders are positioning soldiers and their equipment in anticipation of the historic announcement. The elements need to be in place before leaders in Washington can be made fully aware of what has befallen the United States: 20 percent of its oil production capabilities has been taken from its possession and returned to its rightful owners.

That they have a new border and powerful, new neighbor.

Mission accomplished. And all before the majority of the US population even knows the Free States of America exists.

A few hours yet. By noon, at the latest. It won't be long before the Pentagon and other brass hats inside the Beltway comprehend that something has gone seriously sideways with the First Armored Division. And the Texas Army National Guard. *And* an entire fighter squadron from the Forty-Ninth Tactical Fighter Wing at Holloman. No doubt, desk jockeys and paper pushers in Arlington are scrambling right now, trying to get in touch with the missing units—the very people who have risen against them—only to have those phone calls go unanswered.

All of that will soon change. Washington will hear from Texas soon enough.

———————

THEY TRANSITIONED FROM the state highway to Interstate 20 ten minutes ago and now speed toward Monahans in silence. Gibbs has finished reaching out to his fellow sheriff's deputies in Reeves and other surrounding counties. Those brief conversations were problematic, staccato outbursts filled with profanities and alarmed questioning. Understandably, local authorities are bewildered by the abrupt appearance of military units in the region. Answers are not available, certainly not in these early hours. No one seems to know what's going on, including the few "invading" soldiers willing to talk. A wary stand-off is the result, with one side being substantially better armed than the other.

The landscape outside her window is flat and monotonous, with no landmarks to catch one's gaze. Her thoughts drift. Hayley imagines herself as an android. Engineered. Capable. Task oriented. Devoid of emotions. Data is received from sensory inputs and fed into a central-processing unit. Action results. How much more manageable that existence would be. So effortlessly simple. Whereas only hours earlier she relished the prospect of motherhood, the deeper state operative now combats a gnawing insecurity. How can she ever expect to be a mother? A day after graduating from high school, Hayley fled her family home—dysfunctional and rudderless—for a new life in the military. She was the oldest of six kids. Her mother, crippled by physical and mental illness, did almost nothing to raise a brood that had already lost its father. Guilt for abandoning her younger siblings is a daily sucker punch to Hayley's gut.

This eternal conflict between a regular life and the one she has chosen is a torment. She glances to her left, at Jay Gibbs. Like Sam McGovern in some ways. But different in so many others. Hayley watches him, the muscles that ripple across his face, and feels that undeniable buzz.

I guess I have a type.

The sheriff's deputy, of course, feels her eyes on him.

He asks, "You okay?"

"Yeah. You?"

Gibbs nods. Keeps his eyes forward. They'd passed two convoys of military vehicles and troops heading in the opposite direction, back toward Pecos. His anger is brewing, and he must focus on keeping it in check.

They each fall back into a brief silence. Concentrating on what lies ahead.

Hayley feels the War Hawk snug in its holster at her waist. On the opposite side, she wears a double mag pouch lent to her by Gibbs. He gave her the extra magazines and ammo, too. Besides the Glock 9 millimeter he carries in his service holster, the sheriff deputy is banking on the department-issued, short-loaded M4 rifle fitted with an Aimpoint sight and SureFire X300U Weapon Light.

If it comes to all that.

"We find this guy, do you make a call?" he asks. "Blackhawk swoops in and a half dozen dopes on ropes slide down to make things right?"

Hayley shakes her head. "Going to be just us. Were you hoping I could make a call like that?"

"Not really. Rather punch this fella in the face all by myself."

She smiles.

"Hope you get the chance, Deputy."

Gibbs scratches his chin and squints into a nonexistent sun.

"Well, I guess this is the time when I'm supposed to tell you some story from my childhood. How my old man used to beat my ass for dropping the pigskin in the big game. Or the time I fell in love with The Wrong Woman."

"Did you drop the pigskin in the big game?"

"Hell no. More of a baseball guy, anyways."

"And bad love? You make that up, too?"

He grins, sliding a glance her way. "The frustrated novelist in me."

"You can share a story with me, Deputy. Something real. Made-up. I don't mind either way. I'm not much of a storyteller myself, but I enjoy hearing them."

"Kinda putting me on the spot here. . . ."

"You 'kinda' put yourself on the spot," says Hayley.

"All right, lemme think a minute."

"We don't have a lot of time, cowboy."

"Think I got a good one. Sure."

Winds shove the SUV. Clouds scuttle low on the horizon. She sits up straighter. "I'm ready."

As suddenly as it began, the rain stops.

"Well, I was a senior in high school. Back in Pecos. It was spring, and we just had nothin' to worry about, know what I mean? Me and my buddy, Wes, were just kickin' back, me, him, and his girlfriend, Sasha. Drinking beers. Switching to whiskey when the mood strikes. Yeah, pretty lit. Gets late. We're maybe a little bored. So we decide to drive down to Toyahvale for a midnight swim. Spring-fed pool they got down there, at Balmorhea State Park."

"I've seen it, under different circumstances."

"Yeah, well, that time of night it's closed, of course. And surrounded by a ten-foot-high chain-link fence. Now, climbin' it isn't a problem. Not for three teenagers, no matter how drunk. Doesn't even seem sportin'. At the time, that is."

"So you . . . ?"

"You gonna let me tell the story or what?"

Hayley nods. Waits.

"So I announce that I can climb the fence with my hands tied behind my back. In fact, I bet Wes that I can accomplish such a feat. A hundred bucks, I bet him."

"You really were drunk."

"I really was. And, ya know, I thought I could really do it. With that vainglorious confidence that only the young possess, I believed my Justin boots and sheer bravado would help propel me up that fence. That determination and copious amounts of Jack Daniel's would bestow on me the power of flight. Magical thinking, maybe. But sometimes you gotta believe, right? That the impossible is within reach."

He's got her now. She is listening. Anticipating what's next to come.

"Wes tied my hands behind my back with my belt. I'm shirtless, okay? And just ripped. In the best shape of my life. A feral prince, wearin' nothing but cowboy boots and ragged-ass pair of jeans. Sasha watchin' my every move. Slack jawed. Like, did I *really* think I could do such a thing. Wes smirkin'. Counting down the seconds until I failed."

Gibbs looks toward Hayley as he drives. His eyes blaze. As if he is that teenage kid again. The feral prince. Willing himself up a ten-foot fence with his hands tied behind his back. With nothing but his boots. And a whole lot of gumption.

"So I go at it. With full commitment. I'm going to do this thing. First try, I get no higher than a foot or two before falling back down on my ass. Second try, no higher than that, and I fall on my ass again. Hard. Can't break my fall. Because my hands are tied behind my back, remember? Now I'm mad. Angry. At the fence. That thing determined to deny me."

Hayley waits.

The deputy says, "Wes is laughing his ass off. Countin' the money before it's in his pocket. Ribbing Sasha in the side with his elbow and pointing at me. But she's not laughing. I don't dare look at her but can just feel it. Her willing me up. Forward. Over the fence. Wanting to see something."

Yes. See something special.

Hayley can imagine the girl. Desiring to bear witness of magic in an otherwise drab universe.

"I struggle to get standin' again. Ass sore from fallin'. Fence still ten feet tall. And I go at it. Jammin' the toes of my cowboy boots into that fence and scramblin' up, maybe two feet this time before fallin' again. Down hard. Flat on my back. Probably hittin' my head, too. Wes hootin' and hollerin'. And Sasha crouching over me. An angel askin' me if I'm all right. Was I hurt? Did it make any difference if I was hurt? You try hard enough, then you can't lose."

Hayley knows the coda of the story before he tells her.

"How long before Sasha was your girlfriend, Deputy?"

Gibbs grins in that sly way of his.

"That night and through the whole summer." A broader smile with memory of it. "A real nice summer that one."

HE PULLS OUT from his spot behind the overgrown shrubbery at the abandoned Sunset Motel and drives a mile back to Monahans on Sealy Avenue. Most businesses don't open until eleven, but Oswald remembers seeing a Sonic Drive-In when he first reconnoitered the town. Turning left at Main, he drives five blocks, turns in at the fast-food restaurant's second driveway, and pulls into the first parking stall on the right, closest to the road.

A carhop approaches the driver's-side window, shoulders scrunched against the wind and occasional raindrop. Oswald is the only customer who hasn't already been served. The teenage kid reminds him of his niece. How long has it been since he's been home? One of these days, he promises himself.

"What can I get for you?"

Oswald doesn't want to take too many chances like this. Staying low to the ground is the name of the game. When the shit *really* starts flying, who knows how long it'll be before he can get a meal again.

"Ultimate Meat and Cheese Burrito. Large sweet iced tea."

The girl doesn't bother writing it down.

"That all?"

He grins. "That'll do me."

Carhop turning away from the window, Oswald decides to throw in for broke.

"Onion rings, okay?"

The girl raises a hand vaguely, signaling that she has the order.

Oswald rolls up the window again. The letter box on the restaurant's sign is an advertisement for help wanted. Carhops at $10 an hour, plus tips. Day cooks $12 an hour. He wonders what life working at a fast-food joint might be like. He's too old for carhopping, of course. But a day cook at a Sonic Drive-In seems oddly enticing. So different from driving around the West Texas hellscape with a nuclear device in the trunk of his rental car. Oswald imagines the studio apartment he would rent in this imagined life. Unable to afford a car, his domicile would have to be within walking distance of the restaurant. He knows he could do it. Once all of this business is over and done with, Oswald is ready for a simple life. One with less—at least less substantial—conflict.

After all, he's not getting any younger.

THEY LEAVE THE interstate at the exit for Monahans and transition onto Sealey Avenue. Pass an RV park. A shuttered honky-tonk that has seen livelier days. The inevitable Baptist church. And another

RV park. The roads are empty. Foul weather to blame, she assumes. Hayley watches the scenes roll past. Waiting to feel it. A recognition that she has found their target. Staving off the distressing sense of futility. She gathers up all distractions—the revelations concerning her father, her pregnancy, physical and mental fatigue from these ten marathon days in Texas—and puts them in a box. No time for diversions.

"Blink and you might miss it," says Gibbs.

Hearing this, Hayley thinks he might be reading her mind but then realizes that he is referring to the town.

As they approach Main, she sees more activity on that thoroughfare.

"Take a right."

The sheriff's deputy eases the prowler into the turn.

"What're we looking for again?"

She doesn't need to tell him that she's not sure.

"Kind of surprised there's not any soldiers here yet."

Gibbs says, "Focusing on the bigger fish. Midlands. Odessa. Pecos. Lock down the cities. They'll be in Monahans soon enough."

Hayley clocks his grim expression. The invasion of his homeland is sorry business. Pains him. Nobody asked Gibbs if he wanted no part of the United States.

"We're going to stop this," she tells the sheriff's deputy.

"Yes. I imagine we will."

The deeper state operative appreciates his quiet resolve. The low drama the man exudes, an older and wiser version of the teenager who tried to defy gravity. She turns her eyes forward again, off the deputy, as the prowler rolls past the Sonic Drive-In on their right.

Hayley looks out her window and finds her gaze locking on the man in black, sitting in the front seat of a white sedan parked in the first stall next to the drive-in's second entrance.

———

OSWALD SEES THE sheriff's department SUV approach, his car near the curb and facing north. Thinks nothing of it. Why should he be concerned? He is a painfully normal, middle-aged man waiting for his painfully normal Ultimate Meat and Cheese Burrito. How would any sheriff's deputy know that he has a tactical nuclear device in the trunk of his Ford Fusion?

It's all good.

But as the Reeves County sheriff's department patrol vehicle— what the hell is it doing in Ward County?—draws nearer, Oswald is stunned to find himself staring at the very same young blond woman who has stalked the cabal from its lowest level to top leadership. The absurdly named Hayley Chill.

How the hell . . .?

His stupefaction is so complete, Pete Oswald can only gawk at the passing specter of his nemesis.

———

SHE ISN'T ENTIRELY shocked to see him again. The man in black has been a constant thread throughout her investigation. Turning up at the New Mexico compound and watching from atop the distant ridge. With Major Culberson at the National Guard temporary camp in Balmorhea. He came after her then, pursuing Hayley to El Paso. Was he responsible for the attempt on her life in Dallas? And then their confrontation on the road after he tailed her from the Beverly Crest. When she snatched his truck keys from the ignition, punched him in the face, and left him stranded. Played him like the fool. Old and unable to keep up.

Now he's here. In Monahans. Doing God knows what fucked-up business for his racist cause. A pure, white nation.

One hundred feet past the drive-in and Hayley twists around to see what the man in black will do next.

He saw me. The shock of recognition so plain on his face.

Gibbs asks, "What is it? What did you see?"

She is still turned around in the front seat, watching the white sedan in the drive-in stall receding in the distance.

"That was one of them. A ringleader. He's been chasing me for the past ten days."

"Where? At the Sonic?"

Hayley's eyes zeroed in on the secessionist's vehicle.

"Why isn't he coming after me?" she asks, mostly to herself.

"What? Hayley?"

Gibbs has never seen her like this. Perplexed.

She is quiet.

Still.

Then she gets it.

Quietly Hayley says, "Turn around."

"Go back after him?" He doesn't have any problem with it. Just surprised she doesn't, either.

"He's not chasing me, because he's the guy." Hayley looks to the sheriff's deputy. "He's got the bomb."

———

THE CARHOP IS emerging from the building when Oswald sees the Reeves County sheriff's SUV making a U-turn a block south and return in his direction.

He hits the ignition, puts the sedan into gear, and backs out of the parking stall. As Oswald pulls back onto Main, heading south, he clocks a GMC Yukon across the street pulling away from the curb and following close on his tail. The dark blue SUV escaped his notice until this moment. Glancing in the rearview mirror, Oswald sees the two men in the front seat of the Yukon. More men in the back seat.

Beards. Ball caps. Sunglasses.

Like a neon sign. Special Forces.

Relieved, Oswald realizes he is not alone. Without informing him, the higher-ups in the organization provided "shadow" cover. Instructed to stay in the background. Reveal themselves only if necessary. Like now.

As he hits the gas, Oswald's only regret is that the breakfast burrito hadn't come just a minute sooner.

HAYLEY POINTS. "HE'S running!"

"Got him." Gibbs hits the lights and sirens.

With the dark blue SUV between them and Oswald, the deputy turns the wheel, swinging the prowler to the right of the blocking vehicle.

The Yukon swerves into their path.

"What the hell . . . ?"

Hayley gets it before Gibbs does. "Protection team!"

They can't see into the tinted rear or side windows of the Yukon. Farther ahead, the white Ford Fusion races toward the intersection with Sealy Avenue, turning right.

"Hold on." Gibbs spins the wheel to the right, abruptly steering the prowler into a sharp turn east on Second Street. The Yukon continues north on Main.

Hayley grips the handle over her door.

Once they're through the turn, Gibbs stomps on the gas. Focused on driving, he says, "Grab my vest and one for yourself."

Hayley twists around and reaches to the bench seat behind her, thankful for the absence of a barrier. Retrieves two of the tan-colored vests, one festooned with mag pouches. She quickly slips on the basic, unadorned vest and secures it to her body.

Gibbs says, "Rifle rated. Level-four armor." And once she's set: "Grab the wheel, okay?"

She does, holding them on course as the prowler races up the commercial street.

The deputy gets his arms through the vest and secures it. The two pouches on either side of the body armor are loaded with magazines for his M4, base plates up. In front are pouches for his radio and two more mags. "Here we go," he says as he spins the steering wheel left.

Turning north onto Franklin Avenue, the prowler charges up the short block back to Sealy. The Fusion jets through the intersection just ahead of their reaching it.

As they renew their pursuit of Oswald in the rental car, Hayley looks behind and sees the Yukon on their tail. SOF types visible through the windshield glass.

"Mercs in the Yukon." Her voice is free of emotion. The War Hawk stays in its holster for now.

Gibbs nods. Says nothing, focusing on the white Ford. His police siren making all kinds of a racket.

OSWALD HEARS THE Reeves County SUV first, coming from out of nowhere and falling in behind him. Watching in his rear- and side-view mirrors, he sees the overwatch team closing the distance between them and the sheriff's deputy. Leading out of town, the road ahead is clear. Oswald pushes his four-banger Ford as fast it will go, the sheriff's prowler on his bumper.

He's confident the SOFs in the Yukon can handle Hayley Chill and her deputy sheriff friend.

He wishes he could hang around to see it happen. But that isn't possible. Once he shakes loose these two fucks, Oswald is hitting the road again.

Get hidden and stay hidden.

He's not feeling so clandestine right now, of course. Not with the lights and sirens of the sheriff's vehicle going off like the Bicentennial Fourth of July. The three vehicles—Ford Fusion, Reeves County SUV, the Yukon—all racing at top speed east on the two-lane road.

He thinks that maybe he shouldn't have left his relatively secure location at the abandoned motel. Put off breakfast.

He wishes he had never taken this assignment. That he had stayed with Morale Operations. Because, as much as Oswald is confident the overwatch team will take care of business, there is the matter of Hayley Chill's seemingly indomitable ability to . . . fuck . . . his . . . life . . . up.

Maybe he is gaping in his rearview mirror too much.

Maybe he's too nervous. Too long without a decent cup of coffee.

Maybe Oswald's just too old. Because when he looks forward again—down the road where his gaze should've fucking been in the first place—it's too late.

Just too damn late.

HAYLEY SAW THE flatbed tractor trailer—hauling a 1961 Hooper Hoist oil rig from a drill site three-quarters of a mile north of the road—without really knowing what it was except that it was big and slow moving, pulling out from the service road and across Sealy for the westbound lane. With the long run home to Bakersfield ahead of him, the truck's driver has been popping pills all through the night just to make the pickup in Monahans on time. Interviewed later by local police—a miracle he survived, given the amount of gunfire, even if curled up on the floor of the cab for the duration of the fight—the truck driver admitted his fault. Didn't look both ways but leaving out the part about the methamphetamines.

Didn't see the vehicles on Sealy coming, despite the siren and cop lights.

By the time Pete Oswald moved his eyes from the rearview mirror to the road ahead, simple physics had reduced his options to exactly none. Stopping distance is proportional to the square of the rental car's speed. When he sees the truck straddling the entire road ahead of him, the Fusion has attained a speed of ninety miles per hour. He will travel 98 feet in the time required for senses and motor skills to react, planting his foot hard on the brake. To come to a full stop and avoid impact with the flatbed hauler would require another 386 feet of roadway.

But Oswald's vehicle is 266 feet from the rig truck when he sees it. Though he does indeed stomp on the brake in reaction, another part of his brain—a more primal instinct—knows his hopes of avoiding collision are nonexistent. Consequently, he panics and spins the steering wheel to the right. As if that will do anything but flip the Fusion, side over side, all four tires leaving the pavement for what seems like an eternity.

Jay Gibbs is a better driver, his vehicle's brakes upgraded from stock. Like so many of the prowler's modifications, the Reeves County sheriff's department SUV is equipped to handle challenging situations, on the road and off. The Ford flips ahead of them—the awful sight of it filling the prowler's windshield from end to end—as the sheriff's deputy ably brings the big Chevy Tahoe to a controlled stop.

The Ford impacts the flatbed roof first, stopped hard there by its massive bulk.

Gibbs hits a button hidden deep under the dash that electronically releases the M4 bracketed muzzle up between the prowler's two front seats. Grabbing the rifle, he pops open the door and rolls out into a crouch, facing toward the rear of the vehicle. In the direction of the shadow team's Yukon. In near-simultaneous concert with the sheriff's deputy, Hayley draws the War Hawk and bails out, too, making herself as small a target as possible. She holds the 1911 in the grip of both hands and at arm's length. Waiting for targets.

Those targets come.

When the Fusion had flipped, the bearded man behind the wheel of the Yukon brought the heavy vehicle to a skidding stop fifty feet behind the deputy's prowler.

Four doors pop open, and the four operatives start firing before their feet meet the pavement, without clear acquisition of their targets. The racket of gunfire starts heavy and stays that way.

Full auto. No ammo conservation, Gibbs assesses. *These guys don't expect a long fight.*

On either side of the prowler, he and Hayley return only enough fire to buy them a few seconds to retreat backward, to a precious sanctuary behind the Tahoe's front end. The .45-caliber in Hayley's hands isn't feeling particularly adequate to the job.

"Four guys?" she asks Gibbs as they crouch below the prowler's front end.

"That's what I saw. M4. Couple HK MP5s. The driver I don't know what."

Rounds continue to impact the SUV's rear end with a sickening deluge of metallic thuds and shattering glass.

Hayley's eyes fall on the Fusion, its underside obscenely exposed to them.

"Think he's dead?"

Gibbs shrugs. "I'll keep these boys busy."

"Light 'em up, hombre, and cover me."

Hombre.

He's glad she remembers their first conversation. Wishing this didn't have to end like an Elmore Leonard novel.

"That's the plan," says Gibbs.

They exchange a look. He offers up a crooked smile.

"Interesting if not enjoyable, I guess."

Hayley can't think of any decent reason to smile. "I guess so."

He winks. *Let's do this.*

They stand to a crouch and pour fire.

War Hawk in her grip, Hayley belly crawls toward the Fusion on its side. She waited until Gibbs slammed home a fresh mag before making her move. Rounds ping off the underside of the rental car and off the flatbed. The dismantled oil rig. Skipping off the blacktop pavement.

Seemingly everywhere.

How the hell haven't I been hit?

Somehow, she reaches the wrecked rental car without being shot. Still on her belly, Hayley shimmies around to the front of the car. Protected now from the continuing gunfire, she can see inside the front-seat area of the Fusion through the crushed windshield.

There's no sign of the man in black.

Hayley carefully climbs into the car and inspects the interior, front and back.

Not inside. No bomb, either.

The deeper state operative extracts herself from the crushed Fusion. She works her way toward the back by crawling underneath the flatbed's trailer, to the Ford's rear end.

The trunk is popped open. And empty.

To the erratic drumbeat of rounds smashing into the rental car's undercarriage, the flatbed, and rig parts, Hayley ducks under the trailer and, crawling to the other side, scans the way east.

She sees the man in black running up the side of the road, with maybe a thousand-foot head start. He wears an olive drab backpack strapped to his shoulders.

No time to tell Gibbs.

Hayley takes off after her target.

12

DARKNESS AND DISTANCE

He hears only one of the HKs firing now.

Working to out-flank me. That's what I'd do, too.

Hunkered behind the front of the prowler, Gibbs checks his watch. It's been three minutes since Hayley retreated to the upturned rental car. He hasn't heard any signal from her that she has located the bomb.

If he doesn't move, he's dead. If he dies, so does Hayley, most likely. Then these sonsabitches can do whatever the hell they want.

Gibbs releases the magazine in his M4 and checks its load. Confirming it's light, he slams the mag back home, stands, empties it on the Yukon, then turns and runs at a crouch toward the flatbed, assessing his protection there more robust.

Once he is safely behind the upturned Fusion, Gibbs exchanges the mag in the M4 for another from his vest. A quick check of the rental car's interior confirms that Hayley isn't there. The deputy crawls to the other side of the trailer and looks east, the only direction in which she could have gone. Sure enough, Gibbs sees the deeper state operative running up the side of the road, maybe a quarter mile off.

He may not know much about Hayley Chill, but Gibbs is confident she isn't running from the fight.

If he joins her in the pursuit, the shadow team will follow them and prevail. There is no question of what Gibbs must do. Rearguard protection. Stop them here. At bare minimum, slow them down. Buy the woman some time.

He has wasted precious seconds in evaluating the situation and deciding on a plan. He belly crawls to the Fusion's rear end and drops into a prone position at full extension. With his feet a little more than shoulder width apart and his strong elbow making contact with the pavement, Gibbs searches through the Aimpoint for a target on the north side of the road's frontage.

Finds one in the operative cradling an HK as he runs at a crouch to almost parallel with the flatbed tractor trailer rig. With sight picture and a brief exhale, Gibbs squeezes the rifle's trigger and vaporizes the top half of the man's head.

One down. Three to go.

Gibbs rolls to his left and, after four revolutions, returns to a prone position but oriented south, toward the opposite side of the road.

The man there is a smaller target, in a braced knee position and taking aim with his rifle. Gibbs fires before the other man does and puts a round in his center mass. The operative falls backward.

Gibbs pulls the trigger to lace the downed man with a finishing burst . . .

Nothing.

No fire.

The sheriff's deputy shifts his weight and bangs the mag's bottom in hopes of curing the malfunction. Pulls down on it to confirm the mag is seated, then yanks back the charging handle, sights, and squeezes the trigger. Still nothing.

Gibbs registers the lack of gunfire. Silence that indicates the remaining operatives are on the move.

He releases the magazine and reciprocates the action three times. Slams the mag back in. Tap and pull down. Only a few seconds have transpired since the malfunction, but before Gibbs has time to take aim on the second man, he hears the scuff of feet behind him.

The deputy rolls—evading a burst of gunfire that chews up the pavement where he lay a second before—dropping the M4 as he goes. Because another "failure to feed" malfunction and it's game over. Instead, as he spins himself clear of the underside of the trailer, Gibbs retrieves his backup gun from a holster on his left ankle and comes up in a sitting position with the Sig pointing in the direction of the truck's cab.

A sharp thud to the center of his back. Feels like he's been hit by a baseball bat. Slammed facedown, to the pavement.

The inevitable few seconds of disorientation—time that is all too precious—and then the deputy realizes the body armor has given him only temporary reprieve.

He hears his pistol kicked away, skittering across the blacktop.

Gibbs rolls over on his back. Reaches for his knife. With eyes skyward, into the swirling black clouds. Each second of additional life an uncut gem.

He's pleased he has slowed them down this much. His dad would be proud.

And Gibbs is grateful, too, that Hayley Chill doesn't see him this way. Bear witness to what's to come.

———

THE SIRENS OF approaching police cars—the Monahans Police Department less than four minutes away on Second Street in town—draw the two remaining operatives back to the Yukon. They place their rifles inside the vehicle, on the front seat. Leaving the doors open, they take a position on either side. Arms up, they both wave in a friendly, "seeking help" manner.

Two police vehicles stop short by a hundred feet of Yukon. A policeman emerges from one, standing behind his door and using it to brace his gun hand. The public address speaker on the other vehicle crackles.

"On the ground! Slowly!"

The two SOFs remain motionless.

Gunfire erupts from the south side of the road, where Gibbs had shot one of the mercs. Who was wearing body armor.

That man unloads his M4 on the cop cars.

The other two operatives retrieve their weapons from the front seat of the Yukon and also go full auto.

The Monahans police officer who was standing behind his door is hit multiple times and drops. Despite the heavy fire, the driver of the other police car is able to reverse away from the scene, retreating far up Sealy Avenue.

Both operatives get back inside the Yukon. The driver pulls forward and pauses for the third man to climb into the back seat. Getting around the tractor trailer rig that straddles the road requires swinging wide, off the pavement, before resuming their course east on Sealy. In pursuit of the woman.

NORTH OF THE road is a broad expanse of scattered pumpjacks. The majority of these stripper wells are active, counterbalanced "horseheads" at the end of walking beams bobbing with a steady and monotonous up-and-down action. Other drill sites are dormant, frozen in midstroke. No people appear to be present in this panorama of industrial machines. Just these indefatigable iron locusts, coaxing fewer than ten barrels of Texas crude a day through steel sucker rods.

The only sound is the whirring grind of pumpjack motors. And wind. Always the wind.

Hayley runs across that blighted landscape. The storm's deluges have firmed up the usually loose, granular soil. Intermittent pools of oil-stained rainwater collected by the tire ruts on the unpaved road do not slow her down. Running is her life. Always has been. She saw her target turn in this direction, into the oil field just west of the adjacent sand hills. Her pace is twice what she calculates his to be. The man in black is in here somewhere, and she's going to find him. If he doesn't turn over the backpack, the deeper state operative will kill him.

She is one hundred yards deep into the oil field when the Yukon drives past on Sealy Avenue behind her, then reverses and turns onto the same dirt-and-gravel service road.

THE SILENT, ARMED men have her in front of them, and then she's gone again, darting right and off the road. They drive to the spot and stop. Looking east, they see only the hulking pumpjacks punching at the earth. Up and down. Relentless. The wind blows through their open vehicle windows. Engine idles. Weapons at ready, the driver steers the Yukon off the road and drives across the giving, rain-drenched soil. Slowly. No more than five miles per hour. One man looking to the right. Man in the back and the driver to the left. Find the girl first.

Then Oswald. Wherever the living fuck he ran off.

HAYLEY CROUCHES BEHIND a pumpjack's gearbox, a steel enclosure that is not quite head tall. Excellent cover and just ten feet off the track on which the Yukon currently approaches at a crawl.

That the shadow team got past Gibbs means the sheriff's deputy is dead. She cannot imagine any other possible scenario. Her measure of the man is that certain.

His death must be avenged.

Even a nuclear device, loose in the wild, is a secondary priority.

She doesn't know how many of the four operatives remain alive. Her glimpse of the Yukon turning off Sealy was fleeting. Risking a second observation of the truck as it approaches her location is out of the question. Hayley will go by her sense of hearing alone, listening for the moment when the Yukon is closest to her position. Depending on how many operatives are in the vehicle, the deeper state operative estimates she has approximately three seconds to kill all of them. Failing that, the odds of her surviving diminish precipitously.

The Yukon nears her hiding place. Hayley waits. In control of her heart rate and breathing. Both hands on the War Hawk. Safety off. Muzzle high. Waiting. Only seconds remain.

Sights. Slack out. Pressure wall. Press. Reset.

What her weapons training instructor had taught her the camp in central Oregon. What she doesn't even think about when the shooting starts.

———————

SHE STANDS, ARMS extending as her head clears the top of the pump-jack's gearbox. Gears within the enclosure drive a shaft that tilts the horsehead and walking beam up and down, working in conjunction with the slow-spinning counterweight. All of this massive, industrial-age ironwork obscures her as she stands. Unnoticed by the three bearded men inside the truck.

Hayley fires. Three targets, three quick shots, moving from front to back. A brief pause in search of more targets to acquire. Finding none, she follows with six more shots, two into each man and emptying the gun.

She has slammed home a new mag before the death truck eases to a stop.

So TIRED. AND dirty. He had been running for so long that Pete Oswald worried his heart might burst. And so he stopped running. Walked instead. Let her catch him. What did he care anymore?

He sits now, almost clear of the oil field. The sand hills loom ahead. Otherworldly. Has he been transported to another planet? Oswald wishes it were so.

He removes the heavy backpack. Fucking thing. Goddamn stupid fucking thing. Lies backward, arms spread out. Stares into the sky. Finished.

Goddamn woman. Fucking Hayley Chill.

The sound of gunfire brings Oswald sitting upright again. Three shots. Followed by six more. The shadow team!

Perhaps he's saved. Oswald hopes to God they've killed her. Chop her motherfucking head off. Oswald checks his pants pocket to make sure he has the burner phone.

Good. It's still here.

Oswald doesn't think he's felt such pain in his entire life. After the car accident, every muscle aches. He's pretty sure his wrist is busted. The cut on his forehead is no joke. And then the run.

That motherfucking run.

The only thing he wishes for more than deliverance from this godforsaken desert is the chance to spit on that woman's fucking corpse.

He should stand. Make himself noticed. The shadow team must be looking for him.

Oswald reaches for the backpack and experiences a whole new kind of pain. One he's never experienced in his life. Like a hot poker jammed into the left side of his neck.

HAYLEY IS WALKING east, drawn by the sand hills there if for no other reason than the enticing refuge they offer. If the man in black has disappeared into the undulations and folds of the Monahans Sandhills State Park, she worries that she'll never find him.

She hears a shot. Followed by several more. Close by. She estimates the location is no more than a couple of hundred feet to the northeast of her position. Gun at ready, she jogs in that direction.

Hayley hears her target before she sees him. His gasping and choking are a cruel and desperate beacon. Keeping as low to the ground as possible, she approaches her target's location.

The man in black sits on the ground, legs thrust out before him. In the sandy soil to his right is his Glock. To the left is the bulky, olive drab backpack. In front of him is the snake, a western diamondback with most of its head shot away.

She can see the bite marks on his bloated, right hand from twenty feet away. The man's neck is swollen, too. Already turning black. Having spent enough time in Texas while stationed at Fort Hood, Hayley knows something about rattlesnakes and their bites. The diamondback's venom isn't the most lethal. But, if antagonized, the species can deliver an enormous amount of that venom with a single bite. The zootoxin's progression through a victim's body is exceptionally rapid. Obstruction of the man's airways is imminent. Without immediate medical intervention, painful strangulation is inevitable.

He clutches his throat with both hands.

"Help . . . me."

Hayley moves cautiously forward, keeping the War Hawk on the dying man, and takes possession of the backpack and the Glock. Then she retreats to her original position and squats down. To watch him die.

GOING THROUGH HIS wallet afterward, she finds his Texas driver's license.

Peter Samuel Oswald.

She hears again what Woodside had said.

Oswald.

Hayley looks from the license to the dead man's face. Her father's assassin.

So extraordinarily ordinary.

Both were unaware of the other's true self. Oswald was commissioned to kill Charlie Hicks and never connected Hayley to that hit job in Arlington.

Better this way, she decides.

Not to have known the whole truth until his painful, agonizing death. Hayley would have found some way to prolong that agony. Debased herself. Down to *their* level.

Rage and hate have dissipated, replaced by God knows what.

She hears Oswald's phone vibrate. Hayley reaches and retrieves the device from the dead man's pants pocket. Puts the phone to her ear. And says nothing.

"Hello?" asks a male voice. Predictably gruff. Panicky.

Hayley remains mute. Listening.

"One thousand suns."

More silence from her.

"Did you copy? One thousand suns. This is a direct order from our leadership. It's time. Light that sucker up. This is war. Fuck 'em all."

The call is disconnected.

Hayley stands and flings the burner phone as far as she can throw it. Draping the backpack over her shoulders, she turns east. They will be coming after her. When their precious bomb fails to burn brighter than a thousand suns in the sky, they will search high and low for it. To find out why. The sand hills are the perfect refuge. A place where they'll never find her.

THE DUNES SHIFT with the wind. A valley can disappear overnight, in its place small mountains of sand that creep at across the landscape. With lives of their own. Among the hills, Hayley finds cover in a stand of shin oak. She has lost track of time and is shocked when a check of her wristwatch confirms the noon hour.

Resting, finally, her eyes rove the otherworldly landscape. She feels an uncanny sensation of having been here before. And then Hayley remembers the framed photo in the examination room at the women's health clinic in New Mexico. The granny nurse practitioner, looking up from her Rx pad and catching the deeper state operative in the act of absorption. Unable to tear her gaze away from the desert landscape of wind-rippled dunes. Massive. Undulating.

Los Médanos.

Vividly recalling the scene now. The photograph of the Sama-layuca Dune Fields, southwest of Juárez. The sound of the NP's pen scratching on the pad. A blast of cold air streaming from vents in the ceiling, the temperature in the examination room too cold for comfort. Her false sense of confidence at the time. Of certainty. All of that changed now.

Everything has changed.

Though the rain has stopped, for good it would seem, dark clouds continue to scuttle across the sky. A company of Apache helicopters—eight aircraft a mile off—fly in the direction of what must be Odessa, thirty miles distant. The wind carries the sound of gunfire from the east. Or is it south? In her sudden bewilderment, Hayley recognizes her utter exhaustion. A weariness that saturates her every molecule. Beyond wanting food, water, or sleep.

She is simply done with it.

Running. Shooting. Killing.

Andrew Wilde. The deeper state.

At a finish.

To the soft, disjointed racket of distant gunfire, Hayley slowly keels over. Twin F-15 fighter jets streak low overhead. She pays them no mind. Bringing her hands together and under her head, she lies down and draws her knees in close to her body. The bomb bag is beside her, like a child. Both are safe for now.

———————————

IT'S AFTER DARK when she opens her eyes again. The storm has passed. What clouds remain have split open, releasing a tumult of stars that wheel and dip overhead. For several seconds, Hayley remains still. Just staring into all of that luscious night sky. Listening to the low rumble of what cannot be thunder. What can only be the opening acts of America's Second Civil War.

Hayley unfolds her legs and slowly stands. Leaving the backpack under the shin oaks, she climbs a seventy-five-foot sand dune to its summit. From that vantage point, she can see Midland and Odessa to the east where the explosions erupt with disturbing frequency. Looking west, Hayley can see the town of Monahans and evidence of heavy military presence. Trucks and vehicles and troops in the streets.

She cannot begin to guess what's happened. What *will* happen. All she knows is that the bomb must be kept hidden. It must be kept safe.

Hayley walks back down to her camp.

———————————

HOURS PASS.

For some time now, she hasn't heard any more gunfire or distant explosions.

Hayley cannot hide out in the sand hills forever. Eventually, she will have to walk out of this place. No longer can she deny a terrifying thirst.

Bury it. Bury the bomb.

The little trees are a good landmark with which to locate the device when she is able to return. Hayley begins to dig into the hard-packed soil that has given the oaks firm ground in which to root. A stick is a useful tool. The deeper state operative hasn't been at work long when she hears a helicopter approach from the southeast. At first, Hayley believes the chopper is merely traversing her position. But then she notes the aircraft's deliberate flight pattern over the sand hills and adjoining oil field to the west.

They're looking for me.

Hayley drops the digging tool and gathers her things—backpack, weapons—and pulls them with her under the low shelter of shin oaks. Squatting on her haunches, under those acorn-laden, spindly branches, she can just barely see the outlines of the Black Hawk helicopter swoop back and forth over the area. Low lights inside the aircraft reveal the personnel framed by the chopper's open rearward door. Wearing night-vision gear.

If the Black Hawk is equipped with a thermal sensor package, then it's game over.

As if in answer to her musing, the chopper alters its course slightly, swings around to return to her position, holding directly above her briefly, before moving a thousand feet to the west and quickly landing.

Hayley imagines the soldiers off-loading and humping at double time to her little stand of shin oaks. They'll carry M16s and night-vision goggles.

She's got her War Hawk, a Glock 19, and a nuclear bomb.

Getting in a prone position and making herself as small a target as possible, Hayley waits for them. War Hawk in one hand, Glock in the other.

If I'm going to die, I'm not going to die easy.

And she waits, hearing only the forever wind and her heartbeat.

Then, from the darkness, a female voice . . .

"Hayley Chill?"

They know my name?

She can't see shit. The elusive light from a canopy of stars too diffuse.

Hayley knows they have her position locked. No use pretending otherwise.

She calls out, "Who are you?"

A demand, really. She is, after all, a nuclear power.

"Corporal Wanda Jackson, ma'am . . ."

A tall, thin woman wearing standard-issue ACU emerges from the darkness. She carries her M16 in a cross-body sling, muzzle down. Hands held out wide in a gesture of peace.

". . . United States Army."

Hayley doesn't change her stance. The corporal continues to advance slowly.

"We good, Hayley?"

The others emerge from the darkness. All soldiers. Wearing the same uniform. The American flag patch worn on the right shoulder, star field facing forward, proof of their allegiance to their country.

For the Constitution they've all sworn an oath to support and defend.

Just like her.

"We're good," Hayley can finally say.

Minutes later, after the SADM is secured and Hayley has drunk her fill of water, one soldier asks, "Ma'am, are you injured?"

No one had noticed the blood. Maybe they hadn't because the blood wasn't there before.

The soldier—dark haired and shy, no more than twenty years of age—respectfully gestures toward Hayley's pant legs, soaked through and dark.

She looks. And knows.

———————

WHEN HAYLEY WAKES up from what could have been a short nap, she sees April Wu sitting on the plastic chair to one side of her bed. Her friend, reliably pale and with dark circles under her eyes, stares placidly at her. As if the last ten hours of the deeper state operative's life hadn't been the least bit harrowing. Or the last ten days, for that matter.

"How did you find me?" Hayley is genuinely perplexed.

"Wasn't so hard. I just followed the bodies."

"That's not funny."

April's response is to shrug. Not at all contrite.

"How're you feeling?" she asks.

"Like I almost bled to death."

In the ninth week of her pregnancy, the miscarriage should not have been an emergency. As a precaution, the soldiers loaded her into the Black Hawk and flew Hayley to the nearest medical facilities, at the Ward Memorial Hospital in Monahans. Less than a five-minute hop. After a quick checkup, Hayley was close to walking back out the door when the bleeding became worse. The emergency room doctor on duty was unable to diagnose the issue. Because it was already after midnight by this time, an ob-gyn wasn't available. Hayley's condition became more critical. Before dawn, she was transferred to the much larger medical center in Odessa, forty-five minutes by ambulance. A blood transfusion and the removal of a blood clot in her cervix saved Hayley Chill's life.

Now half past ten in the morning—nearly twelve hours following the final, desperate minutes in the sand hills—Hayley can expect to leave the hospital soon. She hasn't begun to process it all.

April Wu shelves her usual, snarky demeanor, exchanging it for something more genuine.

"You decided . . ." She stops there.

Picking up the slack, Hayley says, "I decided that being a mother couldn't be more challenging than what the deeper state has thrown at us."

"I truly am sorry, then," says April.

Lying on the hospital bed, the deeper state operative stares up at the speckled ceiling tiles. She imagines that she's back at the Monahans Sandhills State Park, protected by the shin oaks. That she is still with child.

"Did they say . . . why? Was it because you were running around half of West Texas and preventing the Second Civil War?"

Hayley shakes her head. "The ob-gyn was kinda sweet, actually. She promised me it had nothing to do with any of that. 'Genetic abnormality,' the doc told me. 'Nature's way of taking care of nature.'"

"Then, for the best, I guess."

"Yeah." Not that it makes it better.

"You know I'm here for you."

Hayley lowers her gaze again to meet her friend's eyes. In them, she can find some measure of hope. Of loyalty and continuation.

"I do."

The door opens. Andrew Wilde enters the examination room unannounced.

He says, "Hello there."

Hayley turns her focus on the man who is the primary link with Publius. Even his typically tan complexion seems slightly washed out by the room's unforgiving fluorescent lights.

With him, she is unemotional. On duty, no matter the circumstances.

"Sir."

Wilde appears mildly confused. "Who were you talking to?"

Hayley looks to the chair to the right of her hospital bed. It's empty. The specter of her dead friend gone again. To wherever ghosts go.

She turns her eyes back to her superior in the deeper state.

"Nobody."

Wilde grimaces, chalking up her odd behavior to her recent brush with medical catastrophe.

"Are they *really* going to kick you out of here soon? Maybe I should talk to somebody."

"That's not necessary, sir. I'll be all right."

He nods. Taking her word for it.

"Well, I guess I can speak for the entire organization by expressing my gratitude for your outstanding work these last two weeks."

"I've been kind of out of it, sir. Is it over?"

"It never really got started. Once the rank and file troops understood what the cabal of officers, rogue elements, and private citizens were expecting of them, the tide turned against the secessionists. The SADM was the wild card. Very fortunate that you gained control of the device."

"Mr. Wilde, I never would've succeeded without the assistance of Deputy Sheriff Jay Gibbs. He sacrificed his life so that I could complete my mission."

"Understood. Good man."

Hayley is silent. The crush of memories all of a sudden too much for her to bear. But she is resistant to betraying these emotions—any emotions—to Wilde. Her face becomes stone.

For the truths she has learned, Hayley has lost much. Her eyes turn again to the empty chair beside her bed. To the person who is not there. The people.

"Well, we'll get you out of here. I imagine it can't be soon enough for you."

"Sir?"

"Got a plane waiting for us. I'll have you back in Washington before dinnertime. How's that sound?"

And leave part of herself here? Hayley feels a momentary panic. The emotional frenzy comes from that place where fear intersects with fate. Is she doomed and, consequently, damning all those with whom she chooses to associate? To possibly love? She imagines herself as Dr. Frankenstein's monster, cast off and adrift on a forlorn ice floe.

Hayley recalls Shelley's line.

Lost in darkness and distance.

But as quickly as that dread swells within her, it scatters again. For all that she has lost, Hayley has regained her father. His nobility restored in her memory of him, a father's daughter experiences resurgent power. Renewed strength.

Not only was Tommy Chill's honor preserved, but so also the nation's integrity.

She is not one alone, but one of many.

Hayley ignores the light-headedness that she will continue to experience for another month, the lingering aftereffects of blood loss and necessary transfusion. All of it will heal. Mended. So that she can fight another day.

She swings her legs off the hospital bed, plants them on the ground.

Hayley rises and stands up tall.

"Ready when you are, sir."

13

WE BEAT THE TURK

FOUR MONTHS EARLIER

Hayley steps off the elevator and traverses the familiar hospital hallway. She has visited so often in these last few weeks—with the end of her tenure as a West Wing staffer and long before she would accept another assignment from Publius—that many faces are known to her, too. Patients. Visiting family members. Doctors and nurses. Technicians and cleaning staff. These people have become friends and many greet the deeper state operative with weary smiles. A knowing tilt of the head. April Wu is well-known, too, on the floor. A popular, shit-dispensing wiseacre who, until she had taken a turn for the worse, is famous for singing the lyrics to "Riders on the Storm" whenever nurses wheel her to her next test. Her next procedure. And, more recently, downstairs, to the hospital chapel.

April's worsening condition has nothing to do with the injuries she sustained in the car accident, but rather is the result of her hospitalization. At some point, she came in contact with someone—a medical provider or well-meaning staff person—that passed along a microorganism of disproportionate lethality. Few effective drugs are available to combat an *Acinetobacter baumannii* bacterial infection, fittingly, a scourge of battlefield hospitals where traumatic injuries are prevalent. Taking hold in April's scalp wound, the bacteria infected her bloodstream.

Medications have helped quell her fever, chills, skin rash, and muscle ache. Still, the patient's confusion and altered mental state—the expected symptoms of a worsening infection—have gone unchecked. While April's doctors are concerned, her response to the last-resort antibiotic, polymyxin E, has been encouraging. Only yesterday, Hayley asked one of them—a white-haired, old-school infectious disease specialist—if her friend was going to die. Taken aback by the deeper state operative's intense, confrontational style, the doctor surmised April Wu would survive, though long-term kidney damage was a strong possibility.

When Hayley enters the private room, April is sleeping. Her pale face is a stark contrast to the dark rings around her eyes. Though a blanket covers the patient, it's obvious her weight loss has been dramatic. The setting sun casts the room in a warm glow. Outside, Washingtonians are reveling in mild spring weather. The president's exposure as a Russian mole and subsequent political upheaval matter not one whit to the uniformed elementary-school kids from Annunciation Catholic School playing in University Yard. Meanwhile, in the Monera kingdom, hydrophilic and lipophilic moieties interact with the outer cell walls of *A. baumannii* bacteria, breaking them down and effectively killing the invading microorganisms coursing through April's bloodstream.

Life, in all forms, goes on.

April's eyelids slowly lift. She observes her visitor without outward expression.

A moment of silence as these two friendly rivals appear to communicate telepathically.

"Did you go to Whole Foods?" asks April, her voice raspy and elongated by a profound weariness.

"I never go to Whole Foods." Hayley digs into her tote and retrieves a small bottle of facial moisturizing lotion of a well-known brand. She places it on the stand next to the hospital bed.

April eyes the bottle with disgust. "What . . . where . . . what is that?"

"Moisturizing lotion. From Walgreens."

"I told you . . . specifically . . . Evanhealy Rose Geranium HydroSoul. From *Whole Foods*."

Hayley stares at her friend, a face of stone.

"I'm dying. Buying me precisely what I requested is the least you could do," says April.

"You're not dying."

"Look at me, for fuck's sake."

"I see you."

April's hand lifts and performs a slow flyover of the length of her emaciated body. "This is a human with a really fucking serious blood infection. They're pumping her with Colistin. That's a DoLR, in case you didn't know. A drug of last resort."

"Why are you referring to yourself in the third person all of a sudden?" Hayley asks with exasperating evenness.

"BECAUSE I'M FUCKING DYING."

"You're not dying," Hayley says again, just as calmly. "I talked to your doctor yesterday. The infectious disease guy."

April is an incorrigible gossip first and irritated hospital patient second.

"White hair? Bad breath?"

"That's him."

"Insufferable. In love with himself. Try getting a word in edgewise. Be my guest."

"He said that you're going to be fine."

"*Fine?!* That man is an idiot!"

Hayley glances at the machine monitoring April's blood pressure and sees that the reading is elevated.

"Okay. You're dying. Just simmer down. Don't get excited."

"God, I hate it when people tell me not to get excited."

"I know." A beat, then Hayley says, "I hate it, too."

Another, longer moment of silence opens up between them. April's manic episode seems to ebb as quickly as it flowed. She looks past Hayley to the golden light fluttering across the room's sterile, white walls. Her face softens. There is acceptance in that expression, and sadness, too.

She knows what Hayley doesn't know.

A person knows.

April's gaze finds Hayley again. A smile forms, sly at first and then more broadly.

"Remember that guy back in Oregon? The Turk?"

Hayley nods. "Sure." She grins, too. "Never could abide by the fact that not one, but two women outscored him on every single test."

"Why did we call him the Turk again? He was a blond-haired, blue-eyed former championship surfer from Redondo Beach."

"Are you kidding me?"

April stares at her friend, blank faced.

Hayley says, "He ate an entire turkey, by himself, our first Thanksgiving in camp. A ten-pound turkey."

"Oh, yeah. That was one, big dude."

"And we beat him, April. Every written and physical test. We beat the Turk."

"Yes. We beat the Turk."

With that happy memory, the patient's eyelids grow heavy again. Hayley watches April drift back to sleep.

Sitting in a chair on the other side of the hospital bed, the deeper state operative can't take her eyes off the face of the only friend she has in the world. More than Sam, April Wu has been the one person with whom she could share every aspect of her life.

Who *understands*.

———————

SHE IS SITTING there still when April wakes up forty minutes later.

"You're still here."

"Still here. What else am I going to do?"

The crack brings a small smile to the patient's face.

"You know, if it wasn't for you, *I* could've been the one to save the US president's life."

Hayley asks, "Oh, you mean the US president who turned out to be a Russian mole?"

"That's the one. I could've worked in the West Wing—"

Hayley interrupts her, saying, "Driven off the Key Bridge while attacked with a knife by your lover, spent the night sleeping in the Lincoln Memorial—"

"Undermined and defeated an entire cabal of deep state conspirators, saved the nation. *I* could've been the one sitting in that chair, staring at you in this bed with those big, pitying eyes."

That one gets no comeback. Only compels Hayley Chill's silence.

April says, "Sorry. Low blow."

"That's okay. You earned it."

"I didn't earn shit. A car fell on my head. And now eighty trillion foreign-born microorganisms are on a fucking rampage in my body. That doesn't make me a Medal of Honor recipient."

Hayley will give her anger all the room it needs.

The golden light has all but disappeared. The room gathers darkness. Outside, in the world, the residents of the nation's capital make plans for happy hour. They wind up the business of the day. Live these few minutes as if they all possess an infinity of tomorrows.

"Want me to flip on the lights?"

April shakes her head.

"I'm going to fucking die, Hay. These little fuckers are gonna take me down."

The deeper state operative says nothing to disagree. While April slept, Hayley witnessed the shadow passing over her friend. She knows it now, too.

Despite what the doctors say, April Wu will never leave this hospital. Not alive, she won't. The infection will rage anew. Nothing in this world can change the outcome. After all drugs of last resort are expended, the only uncertainty will be when.

Not today. Probably not tomorrow. But soon.

"Tell me about Sam."

Hayley recognizes her friend's need to talk about anything but herself. About her illness and infirmity.

"He's good."

"Is the sex good?"

"Jesus, April. . . ."

"It's an obvious question."

"Well, then, can you be *less* obvious?"

"Of course not." After a pause, the patient asks, "Well?"

"It's fine," says Hayley.

"That word again. *'Fine.'* I thought you were really into this guy."

"Sam is great."

"*Great*," says April mockingly.

"It's hard. You know it's hard. Putting us—you and me—in with the regular world. With normal people. It's . . . it's just hard."

"Yeah." April is sideways here. Her agreement rings hollow.

Hayley says, "I'm trying."

"Good. Try hard. Saving the republic doesn't have to be everything."

"Now you tell me. They said otherwise during our orientation. Andrew Wilde acts like saving the republic demands every bit of us. Our lives, if necessary."

"Well, they got mine. Maybe that should be enough."

April says this without bitterness. Begrudging, if anything. Hayley is quiet again, disliking this talk from the patient.

A nurse walks into the room. He's a large man with a broad, open face and a smile that seems to stretch for miles. Before he speaks, the deeper state operative has him pegged as being from the islands.

"How's this one, den? Everything's copa?" the nurse says with an accent that confirms Hayley's hunch.

Without waiting for a response, he checks the IV bag hanging on a pole attached to the hospital bed.

"'*This one*' could use a glass of Penfolds Shiraz Barossa Valley RWT Bin 798 instead of the evil shit you're putting in that bag." April Wu pauses to consider her prospects and adds, "Make it a bottle."

"You mean the evil shit that's saving your life, den?" The nurse shoots Hayley a pair of arched eyebrows. "She act like she hate on me, but I catch 'er giving me a sweet eye."

"Francis says that about every female patient on the floor, and probably some of the men."

"I don't want to be in the middle of this," says Hayley.

Satisfied the IV bag needs no tending and April's vitals check out, the nurse turns to leave. He pauses at the foot of the bed, looking toward Hayley with eyes like saucers.

"She says she's seeing the jumbies up in here."

Hayley hasn't a clue what the man is saying.

"Ghosts," April says flatly.

"Every night. When the unit is quiet? She says they come to her, tappin' their foot like." He gives Hayley a sideways look. Wary. "You slippin' in dis wine den?"

Hayley shakes her head. But she knows that April, who is suprisingly superstitious, wouldn't speak idly of the supernatural. The deeper state operative feels a shudder travel up her back and to the top of her skull.

The nurse turns to face April in the bed and waggles his index finger in a mock threatening manner, wanting no talk of ghosts.

"No more. Not dat!"

Within seconds, the two friends have the room to themselves again. Hayley looks to April, who stares back at her.

Jumbies.

THE ROOM IS almost dark, the sun having set thirty minutes ago. Hayley enters again. She stepped outside to answer a phone call from Sam. They have plans to get together later that night. The deeper state operative intends to tell him (she never could assign the fireman a label of "boyfriend") at this late dinner that she has signed up for mixed martial arts training at a gym in West Virginia. Hayley anticipates his displeasure, but not a scene. He's never been like that.

Sam McGovern is something else entirely. Sam is solid. Kind. A good man.

I must be crazy.

They'll have a late dinner. Return to her place. Then sex, a first in more than a few weeks. And the last for probably a while. Sad sex. Furious sex. Goodbye sex. Hayley plans to leave at the end of the week. Sam is on duty through that entire time, starting tomorrow morning. She'll miss him. The sound of his voice. His smell.

Still, Hayley Chill will go. Escape from all that has transpired here in the past days. The shock of her father's stunning reappearance. His horrendous death.

How many more times must she experience that loss?

April is awake when Hayley steps inside the gloomy hospital room, staring out the window at a day's extinguishing.

"Want me to get these lights?"

The patient shakes her head. "Did you tell him?" she asks.

"Tonight. At dinner."

Hayley feels guilty enough leaving April at this time of need. Disappointing Sam McGovern will be trivial by comparison.

Too many questions here. Too few truths.

April says, "You don't have to feel bad about it, you know. We're all grown-ups."

She always had this ability to read Hayley's thoughts, a testament to their connection. The kind of friendship that the deeper state operative hasn't found elsewhere in adulthood.

"I know," she says, sitting again in the chair by the window.

"We chose this life. No one put a gun to our head."

"I know this, too."

"Hayley?"

Her gaze had drifted without her realizing it. She focuses on the patient again.

"You don't have to come back, okay? To see me here."

"I'll be back."

"But . . . I'm already gone."

Hayley doesn't say anything.

"What the nurse said. Francis? It's true. I saw them. *Dem jumbies*. Ghosts. The dead came to me. A kind of an orientation committee, I guess you could say. My grandmother. A guy from West Point who died in a rock-climbing accident. The old man who lived down the block where I grew up. They told me what to expect. That I shouldn't be scared."

Still nothing from Hayley, who hates to hear her friend talk this way. But who is she to argue? The deeper state operative felt it, too.

A gathering of spirits. The handoff.

Hayley says, "I'll see you tomorrow morning. Got stuff later in the day."

"You don't have to come. I'll be worse tomorrow. This is my last good day. I prefer you remember me like this. Halfway normal."

"The medication is working, April."

"Yeah, well, it better watch its six. The *Acinetobacter baumannii* bacteria is working harder."

Hayley stands.

"I'll bring the Geranium Hydro-whatever-you-call-it tomorrow."

April wants to scream. Kick her feet. Punch something. Bring the roof and walls down with her.

But she doesn't do any of these things. All of that was for another time.

First and foremost, April is a warrior. And warriors must know how to die.

"Evanhealy Rose Geranium HydroSoul, dummy. Don't bother. Believe me, by this time tomorrow, dry skin will be the least of my worries."

Hayley steps forward and takes April's hand in her own.

She says, "If you hadn't been in Oregon, I wouldn't have worked as hard as I did. Our rivalry—our friendship—made me stronger. I needed you then, and I need you now. I wouldn't have found Rafi Zamani without you."

Now it's April's turn to go mute. Expressing deep feelings is not their forte. She barely moves, her nodding almost imperceptible.

Hayley isn't finished.

"I would be alone. So, thank you."

The patient says, "I *love* you, you freak."

The words strike like an earthquake. A shock of recognition. As long as they have known each other, April made only a superficial attempt at fostering a relationship with any man. The deeper state operative never gave the fact much thought, but rather chalked it up to the job. How much more of life has she taken for granted?

When will she ever learn to see the true nature of things?

Hayley says, "I love you, too."

ACKNOWLEDGMENTS

I would like to thank Emily Bestler and the entire team at Atria Books, including Lara Jones, David Brown, Dana Trocker, Milena Brown, James "Jimmy" Iacobelli, Megan Rudloff, and Libby McGuire. The book you hold in your hands would not have been possible without the dedication and assistance of these amazing folks.

I would like to thank my reps, Jordan Bayer (left coast) and Dan Conaway (right coast), for having my back.

Rose Blackwell and Jackson Hauty provided medical know-how at opportune times in the course of writing this book. Thank you, Doc and almost-Doc.

Clint and Heidi Smith once again graciously offered expertise in all things weapons-related.

As always, Christie Ciraulo put first eyes on the manuscript.

Tricia Callahan provided final copyediting duties, as she has on every Hayley Chill book. I couldn't count how many times she has saved me from myself. Thanks, Tricia.

Finally, I'd like to acknowledge my old man, George Thomas Hauty, gone now three decades. Teenage fishing guide in northern Minnesota, Second World War veteran, scientist, and educator. GT always wanted to be a writer but let go of that dream to provide for his family. I inherited the passion and ran with it, banging out one damn thing or another—whether poem, short story, stage play, screenplay, or novel—since high school.

So, thank you, Dad. Good to have dreams. Even better to pass them along.